A KAEMOURI LEGEND

The Dragons' Duel

JOHNATHON DAUGHERTY

The Dragons' Duel
Copyright © 2022 by Johnathon Daugherty

ISBN
978-1-958122-73-0 (Paperback)
978-1-958122-72-3 (eBook)

Table of Contents

Notice to the Reader: If you are under the age of Seventeen or are easily offended by any of the following the material, please do not read this selection.

- Depictions of sex
- Mature or Suggestive themes
- Murder
- Strong or Graphic Violence
- Language
- Betrayal

Chapter 1

In an age of civil war, Japan stands divided as its four great cities, and their clans, vie for power: The Dragon Clan of Shikanaca in the north, The Wind Clan of Sikan to the east, Kaylah's Spirit Clan to the south, and Isura's insidious Wyvern Clan to the west. Of these four, two have fallen, Shikanaca and Sikan; destroyed years ago in an event known as "The Great Destruction" as their scattered remnants now wander the land. As for Kaylah, it struggles to maintain its neutrality as its loyalties waver.

Things seem grim for the nation as Isura stands poised for victory, but hope remains. Ancient texts tell of a savior who would be born bearing the mark of his ancient ancestor. As prophesied, this savior was born in the form of a young man. His name was Sakuris. One of the only remaining survivors of Shikanaca's Dragon Clan, he now travels the land with the ambition to restore his clan to its former glory.

It was a warm, breezy day and Sakuris was spending it down by the river training with his little sister, Kayah; a girl the age of eleven. Sakuris was eighteen and a strong, stout young man he was. His sturdy build intimidated even the best of the Dragon Clan's younger fighters. His long, golden, flowing hair matched the color of his amber eyes. The image he possessed could be summed up in one of Michelangelo's sculptures. Kayah's image was a little less appealing, but still contained an attractive countenance all on its own. Her soft, long, flowing, brown hair was a little darker than her hazel colored eyes. Her girlish figure seemed to be evenly proportioned to her height, though she was often self-conscious about it.

Her brother, Sakuris, seemed to be in a constant state of competition with his friend, Reia, a beautiful woman of the same age, and, despite her short stature, could overcome anything that stood in her way, including Sakuris. Many is the time he stuck his foot in his mouth with her, but no matter what; he always found the mature thing to say to make her forget her anger toward him.

Using ancient manuscripts found within the ruins of his home city of Shikanaca, Sakuris trained himself in the ways of his people. Pushing himself to exhaustion, he feels the overbearing heat of the sun beating down upon him as he stops and kneels down to dip a piece of silk cloth into the river. From his strong brow, he wipes away the sweat as it streams down his strong face, glistening in the sunlight.

Her hair shimmering in the broken rays of sunlight that shone down through the forest, Kayah watches her brother. "Sakuris, you're pushing yourself way too hard, these days. Why don't you give up this foolish quest to be Arch-Dragon? I hate seeing you do this to yourself." She says, watching her brother wipe the sweat away from his face and forehead.

Placing the cloth away in a small leather sack, Sakuris cups his hand and reaches down into the river. Using his cupped hand, he draws some of the shimmering water from the river and brings it to his mouth to slowly drink from, and then turns to his sister as he continues to kneel by the river. "Kayah, one day you will understand why mother and father sacrificed their lives to save us. They knew we would be the only ones to revive the Dragon Clan." He responds, taking his sister into his embrace and hugging her closely.

Kayah looked at her brother. "Tell me, again, how our village was destroyed." She said to him curious about the destruction of their home.

With soft eyes, he looks back at her. "Kayah, I've told you this story so many times before and it's never changed." He says, releasing her from his embrace.

With great curiosity, she looks at him and informs him she wants to hear it again.

Shrugging, Sakuris begins his story. "We were playing in the fields like we always would, you know, even though father would yell us. There was an explosion and-." But he cuts his story short.

"And what brother . . ." Kayah said urging her brother to finish his story.

Sakuris's attention, however, was focused off in the distance of the forest; for a deathly silence had fallen over it. Three arrows suddenly flew at them. Quickly grabbing his sister, Sakuris leaps out of the way. Right after he lands, he reaches for the twin blade that was about his waist, drawing one the short swords housed in the scabbard as he sets his sister aside.

"My, this handsome stranger, certainly, does have fast reflexes, doesn't he, ladies? I might have to ask for a demonstration of just how fast later." A woman remarks as she emerges from the forest. The girlish giggle of two other ladies could be heard as the three of them approached the siblings.

Sakuris looked at the three of them with a defensive stare in his eye. "Why do you dare attack us?" He demanded to know.

The young woman who fired the three arrows at them loaded another one onto the string of the Japanese longbow she carried with her. "I don't think that matters, seeing as how you are in Sikonian territory. If you want to live, I suggest you leave Kaseo Forest." She said to him.

Sakuris looked at the three of them, and then back to his sister. "How careless of us; it seems we've wandered into Sikonian territory, Kayah." He said in a calm voice as he looked back to the female archer.

"Then perhaps you should heed my words stranger, otherwise . . ." The female archer said as she stopped in front of him and motioned to the other ladies that had been with her as they drew their swords.

From behind Sakuris, a voice called out, "Sheileena, enough, the three of you are certainly not good enough to match this handsome outsider. Let me do it instead."

Behind Sakuris was a beautiful young woman leaning against a tree. As he turned to look at her, she appeared quite beautiful to him. Studying the curvature of her form; from the swell of her bosom down to her waist and shapely hips, he could see she was the desire of any man.

"We're not looking for trouble. Please return to the forest and leave us in peace." Sakuris remarked, desperate to avoid conflict. He and his sister had been traveling for days and were looking for anything but a fight.

"You may not be looking for trouble, boy, but it's found you nonetheless." The mysterious woman responds, walking past him to her awaiting companions. The three women looked at the woman whom Sakuris had already guessed was their leader as she stood with them. "However, I might be willing to overlook this little oversight of yours if . . ."

"If?" Sakuris repeated as Kayah stood a little ways behind him.

"If you pay me with your head." The stranger demands as she drew a long knife that rested within the scabbard slung about her waist, resting just above her nicely curved hips. She then ran toward Sakuris with her blade-raised ready to strike, and when she was close enough, brought it down upon him only to see that he had disappeared.

"It seems you can't take a hint." He said as he reappeared, standing on a tree branch behind her, "Therefore; you've left me no choice!" Leaping from the tree branch upon which he had been standing, he charges his blade with the power of wind, ready to strike the opening blow to the female attacker.

"Foolish boy, stop wasting your time!" She retorts raising her sword as she turns to fend off his attack. Clashing steel echoes throughout the forest as their swords bear down on one another. Using his momentum, Sakuris pushes off, flipping over the woman and landing behind her.

Glaring back at him, a look of surprise plays across the woman's face, *"He stopped my blade, his style."* She thought to herself as Sakuris stared back at her.

"My wind slicer didn't work. Who the hell is that woman?" He thought to himself as his sister looked on in disbelief.

Turning to face each other, the two combatants run at the other with lightning speed ready to strike a passing blow. Feeling blood seeping through his gi-top, Sakuris looks to see his clothing had been slashed and the woman had wounded him in passing. *"She wounded me. A scratch, but a wound none the less."* He thinks to himself as he and the woman turn to face each other, once again, "Seems we're evenly matched; let's postpone this, for now. I'd hate to have to scar that pretty face of yours."

Weapon in hand, the strange woman glares at him and scoffs, "I suppose you are trying to be charming."

"I may be a fighter, but, always, first and foremost, I'm a gentleman." Sakuris replies, shaking his head.

In disbelief, the strange woman merely stares at him. "All men are the same, and they only want one thing from a woman. Still, I can't fight a wounded man, so I'm willing to put this match off to a later date." Tension rests over the forest as the two fighters stare in silence.

Breaking the tension, a cry for help echoes in Sakuris's ears. The forest had the scent of death resting upon it. Looking around, the stranger notices the women she had had with her were all dead.

Looking to his sister, Sakuris quickly finds her surrounded and cornered by a group of rival assassins with one holding her hostage and was ready to run to her aid until someone called out from behind them, "Go no closer!" causing Sakuris to freeze in his tracks. On a nearby stone, a stranger sat watching. "So you are two of the surviving Dragon Clansmen of Shikanaca: Sakuris 'the wind sleeper' and his sister Kayah." He said to them

Turning to see who had spoken to them, Sakuris and the woman from before could see he was wearing a half-mask to protect his eyes and, more or less, hide his identity. Staring directly at Sakuris, the small symbol of a wyvern's tail emblazoned the left breast of his Gi.

Beneath the visor, his eyes gleamed in the sunlight as he stared over at the young woman, "And I am judging by your style that you're a Wind Clansman of Sikan." He then returned his gaze toward Sakuris, "However, while I doubt anyone would believe that there were any Dragon Clansmen left in the world, we of the Wyvern Clan thrive on the hunt of new prey. I am Kenyo Sekuroas, the first of the Wyvern Clan elites. I've come to end your lives as were my master's orders." He said letting his eyes glow brighter and with a sinister smile upon his partially concealed face.

Readying his blade, Sakuris prepared himself for the impending challenge. Seeing this, Kenyo merely looked in Sakuris's direction and flashed a bright light from his eyes causing Sakuris's body to convulse with pain. It was so great that it caused Sakuris to open his hand and drop his blade, but somehow, even through all the pain, he managed to use his power over the elements to draw the flame of his nearby campfire into his hands as he raised his arms and began to concentrate. This caused the small flame to ignite into a large fireball between his hands, and the more he concentrated the hotter it burned.

Sakuris looked up at his opponent. "Leave us alone or I'll kill you with this flame." He demanded threatening to ignite Kenyo's body ablaze with fire. Stopping his attack, Kenyo called off his comrades threatening Kayah, and released Sakuris from his power. Hesitating for but a mere moment, Sakuris extinguishes the flame, but Kenyo refused to back down. He drew his sword and ran toward Sakuris with the tip of the blade aimed at his heart.

Recovering his stance and drawing his other blade, Sakuris quickly sidesteps out the way plunging his sword into Kenyo's heart. Kenyo grinned with a sinister grin that would send chills up your spine as he disappeared leaving a log in his place. *"He escaped, damn!"* Sakuris thought to himself as he looked around and then noticed the Wyvern Clansmen had also retreated back to the forest.

Concerned for his sister, he quickly collects his weapons and runs over to her, calling her by name, as he kneels down in front of her and holds her close, "Are you ok?"

With fearful tears in her eyes, Kayah nodded and informed her brother that she was fine. As he comforted his sister, Sakuris looked to see the strange woman kneeling over her dead comrades with a sad look on her face as tears streamed from her eyes. "Kayah, stay here." He says, leaving her where she stood and approaching the stranger from behind, "How well did you know them?"

"We grew up together." She responded, "We were all that was left."

Unsure of what to say or even do at this moment, an expression of sorrow plays across Sakuris's face, "I'm sorry for your loss." Seemed to be the only thing he could think to say.

The stranger merely looked at him from where she was kneeling as he looked on. *"This one doesn't act like the men from Sikan. Could he be different?"* She thinks to herself, but quickly shakes the thought from her mind.

They soon heard an uproarious laughter and a voice speaking from behind them, "Strange how two of the finest assassins of the four kingdoms were so much less than what would be considered . . . effective." Surprised by the new comer, the three quickly turned around to see who had spoken to them.

"How did you know we were assassins?" Sakuris asked curiously. A middle-aged man had been sitting on a stone behind them. They weren't sure how long he had been sitting there or when he had arrived, or how long he had been watching them.

"You mean you don't know? In ancient times, the four original clans of assassin were Dragon, Wyvern, Wind and Spirit. Through their teachings other clans formed and Japan became the nation it is today." He replied, looking at the footprints of the clansmen from before, "Now it seems that, once again, the Wyvern Clan seeks to conquer the land." Sakuris had judged from the way he was dressed that he was a monk or wise-man of some sort, although he could not make out his face.

"Do you know about the one who attacked us?" Kayah said stepping forward.

With a soft smile and a gentle eye, the monk shifts his gaze in her direction. "Yes, child, but to get the full truth of the matter, I suggest you travel to Kayla and visit Master Veroas. He would surely know more than I would. I am but a humble monk after all." He responds listening to the crickets chirp, "Ah, the crickets are chirping early this spring." Stopping to listen everyone diverts their attention to the forest. Returning their attention to the monk all that remained of him was a single white feather.

Looking up at the sky, the woman from before thinks to herself, *"A peculiar fellow he was,"* as she shifts her gaze to the siblings, *"and what of these two? Can they be trusted?"*

Looking to the woman as she mourns over her comrades, Sakuris sighs through his nose as he takes pity on her. "Kayah," He remarks looking at his sister, "grab our things. We make for Kaylah."

"What of her? We can't leave her alone." Kayah responds as she motions to the strange woman.

Looking from his sister to the woman and back to his sister, Sakuris sighs once more. "She's coming with us." He responds as he looks back to the stranger, "Miss, my sister and I make for Kaylah. We'd like for you to join us. The forest gets dangerous at night we'd be better off together."

Shooting a quick glance at Sakuris, she turns back to her deceased comrades and retorts, "Not until I've buried my comrades." rather impatiently, but couldn't help but think that she was beginning to feel drawn to him.

Quickly shaking the feeling off, she motions for him to help her; feeling sympathetic, Sakuris nods and grants her his assistance in burying her three comrades. Since they had no digging tools available to them he used his power over the elements to create holes in the soil deep enough for the deceased women.

He would've helped the female stranger carry them but she pushed him away yelling, "No!" as her body shook and a look of sorrow and anger rested in her eyes, "You'll not lay your hands on them. Please, you've done enough." Sakuris merely nodded and backed away with hands up as he stood at his sister's side.

"She has a real problem with men." Kayah whispered, to him, as the two of them watched the stranger lay her comrades to rest.

"I've noticed that as well." Sakuris responded, *"I wonder what it was like for her in Sikan. Still, it's too bad she's not Shikanacan, they would've treated a woman of her skill like a queen."*

Nodding in agreement, Kayah stands with her brother as they watch the stranger finish laying her comrades to rest as she looked over at Sakuris with tears in her eyes and nodded. Nodding back, he uses the same power from before to return the soil he had moved back into place as it covered the three deceased women. When he had finished, the stranger merely turned back towards the graves and bowed out of respect, and informed the siblings she was ready to leave, motioning for them to follow her.

Grabbing their belongings, the small party begins the long walk through the forest as they proceeded south to Kaylah. Along the way, Kayah looked up at the sky and noticed it had changed into many shades of red, gold, orange, and amber. "Sakuris, look the sun is setting. Isn't the sky beautiful this time of day?" She said excitedly.

"Yes, very beautiful." Sakuris agreed, but his attention wasn't focused on the sky, but rather the woman they met.

Kayah looked at her brother. "Sakuris, I'm hungry. Can't we rest?" She pleads.

Looking at his sister and then at their female guide, Sakuris nods. "Miss, my sister needs to rest and it is getting late." He says to the newcomer. Looking back at the siblings and then at the sky, the woman nods and agrees.

"In my journeys, I happened upon the ruins of Shikanaca, its charred remains littered the ground. Kaemouri-san, how did you and your sister survive?" She asks Sakuris as they sit around a fire he had built for them. It was nightfall and the sky had turned many shades black and dark blue.

Sakuris merely shrugged as he looked at her. "It hasn't been easy for us these last few years. It's been harder on young Kayah here." He responded as Kayah rested her head in his lap, "Honestly I've tried to forget about it. Haven't you?"

The woman merely looked up at the black sky as she thought back to the day Sikan was destroyed. Her brother sat kneeling in front of her holding a blade out for her to grasp, "Dayis, let me fight with you." She pleaded.

Her brother merely shook his head, "No, Saiera, you cannot. As the new head of this clan you must survive to one day remake it anew." He then handed her the sword he was holding, "Now take this sacred sword and go to Kaylah and Shikanaca and enlist the help of anyone you can. I promise we will meet again someday. In the meantime, I'll take care of this demon. Now go, quickly, and don't look back." He said to her as she cried. She then quickly embraced him and said her good-byes before running off into the woods, and with that, her journey had begun.

"Miss, miss are you all right?" Sakuris asked bringing her back to the present. Saiera didn't answer him, but merely wiped away a single tear that had trickled down her cheek and turned away to fall sleep. *"Why is she so resentful toward me?"* Sakuris wondered rather puzzled.

He looked down to see that Kayah had fallen asleep. Raising her head a bit, he puts a rolled up blanket underneath it as he got up from where he was sitting and rested her head on it. He then went a few yards away from where the women were sleeping and looked up into the black sky of the night, shouting, "Mother! Father! I will revive the clan and I will be Arch-Dragon. Your deaths . . . will not have been in vain!" Kneeling down, he then says a prayer to goddess Elayis for his parents. When he had finished he went back to where the women were resting, lay down by his sister and he, too, fell asleep.

When morning came the women awoke and went down to the river to bathe, while Sakuris went into the forest to hunt for their breakfast. Spotting a good-sized forest rabbit, he began to chase after it. After about twenty minutes of chasing, he realized this was not the best way to catch a meal and, instead, proceeded into some underbrush and knelt down to wait for the rabbit to approach his hiding spot. When it did, he had himself a meal. Satisfied with his kill, Sakuris quickly took it back to camp. Building a small cooking fire, he places the rabbit over it, allowing it to cook. *"Kayah might want berries."* He thinks to himself as he proceeds back into the woods where he gathers a variable cornucopia of nuts and berries.

The sun had just peeked over the mountains in the distance and was shining throughout the forest. Sakuris had just finished finding fruit for his sister and returned to camp to see a forest wolf sniffing the morning meal. Not to wanting to lose his hard earned breakfast, he rushes towards the wolf shouting for it to leave. With a growl, the wolf turns his head to face Sakuris before running back into the forest.

Returning from the river, the two women pass by him as he humbly bows before them. "Ladies, your breakfast awaits." He says to them in a charming voice. Looking at him as she observes the assorted meal before her, Saiera could feel her resentment toward Sakuris beginning to leave, but still could not bring herself to fully trust him. Gathering some berries and rabbit meat onto a wooden plate, Sakuris first serves Kayah. Taking the meal into her grasp, she watches Sakuris fix another for Saiera and turn to hand it to her only to see she had already prepared one for herself.

Sighing through his nose, he takes a seat beside her. "You don't have to be so resentful toward me. I have been nothing but a gentleman to you, even during our match." He says to her.

Saiera merely looks at him as she opens the gap between them. "It's nothing personal. I'm just not used to the hospitality you've shown me." She says to him as she begins eating her meal.

Kayah had taken out several green tea leaves from her bag and put them into a small iron kettle, and using a small flask of water fills it half way. "Sakuris, is this the correct amount of water?" She asks her brother, motioning for him to come over.

He merely laughed. "Kayah you've seen me do this so many times before." He responds going over and looking into the small kettle, "Yes, Kayah, just enough. But I have told you green tea is only for special occasions." He said to her.

"This is a special occasion." She responds placing the kettle over the fire.

"Oh, why is that?" He asked her.

She leaned over and whispered into his ear, *"You're in love. You can't fool me."* as she motioned toward Saiera.

Sakuris merely moved his eyes with her gesture and then turned back to her, *"What makes you so sure, squirt?"* He whispered calling her by the nickname he had given her when they were very young. She merely shrugged and said nothing.

Thinking of her own brother whom she had left behind so long ago, Saiera watches the two siblings with curiosity as the three finish their morning meal and share a cup of tea before gathering their things and proceeding onto Kaylah. Walking until the forest suddenly grew quiet, they hadn't known about the fighters that had been secretly shadowing them in the trees. Noticing the sudden silence, Sakuris quickly stopped, "We're not alone." He said as Saiera and Kayah quickly stopped. Saiera drew the long knife from her scabbard once again. Kayah reached for the diamond dagger that was housed in a scabbard hidden under the short kimono she wore.

A few darts suddenly flew at Sakuris as he leapt out of the way, narrowly dodging them. A few more darts flew at Kayah and Saiera. Kayah merely held up hands, "Sidetsute." She chanted, causing the darts to stop dead in their tracks as they fell to the ground.

A young fighter soon calls for his clansmen to stop their attack and approaches the three travelers. In his hand, he carried a Japanese long spear, known as a Yari; that rested on his shoulder. Reaching up, he removes the hood he had been wearing, revealing his face to them, "My people have the advantage in the forest, so don't make any sudden moves." He warned, "So who are you three anyway. You don't look to be from around here."

Sakuris merely looked at him. He wore dark forest green leather armor over what seemed to be a black Gi. His hair was short and neatly trimmed. About his face a neatly trimmed mustache and beard that was shaved down into a gotee. "I guess we've already entered Kaylah. I am Sakuris of the Dragon Clan of Shikanaca, this is my sister, Kayah, and this is-." He said motioning to the woman he had met earlier.

She looked at him, "I am Lady-Master of the Wind Saiera, of the Wind Clan in Sikan. My reasons for coming are my own." She said finishing Sakuris's statement.

The young man studies the three of them, "Wind and Dragon, you say? I heard those clans were wiped out. Still, you don't appear to be hostile. Very well, follow me and I'll take you to the village." He said motioning the way to Kaylah.

Sakuris merely hesitated before following. All three of them did, in fact. "Wait a minute. You're going to trust just like that?" He said to the Kaylan.

The Kaylan fighter merely looked back at him, "You said your name was Master Sakuris, right?" He asked suddenly remembering his place,

"Oops, I'm sorry, I forgot to introduce myself. I am Ryuomi, son of Taylah, and second in command of Kaylah." He said to them. The three travelers hesitate, once again, before deciding to trust the newcomer and reluctantly following him to Kaylah.

When they arrived Sakuris found the nearest hot spring he could and undressed before climbing into it, "Oh yes; that is so much nicer than the freezing cold river." He said letting the warm water relax his tired body. He also noticed the small wound Saiera gave him wasn't even a scratch, before looking up to see Saiera as she approached the hot spring, "Lady Kanz, kobanwa." He remarks watching her strip down and slip into the hot spring.

Stretching within the warm waters of the spring, Saiera dips her long hair into the spring letting the water soak into it. "Pardon the intrusion Lord Kaemouri, but this is the nearest hot spring around and I am in desperate need of a hot bath."

Not wanting to be bothered, Sakuris merely turned around and went to the other side of the hot spring. Chuckling slyly, Saiera swims over to him, putting her arms around his neck. "Don't be so modest Sakuris, we're both adults. What do you say, why not? It's just us out here under this romantic sky of the night. I saw the way you were looking at me in the forest."

Sakuris could suddenly feel himself becoming aroused as his body heat began rising, but whether it was from passion or the hot spring he did not know. Quickly releasing himself from Saiera's embrace, he swam to the other side. "A tempting offer but I really must decline. Besides, I'm not that kind of man." He said not bothering to look at her.

Saiera once again moved over to him. "All men are the same, right?" She said blowing into his ear and rubbing her sex against him. Sakuris's eyes grew wide as he started sweating and felt an erection growing between his legs. "Okay I'm finished." He said quickly climbing out, grabbing his bag as he did and proceeding behind some bushes to get dressed. He finally looked to Saiera not bothering to pay any attention to the assets she had flung on him. "You are positively evil, you know that." He said getting dressed.

Saiera watched him as he did. "*Not once did he lay his eyes on me. Maybe he isn't the same.*" She thought to herself and then giggled a bit, "*He is a handsome one. I'll grant him that.*"

Sakuris quickly left the hot spring walking back up the trail, passing Kayah as he did. "How's the water, Sakuris?" She asked as he passed by.

"It's too hot for my taste." He responded as he continued to walk by not bothering to stop.

Kayah merely watched him. "*Saiera*." She immediately thought to herself as she continued to walk toward the hot spring. The evening air blew against her with a warm breeze as she got undressed and climbed into the hot spring with Saiera. "Miss Saiera, do you hate my brother?" She said to her kind of sternly.

Kayah's statement startled Saiera a little, how would an eleven-year-old know of such things. "Uh, what makes you ask that little one?" She said puzzled.

Kayah merely shrugged, "My brother likes you, but he and I both noticed how resentful you are towards men." She replied letting the water of the spring relax her girlish figure.

Saiera suddenly became nervous. Kayah had certainly hit the nail on the head. "I could see how you two would think that way. May I ask you something?" She responded. Kayah merely nodded in acknowledgment. "Your brother said, 'he wasn't that kind of man.' Is that what all men from your clan were like?"

Kayah merely nodded. "It was, but our laws also state that when a woman reaches childbearing age that it's proper for her to choose a husband. Not so much out of disrespect, but it's how the clan survived for so many years. The women were always treated with decency."

Saiera was surprised to hear this considering the way she acted toward Sakuris earlier. "I take it Sakuris never had the chance to marry before the destruction then." She asked Kayah rather inquisitively.

"No, we were both very young when it happened." She responded to her as she splashed some of the warm water on her face. "What about your clan? What were your views on the subject?" She asked her.

Saiera merely looked down at her own reflection in the spring. "In Sikan, women were the property of men; meant only to bear children and to serve a man's carnal nature. However, there were men like my father who wanted to see a change in the clan, they rose up against our old master and removed him from power, driving him and his followers from Sikan, allowing the women to venture out and find husbands who treated them with respect and decency, and bring them back to the village. Afterward, we began training them in the ways of the Wind Clan. "

Kayah was stunned to hear this, she was unaware there were men in the world who saw women like that. She figured that's why Saiera distrusted Sakuris. "Was that why you were resentful toward my brother earlier?" She asked rather sadly. Saiera merely nodded as she leaned on the edge of the hot spring letting the water relax her tired body.

Kayah merely studied her with much envy. "You have a very nice figure you know. I wish mine looked like that; then all the guys would flock to me as the girls did to Sakuris." She said to her.

Saiera looked at her in surprise. "Kayah, you're not self-conscious, are you? Surely you don't think I always looked like this. Actually, my figure didn't sprout until I was fourteen long after the other girls my age, but I really didn't blossom until I was seventeen. That's when the guys really started to notice me, or so I thought. It was my body they were noticing. I realized this after men started drooling whenever I entered the room." Saiera said attempting to make Kayah feel better as she climbed out of the hot spring allowing Saiera got a good look at her figure. "Wait, you're upset about that. You have the perfect figure for an eleven-year-old." She said to her.

Kayah merely shook her head, "Not in my clan, guys aren't attracted to this. Sure my butt's nice and all. But I have these girlish breasts and these less than nice legs." She said still unhappy.

"*Oh boy,*" Saiera thought and then spoke to Kayah, "Kayah there is nothing wrong with your figure, it's just . . . proportioned to your height." She said to her also climbing out and getting dressed.

As she did Kayah looked at her, "Kanz-sama, compared to you; I have no figure." She said also getting dressed.

Saiera merely looked at her, "Just give yourself time, you're only a child." She said to Kayah. Finally, a small smile played on Kayah's face and she left. Saiera undressed again and took a good long look at her own figure. "*To be honest, Kayah, I wish I had your figure.*" She thought to herself getting dressed again.

Chapter 2

Leaving the hot spring, Saiera went back up to the fort and entered her room to lay down on her bed. Dressed in a simple sleeping gown Kayah came out from the back room to lay down on the bed that was next to Saiera's and closed her eyes, slowly falling asleep. Looking at the young Kaemouri as she slept, Saiera thought of her brother, wondering if he was safe or even alive. She'd not seen him for a long time and was worried about his safety.

Weary from travel, Saiera merely allowed her head to rest on the soft-feathered pillow until she slowly fell asleep. During the night Kayah began to grow restless in her sleep due to a dream she was having. It started off with her and Sakuris in the fields of Shikanaca. This happy memory made her calm down, but the dream soon turned into a nightmare. She saw a man and a woman who were each carrying a child. Behind them, the village was burning as smoke began to rise from the coast. Kayah looked at the woman and realized it was her mother, and the child she was carrying was Sakuris.

Feeling her heart beginning to race in her sleep, she looked over to see her father carrying a younger version of herself. Shikanaca had been destroyed about five years ago. Sakuris was the age of thirteen and Kayah the age of six. She saw her father set her down and draw his blade, and run back to Shikanaca. Her mother set Sakuris down and ran after him. As Kayah looked on she could make out a red demon-like creature. As her parents ran back, she tried to call out to them, "Mother! Father! Come back!" but they didn't hear her as they continued and were consumed in the flame. Frightened from these images the young child quickly woke up crying and screaming.

Her frightened screams and cries woke Saiera who quickly walked over to her and held her in a motherly manner, "Shh, it's ok young one." She said trying to calm her down.

Kayah looked up at her proclaiming, "Mother, father, they're gone."

Saiera looked at her as she held her close reassuring her, "It was just a dream. You're ok now."

Kayah still looked at her, her small body trembling, "I want to go to Sakuris." She said holding tightly to Saiera.

Saiera rose from the bed with Kayah in her arms and walked out of their room and over to Sakuris's and knocked on the door. A few moments later the door slid open, and a groggy Sakuris stood before her. "Saiera it's the middle of the night. This had better not be another seduction attempt." He said, yawning, as he let her in.

"I'm sorry, but Kayah insisted on seeing you." She said to him setting Kayah on Sakuris's bed, "I was awoken by her frightened screams and cries."

Sakuris merely looked at Kayah who now rested on his bed before proceeding into the back and heating some milk for her. He came back out and handed the cup of milk to Saiera. "She's having nightmares, again. They started when Shikanaca was destroyed." He said sitting on the bed next to Kayah. Retrieving the small cup back from Saiera, Sakuris then gave it to Kayah who took it within her grasp and drank it, slowly fallen back to sleep.

With the empty cup in hand, Sakuris carries to the back placing back into his pack before taking out two more clean cups and a small flask of wine, pouring some for him and Saiera. Proceeding back into the front he handed a cup to Saiera who took it as she sat down on the other bed. "Lord Kaemouri, I apologize if I made you feel uncomfortable at the hot spring earlier." She said taking a sip of the wine he gave her.

Sakuris sat down next to her. "I must admit I was caught off guard by what you did." He said to her as he looked at Kayah, gently running his fingers through her hair.

Saiera merely looked at her as well. "I see you trying to be a father to her, but a brother's love isn't enough. She needs the love of a mother and father." She remarks setting her cup down near a candle that rested on a nightstand beside the bed they were sitting on.

Sakuris sat his drink next to hers, responding. "After our parents died, I was the closest thing she had to a father. There was one who was willing to take us in, but in the end it didn't work out. After that we wondered the land surviving as best we could." while still looking at his sister.

Thinking for a moment, Saiera remembers some friends living just outside the city, "I know a young couple a few miles from here. They're farmers and could use the extra help. The husband is also a swordsmith and well-known martial artist. He could use a young man such as you in the fields. Kayah could also help in the kitchen and the home."

Not knowing what to make of her statement, Sakuris merely turns to face her asking, "You would do that for us?" as Saiera nods in response. "What if they wouldn't take us? I couldn't bear for Kayah to have her hopes raised only to be hurt."

Moonlight broke through the thatched roof and made Saiera's long flowing hair shine in its light. "I'm sure they'll accept you. Anyway, when I approached you at the hot spring, what was your first intention?" She asked him.

Her question puzzled Sakuris. He was afraid of giving her an honest answer. "If I were not the man my father raised me to be, I might've taken you, but even then, it would not have felt right." Causing Saiera to smile and sit closer to him.

"Back in Sikan our old master taught the men 'women were merely property meant only to bare children.'" She says to him. Sakuris had suddenly realized the truth behind the resentment she had shown him and wished he could have acted differently when he met her. "As I told your sister many of the men were driven out allowing the women to find others outside the village who treated them kindly and with respect." Saiera continued, "All the women were wed and Sikan prospered. I am the only one not married." She said to him resting her hand on his shoulder. She then took a deep breath. "I'm sorry for my resentment towards you earlier. I know you only wanted to help."

Sakuris looked at her as she did, "No, I am sorry about the way I acted earlier, trying to take charge of the situation."

"No, you were trying to do what you thought was best. I understand" She said to him.

Sakuris merely placed his arm around her shoulder as she touched her hand to his. "So I guess neither one of us has anyone to miss then." He said to her.

Saiera allowed her hand to rest on Sakuris's. "A man's loving touch, something I have not felt in a while." She said to him.

The feel of her hand against his surprised Sakuris; the only woman who had touched him in such a loving manner had been his mother. "Aside from my mother, no other woman has touched me so lovingly, I'd forgotten the way it felt." He remarks as Saiera raises her head, feeling herself, now more than ever, being drawn to him as she pressed her lips to his. They shared the moment as Saiera gave a long sigh of contentment. A second later, Sakuris quickly pulled his head back. "We can't do this." He said to her.

Saiera merely looked at him as his golden hair shimmered in the dim moonlight that shone through the thatched roof. "Sure we can, Sakuris. Kayah's asleep and it's just us."

Sakuris merely looked back at her, "I know, and I want this, but I just can't."

"What's wrong?" She said setting her hands on the bed, "Is it because you are to be Arch-Dragon? Should that really matter?"

"It shouldn't, but I just don't know. If only I had a sign from our clan's spirit." He said to her. He had been deeply troubled indeed. As he wondered about this, the room grew a little brighter as a middle-aged woman appeared before him.

Almost ghost-like, she carried with her a beautiful countenance, "Young dragon, do not trouble yourself over such a trivial matter. You know, plainly well, the answer to the question that you seek." She said to him in a majestic voice, placing a gentle hand to his cheek.

Recognizing her, Sakuris immediately drops to one knee, gasping, "Goddess Elayis!"

With a warm chuckle and a soft smile, the goddess leans forward, cupping a hand under his chin gently remarking "Rise, my child." and bringing Sakuris to his feet. "You are a man of nobility and honor, Sakuris Kaemouri. If a life with this young woman is what you seek, then you have my blessing to do so. Myuranth chose well the vessel of his spirit. The mark on your arm: the dragon, coiled around the sword, is proof of your birthright. Shake off your past life, and start anew. You have my blessing, Arch-Dragon Sakuris Kaemouri."

She then turns to Saiera gently commanding, "Saiera, Lady-Master of the wind, I charge you: Care for the young Kaemouri as he starts his new life, be there for him always; for he will need you by his side. I now leave you both, good luck." before disappearing.

Saiera looked at Sakuris, "So what will be your first duty as Arch-Dragon?" She asked rather curiously as she continued to gaze upon him; he stood strong and proud in the moonlight that was shining through the thatching of the ceiling.

Looking back at her, Sakuris knew without a doubt what it was he must first do. "Rebuild my clan, and slay the demon that destroyed my home."

Looking upon him, Saiera could see the fire burning in his eyes and could hear the determination in his words. "Then allow me, Master Kaemouri, to lend you my aid. My blade demands blood and the ghosts of my people cry out for justice. They too wish to see the demon slain." She responds, rising to her feet and standing next to him.

"Your aid is most welcome, Lady-Master of the wind Saiera." Sakuris responded as he turned to face her, "both in battle and in my bed." He then wrapped his arms around her and took her into his embrace. "Now, shall we finish what we started?" He said to her as his desire for her burned and enflamed his heart.

"Yes, by Elayis, yes, take me" She responded. Sakuris went over to where his sister rested and pulled the covers over her before proceeding back over to Saiera, taking her into his arms.

"Sakuris, easy big boy." She said to him as he carried her into the back and placed her on the bed there. He leaned in to kiss her but she placed her hand to his chest to stop him. "Wait, this isn't the alcohol talking is it." She said to him, making sure their judgment was clear.

He shook his head. "Anyone who gets drunk off that weak stuff must be a really light drinker. We're sober." He replied.

"Then come to me, Sakuris." She said pulling him on top of her by the collar of his sleepwear and kissing him deeply. The two shared the moment, wrapped in passion's embrace as their tongues intertwined with each other.

As they did, Saiera could feel her body heat rising as she felt herself starting to moisten between her legs, signaling her body was ready to receive Sakuris. "*Take me.*" She whispered in his ear as she opened her silk kimono top revealing the swell of her bosom to Sakuris. Eager to please,

Sakuris placed his lips upon one of Saiera's breasts and sucked upon it hungrily. This made Saiera gasp as she threw her hands around Sakuris's head to hold it in place as he continued to suck upon her breast.

Saiera's body heat was rising even more. She so desperately wanted Sakuris inside of her as she hiked up her skirt and underskirt and reached down to undo Sakuris's pants. Sakuris stopped her in the process and whispered into her ear, *"All things come to those who wait."* He teased, but not wanting Saiera to be disappointed, he reached down and slid a finger or two inside of her.

The motion of his fingers sent chills throughout Saiera's body as she gasped from the pleasure she was feeling. "By the goddess, don't stop." She pleaded as she felt Sakuris's fingers moving inside of her. The pleasure was too much for her to stand any longer as she took charge of the situation and rolled them over so that she was on top. "I get what I want, Lord Kaemouri, always." She remarked with a playful aggression as she moved down Sakuris body and removed his pants revealing his erection to her, "and what I want looks very nice indeed."

She moved back up and sat firmly upon Sakuris as she felt his hard shaft entering into her. "Oh my goddess!" She gasped as the feel of his body inside of her sent pleasure through her entire core making her quiver with delight, "You feel amazing."

Rocking her hips back and forth, she felt an even greater amount of pleasure to coarsing through her. The motion of her hips caused Sakuris to stiffen even more inside of her as the pleasure was building for him as well and he was panting heavily. Saiera's body had enveloped him completely as it began to tighten from pleasure. The two embraced each other as they continued their passionate love-making, both on the verge of climax.

Finally when neither could withstand the pleasure any longer, their body's erupted into orgasm together as Saiera's body tensed and quivered furiously. This caused Sakuris to shoot off inside of Saiera as he tensed up and embraced her tightly. Exhausted and out of breath, the two of them laid in each other's arms as they lovingly held each other close.

Sleepily, Saiera finally rolled off of Sakuris as she snuggled in close to him. Feeling her against him, Sakuris merely wrapped his arm around her, from the side she had been snuggling him from, as they gazed lovingly into each other's eyes for a moment or two. Saiera then gave him a light kiss on the tip of his nose. "We should probably get to sleep." She yawned with a sweet smile.

Sakuris merely smiled back as he gently stroke her long soft hair. "Yes, we probably should." He responded as he continued to play with Saiera's hair.

As he did, Saiera merely moaned in content. "That feels nice." She remarked as she felt Sakuris's fingers running through the strands of her hair, gently relaxing her until she fell asleep next to him. Smiling as he gazed down at her sleeping, Sakuris merely kissed the top of her head and he, too, laid back to fall asleep.

When morning came the two awoke to a pleasant aroma coming from an open fire pit. Taking a deep sniff, Sakuris recognized the aroma almost immediately. "Oh man, Kayah's cooking her berry-nut pie." He said letting drool drip from his mouth.

With a chuckle, Saiera wiped it away with a piece of the soft silk sheet. "It's that good, huh?" She asked.

Sakuris got up and dressed his lower half. "A taste you wouldn't believe. You would die for just one bite." He responded as he reached for his gi-top.

Kayah soon entered the room, "Breakfast is read-." She stopped in mid-sentence and in her tracks when she saw Saiera laying naked in the bed and Sakuris without his gi-top on, "Breakfast is ready, unless, of course, you're not hungry." She informed them as she quickly exited the room.

Sakuris quickly dressed his upper half and stepped outside the room and walked over to Kayah. "So . . . good night?" She asked rather curiously.

"Yes, it was very nice." He responded as he leaned against a nearby wall; his face somewhat flush from slight embarrassment.

"Clearly," Kayah responded with a sly grin. "*Bad boy.*" She whispered with a playful motion of her hand.

Sakuris merely leaned his head back aganst the wall he had been leaning upon and took a deep breath through his nose and released it through his mouth, as he walked over to his sister. "At any rate, I think we need more knocking drills." He said as grabbed his sister and began tickling her.

"Sakuris, stop you know I'm ticklish." She said laughing. "Okay, okay, I'll knock next time." She remarked as she continued to laugh as her brother tickled her some more.

Saiera came out and saw the two siblings, and laughed at the spectacle. Sakuris soon released his sister, and then went over and sniffed the pie that was cooling. Reaching for a small cutting knife, he was about to cut it when a small pebble hit his hand. He recoiled his hand, dropping the knife. He then looked back and saw Kayah holding the small leather sling she had made when she was little.

"Touch that pie, and you'll regret it. It's for Ryuomi and Master Veroas, but don't worry I made one for us. It's cooling by the window." She said putting another pebble into the sling. Sakuris slowly backed away and looked at the window where he saw the steaming hot pie. The aroma of it gave him the look you'd see on children's cartoons when the characters float toward the flavorful aroma of food. Before he could take a step toward it Kayah readied her sling once again, "Don't even think about it. It's for after breakfast." She warned.

Sakuris looked down in disappointment and then to his sister. "Do you spend every night thinking of ways to torture to me or do they just come to you?" He asked playfully, sitting down at a nearby wooden table.

Kayah gave a small giggle before answering him. "A little bit of both." She teased as she walked over to where she had their morning meal cooling as she gathered some of the wooden dishes from a nearby cabinet and began preparing plates for each of them.

Saiera walked over to Sakuris tying her tunic closed and sat down beside him, *"I should probably talk to Kayah about what she saw; maybe we both should."* She whispered to him and he nodded in agreement. The sun had just risen high over the fortress as Sakuris motioned for his sister to come sit next him. He then looked at Saiera who had turned redder than the blood run through her veins and arteries.

Kayah went over and sat down beside Saiera, "Listen Kayah, I'm sure you know what your brother and I did last night." Saiera said looking at her.

"I've got a guess." Kayah responded. Sakuris meanwhile had gotten up and brought over the plates of food Kayah had prepared for them. He sat each plate down before them and then went over and grabbed the last plate for himself. Going back over to the table, he then joined the women for breakfast.

"Kayah, are you okay with the idea of your brother and me?" Saiera asked concerned for Kayah's well-being.

"I am, but my brother's life is not my own. It's his decision whom he shares it with. I know he will always be there for me. If a life with him is what you seek Lady Saiera, and if it is what he wants as well; that is all that matters." Kayah responded. There was much wisdom in her words for a girl her age.

Saiera merely smiled at Kayah as she placed a hand on top of her head and ran her fingers through her silky dark hair. "Wise words, little one." She remarked as Kayah smiled at her actions.

"Indeed, our father taught her well." Sakuris remarked as the three of them proceeded to enjoy their meals. He then looked over to Saiera, "Saiera, this might be a good opportunity to talk to her about what we discussed last night."

Nodding in agreement, Saiera looks to the younger Kaemouri, stating, "Kayah, your brother and I have something important we want to talk to you about. We discussed the idea of taking you two to find some people who might be willing to adopt you and be your parents."

Her statement causes Kayah to perk her head up, "You mean . . . I would have a mommy."

Sakuris looked at his younger sister. "Kayah, we don't want to get your hopes up, Saiera offered to take us to see some friends of hers." He said getting up.

Saiera nodded. "That's right; they have fields you could play in and a nice cottage. Sakuris, I forgot to mention to you, the husband has rather large training dojo as well. You could work out there all you want." She said turning to Sakuris who had been pouring wine for the three of them. It was a fine red wine mature in both color and taste.

Proceeding back over to them, he sets the glasses before each of them and seats himself. "A training dojo; that would certainly make my training easier, I wouldn't have to train in the heat of the sun all the time." He said sipping his drink. Finishing his beverage, he dismisses himself from the conversation in order to grab some clean clothes so he may bathe in the nearby hot spring, leaving the women to talk on their own.

"Your brother sure is a handsome one." Saiera remarks as she and Kayah continue to enjoy their breakfast. Its flavorful ballet danced on her tongue making her taste buds sing with delight.

"Yes, just make sure you treat him well, or you'll have me to deal with." Kayah warned playfully as she took another bite of the food before her.

"Oh really, now, very well, show me what you got." Saiera remarked holding up the palm of her hand for Kayah to punch.

Kayah then playfully gave her hardest punch into Saiera's hand. Even for a playful punch, Saiera was still able to see there was a small measure of power behind it. "Not bad. You'll grow to be a fine fighter, someday." She remarked as she lowered her hand back down and began eating at her meal once more. Kayah then slid over closer to Saiera, a look of curiosity playing across her face. "So *how did he do*?" She asked rather curious about her brother's performance.

Saiera quickly gasped. "Kayah! He was nice." She responded finishing her wine, "You're brother's a most impressive man." She then took a moment as she gazed blankly at a nearby wall, playing with her hair.

Kayah watched Saiera as she fiddled with her hair. "You know what Saiera? I could do this great hair job for you." She said going around behind her. Saiera merely put her hands down as Kayah fiddled with her hair. "Let's see, you've got long, soft, brunette colored hair. I know just the thing." She said quickly going through Sakuris's bag to find her hairbrush and a few flowers, "I could do this style that would really make you look attractive to Sakuris." She said as she began brushing.

"Kayah," Saiera said to her "Kayah, I like my hair the way it is. I appreciate the offer, but we need to get ready and I really don't want to look any more attractive than I already am." She said to her.

Kayah had suddenly remembered what they had spoken about the night before. "Right, I'm sorry, later perhaps." She said to her.

Saiera shrugged. "Sure, later would be fine." She said to her, "But right now, you little miss need a bath. And after last night I know I do." She said getting up and leading Kayah out of the room and outside to walk back to the room they had been assigned to originally. As they walked, they noticed that sun was already hanging in the sky at a high altitude. Its rays had broken through the treetops and were shining through to the forest floor. The breeze around the forest blew cool and mild providing the ideal temperature setting for such a spring day.

At the hot spring Sakuris had undressed and already climbed into the water letting it rejuvenate his tired body, "*Oh that water feels good, much like Saiera's touch last night. I never felt as safe as I did with her. You know what, since I'm in such a good mood, I think I'll take her and Kayah shopping later.*

It's been awhile since Kayah was last able to buy something nice for herself. She might as well have something nice to meet Saiera's friends in." He thought to himself looking at his tattered and torn clothing as it lay upon the edge of the spring, "*Then again, I might want to buy some clothes for myself as well.*" He then looked around the forest. "*I never knew such a strong forest clan could exist here in the south. A lot of the men here would be well worth the time and effort to train for the Dragon Clan.*"

Saiera soon approached the hot spring. "My love, it's time to go. Lord Ryuomi awaits us." She said as Sakuris swam over to her.

"Saiera, I hope our little experience last night doesn't change anything." He said to her as he climbed out.

She looked at him as the water dripped down his wet physique. "*Oh, by Elayis, he looks good wet.*" She thought to herself feeling an urging desire coming over her. She shook it off even though she wished they had time for a short quickie, although in bed Sakuris was anything but quick. She watched as the sunlight caused the beads of water that dripped from Sakuris to glisten as it flowed down his strong arm and chest muscles as he dried himself off and got dressed. He then reached down and grabbed his blades, and holding them in the small of his back, slung the strap about his waist.

Saiera watched as his golden hair glistened in the sunlight. The light had also hit his eyes just right turning them from amber to a shining gold color. As Sakuris continued to sling the strap for the scabbard that housed his blades about his waist he tightened it so that it fit snuggly about his hips.

He walked over and embraced Saiera. "Let's go, my dear. We mustn't keep our guide waiting." He said to her as he slid his arm down to her waist. Saiera put her arm around his shoulder and they walked the path that led back to the fortress where Kayah and Ryuomi awaited them.

Ryuomi looked at the two of them, asking politely, "Shall we go now?" though Sakuris was sure he had detected a hint of impatience in Ryuomi's tone.

Kayah who had been standing beside Ryuomi ran over to greet Saiera and her brother. Her hair still wet from the bath Saiera had given her, she then her place on the side of Sakuris opposite Saiera.

Sakuris nodded. "Yes, we seem to be ready. Though I do apologize for the wait you had to endure." He remarked apologetically.

Ryuomi laughed a hardy chuckle. "Nonsense, my friend, no apology necessary. Besides, I could tell in the forest you three had endured a lot in your journeys. I only wish we, of Kaylah, could do more." He responded most agreeably, "Still, we mustn't tarry here, my father is waiting." Ryuomi then motioned for everyone to follow him as he led them through the village.

As they walked Sakuris looked around as he marveled at all the shops around him. There were weapon shops and clothing shops. It was these shops that were of the most interest to him. Even though the blade he had was of good use, it was of pour maintenance and badly needed a good sharpening. He even thought about getting it re-forged with new steel to increase the endurance and strength of it. He wouldn't have the blade removed of course; he still needed the power the blade housed within. He would only have the edges re-forged.

Continuing to look around, he noticed a jewelry shop, wherehe would certainly find something nice for Saiera. Ryuomi soon stopped in front of a house and motioned that they wait outside for him. As he entered he saw his father kneeling in front of a small shrine, he created, in meditation. "Father, the travelers you requested to see are here. They're waiting outside." He said informing his father of his awaiting guests.

His father turned to face him. "Yes, I know. I heard you approaching. Please show them in." He said getting up, grabbing a small short sword as he did so, and went over to sit in the middle of the room. Ryuomi nodded and went back outside where he motioned for the travelers to enter. Sakuris, Kayah, and Saiera walked in and looked around the room. It had the appearance of a dojo rather than a living space. All around the room weapons and scrolls hung from and on the walls.

Sakuris looked around and noticed a few suits of Japanese armor standing in the corners, *"And I thought 'Father was obsessed with his heritage.'"* He thought to himself.

Everyone soon took their seats around Ryuomi's father who was still sitting in the middle of the room. Sakuris looked at him, studying his aging face that was covered in wrinkles as his snow white hair rested tied up in a top knot. "Forgive our intrusion sir, but-" He started, but was interrupted by Ryuomi's father.

"No forgiveness is necessary. I know who you are and why you have come, Master Sakuris. You wish to know of the red demon and the Wyvern Clan.

But first, allow me to introduce myself; my name is Master Veroas Taylah. You three could not have come at a better time. I wish to recruit the skills of the remaining two Dragon Clansman in order to test your strength. You see; we of Kaylah rely on the golden ore that is harvested from the mines in the mountains up north." He said as Kayah looked at him.

"That's foolish; the dragons are assassins, not miners. Why don't you send your own men?" She lashed out forgetting her place.

Sakuris gave her a harsh, dead stare as if saying: Watch your mouth. Kayah looked at her brother's expression and then back to Veroas, "Forgive me, sir. I seem to have forgotten my place." She said quieting down again.

Veroas laughed. "No forgiveness is necessary, but please let me explain young one. We have sent several soldiers up to those mountains, but none have returned and the women of the village are growing restless. I wish for you and Master Sakuris to find out why. We believe that the cause is the ancient demon that has rested deep within the mine's caverns for centuries. The demon is known as Zecuroas and is very dangerous. I know I don't need to remind you two to be careful. Bring the creature's head to me and I'll tell everything you wish to know." He said throwing Sakuris a small pouch full of money. "There's 1,000 gold coins there, 500 for the preparations and another 500 for the fee. You may leave when you're ready. Right now feel free to enjoy yourselves." He said looking around.

Sakuris caught the gold and placed it in the pouch that housed the money he had brought with him, as he and the women got up and left.

Ryuomi watched as Kayah left the pie she made for them where she had been sitting. He then turned to his father. "Father, that was the last of Kaylah's money, are you sure it was wise to pay them that much." He asked concerned.

Veroas looked at his son. "No, but I trust they will handle the assignment that has been placed before them. There is no need to worry, why don't you prepare us something to eat." He said finally noticing the pie Kayah had left, "Oh, it would seem the young one left her pie."

Ryuomi looked at it. "She said it was for us." He told Veroas as he picked it up and carried it with him. As he did, the room became filled with the pleasant aroma emanating from the baked good.

Outside the three friends talked about what they should do next. Sakuris looked up at the bright sky and then at the two of them. "Why don't the three of us go shopping in the market place?" He said to them.

Kayah looked at him excitedly. "Sakuris, really." She said happily, getting as excited as a nine-year-old in a candy store as she bounced giddily up and down.

Smiling sweetly, Saiera nuzzles close to the elder Kaemouri, kissing him on his cheek, stating, "Hmm, you certainly know the way to a woman's heart, Sakuris."

"So why are we standing around here then? We should be going." Sakuris said as he led the way.

Kayah quickly grabbed Saiera's hand and pulled her along as she followed her brother. It hadn't taken long for the three to arrive at Kaylah's market place. A few minutes after they arrived, Sakuris distributed the money equally; leaving the five hundred pieces of gold that had been for preparations alone. After the distribution, the three companions went their separate ways. Kayah went to find any form of children's entertainment she could. As she walked through, she marveled at the wooden dolls and carved artifacts that lined both sides of the streets, but soon heard the distinct laughter of three boys about her age.

She watched carefully as they surrounded and approached her, "Well what have here? What do you think guys? She looks like a lost child to me." One of them said approaching her.

Kayah had guess he was the leader of this threesome of goons. "Hey kid, why don't you go home to your mommy?" The other two laughed as they began to approach as well. Kayah began to feel threatened as they slowly approached and dropped into a cat stance with her arms up and palms facing the sky and her fingers extended outward.

The leader of the goons merely laughed, "Hey guys this one thinks she's a fighter." as he grabbed her butt. She quickly turned and smacked him causing him to recoil as he rubbed his face. "Hmm, I've seemed to have underestimated this one. Guys, I have an idea, let's rob her before we cream her." He said to his friends.

The sting of a punch soon shot through the body of one of the boys threatening Kayah. Turning around to see who had struck him, the young boy became filled with fear as he stammered trying to warn the other two of who it was, but couldn't form the words as he quickly retreated. The young man who hit the goon that ran off quickly stepped in front of

Kayah. The boss goon noticed who he was and cowered in fear. The eleven year old stared him down. "If you dare come near my girlfriend again, I will, personally, relocate your heads." He said sternly.

The remaining two goons looked at who it was. "Akisarah, we didn't know. Let's get out of here." Their leader said running off; the remaining one following behind him.

Akisarah watched as they ran off. "Cowardly jerks," He said turning to Kayah, "are you okay, miss." He said to her.

Kayah looked at him, "There was no need for you to do that. I could have handled them myself." She said rather sternly.

The boy merely looked at her. "Hi, I'm Akisarah, what's your name." He said with sarcastic tone in his voice.

Kayah studied him carefully. "Sorry, I am only used to my brother's help. My name is Kayah." She said getting a look at who helped her, "You know; you're kind of cute." She said as she walked past him.

Turning his head to look over his shoulder, Akisarah remarks "Wait, please, allow me to come with you. The people respect me, and will treat you better."

Kayah stopped as she turned to look at him, responding, "Thanks, I'd like that. Just don't get any funny ideas."

Akisarah bowed humbly. "Milady, I am as gentlemanly as they come." He said to her, but at the same thinking, *"I am going to like this one. She's a fighter, a girl after my own heart."* As he extends his arm toward her

She stared at it. "I don't understand. Do you want me to take your arm?" She said to him and he nodded. Kayah liked the idea; a guy had never been willing to escort her around like this before.

Looking at him as she walked, she felt strangely drawn to him as she studied his well-built physique. She could tell this guy was way beyond cute. His strong build deceived the untrained eye about his age. She then noticed a pair of sticks that resided within a leather scabbard that was strapped about his shoulder, "Kali Sticks?" She asked rather inquisitively as she walked next to her new found friend.

He nodded. "I see you know your weapons, by the way, that stance of yours back there; it was a ginta stance, was it not?" He asked curious of the stance Kayah had assumed.

Kayah had suddenly realized she had given herself away as a Dragon Clansman. "Yes, but please don't tell anyone. My brother would have a fit if he found out." She responded in an almost pleading manner.

Akisarah held up his hand. "Don't worry I won't say anything. I should have let you handle those guys and just watched. They really would've learned not to mess with you. Oh sorry about calling you my girlfriend earlier. But the protective boyfriend bit always scares them away." He said to her. The spring wind blew through his wavy hair as Kayah merely walked closer to him, sliding her arm around his waist. What was this strange feeling that was coming over her? She continued to wonder about this as they walked through the market.

On the other side of the market, Saiera was looking for new outfits to wear. She walked past the clothing booths marveling at all the outfits that ranged from conservative to sexy. She giggled as she thought about the sexy outfits she could buy and only wear for Sakuris. Quickly spotting a booth whose outfits suited what she was looking for, she decided to walk over and began looking through the clothing that hung down from the long wooden beams that ran across the booth, becoming partially distracted by all the hustle and bustle of the crowd going through the marketplace, as all the shopkeepers held up their weapons, treasures, and trinkets. Turning her attention back to vendor's booth, she continued to look through the outfits on display. Some were very exquisite, while others were more modest

The female shopkeeper saw her and quickly anticipated the sale. "May I help you, miss?" She asked pleasantly with a smile as she walked over to Saiera.

The sudden voice startled Saiera as she looked from behind the outfit she was marveling at. "Yes, I want something romantic, but that makes me look a little less figured." She responded.

The shopkeeper instructed Saiera to step into view where she could study her form. Following the woman's Saiera allowed the vendor to look at her for as she circled her scanning her from head to toe. "I think I might have something." She informed her as stepped back into her booth and from the shelf pulled down a long, scarlet-red kimono-dress and handed it to Saiera. "Here try this one on." She said as Saiera took it into her grasp.

"Oh, my," Saiera gasped, marveling at the dress's gold trim. "It looks expensive. I can't take this, it's just too exquisite." She then hastily handed the dress back to the vendor.

"Well at least try it on before you decide." She said urging Saiera to try the dress on as she offered it back to her.

Saiera shrugged and looked around. The shopkeeper pointed to where she could change. Walked over to the changing area, Saiera stripped down to her underclothing and slipped the dress over her head and let it dangle down to her feet. The dress came just short of reaching the ground as it rested on the laced sandals she wore. Stepping from the changing area, she walks over to the shopkeeper who looks at her.

"Miss, you must buy it. It's perfect for you and just the right length, too." She said urging Saiera to buy the dress.

It was midday in the market and Saiera was still hesitant about the dress. "Well, how much is it?" She asked. The shopkeeper had certainly picked out the right thing for her. The dress dangled loose enough from Saiera's blossomed figure to conceal it well enough not to be noticed but tight enough to still maintain the romantic fit she was looking for.

The shopkeeper looked at her, "Normally about forty gold coins, but since business has been slow and it is such a beautiful dress on you I'll sell it to you for half the price." Saiera continued to marvel at the dress it certainly suited her as the shades of scarlet red brought out her tanned complexion.

"I don't know, it's such a beautiful dress. It should be sold to a princess, but certainly not me." She said, but she had seen the pleading look on the shopkeeper's face and she really did want the dress, "Fifteen gold coins."

The shopkeeper perked up, "I'll take eighteen, and not a coin less." Saiera nodded and took out eighteen of her gold coins and handed them to the shopkeeper. She then went back to the changing area and again stripped down to change back into her regular clothing.

Taking great not to damage her new dress, Saiera carefully folds it before proceeding to dress back in her everyday wear. Once dressed she steps out and looks at the shopkeeper. "Uh, by the way, I have this friend, an eleven-year-old who wants to look a little fuller in the chest. Do you have something that might help her?" She asked.

Wanting to know more, the shopkeeper looks at Saiera and asks for a description.

Saiera looked only to see Kayah running up to her with Akisarah close behind. "This is she." Saiera said to shopkeeper pointing down to Kayah.

The woman came from behind her booth and scanned Kayah from head to toe, as she had done with Saiera. "I don't know, but I'll look." She responded as she went back behind her booth and began rummaging through the clothing.

Puzzled by this, Kayah looks at Saiera. "Why did she just do that?" She asked. Saiera knelt down next to Kayah.

"I'm buying new outfits, so I decided to buy one for you as well." She responded noticing Akisarah, "Well it seems you made a new friend, and a handsome young man he is, too. And what might your name be, young man"

"Akisarah, son of Kamikawi, ma'am." He responded with a masculine confidence in his voice as he bows before her.

"Oh, my," Saiera gasped, "such confidence." She then turned to Kayah and gave her a sly look as if to say: Hold on to this one.

The female shopkeeper soon came back with another kimono-dress and draped it in front of Kayah. Its deep violet color matched Kayah's eyes, "Why don't you try it on?" Saiera said showing Kayah where she could change. It was good Akisarah was there. Saiera wanted a young man's opinion considering that's whom Kayah wanted to be noticed by. If the first place Akisarah's eyes went to was Kayah's bust, the dress would have certainly done its job.

Stepping into the changing area, Kayah strips down to her under clothing and slips the dress over her head letting it dangle down to her sandals as Saiera had done. When she looked down to study how the dress looked on her, she suddenly became very aware of her chest, excliaming "I have boobs!"

From outside the three had heard her. *"I think it worked."* Saiera thought to herself.

Akisarah merely shook his head as he let his hand stroke the ends of his kali sticks that were still strapped about his shoulder. *"She may be cute, but she is weird."* He thought.

Kayah soon stepped out and the three stared at her with embarrassed expressions on their faces. "Oops, I guess you heard me." She said as everyone nodded; making Kayah turned redder than a ruby from embarrassment.

Akisarah could only notice how good the dress looked on her. "You know I rather like how that dress looks on her, very scintillating." He said aloud.

"Akisarah!" Kayah gasped as she flashed him a dirty look.

He merely shrugged. "What? I'm a guy. If a woman looks good in something I'm going to notice. It's not like I was staring at you." He responded quite humorously.

Kayah merely smiled at the compliment, cheerfully responding "Well, thank you."

Saiera looked at her. "I like it, just be careful about wearing it around Sakuris. He would probably bite my head off for buying that for you." She said looking around. She and Kayah got a few more dresses and new sandals and left to find Sakuris. Kayah motioned for Akisarah to follow, but he declined and told her he had to get home as he hurried along his way leaving the two women.

Kayah was saddened to see her new friend leave but was happy to have met him nonetheless.

Saiera soon wrapped her arm around Kayah's shoulder and beckoned her along so they may find Sakuris.

Meanwhile, Sakuris had found a weapon shop to look around at and approached it. "Excuse me, sir." He said to the shopkeeper who turned and looked at him.

"Yes, young man, what can I do for you today?" He asked him with a sly grin.

Sakuris unstrapped his swords from his waist and handed them to the shopkeeper. "I need these sharpened. Can you do that?" He asked him.

The shopkeeper took out one of the swords and inspected the blade, "I could, but, with the condition they're in, you'd be better off buying new ones." He lied trying to get Sakuris to buy one of his poorly made swords.

Another shopkeeper called to him, "Young man, may I inspect those!" The shopkeeper who had already been inspecting the blades shot a look toward the one who called to Sakuris that said: This is my sale.

Sakuris reclaimed his blades from the shopkeeper and took them over to the other one who studied them carefully. "He was trying to con you. Never go to him." He said to Sakuris in a low voice, "I can re-forge these seven times over making than sharper than ever, and at a good price. I wouldn't even have to replace the blade."

The last part the man's statement was good news to Sakuris. "How good of a price?" He asked inquiring how much he would have to spend.

"For you young man, 40 gold coins. Considering this is a 50 gold coin job." The shop owner responded.

The ten coin discount was music to Sakuris's ears. "How long would it take for them to dull back down?" He asked.

The shopkeeper looked at Sakuris, "My boy, you asked just the right question. Some of these items I just forged . . . one year ago." He responded in an honest tone.

Another customer came up to the booth. "Trust me, kid. I can vouch for that. He's the best blacksmith here. I've been coming to him for a long time." He said purchasing a twin blade very similar to Sakuris's.

Sakuris thought about it and figured it's worth the risk. He gave the shopkeeper the money and let him work. "It'll take some time. I'll need till tomorrow afternoon. You seemed to have kept these in good condition despite the scratches and worn down edge." The shopkeeper said to him as he heated the metal in a large fire pit.

Chapter 3

Sakuris remained silent as he looked and noticed a nearby jewelry shop. "Let me get back to you on that." He responded as he walked over to Sakuris continued to look around at the weapons in the shop and noticed a long bow made of cherry wood in the back, "Excuse me, how much is the bow right there. The one made from cherry wood." He asked the shopkeeper.

The shopkeeper looked at him and then at the bow, "About 30 gold coins, you want to buy it." He said to him.

Sakuris remained silent as he looked around, noticing a nearby jewelry shop. "Let me get back to you on that." He responds, stepping away and walking over to the jewelry shop to look at the various rings that were on display.

The female shopkeeper looked at him. "May I help you, young man?" She said sweetly with a smile and soft tone of voice.

"Perhaps, I need a ring for an eleven year old girl whose fingers are about half as thick as mine." Sakuris responds as he looks through the rings on display.

The woman handed him a gold ring encrusted with a single emerald in the center. Taking the ring in hand, Sakuris inspects it before looking back at the shopkeeper. "Not to sound picky, but do you, perhaps, have one that's just plain gold?" He asked until something caught his eye: A pendant hanging behind her. Dangling from it was a charm: A star housed in a crescent moon. "Actually, may I see that pendant behind you; the one with star charm." He said handing the ring back to her.

The shopkeeper turned around and took the pendant into her grasp and handed it to Sakuris, who studied the charm closely, "Can you tell me what this charm means?"

Nodding the vendor looks at him replying, "It means friendship."

"Kayah would love this." Sakuris thinks to himself, purchasing the pendant, "By the way, do you sell bracelets; it's for a special woman. It needs to scream 'I love you.'" He asked her.

She looked at him and nodded, "Yes I might have something." She said handing Sakuris a gold bracelet with the same symbol.

Looking the bracelet over, he inspects closely, stating "This is perfect." before purchasing the item. Accepting payment for the items, the vendor hands Sakuris a couple of jewelry boxes; one for Kayah's pendant and the other for Saiera's bracelet. Satisfied with his purchases, Sakuris leaves to find the women. It didn't take long before he saw Saiera and Kayah, who just changed out of the dress she bought. He carefully hid their gifts within the pocket of his kimono sleeve and walked over to them calmly as though he didn't buy anything, remarking, "I was just about to go looking for you. You ready to go?"

Kayah had noticed her brother's blades were missing. "Sakuris, where're your swords." She asked frantically.

Sakuris shook his head. "Calm down I took them to get sharpened." He said reassuring her that everything was fine. She let out a sigh of relief as she embraced him.

Their outing complete, the three returned to the fort, arriving just as night had fallen. Sakuris led the women inside his room and presented them with the jewelry he bought. Marveling at the gifts, Saiera and Kayah both gasped in surprise as their eyes lit up with excitement.

Kayah hugged her brother, thanking him for the pendant. "Sakuris you didn't have to do this." She said releasing him.

Saiera kissed him lightly as she looked at the bracelet. "Sakuris, why don't you come down to the hot spring later so I can thank you properly?" She said still marveling at the bracelet.

After each purchase had been exchanged and shown, the women gathered their things and started out the door when Sakuris called Saiera back over. She walked over to him as he handed her a few herbs and a flask of milk, instructing her that if Kayah has any more nightmares, to crush one of the herbs into a fine powder and mix it in with some warm milk to help her fall back asleep. Saiera nodded, kissed him again and placed the items in her bag before taking Kayah and herself back to their room where they talked about their day before falling asleep.

Alone in his room, Sakuris poured some wine for himself and sat down on his bed, *"Tomorrow Saiera will take me and Kayah to see her friends. I should find something suitable to wear."* He thought before hearing a knock on his door. He went over and answered it to see Saiera standing in the red kimono-dress she had bought for herself at the market place.

The sight of Saiera in the dress left Sakuris speechless as he stared at her with a dumb-founded expression. "You going to stand there and stare or are you going to let me in." She teases as Sakuris quickly steps aside and motions for her to come in.

Stepping inside, Saiera embraces her beloved, asking him, "Shall we go?"

"What about Kayah?" He replies, concerned for his sister's well-being.

"She's fine. She's in her room and its being guarded." She reassures him as he returns her embrace. Reassured of his sister's safety, Sakuris acknowledges he is ready and the two leave to venture down to the hot spring.

Back at Kayah's room Akisarah approaches as the guards carefully watch him. "Lady Kayah's not to be disturbed." One of them states.

Akisarah looks at the guard who spoke to them, "Tell Kayah, 'Akisarah Kamakawi has come to see her.'" The noise outside had awoken Kayah from her slumber compelling her she to walk to the door and see what is happening. Opening it, she is met with the sight of Akisarah and the guard arguing.

"Akisarah, what are you doing here?" She asks, letting him in.

Walking past the guards, Akisarah enters the room as Kayah closes the door behind them. "I thought, perhaps, we could go down to the shore and watch the fireflies go by." He responds invitingly.

Beginning to get the feeling of connection she had gotten earlier, Kayah looks at him, *"What is this feeling I get when I am around him?"* She wondered before speaking. "Well, I suppose I could. Wait here for a second." She said walking over to her bag and taking out some Washi paper and writing on it. Setting it on Saiera's bed, she grabs her diamond dagger and walks over to Akisarah, who was still carrying his kali sticks about his shoulders. "Fair warning, you even look at me wrong and I will hurt you. Now with that said, let's go." She warned him as they walked the door.

He smiled at her, remarking "Fair enough for me." as they walked through the fort and down to the river.

Sakuris and Saiera had arrived at the hot spring. Saiera took off her sandals and sat down at the edge letting her feet dangle in the water as the warm breeze blew through the trees that were veiled in the night's shadow. Sakuris had wasted no time to undress and climb in. "Come on in Saiera, the water's great. Say, you ever had a massage." He said to her letting the water trickle down his wet body. She looked at him and shook her head.

"No, actually, I have not." She responded rather plainly as she looked at him from the spring's edge, allowing her feet to continue dangling in the warm water.

"Would you like one? My father taught me how when I was younger." He said to her letting his arms drift in the water. She smiled and undressed, as Sakuris took her by the hand and helped her as she climbed in.

It was clear to her that being with him made her forget about her life in Sikan. She swam over to him and positioned herself to she was facing him as she flung her arms about his neck. "Hmm, I just want to be with you tonight, but I am curious as to what a massage is." She replied as she lightly kissed him.

Sakuris smiled and swam over to the edge. He reached into his bag and pulled out a small bottle of oil and opened it. He tipped it letting a few small drops trickle into his hand. He then closed the bottle and placed it on the edge as Saiera swam closer to him. He smiled at her as he swam behind her rubbing his hands together. He placed them on her shoulders and began massaging them firm enough to relax her, but gently enough not to hurt her.

Slowly he moved down, massaging her back as she let out a sigh of contentment. "Mmm, Sakuris, that feels good." She said as he massaged her back.

He looked at her lovingly. "My father believed in the healing power of a massage. Accessing the right energy points of the human anatomy, you can alleviate pain, increase stimulation, or render a person unconscious." He said to her, "The style I'm doing now is for relaxation, but I can move on to a more pleasurable form if you wish."

She smiled at him. "I like this form just fine." She replied letting his hands work over her skin. The warmth of the night's gentle wind helped to relax her even more as she allowed the heat of the spring's water to penetrate her very core.

Meanwhile, Kayah was spending the night down by the river with Akisarah watching the fireflies buzz by in silence. Akisarah looked at her silent expression. "Kayah, is something wrong? You've been silent ever since we've arrived." He asked her concerned.

She looked at him sadly. "Sitting here reminds of the nights I would spend by the crystal clear shores of Shikanaca. My parents would take my brother and me down to the coast to watch the fireflies that buzzed there. Their ballet of flashing lights would always fascinate me. I would cry when my father said, 'We had to go.' and insist that we stayed, but he'd take me into his arms and carry me as we went home. That was before. . . Before . . ." She said as tears began forming in her eyes and flowing down her cheeks.

Akisarah looked at her and saw the expression on her face. "Forgive me; I've upset you by bringing you down here." He said getting up to leave.

"No wait." Kayah exclaims frantically taking him by the hand getting the same feeling she had before. What was it about this young man that made her have this feeling? "Don't go, please stay here with me." She pleaded looking up at him.

As Akisarah sat back down, Kayah buried her face into his shoulder letting tears flow from her eyes. Putting his arm around her shoulder, he rocked her gently, whispering, "Shh, you're ok. I'm here and I'm not leaving."

Back at the fort Ryuomi was walking along with his father, "The warriors start their journey tomorrow, father. Once they've slain Zecuroas, gold will flow from the mines and Kaylah will be prosperous once again." He said turning to Veroas. Veroas would have responded, but was stopped when an explosion happened at the front wall.

Akisarah and Kayah heard and saw the explosion from the river. "That's where the northern wall is! There are intruders in the fortress!"Akisarah exclaimed rushing backing to the fortress with Kayah running after him, struggling to keep up.

Saiera and Sakuris both felt the shockwave of the explosion at the hot spring. Saiera looked to see the village was engulfed in flames, exclaiming, "Sakuris, the village, look!"

Turning his attention to the village, Sakuris notices the same thing, exclaiming "By, Elayis, the village!" as the two of them frantically climb out of the hot spring and rush to get dressed before running back to the village.

As they got closer they could feel the intense heat of the flame as the smoke clouded their eyes and impaired their vision. "I can't see through the smoke Sakuris what do we do?" Saiera asked frantically trying to find her way through the smoke.

Sakuris stepped forward and flung his arms forward making the wind rise as it cut through the smoke like the sharp blade of a knife, clearing a path that led through the smoke. "Hurry, we need to move quickly." He said, running on ahead. Saiera quickly ran after him. They arrived at the village at the same time as Kayah and Akisarah. The four of them saw Ryuomi and ran over to him. Ryuomi saw them as they approached and ran over to meet them.

"Ryuomi, what's happening?" Sakuris inquired as the five of them gathered together. Around them, the village continued to burn from the sweltering flames as Isuran forces began pouring through the breach in the wall.

"The village is under siege. Isuran forces have breached our northern wall." Ryuomi responded trying to remain calm as he reported the situation to them.

Willing to lend any aid he could Sakuris immediate asks, "Is there anything we can do to help?"

Ryuomi nodded, responding, "Yes, but we'll need everybody. We need to ensure the safety of the villagers. My forces and I can deal with the Isurans. Sakuris, you and Akisarah help with the fires. Kayah, Saiera, rouse the fort and bring everyone into the open that you can and get a head count." as they separated.

Quickly running to a nearby burning building, Sakuris began to form a shapeless pool of water in his hands, by gathering water vapor out of the air, and, aiming it at the base of the flame, let off a powerful yell releasing a strong jet of water at the flame slowly extinguishing it. Lowering his hands, he is thrown to the ground by a powerful flame bursting through a nearby window. As he lands his gi-top opens up and brushes against a dying flame, catching fire. Four of the villagers saw this and rushed over to help him, carrying wooden buckets full of water. Two of them helped Sakuris remove his gi-top and doused the flame out with water.

Looking at the villagers, he nods thankfully before collecting the water in the remaining buckets, from the other two villagers, and forming it into a rain cloud moving it above the burning building using his hand to steady it. He quickly dropped his hand and released a down-pour of water onto the home extinguishing the fire, but the relentless blaze would not back down as burning debris collapsed into the home, and the faint cries of a child could be heard coming from inside. Hearing them, Sakuris quickly douses himself with water and runs inside the inferno.

While Sakuris battled with blazing inferno, Saiera and Kayah were bringing every one into the open and started helping to douse the immense blaze that had befallen Kaylah. The villagers who were with Sakuris continued to work to douse the flame trying to buy Sakuris enough time to rescue the child within. Inside the home Sakuris could feel the intense heat of the flame as he frantically searched through the home trying to follow the cries for help as they became louder. As he got closer to where they were coming from, he continued to search through the home as it burned. Back outside, Saiera rushed over to help the villagers who had been fighting the blaze as flames continued to burst through open windows.

"That crazy fool, he's going to get himself killed!" One of them called over the noise of the flame.

Saiera quickly looked at him. "There's someone in there?" She exclaimed hoping he wouldn't say it was Sakuris.

He looked back at her, still working to douse the fire and responded, "Some traveler named Sakuris."

Saiera suddenly felt her heart beginning to race before rushing to get into the home, but all four of the villagers held her back. All she could do was watch helplessly as the home continued to burn. Her heart began racing so fast, it was as if it was trying to escape through her chest. Minutes later, Sakuris crashed through a window clutching a young child with a flame quickly following out behind him.

With a hard landing, he gashed his arm on a small sharp stone as it deeply cut into his right arm ripping his flesh from his shoulder half way down his upper arm. The child he had been clutching was wrapped in wet blanket. Both of them were choking as fresh air rushed back into their lungs as the five wannabe firefighters rushed over to help them. Saiera quickly took the child into her arms and flashed a cold stare at Sakuris. "Are you crazy?" She demanded to know.

He looked at her as he continued to cough finally getting air into his lungs, "Yes, but not suicidal." He responded using a phrase he was fond of using when he was younger.

He quickly clutched the burnt remains of his upper-body wear and placed it over his wound as it quickly became stained red from his blood.

While all this was going on, Ryuomi and the forces of Kaylah were doing the best they could to fend off the Isuran attack on the fortress, as Saiera announced the presence of the child.

Hearing the announcement, a female villager rushed over. "Show me the child please." She pleaded.

Saiera pulled back the blanket revealing the face of a young girl. "Are you the mother?" She asked.

The woman quickly nodded as she took her daughter into her arms and looked at her and then back to Saiera. "Thank you, young woman." She said to her quickly taking her daughter into her arms.

Saiera shook her head. "Thank Sakuris here; he was the one crazy enough to go into the flames to find her." She replies, turning to Sakuris.

The child's mother looked at Sakuris. "Thank you, young man, I am eternally grateful. Is there anything I can do to repay you?" She asked eager to return the favor, but Sakuris shook his head as blood trickled down his arm from underneath the wadded up clothing.

The woman looked to see the blood running down his arm. "You're injured!" She exclaimed looking at Sakuris's arm.

Sakuris looked down at his arm, "I'll live; it's just a scratch." He said to her.

The woman looked at him in surprise. "That's no mere scratch, it needs to be stitched, please sit down and let me take care of it." She said reaching into her kimono sleeve pocket and pulling out a needle and some thread.

Sakuris sat down on a nearby stone as the woman worked quickly to sew his wound closed while everyone else worked to douse the fire throughout the night. By morning the flames had died down and extinguished themselves. Sakuris looked at the woman as she finished stitching his arm closed. "Thank you." He said to her as rays of sunlight flooded all over Kaylah revealing only the remains of burnt houses.

The Isuran forces were also driven back by the Kaylahn soldiers. Despite this, a looming feeling of dread hung in the air as though this was merely the calm before a bigger storm. Suddenly, as the rest of the Isuran forces were pushed back out of the fortress, Sakuris and Saiera beheld a familiar sight. It was the demon that had destroyed their homes now marching through the opening in the Kaylahn wall.

"It's . . ." Saiera began but stopped her sentence when she saw Sakuris approaching it with a cold stare in his eyes. She could sense his intent as she watched him draw forth his two sacred blades and join them together at the handles. "Sakuris, no, beloved, you can't defeat it on your own!" She pleaded as loudly as she could hoping he would come to his senses, but he continued his determined approach towards the demon as it began attacking the Kaylahn forces who tried to combat it "Sakuris! It'll kill you! Please don't go!" Saiera pleaded once more as she cried out after him.

Ignoring her, he continued his determined march toward the creature. "Nii-Sama!" Kayah cried as she ran up to him, "Nii-Sama, you can't."

"Kayah!" Akisarah called as he ran up to the two of them.

"Akisarah, take my sister somewhere safe." Sakuris instructed their new friend as he continued his march onward, thinking, *"Mother, Father, this is for you."* Joining his weapons together, he quickly dashes out into a sprint toward the creature, and charges them with power, causing the blades to glow a bright blue color, and shouting "TWIN-SILVER FANG ATTACK!" unleashing all the power he could from them once he was within range of the creature.

In awe from his actions, Saiera and the others could only watch as Sakuris continued to approach the creature as his weapon's sustained their beam of energy. Having been struck by the sacred power of Sakuris's weapon the creature reeled out in pain as it began to recoil and slowly withdraw from the area.

"Die, you monster!" Sakuris shouted as fire burned in his eyes and rage enflamed his heart igniting his soul ablaze with a lust for vengeance, but the power of a single sacred blade wouldn't be enough to fall the monster as it withdrew from the Kaylahn fortress and disappeared from sight.

Lost in his rage, it took a moment for Sakuris to realize what had happened, and when he did he fell to his knees and for the first time since the death of parents allowed a stream of tears to finally flow down his face as he broke down from sorrow with everyone, including Saiera and Kayah, gathering around him. Some even brought blankets to cover him with as they helped him to his feet.

Chapter 4

With Saiera at his side, Sakuris stood up and looked around as wiped the tears from his face and composed himself. Ryuomi soon approached them. "Bold move standing up to that demon by yourself, Master Kaemouri." He said complimenting Sakuris's bravery.

Separating his swords, Sakuris houses them back in their scabbard, responding, "It was reckless."

Looking in the direction of the northern wall, Ryuomi chuckles, "At any rate, it might make Isura think twice before deciding to attack here again."

"Nii-sama?" Kayah asked as she approached Sakuris with Akisarah closely following.

"Kayah," Sakuris said relieved as he took his sister into his arms and held her close to him, "are you injured?"

Kayah merely shook her head and informed her brother she was unharmed. Looking to Akisarah, Sakuris knealt down in front of him to look him in the eye. "I owe you a great debt, my young friend. You kept my sister safe when I was unable."

Akisarah merely bowed before Sakuris, responding, "I'm just glad I could be of assistance. If you'll excuse me, though, my people need me." as he turns to leave with Ryuomi following close behind him.

Kayah looks to her brother who had gone back to observing the damage. "Brother, what do we do now?" She asks him.

He looks at her from where he was standing, stating in a stern tone, "We do nothing. You, little miss, are going to explain to me what you were doing out with him so late at night and alone."

Kayah looks down sadly, "Yes, I expected that. He came to me last night and asked me to go to the river with him to watch the fire flies, like we used to do back at Shikanaca, remember."

Sakuris's heart became filled by a sudden loneliness when Kayah had reminded them of their past and he slowly nodded, "Yes I remember. He didn't touch you, did he?"

Kayah shook her head and explaining the events that had taken place at the river.

Though Sakuris had slowly started to trust Akisarah, he was still amazed at how he had not taken advantage of Kayah's childish nature.

Holding the two women close to him he laughs momentarily and leads them onward. "Come on you two; let's go help them clean up." He remarks as the three of them walk through the remains of Kaylah.

"Sakuris, I still wish for you to meet that young couple." Saiera gently reminds him.

"Let's get some fresh clothing on, first." He replies, with a nod, pointing out how torn his clothing had become. Though some of the rooms had caught fire, only the one Sakuris rescued the little girl from had been occupied.

Returning to their rooms, the three travelers removed their dirty, smoke scented clothing and changed into more appropriate attire, before meeting at Kaylah's gate, and leaving the fortress town to meet the young couple, of whom Saiera had spoken.

About a mile down the road, the three of them got caught in a downpour of rain. Saiera knew they were close and urged her two companions to continue. As they walked Saiera's thin red silk clothing became see through. Sakuris looked at her as she held her head down.

"Sakuris, about what happened between us . . ." She said to him.

Motioning for Saiera to be still with her words, Sakuris continued to look at her as they walked. "Say nothing more, Saiera." He responded and then turned to Kayah. "Kayah, that Akisarah kid is a handsome one. You should hold on to him for as long as you can. Friends like that are hard to find." He informed her as the three of them walked. The rain fell hard upon them causing them to become drenched.

Kayah looked over to her brother with a sad expression, "You are speaking of Reia. I hope she made it out of Shikanaca; I would hate to have lost her, along with so many other brave soldiers. She was the best female we had."

"I know, Kayah. I know." Sakuris remarked as they continued to walk through the rain. Kayah's statement had drawn Sakuris's attention back to the day he had met Reia, making him worry how he would feel if he ever saw her again.

Saiera suddenly broke his concentration. "Sakuris, I hope your friend is all right." She said to him with a smile.

Sakuris remembered that even though Reia was short in size, she could cut him down easily if she tried. The two of them had sparred together many times always with the same result.

Lost in her thoughts, Kayah wondered about Akisarah and the feeling she would get whenever she was around him. It was a feeling she would have to talk to Saiera about for despite her efforts to discern it, it was always elusive to her as it clutched at her heart like the talon of an eagle causing her to stop and dwell on it. Sakuris and Saiera both turned back to see her letting each raindrop hit her as they fell. Sakuris would have approached, but Saiera recognized the expression on Kayah's face and realized it was a woman's problem that Sakuris could never understand.

She held him back and motioned she would approach her. "Kayah, is something wrong." She said in a low tone as she knelt beside her.

"Miss Saiera, how did you know when you were in love with my brother?" This sudden question had caught Saiera off guard and she motioned for Sakuris to go on ahead. Unsure of what to make of the situation, Sakuris nods in agreement and leaves the two women alone to speak.

"Does this have something to do with Akisarah?" She asked hoping Kayah would give her an honest answer.

"When I was with him, I would always get this indiscernible feeling. I have tried to clear my head of it so many times and even attempt to clear up the feeling itself, but it always seemed blurred. What is this feeling? I must know." She said raising her voice a bit letting tears flow from her eyes.

Saiera quickly embraced Kayah letting her rest her head on her shoulder. "Shh, this is a feeling you can't understand now. When you're older it'll become clearer. It was the same feeling I had gotten when I was around your brother. It is still unclear to me as to what it is, though I have a better understanding of it after spending time with him." She said as she stroked Kayah's soft hair that had become wet from the rain.

Having left the two women to speak amongst themselves, Sakuris had taken the brief rest to meditate. He took the same ginta stance Kayah had, when she confronted the boys in Kaylah, and closed his eyes. He remembered the practice of Seltah his father taught him when he wanted to reach the unreachable. He closed his eyes letting his mind become open and could soon hear his father's voice speaking to him.

"My son, you have remembered the sacred teachings passed only from father to son." It said to him.

"Father, Kayah misses you and mother. She is not sleeping well, I have had to come to rely on medicinal herbs mixed with milk to help her sleep, but I know longer wish to secretly pump her small body full of tranquilizing herbs. The effect it might be having on her worries me." He said speaking to his father mentally letting his breathing become slow.

"Kayah is deeply troubled my son. Her thoughts dwell on a young man. She is seeking guidance from the young woman you met in the forest." His father said to him.

"How did you know of Saiera?" Sakuris asked puzzled as he continued to maintain the telepathy with his father.

He could hear his father's small laugh. "I have been watching from the other side, my son. You were also never able to hide anything from me. You mustn't worry about your sister, she has her fate and you have yours. However, your path has rarely been easy and this fate might not be what you want. Now tell me what lies beyond your fists." His father's voice said speaking to him mentally.

Sakuris opened his Seltitian mind further as if trying to reach through time itself and soon saw images he could not comprehend. He saw two dragons coming from the sky and fighting each other; one a shimmering gold, the other a dark black. Was this the fate set for him? He then saw an explosion as the gold dragon wrapped itself around the black one and drove it into the ground.

He heard his father's voice again. "What lies beyond, my son?" It asked.

Sakuris opened his eyes and let only two words escape from his mouth: My fate.

Saiera, meanwhile, was still doing her best to help Kayah discern her thoughts about Akisarah. "This feeling you have been having is something you should discuss with him, Kayah. Sakuris should know as well." She said still embracing her; the rain continuing to fall around them.

"No, Sakuris is not to be brought into this." Kayah responded breaking free of Saiera's embrace.

Saiera looked at her. "I think it would it wise if you told Sakuris." She said to her.

Kayah merely shook her head. "No, please don't tell him." She pleaded still letting tears flow down her olive colored skin.

Saiera looked at her and nodded taking Kayah by the hand and leading her down the road, responding, "Very well, I won't say anything to him."

They walked down the road to where Sakuris had been meditating. He looked at them and then to Kayah who dried her tears on her already wet clothing. He could sense the secret she hid from him; his father had been right. He didn't bother to confront her about it. This was something she would have no choice but to face on her own. He could not help her this time.

Saiera merely walked past Sakuris still holding Kayah's hand as she led them down the road. Just another mile down the path, they came to a fairly good sized log cabin. Releasing Kayah's hand Saiera approaches the door and knocks firmly upon it. The rain poured down hard upon them as Saiera listened for footsteps inside while the two siblings stood behind her, waiting to meet their potential parents.

A few minutes later, footsteps could be heard approaching the door as it slowly opened. A middle aged man, who appeared to be in his mid-thirties stood looking at Saiera. His jet-black hair matched his well-maintained facial hair. He wore a black gi, a fighting suit worn when sparring. Black, silver studded gloves concealed his hands. He took a careful look at the visitors and recognized Saiera. "So you've returned Saiera and you've brought friends I see." He said to her motioning to the siblings who stood behind her.

She nodded as the rain continued to fall on them. "Hello, Sinileass, it has been awhile, may we come in; it's wet out here." She said to him not meaning to sound rude. Sinileass gave a small smile and let the three of them in.

Inside the cabin, Sakuris took a look around and marveled at the weapons displayed on the walls. *"It's so much like Shikanaca."* He thought to himself. He was always fascinated with the weapons that had been displayed on the walls around Shikanaca's dojo.

Sinileass looked around and then called into the kitchen, "Reia, we have guests, bring food and wine."

Upon hearing his friend's name, Sakuris had forgotten his obsession with Sinileass's weapons and quickly showed himself into the kitchen where he caught sight of Reia who had been doing some cooking. "R-Reia," He said stammering to get her name out, "Is it really you?"

Reia looked from her cooking over to him and caught sight of his amber colored eyes. "Sa-ku-ris, it can't be you. I saw your home burn as I made my escape." She said pulling her glance away from him letting tears flow from her eyes clenching her fist closed so tight her arms trembled. She turned away from him showing only her back to him.

Sakuris went over and placed his arm on her shoulder, but she turned around and knocked it away. "Don't touch me. Don't even come near me." She ordered him, leaving the room and going up a flight of stairs that led to her room.

Sinileass entered the kitchen. "Are you Master Sakuris?" He asked approaching Sakuris, but he paid him no mind as he took out a small flute that Reia had made for him when they were young and stared at it.

He stood dazed as he stared at wooden instrument. *"Reia, I thought 'You were dead.', but now I find you alive."* He thought to himself as closed his hand around the wooden instrument and, letting a single tear roll down his cheek.

Sinileass stared at him, "Young man, young man is something wrong." He asked as Sakuris merely stood stone silent. "Young man, can you hear me?"

Sakuris merely ignored him and brought the wooden flute up to his lips and blew softly across the opening as he let an enchanting tune escape from the instrument letting it echo throughout the home, *"Reia, hear our song and remember. I know you know who I am."* He thought as he played.

"That's Reia's song. Why is he playing it?" Sinileass thought as he watched Sakuris play the instrument, "Young man, please don't play that if you're not Sakuris." He said to him.

Sakuris took the flute from his lips and looked at him. The gaze that he held in his eyes at that moment could make even the strongest man cower at the very sight of him, "I am Sakuris." He responded. The same song Sakuris had played could soon be heard coming from Reia's room, "Shh, listen to the language she speaks."

Sinileass listened to the song. "I see, you two communicate through notes and rhythms, fascinating." He said as he listened, "What is she saying?"

"She's saying,' I can't believe you're alive. It's been five years since the Great Destruction.' Those are the words hidden within the notes." Sakuris responded as he listened.

"Are you going to go to her?" Sinileass asked looking at him.

Sakuris shook his head, "No, we'll leave her be for tonight. Seeing me here has upset her." He responded in a plain manner.

Sinileass merely looked at him. "My name is Sinileass. I just thought I let you know. My wife, Kyusa, is upstairs enjoying a hot bath. She'll be down soon." He said looking at Sakuris.

"Do you know where I may change and rest, sir. My sister and I have had a busy night and I wish to get some sleep before I have to head back out. So if you may kindly show me a room. I don't mean to be a burden, but my sister and I have nowhere else to go. That's why Saiera brought us here." Sakuris responded quite openly.

Sinileass nodded, "I know, Saiera told me what happened to your parents, it's most unfortunate. There's an empty bedroom upstairs. You may bathe and change there. It's the first door on the right as you turn to your left."

"Thank you, your hospitality is most gracious." Sakuris said with a low bow. He then walked out of the kitchen and into the main room and proceeded upstairs to the bedroom Sinileass had mentioned.

Walking into the main room, Sinileass looks to Saiera. "That Sakuris is a quiet one, he is. Still much pain I sense in his heart almost as if something was eating away at his soul. He also seems to hide a great deal of anger over the loss of his parents even over the course of the last five years." He said sitting down in a chair on the other side of the room.

Saiera looked to Kayah who had fallen asleep in her lap and then at Sinileass. "Please say nothing more on the subject, I am here out of his sister's best interests." She said to him stroking Kayah's, still wet, soft hair as she slept.

Sinileass merely nodded, "Right, you wish for Kyusa and me to become their foster parents. Some extra help would be useful with harvest time rapidly approaching, and Kyusa has been saying, 'She's needs more help in the kitchen' plus with the two of them here, Reia could spend more time on her studies. Still, this is something I'll need to discuss with Kyusa, but that can wait darkness has come and it's getting late. Why don't you go up and get some sleep? I'll take Kayah up and put to her bed myself." He said standing up.

Saiera stood up and handed Kayah to him. "Make sure she's close to Sakuris's room. She has nightmares and needs to be given a mixture of milk and herbs to help her go back to sleep." She informed him. Taking Kayah in his arms, Sinileass nods in reply.

He took her upstairs to Reia's room and knocked on the door. Cracking the door open, a half dressed Reia peeks around from behind. "I just wanted to say 'good night.'" He said to her.

Reia nodded. "Good night, sir." She responded as she closed the door.

Sinileass heard the door close behind him as he left and entered the room across from Sakuris's. Walking over, he places Kayah on one of the beds and pulls the covers over her. As she slept he got a good look her; having a young girl that he could call his daughter would certainly be nice.

He's tried so many times to have a child with Kyusa, but she had always miscarried. Exiting the room, he blows out the nearby candle and gently closed the door behind him before proceeding to his room where Kyusa had just finished bathing, "We have guests, my dear. Saiera's here with some friends of hers. I didn't want to keep them up all night, so I gave them rooms to sleep in." He says to her as he enters and lightly kisses her.

Kyusa was a woman in her late twenties; her fair skin matched the outfit she wore. She had long soft flowing blonde hair, which she always kept tied up in a bun that matched her chestnut colored eyes. Looked at her lovingly, Sinileass smiles upon her "The boy Reia would always talk about, Sakuris. He's one of our guests." He said to her as he changed and slid into bed.

Kyusa looks at him as she slides in next to him, "Reia must've been happy to see him then."

Sinileass merely shook his head as he looked at her, "No, she was just the opposite."

Outside the sounds of the nocturnal creatures could be heard: The hooting of night owls, the croaking of frogs, the chirps of crickets, and the creaks of bats that flew through the trees as to catch their prey.

Sakuris had finished changing when Saiera entered the room. "Everyone's asleep my love, it's just us." She said untying the straps that held her Kimono closed; letting it fall open.

Sakuris merely went over and embraced her. "I'll be leaving for the mines soon to slay the demon. Make sure Kayah's safe, I must go alone." He said as he kissed her lightly not taking notice to her wide open Kimono.

Saiera looked at him disappointingly as she tied her Kimono closed, pulled back from her beloved's kiss before sitting on the bed. "Please don't go alone. It's too dangerous, let me go with you." She pleads with him.

Sakuris merely shook his head, "I can't, I'm sorry." He said sitting on the bed next to her. He turns her head toward him to kiss her, but she stands up.

"Suddenly I'm not in the mood." She says grabbing some clothes and going over to pour herself a hot a bath.

Sakuris merely watches her as he exits the room and closes the door behind him. *"Forgive me, Saiera, I don't want to see you get hurt."* He thinks to himself as he walks down stairs and exits the cabin. He makes his way to the mines, stopping off at Kaylah to retrieve his newly sharpened weapons.

Saiera, meanwhile, had slipped into the hot bath she poured for herself and looked around the room as she thought about her brother, making her realize just how much she missed them. Would she ever see him again? Was he even alive? These are a few of the many questions that ran through her mind. She laid there thinking about him as she let the hot water relax her tired body. Her thoughts about Dayis soon changed to memories of Sikan. How the men of the village would try to force themselves onto her.

She felt a slight shiver in her spine as she thought about them letting her hands work nimbly over the various scars that had been placed upon her. Until she had met Sakuris, she had never known true love. All she knew before that time was to watch what men she trusted. She laid there thinking about how kind Sakuris had been to her, even during their brief duel, and she had only shown resentment toward him.

The water had begun to grow cold, but she didn't care, she felt safe within it. She could be who she wanted to, not worrying about the various rape attempts of the Sikonian men or the resentment she had had toward Sakuris. Her mind was, for once, totally at peace. Time had no meaning for her and for once she could be herself. After she had finished bathing, she climbed out, dried off, and got dressed.

In the meantime, Sakuris had just arrived at the mines and decided to stop and rest before proceeding to enter. He hadn't rested long before going in. It was pitch dark inside, and Sakuris had trouble seeing even with the meager torch he had brought in with him. Realizing it was going to be hard finding his way through he put the torch out and had to rely totally on his other senses. He closed his eyes and tried to imagine what it would look like inside. Suddenly something clicked and the mines were as clear to him as daylight. Had he unknowingly tapped into his Seltitian powers; which were now guiding him?

Along the walls he could see the marks that had been made by miners, probably used to mark where they had mined. As he continued to travel deeper, he could feel the intense heat of the lava that flowed through the caverns around him, "How could anything survive in this environment?" He asked aloud talking to himself as he continued to walk through. A little while later, he had approached a cavern that had been sealed up by a cave in. Studying it, he looks over the rubble curiously as he places a hand to it. Through the rubble he could feel the air of demonic influence coming from the other side, thinking to himself, "*This is it.*"

Summoning his seltian powers, he gave a powerful yell and rubble exploded into a fine powder, revealing a hidden chamber. Entering the room before him, Sakuris saw no sign of the demon, but could still feel the evil presence lurking in the chamber. He suddenly felt an intense heat on the back of his neck as if something had been breathing on him.

"Who dares enter the forbidden chamber of Zecuroas?" The demon remarked harshly, demanding to know Sakuris's identity as it appeared behind him.

Turning to see the immense demon, Sakurs instantly become petrified at its ghastly sight. He would have spoken, but he had been scared speechless as he quivered in fear at the sight of the demon.

"What's wrong human, can't you speak?" Zecuroas growled as he stared at Sakuris, with his hollow black, demonic eyes. Swallowing hard as he slowly reached for his blades, Sakuris prepared himself for combat, but before he had the chance to draw them, Zecuroas grabbed his arms and picked him up. "Another, insolent human who thinks he can destroy me." He growled as he threw Sakuris into air and spun around hitting him with his long stone-like tail.

"Sakuris, NO!" Kayah shouted suddenly waking up from her slumber, "Miss Saiera!" Having heard Kayah's screams, Saiera quickly entered the room to see her trembling with sweat dripping from her forehead as tears rolled down her eyes. "It's Sakuris; he's in danger." Kayah sobbed as she felt Saiera coming over and putting her arms around her.

"Shh, it was only a dream." She said trying to reassure Kayah. Saiera knew, however, Sakuris was in danger. She had felt the same premonition as though it had been a blade piercing through her very soul. Letting herself be held, Kayah could feel the warmth of Saiera's body on her own as it both calmed and comforted her. Her breathing seemed to be in rhythm with Saiera's heartbeat allowing her to fall back asleep in her arms. Feeling the young Kaemouri child falling back asleep in her arms, Saiera laid her back down in bed and placed the covers over her once again.

Taking a moment to look around the room, Saiera thinks to herself, *"Please return to me, Sakuris. Not just for me, but for Kayah as well."* Figuring it best, Saiera decides to stay with the young Kaemouri as she lays down to fall asleep beside her. Whatever fears they had of Sakuris, they would face them together, side-by-side, as Dayis had done for her when she was a little girl.

"Damn, that hurt." Sakuris said, getting up after he had hit the ground. He felt a sharp pain racing through his body from where the blow had struck him. It felt like his body had been crushed, as he felt around his chest to check for broken ribs, miraculously, he had none.

He quickly reached back and drew both of his blades and joined them together at the handles. "My turn, you bastard." He said to the demon as he rushed toward him.

Raising his immense arm, Zecuroas counters with a powerful back fist, knocking Sakuris to the ground causing him to relinquish his weapons as they slid into the wall of stone.

In pain from the palpable hit he had just received, Sakuris struggles to crawl towards his weapons. *"Damn, how am I going to defeat this thing?"* He thought as he quickly began to think back to what Veroas had said wanting to test the strength of the two remaining Dragon Clan members. Then he remembered Zecuroas' chamber had already been sealed. Why would Veroas want to hire him to kill Zecuroas? *"It was a set up. He knew I wouldn't be able to kill this demon. He merely wanted me out of the way."* Sakuris thought to himself, *"But why."*

Feeling the demon approaching him from behind, Sakuris turns on his back to see his opportunity. Hanging above Zecuroas' head was a piece of stalactite. Siezing the moment, Sakuris fires a powerful blast of frost into the demon's eyes, blinding him. Grabbing his weapons from behind them, he uses their power to bring down the large stone spike from the ceiling and onto the head of the demon crushing his skull beneath the weight of the massive rock formation.

Standing up as blood ran down the side of his mouth, Sakuris stands before the corpse of the demon, it's head surrounding by broken fragments of stone. Using a focused beam of energy from his blades, he severs the wounded head of the demon from its lifeless body and wraps it in a clean cloth which he then ties to his bag.

His task complete, Sakuris leaves the chamber and begins the long trek back to the entrance of the cave. Using his Seltah as a guide once more, he looks around, noticing lava flows are gone and that the temperature had decreased significantly. *"The lava flows must've somehow been connected with Zecuroas."* He thinks to himself, walking back to the entrance of the cave, exiting the mines.

Journeying back to Sinileass's cabin, Sakuris quietly enters the home and proceeds up to his room. Entering to see Saiera not waiting for him, he walks over to Kayah's room and looks in to see her asleep next to his sister. Seeing the two of them sleeping peacefully, Sakuris feels warmth in his heart as he walks over and lightly kisses their foreheads.

Stirring from his touch, Saiera awakens to see her beloved standing over her. *"Sakuris you've come back my love."* She whispered to him. Sakuris nodded as he kissed her again. Rising from the bed, Saiera pulls Sakuris out of Kayah's room and into theirs refusing to let him relinquish the kiss he had given her as she returned it with a heavy sigh of content, embracing him as they entered his room.

Wrapping his arms around her waist, Sakuris lifts her in his arms letting her legs wrap around him. Nudging the door closed with his foot as he carries his beloved to the bed, Sakuris wastes no time opening Saiera's kimono and cupping his hands around her breasts. Throwing her kimono to the side, Saiera allows her dear Sakuris to lay her upon the bed keeping her legs wrapped around him, and using her feet to slide his pants and underpants off as she opens his gi top and throws it aside.

"She is certainly good with her feet." Sakuris thought himself as he moved lips down her neck and kissed in between her breasts.

He had known from when they last made love this is where she liked it. Slowly and romantically he slid his lips to the top of her right breast greatly stimulating her nipple. *"Sakuris."* She said in barely a whisper as she felt the pleasure he had given her. She used her legs to bring his body closer to hers sliding her skirt and underskirt off ready to receive her beloved into her until Kayah's voice came through the door.

"Sakuris I had another nightmare." She said sensing her brother had returned.

"Damn, she has bad timing." Saiera thought to herself. She had just begun to enjoy herself when Kayah called for her brother.

Sakuris looked at his beloved. "I have to go." He said to her as he got up from on top of her.

Saiera took her legs from around him as he did. "I know. I'll be here when you get back." She said to him getting up and wrapping herself in a blanket.

Grabbing his clothing, Sakuris quickly dresses himself and walks over to exit to room. "Come on Kayah, I'll get you some milk." He says to his sister, gently closing the door behind him. Lifting her into his arms, he carries her to her room and sets her on the bed. He then goes back to his room, grabs a wooden cup, a flask of milk, and an herb. Pouring some milk into the cup, he crushes a small amount of the herb and mixes it. Carrying the mixture back to Kayah's room, he hands it to her, allowing her to drink from it.

Sakuris merely looked at her as she does. "You know, Kayah, you should work on getting rid of these nightmares of yours." He said to her as she handed him the empty cup.

"I'm sorry if I am being a burden on your relationship with Saiera." She said sadly as Sakuris sat down next to her.

"Kayah, no, you're my sister, you're more important to me than anything right now. Saiera understands I have to take care of you. It'd be no different if it was her who was taking care of a sibling, understand." He said to her as he embraced her.

Wrapped in her blanket, Saiera watched the two from the open doorway and thought of her own brother. *"Oh, Dayis, I miss you so much.*

Please return to me." She thought to herself walking back to Sakuris's room and getting dressed.

When she had fully clothed herself she bent down to recover possession of her long knife and stood up as someone suddenly grabbed her from behind and held a knife to her throat, "Hello, my dear, remember me." A familiar, but sinister voice said to her.

"Kenyo, I remember you. You tried to kill me and Sakuris that day in the forest. How did you find us?" She responded.

Kenyo smiled evilly as he tightened his grip on her. "As I said, my clan thrives on the hunt of new prey. Now, call to Sakuris. Let him hear your pleas for help." He said bearing the blade closer to her lightly colored skin.

"Bastard, let me go." Saiera demanded before calling out to Sakuris for help.

Kenyo gave a small evil laugh, "That's right, let him come to you." He said smelling her hair, "Mmm, you smell good."

Saiera would've smacked him if not for the blade at her throat, "Remember that smell. It'll be the last thing you sniff before Sakuris kills you." She responded before calling for help once more, louder than the first time.

From Kayah's room Sakuris heard his beloved's plea for help. "Saiera? Saiera!" He called back reaching for his blades, but remembered he had left them in his room, "Smart thinking, Sakuris. Letting you hormones get the best of you." He said to himself.

Kayah quickly reached into her bag and grabbed her dagger. "Sakuris, my diamond dagger." She said handing it to her brother, "Go, quickly."

Sakuris grabbed the dagger from Kayah's hand and rushed over to his room. "Saiera!" He exclaimed when he saw Kenyo holding her hostage.

He proceeded to take a step forward when Kenyo bore his dagger closer to Saiera's skin. "Hold it, Sakuris, come no closer, or she dies."

"Sakuris," Saiera pled with tears in her eyes, "Help me."

"It'll be okay, Saiera." Sakuris responded as he brandished Kayah's dagger, ready for a fight.

At this point, having been awoken by Saiera's cries for help, Sinileass had also rushed into the room with weapons at the ready.

"Let her go, Kenyo." Sakuris demanded, "You're outmanned."

Kenyo merely laughed a sinister laugh. "Outmanned? Me? Never. However, if you wish to save her, then bring your Sacred Blade to Isura in three days, if not, she dies. Remember, three days." He then threw a crudely fashion smoke bomb down allowing himself to disappear with Saiera in a cloud of smoke.

The only trace of them that had been left were Saiera's screams of fear fading into the darkness.

"Saiera!" Sakuris cried rushing to the nearby open window and shouting into the night, "Kenyo, you bastard!"

Sinileass merely stepped up behind him and placed a hand on his shoulder. "Sakuris, come, there's nothing more we can do here. Best we get some sleep. In the morning we can work on a way of getting her back.

Sakuris merely nodded as he stared out into the darkness that now veiled Kaseo Forest. "Yes, I suppose your right." He responded as he turned from the window and proceeded to follow Sinileass out of the room.

As the two of them exited the room, Kayah was in the hallway to meet them. When she didn't see Saiera with them, she began trembling with fear as tears began streaming from her eyes. "Miss Saiera?" She asked in concern for Saiera, trying to hide the fact she was crying.

Sakuris merely shook his head. "I'm sorry, Kayah. I wasn't able to help her." He then took Kayah into his embrace and stroked her soft hair, "We're gonna get her back, though, Sinileass and I, okay."

Kayah looked up at her brother with sadness in her eyes and nodded. With a look of reassurance, Sakuris uses the sleeve of his Kimono dry the tears from his sister's eyes as hurries her back to bed. With Kayah safe in her room, the two men return to their respective rooms to fall asleep for the night.

Chapter 5

Morning came quickly for Sakuris and the others. Reia and Kayah had already been preparing the morning meal in the kitchen with Kyusa, and the men, had who already broken the news to Kyusa about Saiera, were currently devising a plan to get her back.

"You know, as well as, I do it's probably a trap, my boy." Sinileass remarked as he and Sakuris continued their discussion.

"Yeah, you might be right about that, but at the same time, I can't leave Saiera in the hands of that bastard, either." Sakuris responded quite openly.

"At any rate, it's a good day's ride from here to Isura, if we take the pass through Mt. Iyea." Sinileass pointed out on the map that was sitting on a table between them.

"That pass is bandit territory." Sakuris remarked studying the map before him, "Still, I doubt we have much of a choice if we want to get there in time."

"Boys, breakfast!" Kyusa soon called as she and the other two women brought out plates of food for both the men. The aroma of eggs and cooked meat filled the room as the plates were presented to the men. Kayah had even made some of her berry nut pie that Sakuris was so fond of eating.

"Thank you, ladies." Sinileass responded as Kyusa handed him his plate with a warm smile and loving gaze.

Reia merely handed Sakuris his plate without so much as saying a word. Sakuris graciously accepted it from her and thanked her properly, but said nothing else, other than "Itadakimasu." as he solemnly began eating. In Japan. Saying: Itadakimasu is similar to saying grace in other parts of the world. It's a way of showing thanks for the meal one was about to eat.

Having served the men with their meals, the women returned to the kitchen and prepared plates for themselves before returning to front room. As everyone ate, not a word was spoken as tension hung heavy in the air over thoughts of Saiera; not to mention the tension that was now lingering between Sakuris and Reia.

"Will you boys be leaving after morning meal?" Kyusa asked finally breaking the silence as she sat next to her husband.

"Probably should." Sinileass responds, looking over to Sakuris who was still fixated on the map as he ate.

Kyusa had also been studying him as well, *"Look at him, Sinileass. Have you ever seen such focus?"* She whispered curiously.

"He's had a hard life. Saiera is probably the first friend he and Kayah have had in a long time." He whispered in reply as the two of them continued to eat.

"Nii-sama?" Kayah said aloud as she finished her meal and moved to sit next to her brother.

Smiling at her, Sakuris ran his fingers through her hair, replying, "Hey, Kayah with a warm smile and a soft chuckle as he finished his meal with everyone else.

"Come on, girls," Kyusa began as she stood from her seat, "Let's let the men have their privacy." Collecting the dishware she and the other women carried it back into the kitchen to begin clean up, leaving the men alone to finish preparing for their trip to Isura.

"Now you're sure the mountain pass is the fastest way to Isura?" Sakuris asked curiously as he and Sinileass finished packing their gear.

Looking at him as he finishes packing his gear, Sinileass closes the rucksack he was to carry with him, and reassures the young Kaemouri about his decision and ability to venture the mountain pass.

Having gathered their belongings, the two men say their good-byes to the women and leave the cabin. Walking to a nearby stable, Sinileass picks out two of his swiftest steeds and, with two of his best saddles and riding crops, readies them for travel.

Once situated, the men mount up and ride out onto the dusty, gravel road leading to Isura. "Sure you're ready for this, my young friend?" Sinileass asked courteously as he and Sakuris rode out onto the road.

"No, but I don't have choice, do I?" Sakuris responded with much honesty as he nudged his horse and started down the road.

Watching him with a smile, Sinileass chuckles to himself, "No, I guess not." He, too, then nudged his horse and rode off after the young Kaemouri.

They hadn't ridden far before coming to a fork in the road. "Which way, Sinileass, left or right?" Sakuris asked as he listened to the birds singing in the trees before suddenly going quiet, "Wait a minute, something's wrong. It got too quiet all of a sudden and quiet makes me nervous."

Sinileass looked around before proceeding down the left path and realized Sakuris was right, "Sakuris, be cautious, this mountain belongs to the Fire Clan of Neiheroghi Village, so stay alert."

Dismounting his horse, Sakuris draws both of his blades leaving them separate this time. Not wanting to leave his young friend out on the road by himself, Sinileass dismounts, as well, and drops into a fighting stance. The silence was broken when a blunted arrow flew straight at Sakuris, knocking the young Kaemouri unconscious.

When he awoke again, he found himelf next to Sinileass. *"Ooh, what the hell happened?"* He thought as he looked up to see his hands had been tied and he was hanging by them from a long post, stripped of his weapons. His horse was also missing. *"Sinileass wake up, look."* He whispered nudging Sinileass with his foot.

Waking up, Sinileass looks around through blurred vision as his eyes came into focus, *"Ooh, what hit me?"* He remarks finding himself in the same predicament. Both of them then saw three men approaching; two of which had crystals laced about their necks. *"The shadow brothers."* Sinileass whispered to himself as he saw them approach. He then turned to Sakuris who had been struggling to get himself free and nudged him. *"Stop, stop, look."* He said to him as he motioned his head in the direction of the approaching men.

Sakuris looked to see the same three men as they got closer and then right up into his face, "Here they are father, the men from the forest." One of the sons said to his father.

Sinileass continued to stare at them. "Doratoas and Doreto, the shadow brothers." He remarked aloud.

Sakuris looked at him. "You know those two?" He asked puzzled.

"Only by reputation," Sinileass replies keeping his eyes focused on the two brothers, "they belong to the Summoner Clan of the west. The crystal about their necks gives them power over the shadows. The tall one there is Doratoas, the shorter one is his younger brother, Doreto; and the third one is their father, Fei Ling."

Sakuris thought back, he had heard the name Fei Ling before. But before he was able to decipher where he heard it, Fei Ling stepped forward and looked at Sakuris's arm. *"Oh no, please don't find the crest."* Sakuris thought to himself.

Fei Ling raised the long sleeve of Sakuris's tunic up his arm and found what he had been looking for. The crest Sakuris had been born with, the dragon encoiled around a sword. "The son of Kalas and Kyuroas." He said as he stared Sakuris in the eye, "My sons, you should be proud of yourselves. You've brought before me the future Arch-Dragon of Shikanaca himself."

Sinileass quickly turned to Sakuris as he dangled, asking with a shocked expression, "Arch-Dragon, what is he talking about?"

"I was meaning to tell you about that." Sakuris replied to him.

Fei Ling then turned to his two sons. "Cut them down and let them be on their way."

"But father . . ." Doaratoes began but was interrupted when Fei Ling motioned for him to be silent as he repeated his statement. Doing as their father instructed both the brothers cut Sinileass and Sakuris free of their bonds causing them to drop, as they landed on one knee.

Both fighters stood up rubbing their wrists, momentarily. "Our weapons and horses." Sakuris said in almost a demanding tone. Fei Ling then motioned for his two sons to bring Sakuris and Sinileass what was theirs.

Both sons quickly left and returned with what belonged to Sakuris and his companion. Once each fighter had what belonged to them, they mounted their horses and rode off. The two sons watched as Sakuris and Sinileass rode off into the distance. "Father why did we not kill them and get it over with?" Doreto asked turning to his father.

A cold stare in his eyes, Fei Ling looks to his son, "Kenyo's orders were to make sure they arrived at Isura." He said to him before leaving to return to his home.

Night had fallen when Sakuris and Sinileass had arrived at Isura's front gates where Kenyo had been awaiting them. "You have arrived early. I like punctuality in a person. Now if you please, relinquish your blades to me." He said extending his hand.

Sakuris merely sat on his horse staring coldly at Kenyo. "You show me yours, and I'll show you mine." He retorted very impatiently, noting that Saiera was not present for the exchange.

"We of the Wyvern Clan may be ruthless, blood thirsty, unscrupulous, murderous villains, but we always keep our word, now . . . your blades." He said to him in a rather cold tone of voice.

"The girl first." Sakuris retorted once again in an even sharper tone of voice.

"The blades, or no deal, Arch-Dragon." Kenyo demanded impatiently.

Sakuris merely shrugged and looked over to Sinileass and then back to Kenyo. "Very well, then, keep the girl." Sakuris responded as he began to turn his horse to walk away from the exchange.

Frustrated by Sakuris's unwillingness to cooperate, Kenyo merely growled through his teeth. "Fine!" He shouted. Turning to two henchmen who were behind him, one of which was leading a horse by the reins, he calls out "Bring her!"

Doing as his master instructed, the henchman lead the horse forward, with a bound and blindfolded Saiera sitting atop it. Nodding to his henchmen, Kenyo dismisses them as they bowed and rode off.

"Saiera!" Sakuris exclaimed wanting to rush towards her but Sinileass placed his hand on the young Kaemouri's arm, instructing him to keep a cool head.

"Sakuris?" Saiera called turning her head about.

"I'm here." Sakuris responded, "I've come to take you back with me."

"What a touching reunion. The swords now." Kenyo demanded.

"Send her over first and then I'll come to you." Sakuris responded in as a calm a voice as he could.

"I'm through playing games, Arch-Dragon!" Kenyo shouted angrily. "Give me the swords, or she dies!" He demanded holding a dagger to Saiera's throat.

"Sakuris, just give him the swords." Saiera pleaded. She had no intention of dying this night.

This was a situation Sakuris was ill equipped for, and he knew it. On one hand, he didn't want Saiera to die, but on the other, his father had entrusted him with his clan's most powerful possession; there was also one other possibility: Kenyo could be bluffing. Sakuris knew that if Kenyo killed Saiera then he would have no reason to make the trade and Kenyo would have to walk away empty handed.

"Well, Arch-Dragon?" Kenyo demanded as his patience grew shorter and shorter.

Sakuris merely smiled and self-assuredly, chuckled "You're bluffing."

Kenyo then gripped the dagger tighter to Saiera's throat as its edge bore down on her porcelain skin. He was ready to do the deed as Sakuris watched him from horseback, but at the last minute he sheathed his weapon and looked at Sakuris. "Fine, come and get her." He responded in a disgruntled tone of voice.

"Heh, I knew it." Sakuris remarked rather smugly as he began to approach Saiera with Sinileass following close behind. Once he was close enough to her, Sakuris removed Saiera's blindfold and looked her in the eyes. "Saiera, are you okay? He didn't hurt you did he?" He asked concerned for her as he placed his hands on each side of her face and kissed her.

Saiera merely reassured her beloved that Kenyo hadn't harmed her as Sakuris placed his forehead to hers. "Sinileass is gonna take you back. Wait for me. Wait for me." He instructed her as he handed the reins of the horse she had been riding to Sinileass who then cut Saiera's bonds and began to lead her away from the area.

Watching carefully as Saiera was led away and he could tell she was safe, Sakuris turned his attention back to Kenyo. "I should kill you now." He said in an extremely harsh tone of voice.

"Why wait?" Kenyo retorted leaping from his horse and knocking Sakuris off his as both men landed on the cold, hard ground. Having landed on top of Sakuris, Kenyo held his dagger up ready to strike a death blow. "I should've done this from the very beginning!" He shouted ready to bring the blade down upon Sakuris.

"You talk too much." Sakuris retorted as he countered with a fingertip jab and plunged his fingertips into Kenyo's throat.

This caused Kenyo to drop his dagger and recoil as he began gasping for air. Realizing the dropped dagger had landed next to him, Sakuris quickly grabs for it and plunges it into Kenyo's heart. "And this time, stay dead." He demanded as Kenyo gasped for one last breath of air and fell, from atop Sakuris, landing lifeless upon the ground.

The fall off his horse and the landing on the ground had left Sakuris winded as he took a minute to catch his breath. He then turned his head to see Kenyo's lifeless corpse still lying next to him with his dagger still plunged into his heart. "Looks like you finally got the point." Sakuris chuckled as he slowly stood to his feet and dusted himself off.

Hurrying over to his horse, he mounted up so could he could ride to catch up with Saiera and Sinileass, but as he turned to leave something caught his attention behind him. It was almost as though a sinister presence had been watching him. An old familiar feeling soon overtook him as fear gripped tightly to his heart. Daring to face what he was sensing, he turned his horse back toward Isura and scanned the area.

What was this old familiar feeling, and why was he now sensing it? "I know you're there!" He dared to call out, "Come on out and show yourself." A sinister laughter and the slow sound of clapping could soon be heard coming towards him from the darkness.

It finally dawned on Sakuris who this presence was as his eyes widened with surprise at the sight of the figure approaching him. "You!" He exclaimed.

"Hello, my old friend." The approaching figure responded, "It's been a while." The clapping sound soon disappeared as the approaching figure stopped face to face with Sakuris.

"Yes, it has, Ketsuro-san." Sakuris responded as he stared at his old friend; a man named Kenzji Ketsuro whom Sakuris had known as a boy before the destruction of his village.

Ignoring Sakuris for the moment, Kenzji walked over to his dead comrade and scoffed, "Worthless." He then knelt down and placed his hand upon Kenyo's corpse. Using a dark power known as Kyuroksho, he allowed his dark aura to spread over and through it causing it to be consumed by a rotting darkness from the inside out until nothing of it remained.

"Such is the price for those who fail, Lord Norakatsu." He remarks, standing to his feet. Not bothering to turn completely around, Kenzji simply shifted his gaze toward Sakuris. "We will meet again, my old friend." He said walking away.

"Wait!" Sakuris called stepping forward but Kenzji ignored him as he continued to walk away from the area. "Who's Norakatsu? What is going on?" Sakuris called once more, but Kenzji had already slipped away into the darkness.

Confusion filling his mind, Sakuris climbed back atop his horse and took one final moment to scan the area before deciding it was safe to leave. As he rode through the forest, he kept a close eye out for his two companions, hoping he would soon catch a glimpse of them.

Thoughts of the night's events stayed with Sakuris as he rode. Around him he could hear the chirping of crickets and the croaking of frogs. Above, the stars shone down through the trees as their light pierced through the veil of shadow that blanketed the land. Feeling the cool wind blow across him, Sakuris shivered under his clothing as his teeth chattered from the cold.

Desperate to stay warm, he held himself tightly and rubbed his hands along his sides to generate warmth. Up ahead, something caught his eye: The glow of a camp fire coming through the trees; a glimmer of hope to Sakuris's eye.

Nudging his horse from a walk to a trot, he quickened his pace toward the fire, but whose fire was it? Slowing his horse back to a walk, Sakuris cautiously approached, and in the fire's light could make out the silhouettes of his two companions. Like a wave, relief washed over him as he released a heavy breath and quickly rode to rejoin his friends.

"Sinileass?" Saiera remarked as she saw Sakuris approaching, but was unable to recognize him in the dark.

Looking in the same direction as Saiera, Sinileass merely stood close to her trying to make out what he could in the darkness.

"Stay your hands, my friends. It's Sakuris." Sakuris announced as he got close enough to see them waiting for him.

Her eyes widening with excitement, Saiera gasps with glee as she rushes over to her beloved. "You made it." She cheers, happy to see him safe.

"Yes, and I apologize for the delay." Sakuris responds, dismounting from his horse and taking Saiera into his embrace.

Pleased to see his friend safe and sound, Sinileass slowly approached the two of them, "Good to see you made it back."

Safely regrouped, it was time for the small party to take rest as it grew late into the night. Near the warmth of the campfire, Saiera had already fallen asleep while Sakuris sat staring at his weapons as his thoughts dwelled on the events from before. Sitting across from him, Sinileass watched him through the light of the fire as it whipped about. "You seem troubled, my young friend." He remarked taking note of Sakuris's solemn expression.

"My father entrusted me with these swords before he died. They are my clan's legacy, dating back to ancient times, and it's most powerful treasure. Tonight, I was willing to sacrifice that trust for the love of a woman I barely know. I don't even know who I am anymore." Sakuris replied with sorrow in his voice as he continued to gaze at his weapons in the glow of the fire.

Sinileass merely chuckled as he picked up a nearby stick and used to stir the fire around a bit. "Growing up isn't always easy my friend. Sometimes we're put into situations where it's hard knowing the right thing to do. Not every decision is so black and white. Sometimes it comes down to doing what we can and hoping for the best." He responded as his stirring of the fire caused it to flicker and lash about before them.

"Tonight, I saw someone from my childhood. A boy I had known, named Kenzji Ketsuro." Sakuris remarked, shifting his gaze from his swords to the fire.

"A friend?" Sinileass wondered, continuing to stir the fire before them, but Sakuris remained silent as he stared into the fire. Feeling hungry, Sinileass reached into the knapsack he had with him and pulled out some dried meat and bread that was wrapped up in a clean animal skin. "Here, my young friend," He said breaking off some of the bread and meat and presenting to Sakuris, "you'll feel better if you eat something."

Sakuris was feeling hungry and accepted the food being offered him. As he ate, so many questions raced through his head. Just what had he and his sister gotten themselves in to? "I'm sorry I didn't tell you about my past before, Sinileass, and now I fear I have placed you and your wife in danger because of it."

"The past eventually catches up to all of us, young Kaemouri. Who knows, perhaps it was fate that we met." Sinileass responded, "At any rate, what will you do now? Tonight has brought you many questions it seems."

Lain back, Sakuris rested his head on his knapsack and looked up at the stars. "Yes, but I know where I can get some answers. Tomorrow, I ride for Kaylah." He responded, turning away from Sinileass to fall asleep for the night. Sinileass merely smiled with a chuckle as he also laid down to fall asleep.

Back at Isura, Kenzji knelt before a dark presence as it loomed over him. "So Kenyo is dead, and you failed to obtain the sacred blade. Kenzji, that is unforgivable." A harsh voice commented coming from the darkness.

Kenzji remained kneeling as the dim light of candles shone through the room. "Kenyo's death is of no consequence, Lord Norakatsu." He remarked harshly.

"I need that weapon Kenzji. Out of the sacred blades it is the most powerful. With it, I could secure my rule over the four kingdoms indefinitely!" Norakatsu shouted angrily.

"And what of the fourth, the one hidden away by Myuranth himself," Kenzji asked curiously as the candlelight flickered about him.

"Don't worry, it'll be in our possession soon enough." Norakatsu remarked turning to a young woman, veiled in shadow, next to him and brushing a hand along her cheek as she grinned sinisterly.

"Why you insist on keeping that 'woman' around is beyond me." Kenzji remarks condescendingly, watching the shadowy woman disappear from sight.

"Watch your tone, son of Ketsuro, it's because of her we're as close as we are." Norakatsu retorted.

"And the research my father stole from the late Lord Kaemouri." Kenzji remarked arrogantly. He then looks at Norakatsu. "What of the other two weapons?"

"All in due time, now leave me." Norakatsu responds as he turns from Kenzji.

With an air of annoyance fluttering around him, Kenzji stands to his feet and, with a masculine poise, walks out of the room. "*Lord Norakatsu continues to keep that 'woman' by his side. Yet she has done nothing to bring the weapon that was hidden away. Meanwhile I'm forced to use my fire clansman to do his dirty work.*" He arrogantly thinks to himself as he walks down a long corridor leading to another part of Isura Fortress; his youthful face and long, dark hair shimmering dimly in the candlelight on each side of the corridor.

His clothes are of Shikanacan design and fit perfectly to his well-toned physique. He is tall and walks confidently with every stride he takes. At his side, a Tachi rests housed within a wooden scabbard wrapped in leather and sealed with beeswax. The Tachi's hilt is of ornate design and engraved on the tsuba, or handguard, of the weapon is his family name, Ketsuro. By appearance, it was easy to tell he came from a family of power.

In truth, his father, much like Sakuris's, had been a clan elder before the great destruction that destroyed Shikanaca and Sikan. However, he was prideful and greedy, and was easily swayed into allying with Isura's dark master, and for this crime was sentenced to death and his children, Kenzji and Tesarah were banished from the region.

"Nii-sama!" A young girl cheers as she sees Kenzji come into the room, running over to hug him. With warmth, Kenzji smiles upon her.

"Tesarah, you should be sleeping." He warmly replies, runnimg his fingers through the young girl's long flowing hair.

Laughing with girlish glee, Tesarah runs over to the bed and hops up on to it. "You got to tell me a story first, you promised." She teases as she covers herself with the bed's soft blankets. In truth, despite Kenzji's shadowy disposition, his relationship with his sister, Tesarah, was no different than that of Sakuris and Kayah.

Smiling with warmth, Kenzji chuckles and proceeds over to the bed; next to it is a wooden arm chair with a single cushion for comfort. As he sits in the chair, Kenzji can feel the hardness of the wooden frame upon his back and the softness of the cushion underneath him. This was most often the way he would tell young Tesarah bedtime stories.

"I want a scary one." Tesarah giggles as she looks at her older brother with wide eyes and a big grin on her face.

Again, Kenzji chuckles as he thinks of a story he can tell her. "Let's see, what kind of story can I tell that would be scary enough to strike fear into your heart, Tesarah?" He asks curiously, and then looks at her with a look of playful wickedness and laughs a playfully sinister laugh, "Oh, I know. I know exactly the story." He then playfully uses his hand to claw at Tesarah's stomach making her laugh.

"Tell me, brave Tesarah, do you know of the haunted grove?" He asks with playful sinisterness.

With a look of childish fear Tesarah brings the covers up to her face and shakes her head with a gasp as Kenzji sits back in the chair. "Well then, young one, prepare yourself as I tell you the legend. It seems somewhere in Kaseo Forest, there's a grove that no one dares to venture. They say a spirit lives there; transparent as the sea, brighter than the sun, and as beautiful as Elayis herself." Kenzji begins as he tells his story, "But beauty, my daring young child, can often mask a darker intent. For this spirit is not as benevolent as it appears, you see it feeds on the negative emotion of humans. This is why no one dares to enter this grove for fear of a slow and terrifying death." Kenzji than throws his arms up in a frighteningly playful manner causing Tesarah to throw the covers over herself.

"No, stop, it's too much." She responds with sarcasm, but it is too late and Kenzji laughs with a sinisterly playful laugh.

"I'm afraid it's too late for that, bold Tesarah. The story has begun and there's no stopping it." He replies as he proceeds to continue the story, "Now where did I leave off, oh yes, slow and terrifying death. First the spirit lures in travelers with a false benevolence; then it entrances them to bend them to its will, and finally . . ." Kenzji continues as he claps a single thunderous clap causing Tesarah to scream in fright, "Just like that, and the poor adventurer never knew what hit them."

"D-does the spirit still roam the grove?" Tesarah asks, with a stutter, as she holds the blankets close to her.

Kenzji merely chuckles. "It's only a story, little one, besides even if it were true, you have me to protect you."

"Onii-sama is the best. I bet you could use your power to bend that spirit to your will instead." Tesarah cheers excitedly.

Kenzji chuckles again as he rubs to top of his sister's head. "Maybe," He responds, kissing his sister lightly on the forehead, "now go to sleep."

Doing as her brother instructs, Tesarah lays back on the bed and lays her head upon the soft pillow as she gently closes her eyes to fall asleep for the night. Kenzji then tucks her in and gives her one last good night kiss on her forehead before leaving her to fall asleep.

His sister safely tucked into bed, the young Ketsuro returns to his room and changes into some sleepwear to retire for the evening as he rests himself upon a soft feathered bed to fall asleep for the night.

Morning seemed to come quickly over Kaseo as Sakuris awoke to see the blazing fire from the night before was now nothing more than a smoldering pile of dying embers. It was still quite early and his companions were still asleep as the sun peeked above the horizon while a misty haze rested over the forest. The morning air blew quite cool as it rushed through the tree tops making the leaves dance in its presence. As diligently and as quietly as he could, Sakuris packed his gear onto his horse and prepared for his journey back to Kaylah, the head of Zecuroas still resting in a separate bag that was tied onto his horse's saddle.

"Sakuris?" Saiera moaned as she stirred in her sleep and slowly woke to see him packing. The sound of her beautiful voice made Sakuris freeze in his tracks as he looked back at her. "What are you doing?" She asked rather curiously.

Sakuris merely smiles as he goes over to her and lightly kisses her forehead. "Beloved, I need you to return with Sinileass back to his cabin. I'll meet up with you two there later, right now, I need to go to Kaylah and fulfil the contract I had made with Master Veroas."

"Let me come with you." Saiera pleaded as she sat up and looked him in the eyes.

Standing over her, Sakuris smiles warmly. "No, my beloved, I think you've had enough excitement; it's best you return with Sinileass and get some rest. Besides, I need someone to watch over Kayah, and she trusts you. I know she'll be very happy to see you." He responds plainly as he tries to help Saiera understand why she cannot go with him.

Reluctantly, Saiera agrees with him and gives him one last kiss before watching him mount his horse and ride off into the forest toward Kaylah. *"Come back to me, my love."* She whispers to herself as she watches him disappear down the wooded trail.

"He'll be okay." Sinileass assures her as he steps up beside her. His voice startles Saiera making her jump in her skin. Chuckling, he apologizes. "Come on, we should be heading back as well." He says to her as he steps away to begin packing his belongings.

Sadly, Saiera stares off into the direction Sakuris had rode off in, before slowly turning away to begin getting her stuff together. The dying embers of the previous night's fire were finally snuffed out by the morning wind blowing through the forest as Saiera and Sinileass packed up their small camp and placed all the gear onto the backs of their horses.

Still saddened by Sakuris's choice to leave her, Saiera climbed onto her horse and looked back in the direction Sakuris had ridden. "I wouldn't worry too much about our young friend, Saiera." Sinileass remarked as he nudged his horse into a walk.

Saiera watched him and then slowly followed him down the road. They were still at base of the mountain and had to venture the mountain pass to get back Sinileass's cabin. Sakuris would be riding in the same direction and there was a chance of the group meeting up again.

Back at the cabin, the women were eagerly awaiting the return of their loved ones as they went about the morning chores of cooking and laundry. Kayah had learned much about doing laundry from a woman she and her brother had stayed with, after the destruction of their home, named Yu-Ka-Mi.

With a smile, Kyusa watched over Kayah as she hung the laundry up to dry. Reia, meanwhile, was busy preparing the morning meal. Over the forest, the haze was beginning to lift as beams of sunlight broke through the treetops and shone down onto the forest floor. Throughout the forest, the sounds of the woodland critters could be heard coming through the trees: From the chirping of crickets to the birds singing high up in the trees.

"Kayah, once we've finished with laundry and have had a proper meal, you can come out and play if you want." Kyusa remarked as she and Kayah neared the end of their task.

"Thank you, Miss Kyusa." Kayah replied cheerfully as she hung up the last of the laundry she had been holding.

Reia soon came out and announced that breakfast was ready. With hunger in their bellies, both Kayah and Kyusa finished hanging the last of the laundry and proceeded into the forest home with Reia to have breakfast. The meal itself consisted of eggs, some meat, and forest berries. As the three of them enjoyed their meal, sunlight began to spill into the few windows of the home while a cooling breeze blew through tree tops making the leaves rustle within the wind. In the trees, birds sang sweetly among themselves while the woodland critters scurried across the forest floor. It was, truly, a peaceful morning.

A knock soon came from the door interrupting the women's pleasant breakfast. Not expecting visitors, Kyusa walked over to a nearby window and peeked outside to see Saiera standing with Sinileass. Letting out a sigh of relief, she walked over and opened the door for them. "Saiera, it's good to see you back safely." She remarked as Saiera stepped inside with Sinileass following in behind her.

"Lady Saiera!" Kayah exclaimed cheerfully, rushing over to Saiera and hugging her. The feel of Kayah's arms around her was not something Saiera was used to as she gasped in surprise but looked down at the child and smiled as she wrapped an arm around her. Noting her brother wasn't with him Kayah looks up at Saiera asking, "Where's Nii-sama?"

"He's safe, little one. He had to travel to Kaylah for a bit, but he'll be back, don't worry." Saiera responded reassuringly.

"Well if you two are hungry, Reia has prepared a nice meal. It's in the kitchen, help yourselves." Kyusa remarked as she and Sinileass embraced and lightly kissed.

"Breakfast sounds nice." Saiera remarked as she removed her footwear and placed them next to the door.

"Thank you, wife." Sinileass responds to Kyusa as he and Saiera proceed into the kitchen to prepare themselves some food for the morning.

As they did, Saiera remained quiet as her thoughts dwelled on Sakuris. "Something troubles you, Saiera?" Sinileass asked concerned for her. She looks at him and merely shrugs as she remained silent. "It's Sakuris, isn't it?" Sinileass asks once more trying to get Saiera to respond.

"Yeah, I was just thinking about him, that's all." She finally says as she finishes preparing a meal for herself. She then turns around and leans on the wooden counter.

"He cares greatly for you, you know." Sinileass remarks as he finishes preparing his plate and sets it on the counter. Walking over to Saiera, he stands next to her and proceeds to, also, lean on the counter. "And I think you care greatly for him."

With a small chuckle, Saiera smiles and nods her head. "I just hope he's okay. There's so much about what's going on that we don't know."

"Those were his thoughts, as well. That's why he's going back to Kaylah. He believes he can find the answers he seeks there." Sinileass responded, "Still, with Kaylah's struggle for neutrality, it's uncertain if they can be trusted at this point."

"You and Kyusa are Kaylahn, and I trust you guys fully." Saiera responds as she turns to take a bite of food from her plate.

With a chuckle Sinileass walks over to where his food was sitting and takes a bite from it. "Yes, that's true. She and I are Kaylahn, but we've no desire to be involved in this war." He responds as he swallows some eggs.

"It may be too late for that." Saiera remarks as she continued to lean upon the counter.

"Yes, and now that the Wyvern Clan knows you three are here it's only a matter of time before they try again." Sinileass remarks carrying his plate over to where Saiera was standing and places it down next to hers, "Still, seeing as how the siblings have nowhere else to go, Kyusa and I will allow them to remain as long as they need. Now come, let's join the others in the other room." Grabbing his plate, Sinileass then heads out into the other room as Saiera remains against the counter for a moment more before grabbing her plate and walking out to join Sinileass and the others.

Back at Kaylah, the clean-up from the previous attack continued as Sakuris was allowed to enter the fortress. On horseback he rode through and beheld the activity around him. Carpenters were repairing the homes that had caught fire as stone carvers worked with lumber workers to help rebuild the wall that had been damaged.

"Ah, Master Kaemouri, welcome back." Ryuomi remarked noting Sakuris's return from a short distance away.

Turning his attention to the sound of Ryuomi's voice, Sakuris rides over to him. "Lord Taylah, I need to speak with your father." He then showed him Zecuroas's head still tied to his saddle.

"Wait here for a moment." Ryuomi instructed him as he stepped away for a few minutes before returning on horseback, "Father is in the main house, right now. Follow me, and I'll take you to him." Leading the way, Ryuomi escorts Sakuris to his father's residence. With watchful eyes and a low level of trust, Sakuris proceeded to follow behind Ryuomi as he led him to see his father. Sakuris's caution of trusting the Kaylahn was not uncommon. It was well known throughout the land that their loyalty waivered to and fro. Still, if he was to gain the answers he sought, Sakuris would have no choice in the matter.

As the two men rode, a heavy tension hung on the air between them. "The clean-up is proceeding on schedule." Ryuomi commented trying to break the tension, "Though our wall will take some time to rebuild."

"What will you do in the meantime?" Sakuris asked curiously.

"We've posted extra guards to help with security. Still, with that demon that attacked, there's no telling how useful they'll be. That was the demon that destroyed your home, wasn't it, Lord Kaemouri?" Ryuomi asked as they neared their destination.

"Yes, it was." Sakuris remarked as the two men stopped their horses in front of the main house.

"Well, at any rate, we'll just have to make do with what we have. Father's inside, wait here, and I'll inform him of your return." Ryuomi remarked as he dismounted his horse and went inside the building.

Dismounting his horse, Sakuris stood next to it as he surveyed his surroundings. He then spied young Akisarah coming up to him. "Master Kaemouri, ohayo." He remarked wishing Sakuris a good morning as he bowed before him.

"Ohayo, young Akisarah." Sakuris responded returning Akisarah's bow.

"I am glad to see you safe, sir. May I inquire about Kayah's safety?" Akisarah asked, humbling himself before Sakuris.

"She is safe, my young friend." Sakuris responded as Ryuomi stepped back outside.

Noting his presence, Akisarah turned and bowed. "Master Taylah, Ohayo." He remarks wishing Ryuomi a good morning.

With a gruff look in his eye, Ryuomi turned toward young Akisarah and bowed back but did not return his greeting. He merely turned his attention back to Sakuris. "Father is waiting, Master Kaemouri." He then turns his attention back to Akisarah, "You should be helping with the clean-up, son of Kamikawi."

"Yes, sir, good morning to you both." Akisarah responded as he bowed and left the two men to return to assisting with the clean-up.

Watching him as he leaves, Ryuomi merely chuckled. "Don't mind young Akisarah. He's a good kid, and an even better fighter. There's great potential for him to have a future among the Kaylahn ranks. Come, let's not keep my father waiting." He remarks as he leads Sakuris inside.

Once inside the room the two men stand before Veroas who was sitting in the center of it. "Welcome back, son of Kaemouri. Ryuomi informs me, you completed your task." He says to Sakuris. Having untied Zecuroas's head from his saddle and bringing it in with him, Sakuris holds it up for

Veroas to see. "Very well, you've kept your word, so, too, shall I keep mine." Veroas remarks observing the head as Sakuris threw it to the ground before him, "Sit before me, and ask whatever questions you may have, my friend."

"I prefer to stand, thank you." Sakuris responded assertively, "As for my questions, I do have a few. First, what can you tell me of the Wyvern Clan?"

"Much like our clans, Lord Kaemouri, they date back to the time of our ancestors. They are currently ruled by a tyrant named Norakatsu." Veroas responded.

"And the red demon that attacked my village." Sakuris asked beckoning Veroas for more information.

"No one is quite sure where it comes from. There are rumors that Norakatsu has someone with demonic powers at his side, but no one knows who." Veroas responds.

Despite Veroas' response, Sakuris had a good idea of whom he spoke. "What can you tell me about this Norakatsu?" Sakuris wondered.

"Very little. He tends to keep to himself, and prefers to let his underlings do his dirty work. There are rumors going around that he is searching for an artifact of power, however." Veroas responded.

"Artifact?" Sakuris exclaimed curiously. He interest was fully piqued at this point.

"Yes, speculation is going around that it could be the lost sacred blade that was meant for Isura. Do you know of it, Lord Kaemouri?" Veroas responded inquiringly.

"My father once spoke of it, but I was very young, at the time." Sakuris remarked as he viewed Veroas from across the room, "It's supposed to be hidden on an island of some sort, I believe."

"That's the story, my friend, unfortunately, ancient texts speak very little of it. It's rumored that before his death, your ancestor, Myuranth, used his power to forge four weapons of power. Your twin-silver fang is one of those weapons. Ryuomi carries the spear meant for Kaylah and our Sikonian friend possesses the long knife meant for Sikan." Veroas responds.

"Father, why is it Myuranth would hide away the weapon meant for Isura?" Ryuomi asked finally speaking up.

"Because, like Norakatsu, Isura's original leader, Lagiera, was also a tyrant. What most people don't know however was that both men possessed vast amounts of power within them, and that when they killed each other in a fateful bout one evening, they both vowed to return to finish what they had started, drew their signifying marks upon the sand, one of which rests on your arm, Master Kaemouri." Veroas responds motioning toward Sakuris. He then chuckles as Sakuris lifts his sleeve revealing the mark. "Yes, I know who you are, son of Kaemouri and descendent of Myuranth."

"Father, if Sakuris possesses one of the marks then it stands to reason Norakatsu possesses the other." Ryuomi remarks logically.

"A logical conclusion, my son. Unfortunately, however, Norakatsu was born far earlier than young Sakuris here. That has given him more time to hone his abilities and amass his forces." Veroas responds directing his attention to Ryuomi and then back to Sakuris, "My friend, I'm afraid you find yourself at a grave disadvantage."

Outside, the sun was beginning to set as the three men continued to converse among themselves. "Regardless of the circumstances, young Kaemouri, you were chosen by your ancestor to finish what he started in the past. This is a grim fate, my friend, but one you must rise to meet." Veroas remarks taking note of the setting sun outside a nearby window, "The sun is beginning to set, my friend. I can have accommodations arranged, if you wish."

"No, I'll return to the forest, tonight." Sakuris responded, "But thank you, anyways." He then turned and proceeded to exit the room with Ryuomi watching him leave.

Once Sakuris had left and closed the door behind him, Ryuomi turned back to his father. "Father, are you sure that wasn't too much information." He asked curiously.

"I told him no more than was needed, my son. What he does with the information given him is his choice." Veroas responded.

Above him, the sun was setting below the tree line as Sakuris took the dusty trail back to Sinileass's cabin in the woods. He was weary from the day's travel and was ready to fill his belly with a hot meal and get a good night's rest. The wind blew warmly that night as the sun finished setting and the stars began to shine. The moon remained completely veiled in shadow as Sakuris arrived back at the cabin. Inside, the only light he could see was a dim candle lit in the window, but he was sure he could make out someone walking around in the cabin.

Taking note of this he rode around to Sinileass's barn and stabled the horse he had been riding. Grabbing his gear, he made his way to the cabin's back door. That morning's laundry had already been collected and the day's remaining chores had been completed as Sakuris entered into the cabin and announced his presence.

Hearing his voice, Kayah stirred awake in her bed. "Nii-sama?" She questioned hearing her brother announce his presence again. "Nii-sama!" She cheered happily as she sprang from her bed and rushed out the room in her sleepwear. Saiera and the others had also been woken by Sakuris announcing his presence and went to see him.

Pausing at the top of the wooden staircase, Kayah looked down to see her brother coming into view. "Nii-sama!" She cheered with glee as she rushed down to greet him with a hug.

With a smile, Sakuris chuckled and hugged her in return. "It's good to see you again, Kayah. Any nightmares tonight?" He asked with a low tone of voice.

Kayah shook her head. "No, Nii-sama." She responded as Saiera and the others soon arrived at the top of the stairs and looked to see the two siblings in the middle of the room.

"Sakuris!" Saiera cheered as she hurried down the stairs to see him. Rushing over to him, she threw her arms around her beloved and held him close to her, "Thank Elayis your safe."

Sakuris merely held Saiera in his arms. "I'm okay, Saiera, but hungry." He responded as his belly growled with hunger.

Hearing this, Saiera chuckled. "Come, I'll prepare you something to eat." She remarked as she took Sakuris by the hand and led him into the kitchen.

"It's good to see our young friend back safe." Sinileass remarked as he turned toward Kyusa and Reia. Reia merely scoffed and returned to her room for the night.

"Come, husband," Kyusa beckoned as she took Sinileass by the hand, "we should leave them be." Looking at his wife, Sinileass smiled as he gazed into her emerald green eyes and ran his fingers along her aging facial skin. With a nod, he called for Kayah who was still downstairs. Hearing him, Kayah quickly raced up the stairs as the three of them returned to their rooms.

Down in the kitchen, Saiera worked tirelessly to prepare a satisfying meal for her beloved Sakuris. "Were you able to speak with Veroas?" She asked curiously.

"Yes, but now I am left with more questions." Sakuris responded as Saiera finished preparing his meal and brought it over to him. On the plate she offered was an assortment of berries and garden vegetables along with a properly cooked cut of meat.

"Here, my love, eat this." Saiera remarked handing him the plate. Sakuris had been standing next to a nearby counter as he accepted the plate and leaned against the counter top to eat. "What did he say?" Saiera wondered as she watched Sakuris eat.

Making sure to swallow the food he had been chewing first, Sakuris looked at her and responded, "He spoke of the sacred blades and my ancestor." Feeling overwhelmed with fatigue, he stretched and yawned as he finished his meal and set his plate aside. "Thank you for the meal, Saiera. It's most appreciated, but I'm exhausted from travel." He remarked

Saiera smiled and once again took him by the hand. "Come, let's retire to our room, then. You'll feel better once you've had a night's rest." She responded as she led him out of the kitchen and back upstairs to their room. Once there she helped Sakuris over to the bed as she helped him lie down. Feeling her desire for him overtaking her, she grinned slyly at him as she leaned forward to kiss him, only to see he had quickly fallen asleep.

Saddened she wouldn't get to have him tonight, Saiera was content to merely smile and gaze lovingly at him as he slept. She then leaned forward and whispered in his ear. *"Thank you for coming to rescue me."* She then kisses him lightly on his forehead and climbs into bed to snuggle beside him as she falls asleep for the night.

It was a pleasant night in Kaseo Forest. Through the trees, the wind blew warmly while the crickets chirped and the fire flies buzzed, putting on a spectacular ballet of flashing light, and the stars shone brightly as darkness blanketed the land.

Chapter 6

In the morning, Sakuris awoke to see Saiera vomiting into a small wooden bucket. "Saiera?" He asked going over to her.

"Oh, I am not well this morning. I have been throwing up like this all morning and for some reason I am the mood for sushi and berries." She said to him wiping her mouth clean.

Sakuris merely knelt beside her and rubbed her back. "Don't touch me!" She demanded as she raised her voice. This was unlike Saiera. She hadn't spoken to him that way since the day they had met. She then gasped in pain as her hand brushed against her breasts.

"Saiera?" Sakuris exclaimed, "What's wrong, my love?" Sakuris was feeling powerless at this point. He didn't know how he could help Saiera.

"My breasts hurt. Sakuris, I don't know what's wrong." She responded.

"Wait here, I'll go get Kyusa." Sakuris remarked as he quickly left the room to get help for Saiera.

"Reminder to self: hit him later." Saiera thought to herself as she continued throwing up. When she had finally finished she looked into the bucket. "I don't remember eating that." She said to herself and then wiped her mouth.

Sakuris soon returned with Kyusa coming in behind him. They both looked to see Saiera on the floor clutching her tender bosom in her arms as she sat in pain.

"Saiera, oh dear, you don't look well." Kyusa remarked as she rushed over to her and placed a hand on her forehead, "No fever, that's good." She quickly looked to Sakuris. "How long has she been like this?" She asked curiously.

"According to her all morning. I just woke up not too long ago and found her throwing up." Sakuris responded, "Is she alright?"

"She needs to see a doctor, right away." Kyusa responded as she turned to Saiera, "Saiera, can you walk dear?"

Confident she could, Saiera nodded and allowed Sakuris and Kyusa to help her to her feet as they helped her downstairs where the others were going about their morning. Sinileass looked at her as she came down the stairs, "Saiera, are you feeling okay?" He said to her in a polite tone of voice.

Saiera suddenly felt her mood swing. "Do I look like I'm feeling alright?" She snapped at him.

The hustle and bustle that had been heard in the room suddenly got quiet and everyone looked at her, including Sakuris and Kyusa who were still helping her stand. "Saiera!" Sinileass exclaimed looking at her rather dumbfounded.

What made her lash out him so irrationally? Saiera merely looked around as she shook herself loose from Kyusa and Sakuris. "I'm going into the village. I'll be back later." She said leaving out of the house letting the door close behind her. "*What the hell happened back there?*" She thought to herself now realizing she had lashed out at Sinileass for no good reason.

She thought of ways to apologize to him as she walked down the road and entered a nearby village. It was smaller than Kaylah, but all the hustle and bustle that was going on inside would make you think otherwise. As she walked around the village, Saiera took in all the sites and looked through everything that was on display throughout the markets. Suddenly feeling sick again she rushed to a nearby barrel, and began vomiting into it, "Ugh, maybe Kyusa was right, I should see a doctor." She said to herself as she wiped her mouth clean and stood up.

She walked to the nearest clinic she could find and entered. The doctor who was there looked at her, "Can I help you miss?" He said to her.

Saiera looked at him. He had a middle aged physique and small wrinkles in his forehead and a weak smile," Yes, I have been having nausea all morning, my breasts are tender, and I've been having some stomach cramps, as well." She said realizing she had not told Sakuris about the stomach cramps.

The doctor took her by the hand and led her to a bed as he helped her lay down, "Stomach cramps, huh. Hmm, uh, don't take this the wrong way, but can you lift your top up for me." He said to her.

Saiera suddenly felt another mood swing and grabbed him by the lapel of his kimono, "Look, I came here to be examined, not to have my body drooled over." She said to him sternly.

"I just need to examine your stomach." He said to her hoping she wouldn't she kill him.

Saiera slowly let him go wishing he had been a female. She would have felt more comfortable being examined by one given her past history with the Sikonian men as She opened the lower half of her kimono top baring her stomach, "Any higher or lower, and I will kill you." She said to him.

He looked at her as he rubbed her stomach. "Does it hurt when I do this?" He asked her trying to hold his composure. He wasn't ready to show her any fear he may have had.

She shook her head, "No, not really, wait, now it does." She said to him in pain as she gave off a low scream.

The doctor held his hand out to her. "Can you try to sit up for me, please?" He asked her as she clutched his hand and rose up. He then turned and took a small candle that had been burning on a small table beside him and held it to her eyes. Her pupils shrank in size as he held it closer and then returned to normal as he took it away, "Well that's normal, I don't know I can't seem to find anything wrong with you, except. . ." He said cutting his sentence short.

Saiera looked at him. "Except what, tell me." She responded almost demandingly wanting to know what was wrong with her.

"Except that your symptoms suggest you're pregnant, young lady." He said to her.

Saiera felt another serious mood swing as she grabbed the lapel of his kimono once again. "How the hell can I be pregnant? I have never . . ." She then thought back to her first few nights with Sakuris, "oh right." She said slowly releasing her grip.

The doctor thought she was going to kill him. "Tell you what, lady, let me live and I won't charge you for the examination." He said to her starting to panic.

Saiera stood up and walked out the door, not bothering to apologize to him. Even though she was relieved nothing was wrong with her, the fact that she was pregnant troubled her more. How would she tell Sakuris?

A baby, oh no, what am I going to do? Sakuris is going to go crazy when I tell him. " She thought to herself as she walked back to the cabin and entered. She looked around at everyone and then to Sinileass. "Sinileass I am sorry for the way I acted earlier." She said to him and then turned to Sakuris and Kayah. "I need to talk to you two upstairs." She said to them as she went up top. Sakuris and Kayah stood up and followed her to Sakuris's room. After they had entered, Saiera closed the door behind her and looked at the two of them. "You are not going to believe this. Hell, I didn't believe myself, but . . . I'm pregnant." She said to the both of them rather hesitantly.

Sakuris merely stood stone stiff as Kayah looked to Saiera rather excitedly, "Miss Saiera, that's wonderful." She said to her with a very happy tone in her voice. She and Saiera then looked to Sakuris who suddenly passed out from the shock.

They both rushed over to him as he regained his composure and looked at the two of them, "P-p-pregnant," He stammered, "d-d-did you just say you were pregnant?"

Kayah looked at her brother "Look at it this way Sakuris; at least it's not me." She said laughing.

Sakuris looked at her. "Oh no, I forgot about you, do me a favor, no dating until I'm dead." he said to her and then turned back to Saiera, stating, "I need a drink." As he went over and took out a wooden cup and a flask that contained a strong drink known as mead. Sakuris poured some for himself and drank it in one shot as he set the empty cup down.

Saiera went over to him and put her arm around him. "I know this is going to change things between us." She said kissing him on his cheek.

Sakuris could only stare into the empty cup. "This changes everything," He responded, "We're going to have a baby. I mean, a baby." The news was hard for Sakuris to process. On the one hand, he cared for Saiera, but on the other, the news of becoming a father in the middle of a war he knew little about frightened him.

Kayah ran over to her brother and hugged him. "Oh, Sakuris, you're going to be a father." She said as Sakuris picked her up. "Remember that's your niece or nephew inside her." He said to her as she fainted in his arms having forgotten that fact. "It runs in the family." Sakuris said as he placed Kayah on the bed.

Watching Sakuris with his sister, Saiera realized having a child with him might not be so bad. He was always a good father to Kayah despite the fact he was still her brother. She only hoped she would have a little girl much like Kayah.

Sinileass soon opened the door and entered the room, "Pardon my intrusion. Sakuris, I just thought you'd like to know Kyusa and I have been having a little discussion of our own, and we would be willing to have you and Kayah stay with us for as long as you need." He said acknowledging their decision to adopt him and Kayah, "Now what's all this about a baby, Kyusa and I heard all the chatter from downstairs."

Saiera merely looked at him with an embarrassed expression and shrugged. He looked at her happily, "Saiera that's wonderful. Who's the father?"

Sakuris stepped forward and hesitantly raised his hand. "That would be me, sir." He said to him. The idea of being a father however was not something Sakuris was prepared for and he needed time to process it. "Excuse me, I need to go get some air and clear my head." He remarked leaving the room and walking downstairs. Kyusa and Reia had been busy preparing something to eat for the afternoon and had taken noticed of Sakuris leaving.

Once outside the small cabin, Sakuris allowed the day's warm wind to blow across him as sunlight poured down onto the forest. Finding a nice trail to traverse, Sakuris ventured away from the cabin a short distance and found a nice spot to meditate in. He was going to commune with his father again.

Closing his eyes, Sakuris dropped into the proper stance and began to focus his thoughts on his father. "*Father, I need guidance. The fate I was shown earlier, that was only a possible fate, correct?*" Sakuris said to his father through the power his Seltitian mind.

His father's voice came through, "*One possibility, yes, but it is a possibility you must decide on. If you love your sister and Saiera, you will find that even though it is only one fate of many. It is the only way to win. The demon-dragon you will be forced to fight cannot be destroyed by any other means. No mortal weapons can kill him, not even the power of your sacred blade can harm him. I am sorry this is the fate that has been chosen for you, so shall it be written, so shall it be done.*" The voice quoted.

"*Damn what has been written, I will not leave my sister. I promised myself as I watched you and mother die I would protect her at whatever the costs.*" Sakuris rebuttled against his father's statement as his father's voice came through Sakuris's mind.

"That cost may be your life, my son. I will not force you to accept the fate that has been set for you. You possessed the mark, you inherited the sword, you and Kayah where the soul survivors. It is all happening as it was foreseen." It responded.

"Father, Reia is alive." Sakuris said informing his father of Reia's survival.

"This may change everything." His father responded rather concerned for the future.

"Sakuris!" Sinileass called trying to find him.

Sakuris quickly opened his eyes as he closed off his Seltitian mind. "I'm here!" He called back as he turned towards Sinileass's voice; thoughts of his father words still running through his mind.

Sinileass followed Sakuris's voice to where he was, "You Dragon Clan members are sneaky ones; that you are." He said to him as the two men faced each other, "So, a baby is it, and here I thought Saiera would never find someone to give herself to." Sinileass pauses for a minute and takes in a deep breath through his nose as the aroma of the surrounding forest fills his nostrils. "Still, more important matters lie before us, young Kaemouri. Were you able to find the answers you sought from Kaylah?"

"Yes, and no," Sakuris responds solemnly as Sinileass gazes at him with a puzzled, but attentive look, "It seems I was left with more questions than answers. I was, however, able to learn the name of the one responsible for Shikanaca's destruction."

"That's always the trouble when seeking information, my friend. Sometimes it leaves us with more questions than answers, as you, yourself, stated; but more important than information is what you do with it. So tell me, young Sakuris, what will you do with the information you have received?" Sinileass responds plainly.

"What I intended to do from the start: Revive my clan." Sakuris answers with an assertive voice as he turns from Sinileass and looks up at the sky.

"And after you've done that?" Sinileass quickly asks trying to get Sakuris to see further ahead into the future.

"Kill Norakatsu." Sakuris quickly responds in a harshly determined tone of voice.

"Is revenge all that is on your mind?" Sinileass remarks as he steps forward and stands next to Sakuris. Sakuris merely remains silent as continues to stare at the sky. "It's plain to see the past still haunts you, my friend, and it's good you would rather rise to meet it than run from it, but there are other ways besides revenge." Sinileass chuckles for a minute, "But what do I know? I'm just a silly old man. Maybe you younger types have life more figured out than I do."

"No, there is wisdom in your words, my friend," Sakuris responds, "if revenge is not the answer, then tell me: what must I do?"

"I'm afraid this path has been set before you, not me, my friend. It is up to you what you decide. Just know whatever that may be, Kyusa and I will do our best to provide what aid we can. You and your sister will have a place here with us for as long as you need. At any rate, you cannot challenge Norakatsu now as you are." Sinileass remarks as the two men gaze at the morning sky with the wind blowing warmly across their skin, "Such a pleasant spring morning."

Sakuris chuckles for a moment at the last part of Sinileass's statement. "Changing the subject?" He remarks humorously.

"Just trying to take your mind off things," Sinileass responds truthfully with respect, "come, my friend, Saiera will need you now, more than ever." He then turns to walk back inside the small cabin.

Sakuris chuckles once again as he turns to follow Sinileass. "I suppose you're right." He remarks as the two men begin the short trek back to the small cabin in the woods.

Back inside the cabin, the women had been talking amongst themselves while Sakuris and Sinileass were outside. "So, a baby is it, Saiera?" Kyusa remarked, "Well, I think it's wonderful news, and young Sakuris seems like a very capable young man." She then looks at Reia. "Reia, you knew Sakuris before the great destruction, did you not?"

Still in disbelief, Reia merely shrugged and remained silent. She didn't want to believe the person she had long thought dead was now back. She merely ignored Kyusa's question and walked back upstairs to her room. "Reia?" Kyusa called as Reia disappeared from sight.

"She'll be alright, Kyusa." Sakuris remarked as he came in with Sinileass, "She just needs time is all."

"Nii-sama?" Kayah remarked as she approached her brother, "Why does Miss Reia not believe it's you?"

Kneeling before his sister, Sakuris places a hand to her shoulder. "It's been a long time since the destruction of our home, Kayah. Reia's lived with the thought that I've been dead all these years. In her mind, I'm just a guy who claims to be someone I'm not." He responds as he stands to his feet and looks up to the second floor, "At any rate, we'll have to find a way to convince her and bring her back into the clan." He takes a breath through his nose and exhales. "So few of us remain now."

"She makes three." Kayah commented.

"No, Kayah, she makes four." Sakuris corrected her. His thoughts dwelled on Ketsuro-san. Truth be told, with Ketusro and his sister, Tesarah, there were five remaining pure blood Shikanacans accounted for, and with Saiera carrying his child, one future half-blood Shikanacan.

"Who's the fourth?" Sinileass interjected. Sakuris looked back at him over his shoulder, "Was it the man you spoke of in the forest?"

"Yes, his name is Kenzji Ketsuro. His father, like mine, was a village elder. He was bought off early on in the war. We believed it was him that was responsible for the attack on our village." Sakuris responded as he told everyone present the truth about his past with Kenzji and his father, Lord Ketsuro.

Stunned with disbelief, Sinileass took a deep breath through his nose. "That's quite the story my friend. Still, it's easy to see how Kenzji might've been persuaded to serve under Norakatsu. As a child who had just witnessed his father be executed, only for him and his sister to be exiled right after, he would've been easy to manipulate."

"Yes he would've, but he harbors the same dark power as his father, and is just as dangerous." Sakuris responds as he goes over to a nearby wooden sofa with Kayah and sits down, crossing his legs in a confident, figure four, manner. Kayah merely hops on the sofa next to her brother and sits patiently beside him.

Taking a seat in a chair made specifically for him, Sinileass sits down with a straight posture and crosses his legs in much the same way Sakuris had. "Such a tangled past for someone so young. What will you do?" He asked curiously.

"As I said outside, reviving my clan is still my main priority." Sakuris responded as he looked over to Sinileass.

Kayah merely laid her head on Sakuris's arm and hummed cheerfully to herself as she allowed her legs to dangle back and forth while the adults talked among themselves. Outside the sun moved slowly across the sky as morning gave way to afternoon and the forest was alive with the sounds of the woodland critters as they scampered about their day.

It was a pleasant day in Kaseo Forest as afternoon meal time slowly approached. Reia remained hidden away in her room leaving Kayah to help Kyusa with meal preparations. To take Sakuris's mind off things, Sinileass had invited him to spar with him in his dojo. He wanted to gauge Sakuris's abilities himself.

"Now, son of Kaemouri, do not hold back." He remarked dropping down into a defensive fighting stance.

"No openings at all." Sakuris thought to himself, studying Sinileass's stance. Making the first move Sakuris struck first with a basic front kick to Sinileass's waist. A simple low block was all that was needed on Sinileass's part to stop the technique as he countered with a finger-tip jab to Sakuris's throat.

Sakuris countered with an inside block, pushing Sinileass's hand out of the way as the two men exchanged blows in a splendid ballet of physical techniques. "You fight well, son of Kaemouri, but if all you rely on is the physical . . ." Sinileass remarked as he opened the gap between the two of them and launched a bolt of chi energy at Sakuris. Caught off guard, by the attack, Sakuris took the full force of the bolt as it sent him down to the ground, "Then you have a long way to go." Sinileass remarked finishing his statement as he stood over Sakuris and offered a hand to help him up.

Hesitant at first, Sakuris merely looked at Sinileass's extended hand. "Come on, now, lad." Sinileass beckoned as he once again offered his hand to Sakuris. Taking Sinileass's hand into his own, Sakuris allowed himself to be helped to his feet as the two men stood facing each other. "Now then," Sinileass began as went back to his starting position, "again."

Sakuris got back into his starting position as the two men prepared themselves for a second bout. "Begin." Sinileass instructed as Sakuris once again made the first strike, this time using a combination round house and spinning back kick. As soon as he did, Sinileass merely used foot work to evade both the kicks and readied himself for a third kick, but Sakuris had something else in mind as he charged one of his fists with the power of wind. Coming out of the spinning back kick and turning back to front, he used a palm strike to unleash a powerful blast of wind to send Sinileass to the ground.

Pressing the advantage, Sakuris quickly took position of dominance atop Sinileass and readied a second charged blow. "Enough!" Sinileass called stopping the bout before Sakuris could unleash his attack.

Backing up from Sinileass, Sakuris ended his attack and stepped back to starting position. "You Shikanacans command the elements, I see." Sinileass remarks standing up to return to starting position.

The afternoon passed rather quickly as the men continued to spar in the dojo and sun gave way to moon as night fell upon the forest. Thirsty and sweaty, the two men left the dojo, exhausted from training, and returned to the cabin where they may rest and take water.

It was early evening and Sakuris was upstairs in his room changing out of his training gear into some night time wear. Seeing the weapons his father had entrusted him with nearby, he merely held them up and once again reflected upon who he was, where he was going, and what it was he had to do.

Saiera, meanwhile, had decided to pour herself a hot bath to soak in as she let her thoughts drift. As she laid, soaking, in the tub, she could feel the water warming her in even the deepest crevices of her female anatomy. It had relaxed her so much; she could feel herself slipping off into the land of slumber, but despite her efforts to try to sleep, thoughts of her past kept her awake. Like Sakuris and Kayah, she, too, lost loved ones on the day of the great destruction. Her father perished saving the sacred blade, she now carried with her, and she was forced to leave her brother behind.

All she could do was let tears flow from her eyes, and she slowly began toying with the thought of submerging her head in the water in which she lay. She would have done so had she not thought of the friends she had made. Friends like Kayah and Sakuris, whom she now loved very deeply. Thinking of them brought a smile to her face and gave her renewed hope. She had lost one family but gained another.

Her thought cycle was soon broken when she heard a knock at the door. Everyone else had fallen asleep for the night and it was just her awake. So she stepped out of the tub, dried herself off, and got dressed. She stepped down the stairs and answered the door to see Akisarah standing in the doorway.

"I'm looking for Kayah." He said politely bowing humbly before her. He was dressed in simple clothing but his hair was straight and he stood with confidence. Every word he spoke was articulate and clear. It was clear that, for a boy his age, he was quite the well-groomed young gentleman.

Smiling sweetly back at him, Saiera motions for him to come inside. Acknowledging her gesture, Akisarah thanked her and stepped into the cabin. Saiera's thoughts suddenly dwindled away and she instructed him to wait a moment as she called Kayah down. Seeing him here would make her happy, or would it? Saiera thought back to the talk she had with Kayah on the road. She had known what the feeling was that Kayah would get when she was around him. It had been too late to change her mind; Kayah had already come downstairs and saw Akisarah standing there.

He looked up her with a smile. "Hello, Kayah, I heard I might find you here." He said walking past Saiera. Still dressed in her night time wear, Kayah became embarrassed and rushed back into her room to put on something more appropriate as she closed the door hastily behind her and leaned back against it. "Oh no!" She exclaimed, examining the clothing she was wearing. "Okay, Kayah, don't panic." She remarked aloud as she rushed to find something more suitable to wear.

Saiera soon knocked on her door and stepped in. "Miss Saiera, you have to help me. I can't let him see me like this." Kayah said in a panic as she continued to frantically search.

Saiera quickly went over and placed her hands on gently on Kayah's shoulders. "Kayah, slow down a minute. Take a breath." She said gently kneeling before her. Doing as Saiera instructed, Kayah took a deep, relaxing breath to calm herself down. "There, you okay now?" Saiera asked as Kayah nodded her head. "Okay, let's find you something to wear." Saiera finished as the two of them began to go through Kayah's clothes.

Downstairs, Akisarah waited patiently for Kayah to come back down. He had spent the day helping with the clean-up in Kaylah and wanted to see a friendly face, and found the Kaylahn boys to be somewhat beneath him. Stepping back out into the front, Kayah emerged from her room and proceeded down stairs more appropriately attired. Saiera had even taken a few minutes to straighten her hair for her.

"Apologies for the wait, Akisarah." She said sweetly as she walked down the stairs. The sight of Kayah took Akisarah's breath away leaving him at a loss for words. "Say something, silly." Kayah teased as she approached him.

"I can't find the words." The young boy responded as Kayah stood before him.

She smiled sweetly at him making his heart beat in his chest. "Well, you look very handsome tonight." She responded.

"Thank you." He responded as he watched Kayah walk around him only to stand before him again.

From upstairs, Saiera watched the two children with a smile as the connection between them slowly seemed to strengthen. "Kayah," She called gently, "will you come up here for a moment?" She felt remorseful for breaking the connection, but what she had to say to Kayah may determine the fate of her relationship with Akisarah.

Turning from Akisarah to look up at Saiera, Kayah returned upstairs so that she may speak with her. "Yes, Miss Saiera?" She said plainly as she stood before Saiera.

Saiera knelt down beside her. "*I'm sorry, but that feeling you have been having when you're around him, I think it's time you figured out what was. Can you tell me what you think it is?*" She asked in almost a whisper.

Kayah shrugged. "*I don't know. Why are you bringing this up now?*" She responded in the same, almost a whisper, tone.

Saiera merely held Kayah close and whispered in her ear, "*Because that feeling you've been having . . . is love, Kayah. Though you might be too young understand it right now. I can tell by the way you act around him, look at him, the way you move around him, even the way you talk to him. All these things determine if you're in love. When I'm with your brother, I feel the same strange feeling. I love your brother completely; so what I want you to do, go back downstairs, and tell Akisarah everything. Tell him how much he means to you, how he provides you with a sense of security and safety, everything. But just don't come out and say it, you might end up scaring him off, and we don't want that. You got to hint around, and speak casually about it. Do you understand?*"

Kayah merely looked at Saiera. "*But what if I mess up and end up making a fool of myself?*" She asked puzzled.

"*Nonsense, Kayah, I'll be here to guide you.*" Saiera replied looking at Kayah with motherly eyes. Kayah nodded, acknowledging she understood. She knew she would have to tell Akisarah one day. How he would react is what she didn't know? Saiera smiled at her warmly and encouraged her to go back down stairs and talk to Akisarah.

The two women looked to see Akisarah downstairs waiting patiently. Kayah could only look at him in his splendor and think of what Saiera had said, but realized it was easier said than done. She didn't know what to say as she merely walked past Saiera and back into her room. Saiera watched as she did, she wanted to say something but remained silent. *"Maybe now isn't the time. She is only a child after all. But it's only right Akisarah should know. Oh what do I do? I wish Dayis was here. He'd know what to do. He always did?"* She thought to herself as she looked downstairs, at Akisarah.

He merely looked back up at her as she motioned for him to come upstairs. Doing as instructed, Akisarah went on up and allowed Saiera to show him an empty room he might rest in. It was a small room that was next door to Kayah's, and the last one that remained empty. Humbly thanking her, Akisarah went in and changed before lain on the bed to fall asleep. Saiera then went to Kayah's room and opened the door to peek in on her. She had fallen asleep and was dreaming about the day she would tell Akisarah everything.

Smiling at how peacefully Kayah looked sleeping, Saiera merely shut the door and returned to Sakuris's room to be with him. Being careful not to disturb her slumbering lover, Saiera closed the door behind her as she entered the room. She was dressed in sleep wear and didn't need to change clothes. Feeling sleep overtaking her, she stretched and yawned as she walked over to the bed where she saw her beloved Sakuris dreaming peacefully. Gently pulling back the blankets on her side of the bed, Saiera eased herself onto the feathered mattress and snuggled up close to him as she gently wrapped her arm around him.

Gently stirring at her touch, Sakuris smiled and moaned contently as he rolled over to look upon her. "Hey, Saiera." He said gently kissing her forehead.

"I was hoping not to wake you, my love." She responded gently.

With a gentle chuckle and moan, Sakuris stretched and yawned. "Worry not, beloved. It's awful late, though, why are you just now coming to bed?" He asked curiously.

"We had a visitor for young Kayah. Seems she made a new friend in the young Kaylahn from before." Saiera responded.

"Young Akisarah?" Sakuris asked as Saiera affirmed he was correct, "He's a good kid, with much potential. I'll be watching him very closely."

"You wish to make him a part of your clan?" Saiera asked curiously.

"If he proves himself, yes." Sakuris responded as he once again kissed Saiera on her forehead, "Now get some rest. Morning will come quickly."

"Hold me till I fall asleep." Saiera said plainly as she turned away from Sakuris and allowed him to snuggle closer to her as he held her in his arms allowing her to fall asleep in them. He, too, then closed his eyes and fell back asleep.

In Kayah's room, Kayah had been thinking about what Saiera had said. Was she really in love? Would she ever be able to tell Akisarah? What if he didn't feel the same way? These were only a few of the many questions running through her mind as she slept. She had only wished she could have Akisarah next to her to feel the warmth he gave her the night they went down to the river in Kaylah.

She decided that instead of letting him come to her she would go to him. Just to see him. That's all she would do, just go to see him. No harm could from just going to see him, right? With a determined look she woke from her slumber and walked out of her room quietly closing the door behind her so not to wake anyone; with a small candle resting in her grip. The small flame it produced radiated just enough light.

Without knocking, Kayah entered Akisarah's room where he lay sleeping and walked over to his bed. She looked at him under the light of the candle. His handsome countenance radiated in the light. His slow breathing almost seemed rhythmic with the pulse of the flame and for once Kayah knew where she belonged and who she belonged with. She soon saw Akisarah stir in his sleep and she quickly exited the room dropping the candle she had carried with her. The flame of the candle extinguished itself as it hit the floor with a thud.

The thud of the candle as it hit the floor woke Akisarah fully, "Who's there?" He asked in a frightened voice but received no answer. He gripped one the Kali sticks he had resting under his bed and walked toward the door as he stepped on the candle. Feeling it under his foot, he knelt down and took it into his grasp to examine it. The scent of Kayah's sweet smelling perfume rested on it, "Kayah." He said recognizing the smell of the perfume. He then walked out his room and over to hers. Entering, he found her lain in her bed pretending to be asleep. Walking over, he gently nudges her awake whispering, "*Kayah.*"

Pretending nothing had happened she turns and looks at him whispering, *"Akisarah, what are you doing in my room?"* in response.

He merely held up the candle, replying *"I think you dropped this when you ran out my door."*

Her face flush with embarrassment, she took the candle from his hand and set it aside. *"Akisarah, I'm sorry, but I had to see you, just a small amount of time."* She whispered putting her hand to his face. His smooth skin felt like the steel of a newly forged blade, warm yet cool, *"The feeling of safety I get when I'm around you. I had just look upon your face one more time, to get that same feeling. I care about you Akisarah. I care about you very much."* She said resting her head in his shoulder letting tears flow down from her eyes as she put her arms around him.

Not knowing what to say or do, Akisarah merely put his arm around her and let her cry into his gi-top. Her words almost seared into him like a flame burning his soul to almost nothing. He had never heard those words from a girl before, especially one of Kayah's age. He wanted to speak; to say a few kind words to make her feel better, but not a word came out.

He realized there was nothing he could say or do. So he did nothing except let her cry in his shoulder as he gently stroked her hair, even he knew he was too young to understand the concept of love and all its complexities. Their childish minds merely led them through a maze of twists and turns that led to nothing but dead ends. *"Kayah."* He whispered as he gently stroked her hair and held her.

He toyed with the idea of staying with her for the night, but wondered if he should. If Sakuris were to see the two of them together in the morning, it might drive him into a frenzy. He certainly did not want that any more than he wanted to get Kayah in trouble with her brother. *"Akisarah, please stay with me tonight."* Kayah whispered lifting her head up to look into his eyes; his soft chestnut colored eyes. Akisarah took his hand and wiped away the remnants of the tears that lingered on Kayah's face.

His touch gave her the warmth she had been seeking, that feeling of safety. Gazing into his eyes, it was almost as if she were peering into the depths of his soul. *"Please don't leave me."* She whispered pleadingly as she once again put her hand to his face. Kayah's pleas for company and longing for the feeling of safety only he could provide for her made up

Akisarah's mind. He would stay with her; with the young woman who cared so much for him.

He merely held her as she fell asleep in his arms; the feeling of his rhythmic pulse was in complete resonance with Kayah's breathing. He laid her back down on the bed and found a spot for him to sleep on the floor. Kayah looked down at him, *"You want a blanket."* She whispered to him holding up the top cover on her bed. He nodded as he watched Kayah pull off the top cover and hand it to him.

Slowly he laid his head down and sank back to sleep. Kayah was happy he decided to stay; she would feel safer with him around. She wondered however if telling him how she felt was the best thing for the both of them. She certainly did not want to jeopardize her friendship with him. By now it was too late; she only hoped that they would still remain friends.

Outside the cabin, night drug on, as an ominous silence fell upon the forest. Unbeknownst to the sleeping inhabitants, danger lurked outside the home as multiple intruders stealthily entered as they moved quietly from room to room. It was clear they were searching, but searching for who, or what.

They soon found who it was they were looking for as they entered into Kayah's room and saw her sleeping in her bed. A couple of the intruders remained outside her room as a lookout while the remaining two crept past the sleeping Akisarah and towards Kayah. With a wicked grin they stood next to her bed and began reaching down to grab ahold of her.

She stirred for a minute in her sleep as she lazily opened her eyes and saw them standing over her. She tried to scream, but one of them covered her mouth to muffle the sound as Kayah struggled on the bed. Awakened by the commotion, Akisarah quickly stood his feet and tried to call out but was grabbed from behind as a hand covered his mouth and both children were drug out of the room, and as quickly as they entered, the intruders left with both of the little ones with no one being the wiser. All that was a left was a note instructing Sakuris where to come to retrieve them.

Chapter 7

The two of them were taken by horse back to a temple outside Neiheroghi Village, the home of the infamous fire clan, where they were placed in cages. Their hands were bound and the cages shut tight with leather straps. They were made of a Japanese bamboo, very strong. The smell of the air in the temple had a rather unique must about it. It reeked of evil and the stench of animal feces. A nameless fighter soon stepped in and went directly to Kayah. His eyes had a familiar aura about them. Kayah knew she had seen this fighter before, but from where. His dark pale skin and pale green tunic and black pants gave him away as being an ex-Dragon Clansman.

Long hair that had been tied into a pony tail rested about his head as it flowed down to his shoulders and with a cold voice he spoke. "At last my powers of Kyuroksho have brought me something of use." That word, Kyuroksho, caught Kayah's attention immediately. He possessed the demon side of Galtineah, the power to control the Kyuroksho. Her brother possessed Seltah, the all-knowing. Achieved together they formed what the elders deemed as Seltesh, the absolute of Galtineah.

With a nod of his head, the Fire Clansmen left him with the two children. Kayah merely looked at the fighter in stunned silence. Where had she seen him before? She looked closely at the fighter as she scanned him from head to toe and suddenly found what she had been looking for; a scar about his hand from where Sakuris had slashed him. "Kenzji Ketsuro, a treasonaire extraordinaire of sorts. Why have you brought me here? Your dispute is with my brother." She said in a rash demanding voice.

Kenzji merely looked at her. "You're abosultely right, dear Kayah, and it's a dispute I intend to settle. You two are insurance to make sure he comes." He responds in a cold tone of voice.

Outside the temple, the sun had risen over the forest, ushering in the new day. Akisarah scanned Kenzji over as he attempted to size him up. From his height and build, Akisarah guessed he was as strong as Sakuris and a few years older. He then looked to Kayah, "Kayah, what is he talking about?" He asked her hoping she could shed some light on their dark situation.

"He was the other candidate for Arch-Dragon-" She began but was cut off when Kenzji looked at her coldly.

"Candidate!" He shouted, "I should have been the Arch-Dragon, I had everything: power, strength, wisdom. I could defeat an army of soldiers, and they chose your brother over me; that stupid, lazy excuse of a dragon." He said in even colder tone of voice, "Well it's my time come now. I'll kill Sakuris and with him the Kaemouri family blood line." He smiled a sinister smile before laughing victoriously and maniacally.

"My brother bears the mark of the golden one! He's the chosen one, Kenzji. You know this as well as I!" Kayah retorted.

Cutting his laughter short, Kenzji looks to Kayah and scoffs. "Mark or no mark, it makes little difference to me."

Kayah didn't blink an eye or stir in her cage. She looked over Kenzji's figure carefully and spotted her dagger slung about his waist. She looked at Akisarah and motioned to it with her chin. Akisarah looked and spotted it as well. Kenzji's younger sister, Tesarah, soon walked in and proceeded over to Kenzji. "Nii-sama, our master wishes to see you." She remarked noticing Kayah and Akisarah in the cages. Tesarah was actually a few years older than Kayah. She was tall and slender with long legs. Brown hair flowed down to her waist, her green eyes and soft lips combined with the curvature of her figure made her both beautiful and desirable. "Kayah?" She asked stepping towards Kayah.

"Tesarah, step back." Kenzji instructed his sister as she looked back at him.

Peering over at his cage, Tesarah sees Akisarah. "What's this? A gift for me, dear brother. He's a handsome one." She peers back over to Kayah, "Have you had him yet? No, of course not, Sakuris would throw a fit. The thought of his only sister sleeping with someone at such a young age would be enough to throw rage into any brother."

"Tesarah!" Kenzji interjected with a harsh tone, "Tell our master, I'll be with him shortly."

Akisarah merely studied the young girl and her older brother. Who were these two to Kayah, and why had neither she nor Sakuris brought them up before? He thought to ask but did not want to pry where he shouldn't. Kayah merely looked back at the girl. "Tesarah, you're not the type to be doing this, so why are you here now." She asked rather inquisitively.

"You serve your brother. I serve mine" Tesarah responded looking over to Kayah. She then looks to Kenzji and back to Akisarah. "Brother, don't rough up this one too bad. I kind of like him." She remarks reaching her hand in to cup Akisarah's cheek. "Hey cutie, forget about Kayah here. Come with me instead."

"Bitch-girl, you know nothing of me and what I feel for Kayah. I would never dishonor the Kamikawi name by going with you . . . or him." He said motioning to Kenzji with a slight turn of his head and then sinking his teeth into Tesarah's hand.

Tesarah's hand recoiled as she cried out in pain, "Brat, I'll make you pay for that." She said sternly shaking his cage. He bounced around inside of it for the small minute or two she had shaken it.

Kayah laughed girlishly inside her cage, "Way to go Akisarah." She said underneath her laughter.

Akisarah laughed along with her and then looked to Kenzji. "Wait till I've gotten out here and have been reunited with my Kali Sticks." He boasted confidently.

Kenzji then held up a pair sticks. "You mean these. Even if you could manage to get to them, what could you do?" He said to him sternly, "Even more pressing what makes you think you can out of there."

Akisarah looked at him as he smiled. "You're not the only one with special gifts, you know the ropes that bound my hands and the strap that holds may cage closed . . . I've cut them." He retorted arrogantly.

Kenzji looked to see if the strap had been cut. Akisarah waited until he close enough before kicking the cage door into his face. Kenzji reared back in pain throwing his hands to his face as he felt the pain of a broken nose. Akisarah saw the opportunity he needed to reclaim his Kali Sticks. He flung out his hands and they flew straight into them. He then took a few swings at Kenzji's head knocking him out cold. Then turning to Tesarah he threw a few thrusts to her abdomen severely knocking the wind out of her. Quickly taking the few precious seconds it would take for the two incapacitated fighters to recover he undid the strap to Kayah's cage and helped her out. He then went behind her and untied her hands.

Kayah quickly reached down and grabbed her dagger before the two of them ran out of room as fast as their small legs would carry them; realizing Kayah would be too slow to keep up with him, Akisarah took her into his arms and continued to make the escape looking back at only random intervals to make sure their captors weren't following them.

"My hero," Kayah said to him as they ran, "you are so courageous."

Akisarah laughed at her comment. The temple they were in was like a labyrinth, full of twist and turns and dead ends. Akisarah put Kayah down and extended a hand to a wall and closed his eyes opening them once again as they flashed a bright light causing the wall to explode; leading them outside, where, by some luck, horses were waiting for them. Akisarah climbed onto one and then looked at Kayah. "Quickly get on the other one." He said to her.

Kayah looked at the horse and then to Akisarah, "I can't ride." She lied just wanting an excuse to ride with him. Akisarah extended his hand and she took it as he helped her climb up onto the horse. She sat herself firmly in front of him, allowing him to put his hand around her waist as nudged the horse hard enough for it to gallop off into the distance.

"How is it in ten years you never learned how to ride?" He asked her as he spoke over the pounding of the horse's hooves.

Kayah smiled and looked at him. "I have a confession; I lied. I wanted to ride with you." She responded confessing to her little fib.

Akisarah merely held her tighter as they continued to ride through the forest. "Hmm, you certainly had me fooled about that. I have a confession as well; I was hoping you didn't know how to ride. I wanted you ride with me as much as you did." He responded.

Kayah's flowing hair whipped in the wind as they rode. Kayah soon realized they were not going back to Sinileass's home, but merely deeper into the forest. "Akisarah, where are we going?" She asked rather curious of their destination.

"My special place, I'll show you, it's the most beautiful spot you will ever see." He said to her smiling. Kayah merely put her hand over his; she knew at this moment that despite her young age she had fallen in love.

Back at the cabin the woods, the others had begun to awaken. Wanting to check on Kayah, Saiera quietly knocked on the door and cracked it open to peek in on her. "Kayah?" She asked quietly as she entered the room.

When she received no answer, she made her way to the bed. "Kayah, time to get up little one." She said as she pulled the blanket back to find only an empty bed, "That's odd."

She then turned to step out of the room when she spotted the note that was left. "What's this?" She asked aloud as she picked it up and read it. "Oh my goddess!" She exclaimed and as loudly as she could cried out for Sakuris.

The other adults quickly rushed up to see Saiera in tears on the bed. "Saiera, beloved, what is it?" Sakuris quickly asked concerned for her.

Through her tears, Saiera did her best to respond, "I . . . I came in to check on Kayah, and I found this." She then handed the note to Sakuris who then proceeded to read it.

"Saddle the horses." He quickly instructed, turning to Sinileass.

"Right away." He responded as he quickly left the room and hurried to complete the task set before him.

Saiera was still in tears on the bed as Sakuris sat beside her and wrapped his arms around her letting her cry into his shoulder. "We'll get her back, love." He said doing his best to reassure her.

Quickly remembering about Akisarah, Saiera shook herself loose from Sakuris's embrace and ran to the room she had let him rest in and found that he too was missing.

"Saiera, what is it?" Sakuris coming into the room behind her.

"Akisarah was here last night, but he's gone too. They must've taken them both." She responded as she fell to her knees.

"Then we'll get them back, both of them." Sakuris responded as he knelt beside Saiera and gently rubbed her back to comfort her.

"Sakuris, the horses are ready!" Sinileass soon called from downstairs.

"Saiera, you and the other women stay here in case they manage to find their way back. Sinileass and I will head out to try to find them." Sakuris said to her beloved as she gave him an approving nod in return.

"I'm coming with you." Saiera remarked as she dried her tears

"Saiera, no, Sinileass and I . . ." Sakuris began but soon cut himself off when Saiera shot a cold stare his way as fire burned in her eyes. She would not be told: No. Not this morning, she wouldn't.

Sakuris merely stepped back a few steps. "Okay." He remarked as Saiera stood to her feet, and the two of them hurried down to meet with Sinileass.

Back in the woods, the pre-teens soon road to a cliff that provided a view spanning from Kaylah to the ruins of even Sikan.

Kayah looked out from the horse she had been riding around as Akisarah held her in his arms. "Oh, Akisarah, you're right it is beautiful," She said soon spotting the ruins of Shikanaca, "but I prefer to leave."

Akisarah was puzzled as to why and looked at the ruins of Shikanaca and realized why, "Very well, I apologize if I upset you by bringing you here." He responded.

Kayah shook her hair out of her face. "No, I'm glad you showed me." She said to him as he rested his head on her shoulder. Turning her head and lightly kissed him on the cheek as she dismounted and began to walk off.

"Kayah, where are you going?" Akisarah asked watching her go behind some bushes.

"I have to go." She said lowering her skirt and underskirt and squatting.

Akisarah turned his head as he continued to study the view, *"This place always brought peace to my mind, but could it, now, have brought me more."* He thought as he watched Kayah finish up and redress her lower half and come from behind the bushes.

"Oh, that felt good, I have been holding that in all morning." She said to herself.

Akisarah helped her remount the horse and they rode through the forest a little more, this time slowing the horse's pace.

They soon rode up to a small river. Kayah perked up with delight and told Akisarah to stop. Akisarah did so and Kayah climbed off. "Oh I remember this spot. This is where Sakuris and I met Saiera." She said to Akisarah as he dismounted. He went over to the stream and took his kimono top off and dipped it into the water and wiped his face off.

"Akisarah, could you go somewhere for a minute? I wish to bathe." Kayah said realizing she was dirty from sitting in the cage.

He gave a low formal bow, "For you my lady, anything." He responded as he walked from the river and grabbed his Kali Sticks from a rolled up blanket that was on the horse they rode on, "I'll find us something to eat." He then walked off a short distance, straying only far enough to keep Kayah in his sight. He would not wander too far away, and chance having her taken from him.

At the small river Kayah undressed and climbed in, "This water is cold!" She called shivering. She bathed rather quickly to prevent from having to remain in the water for too long. She quickly climbed out and got dressed. "Why couldn't there be a hot spring here?" She said and then looked at Akisarah as he came back with a small rabbit. "On the other hand, maybe I can make a hot spring of my own." She said to herself and went over to Akisarah and embraced him as she pressed her lips to his.

Startled by Kayah's actions Akisarah pulled back and released himself from her embrace, "Kayah, what were you doing?" He asked with a start.

She looked at him, flush from embarrassment. "I'm sorry, I shouldn't have done that. I just . . . oh, never mind."

Akisarah pulled her toward him and took her into his embrace, *"It's ok, just please don't cry."* He whispered to her softly as she rested her head on his shoulder letting herself be held. His warmth gave her the same sense of protection she had gotten their first night together, *"Besides what would Sakuris have done if something happened between us?"* He said to her.

"Oh, Sakuris, this is my life, not his. Akisarah I want to be with you, to hold you in my arms and feel everything about you." She responded.

Her love for him strengthened Akisarah completely. He could feel her rhythmic pulse against his. A feeling had arisen inside of him, a feeling of warmth and purity. It was like a new strength he had never had before. He felt like he could sacrifice his own life to protect her. Had he fallen in love despite his young age, or was his mind merely toying with him? Kayah's small body in his arms passed warmth to him as he stood holding her while they shared the moment. They soon heard horses riding near where they stood, and quickly took cover in some bushes.

A voice soon called out. "Kayah, Kayah are you here? Akisarah, where are you two?"

Kayah recognized it to be her brother's, "Sakuris! Sakuris we're here." She called to him. Sakuris turned his head to the sound of his little sister's voice and saw her stand up from behind the bushes she and Akisarah had been hiding.

Akisarah stood up also revealing himself. Sakuris quickly ran over to his sister and took her into his embrace. "Oh, thank Elayis, you're safe. I felt sure I had lost you." He said hugging her tighter.

"Sakuris, Sakuris, you're squishing me." She teased as he let her go.

He looked over to Akisarah. "I should be thanking you, I guess. I might have lost her if you had not been around." He said walking over and extending an open hand to him, "What do you say, friends?"

Akisarah placed his hand in Sakuris's. "Friends, your sister means a lot to you, I see. I want you to know, whatever happens, I'd protect her with even my life." He said as he firmed his grip on Sakuris's hand.

"Hey, you have a firm grip. I like that, shows strength." Sakuris said as Akisarah released his hand.

Saiera soon walked up beside Sakuris, "Oh, thank Elayis, you found them." She said aloud as she looked at Kayah. Her slight look of guilt tipped Saiera off about her kissing Akisarah. "Sakuris, can you take Akisarah somewhere. I need to speak with Kayah." She said to turning to Sakuris.

Akisarah agreed that Sakuris should take him somewhere and said to him, "Come on, Lord Kaemouri, I'll show you how to use Kali Sticks."

When the two men left, Saiera turned to Kayah. "What happened?" She asked calmly and with a low voice so not to be heard.

Kayah approached her. "I . . . I . . . I kind of kissed Akisarah. I couldn't help it. It's just being held by him, I had to." She said sadly lowering her head.

Saiera took Kayah and held her in her arms. "Kayah, please don't try to understand what you've been feeling. You're just too young." She said and gave a long exasperated sigh, "Did you at least tell him how you felt before kissing him?"

"Yes, in my room last night." She responded.

"Your room, no, Kayah, what were you thinking. If Sakuris had found you two together, he would have been furious." Saiera said frustrated.

"I don't care, Sakuris doesn't run my life. He's not my father . . . even though he tries to be and for that I love him, but this is something I need to figure out for myself. That's why I asked Akisarah to stay with me last night." She said to her.

"You did what? Kayah, think with your head, not that opening between your thighs, girl. That was my mistake. I thought I clearly understood what I felt when I was around Sakuris. But I was wrong, it wasn't until after our first night together that I realized I loved him." Saiera said almost raising her voice.

"Miss Saiera, please keep your voice down." Kayah said trying to calm Saiera down.

"Kayah, why would you even consider having him stay?" Saiera asked rather hastily.

"It was a stupid thing to do, I know, but I get lonely at night. He came to me last night after I went into his room to see him. When I saw he was about to wake up I panicked and ran out of the room and dropped the candle I had with me. He came to find out what happened and I told him everything, ok. That's what I was I thinking." Kayah said in tears and sobbing.

Saiera quickly took Kayah into her arms and laid her head on her shoulder, "Shh, Kayah, I'm sorry. I shouldn't have reacted like that. It's just may not have been the best circumstances for you to tell him. Who knows what would have happened?" She said with a short sigh and then gave a small laugh, "Did you, at least, make him sleep on the floor?" She said with a small laugh.

"No, he chose to." Kayah responded with a small laugh.

Meanwhile, Sakuris was having his own talk with Akisarah. "I appreciate you risking yourself to get you and Kayah out of that temple, but next time, don't do anything. Kenzji's dangerous, you got lucky this time, but if, or I should say when you meet him again, you need to be wiser than you were." Sakuris said walking a few steps away and drawing one of his blades and tipping his finger with it, "However, I wonder." He then threw the blade at Akisarah with such skill that he had no time to react and was struck by the blade as the tip entered him, and he fell limp to the ground being overcome with slumber.

Sakuris walked over and stood over him. "I've just put you in a dream state. My blade did not harm you and I assure you when you awake, the wound will be gone." He said as Akisarah slowly blacked out.

Akisarah awoke to find himself alone in a different place; a place of blackness and pure emptiness. Sakuris soon appeared beside him. "Welcome to the Seltitian Planes. Here, we, the men of Shikanaca, can come and train without fear of hurting each other in a way known as mind fighting. Women dare not come here; the effect of this place on them is too great and severely dangerous." He said as Akisarah merely looked around.

"I see nothing but blackness, why?" He asked rather curious of the place.

Sakuris put a hand to his shoulder. "You have not chosen an arena." He responded smiling.

"An arena, for what, I don't understand. Why have you brought me to this place?" Akisarah asked with an even greater interest.

Sakuris said nothing and merely dropped into a ginta fighting stance, "This is where your training begins. Fight me and prove your strength. You want to protect Kayah one day, then fight and defeat me. I see the way you look upon her. You are hiding something from her." He responded.

"I won't fight you, Sakuris." Akisarah said to him.

"Too late, the arena's been chosen. Look around, notice a scenery change." Sakuris said motioning to the change of the scenery. Akisarah looked and found himself surrounded by a large forest and when he looked back Sakuris was gone.

He looked around panicked. On instinct he drew his Kali Sticks, "Sakuris! Where are you? You can't win hiding." He called.

Sakuris's voice suddenly rang out in his mind, "I am not hiding Akisarah. I am in the black tower at the center of the forest. It's three days' journey from here to there. I didn't specify the conditions for defeating me. Unfortunately few have ever survived this arena. But if you are as strong as you think you are, I trust you'll make it. I give you these items to work with; the first, of course, being your Kali Sticks. They are stronger and have been tipped with spearheads. The second, a white wolf, named blizzard, to be your guide. You won't find her, she'll find you. But she is not the only white wolf that roams this forest. They are several and most of them will tell you they're blizzard, but only one will speak the truth. How you will know truth from deception is for you to decide. The last item is a pouch of Shikanacan gold coins. This will serve as your money. The nearest village is almost a day's travel."

Akisarah looked around, "It would have been a little bit fairer if you had given me some food and water, you know." Akisarah said rather crossly.

Sakuris's voice rang out again, "What do you need that the forest can't provide. But be warned, some of the plants bare good fruit and some don't. Be careful which one you choose. I leave you with this last piece of advice, be careful who you trust. Some will help you, others will deceive you." and with those words spoken, silence.

Akisarah couldn't help but wonder why Sakuris would put him through this. He looked around for two of three items Sakuris left him. The money was in a pouch strapped about his waist. His Kali Sticks had short, diato-shaped spearheads on them. Akisarah soon felt hunger coming onto him as he began walking through the forest in search of food, "Some plants bare good fruit, the other's bare rotten. What kind of riddle is that and how am I supposed to know the difference. He's punishing me, I know it" He griped as he walked through the forest.

Food seemed to be hard to find on the outskirts so Akisarah decided to travel deeper to search. "A bow might have been nice if I wanted to kill a deer. That would feed me for a week, maybe longer. I don't have any camping supplies either." He complained as his stomach grumbled from hunger, and he continued to walk through the forest as hunger began to set in even more.

Sakuris merely watched him with an open Seltitian eye in the black tower. *"Why hasn't he found food already? Our weakest fighters didn't even take this long. Did I overestimate this one or does he overestimate his strength?"* He thought to himself. He hadn't even taken this long to find food. Then again, he didn't survive the journey either. He merely watched Akisarah through the powers of Seltah as he came upon a village. *"Well here we go, he's at a village. He will certainly find what he needs there. Should I have warned him about killing the white stags that run through the forest? No, I think he needs to figure it out for himself."* He thought as he sat in his hiding place atop the tower.

At the village, Akisarah wondered around for a bit trying to find food and shelter. Finally giving in to his hunger, he collapsed to the ground and merely stayed there clutching his stomach. A young girl about his age approached him. "Are you ok young man?" She asked.

Akisarah looked at the girl who spoke to him and to his surprise she carried a strong resemblance to Kayah, "Kayah." He said to her.

She stepped back, "No, my name Tansienia. You don't look well." She said to him as she held her hand out to him, "Please come with me. I'm sure mom wouldn't mind another for dinner." Dinner, the word repeated itself in Akisarah's mind, but he remembered Sakuris's warning about being careful who he trusted.

He stared at Tansienia's hand hesitant about gripping it. "Well, are you hungry or not?" She asked in a rather innocent and girlish voice. The thought of food continued to ring in Akisarah's mind, but was she to be trusted.

Sakuris continued to watch him from the tower. *"He's smart; he hesitates to take this young woman's hand. But the need for food makes a person weak. I love these will he-won't he situations. I even trusted her only to find out she had deceived me. Her robbery attempt left me short twenty coins. Will Akisarah fall into the same trap? Probably, I told him the village was a day's travel. My father even gave me the same time and I was fooled by the illusion Tansienia created. Then again, my hunger wasn't for food, but rather lust. I was fifteen at the time. She appeared to me more beautiful and desirable than Saiera. I couldn't help it; I just had to have her; the curvature of her breasts, her soft lips, the roundness of her butt, those long desirable legs. Her flowing gold hair and chestnut colored eyes. I failed my test against temptation. Will he do the same? I gave her the appearance of Kayah to test him greater. He'll give in; no one has ever survived their first attempt here. In father's case it was mother who he failed his first attempt to."* He thought as he watched.

Akisarah looked at Tansienia; her eyes seemed so trusting to him as she continued to hold out her hand. He was hungry, but remembered what Sakuris had said about the village being a day's travel. He had only been traveling for a few hours, or did Sakuris put him closer to the village than he thought. Should he or shouldn't he, decisions, decisions. She continued to hold out her hand to him. "Can you speak?" She asked him.

Akisarah nodded his head, "I appreciate the offer, but this can't be real. He said it was a day's travel to the nearest village. I've only been traveling for a few hours. Surely you don't expect me to believe there is hot food and shelter waiting for me, do you?" He said suddenly speaking.

Tansienia's image suddenly turned into a white wolf. "Greeting's young traveler, I am Blizzard. It was clever of you to see through my deception. Even Sakuris failed his first attempt; I can honestly show you to food, though. Not here, but close. My den is not far. There you will find food and comfort." She said to him.

Akisarah looked at her. "Sakuris also warned me that many wolves will tell me they are Blizzard. How do I know you are the one I seek?" He asked still not trusting the situation.

Blizzard turned her head. "Look about my neck, you see the mark of the snowstorm. I'm the only white wolf in the forest that possesses this mark." She responded showing him the mark she spoke of. Akisarah hesitated for a moment, Sakuris never told him about the mark and he wondered if he should trust this wolf.

Sakuris continued to watch from the tower. *"Akisarah might be too smart for his own good. Of course, that's the wolf he seeks. I hope he makes the right decision. That was my second failure; my untrusting nature caused me to lose the guide father set for me. Only the guide I had was the white wolf, Phoenix. The mark each wolf bares on its neck proves its identity. It took me almost four days to make it to through the forest and to the black tower but by then it was already too late. Father pulled me from my slumber, once again. He even failed his second attempt, the wolf he had gotten was named Blaze and about her neck she bore the mark of the flame."* He thought as he watched Akisarah follow the wolf into the forest, *"I have hope for him yet."*

Akisarah walked through the forest with blizzard, her size surprised him. She was much larger than a normal wolf. His need for food made him weak and he stumbled a few times. Blizzard looked at him, "Get on, I'll carry you." She said walking back to him and lowering herself for Akisarah to get on. Akisarah climbed on and let Blizzard carry him through the forest with swift speed. He soon spotted a rather large deer.

"Wait, Miss Blizzard, is it safe to kill and eat that deer over there." He said to her pointing out the deer.

Blizzard looked at him. "That is no deer, but one of the White Stags that roams this forest. They are forbidden to be killed by even the animals. I assure you that good food awaits us." She said not stopping as she continued to run through the forest.

She soon came upon a small cave. A small pack of wolves waited for them as one stood outside the cave. When he saw her approach he gave a loud howl to let the other's know Blizzard was back. The wolves in the cave went out and sat patiently as Blizzard approached. Akisarah saw this and out of curiosity asked Blizzard, "Those other wolves seem to respect you."

Blizzard laughed a small wolf-like laugh and responded, "I am their Alpha."

"Alpha, what's that?" Akisarah asked; he had never heard of such a thing.

"Alpha's are the leaders of the pack, the one who announced our approach is my Beta. When I die, he will take my place. The other three are Omegas. They are, what you humans would call, the low men on the totem pole." She responded as she drew nearer to the cave and eventually ran inside of it.

Akisarah climbed off and looked around. He saw a small bed of Animal furs waiting for him. He wasted no time in sitting on it and wrapping himself in a few of the furs. Blizzard watched him as he did. "You humans, always consumed by the need for warmth. That's what gives us wolves the advantage over your species. Night has fallen; you should try to get some rest." She said walking past him and going over to the beta who announced their presence and in a telepathic link spoke to him. "What do you think of this one, mate?"

The beta went over and sniffed Akisarah. "He smells like one of Sakuris's." He replied using the same telepathic link. Blizzard laughed the same wolven laugh. She then went over and laid down in a corner. Her mate went over and laid beside her.

She looked at him. *"Soon, Red Fox, this one will reach the black tower where Sakuris awaits. I was amazed at how he passed the first two tests so easily, but more will follow and they will surely take their toll on him."* She said to him in a whisper and fell asleep. Red Fox gently nudged his mate and fell asleep as well.

Even though he had been hungry, Akisarah's thoughts merely dwelled on Kayah. Sensing his troubles, one of the wolves went over to him. "Something troubles you traveler." She said to him calmly.

He looked at her. "Hmm, growing up, I guess. Why did she tell me that? Why did she even kiss me?" He said almost forcing out the questions.

The wolf looked at him. "Mating season for you humans I see. It's strange; you look so young to be looking for a mate. I thought humans were not allowed to let their pups mate until they were fully grown." She said to him.

"May I stroke your fur? I have never been this close to a wolf before." Akisarah said breaking off the subject.

The wolf leaned her head down as if to say: Yes. Reaching up, Akisarah petted the fur on the wolf's head. Its feel was unlike anything he felt before. It was warm and soft, it reminded him of his safe bed in Kaylah. He realized then how much he missed his parents. He had only been away for a day and already he missed them.

He couldn't help but feel himself getting trapped in a war that was to be fought by adults. Why did Sakuris bring him to this damn place? He wanted to be in his mother's arms and listen to his father's stories. He would give anything to return home. Slowly he realized that if he ever made it out of here, he would be changed forever. He would somehow be stronger, faster, and smarter than most Spirit Clansmen. Slowly, his eyes closed as he fell asleep. The wolf who spoke to him laid beside him sharing the warmth of her fur with him.

Chapter 8

Sakuris watched from the black tower as Akisarah slept. *"His feelings dwell on his parents. That is not a good sign, he's breaking himself more than I thought. He wasn't ready for this. But, then again, who is? No one's ever ready, it took me three attempts to pass this damn thing. I can only hope he does it in one. I should prepare myself for Akisarah's trial. It would only be fair to be at my best. I'd expect nothing less from him, therefore; I will give him nothing less."* Sakuris thought to himself closing off his Seltitian mind. Before him sat three burning candles, each burning a different color. Below, each candle had a sign that led somewhere else. Sakuris could determine which place to commence his training by blowing out a specific candle. One burned blue, another burned red, and the third burned a golden yellow.

Not knowing what kind of challenges the choice he made would leave him, Sakuris thought long and hard before making his decision. He blew out the blue candle. The air in the room grew cold and a mist fell upon it. Sakuris found himself being put into state of slumber, into a deeper world of dreams. He awoke to find himself atop a high mountain where the air was surprisingly warm and breathable. He took a good look around. "Maybe I should have chosen red." He said to himself with a small chuckle. What he saw next he would never have imagined could happen. A doppelganger of himself was waiting for him.

Sakuris stared at his doppelganger as if staring into a mirror. Suddenly and without warning the doppelganger attacked him throwing a series of high and low blows mixed with a flurry of kicks. Taken by surprise, Sakuris didn't have the reaction time he needed to counter the attacks as each blow landed a direct hit at their assigned targets. Some went to his stomach, others to his face, and the rest to his legs.

Sakuris staggered to regain his composure, "I get it. If can't conquer myself, than I can't conquer my opponents. Is this what Sinileass meant?" He said to himself. He had only enough time to think about this before his doppelganger began its attack again. This time Sakuris had been ready. He countered all of his doppelganger's moves easily and swiftly. The fighters fought each other with great skill both equal and unique.

Once again Sakuris's doppelganger had gotten the best of him. Sakuris could feel blood running down the side of his mouth. He merely licked it away and spit it out, *"Damn, and I thought Reia was hard, how am I to be an opponent, when the opponent is me. After all, father always said, 'your hardest opponent was always yourself.'"* Sakuris thought to himself. He watched the doppelganger and looked at its stance. There was one tiny flaw, the same flaw Sakuris always had, it left its guard down at its left flank.

The number one rule of combat is never attack with your flank unguarded. Sakuris was out of breath, but the doppelganger stood motionless without breathing. Not wanting to be surprised by his opponent again, Sakuris took to the offensive and threw his own series of kicks and punches and strikes. He suddenly heard a voice whisper to him inside his head. It was his father's, *"The true warrior is at peace with himself and never raises his fists."*

Sakuris had been caught off guard by his father's voice, *"What am I supposed to do let him attack me."* He asked his father.

"Yes, only through peace can victory be achieved." His father said to him and then was silent.

Lowering his fists, Sakuris dropped his stance. The doppelganger quickly threw several blows and kicks. Allowing each one to strike, Sakuris remained motionless as his opponent continued its relentless barrage of attacks. "Why do you not fight back?" It suddenly asked stopping its attack.

Battered and bruised, Sakuris looks to his opponent, replying, "We have nothing to fight about." His doppelganger suddenly bowed and united himself with Sakuris.

Suddenly as fast as he got to the mountainous area, Sakuris found himself back in the black tower where Akisarah had just arrived and was outside. Sakuris looked down at the bottom level where he saw Akisarah entering. *"Three days already, I had been in a dream state for that long. I was only there a few hours. Does time pass that slowly there?"* He wondered, but paid no mind to the time that had passed and went down to meet Akisarah in the large dojo at the base of the tower. "You've come at last. I didn't think you'd make this far your first attempt. Not many do, now let's see how much stronger you've become." He said to Akisarah dropping into a fighting stance being sure to leave his flank guarded.

Akisarah had looked much different than he did when he first entered the dream world three days ago. He had grown stronger and wiser. He lowered into a fighting stance as well. He wondered if his Yoejitsu fighting style would match up to Sakuris's Galtineah. This was the time to find out as Sakuris quickly made the first move. He rushed at him and threw a punch directly at Akisarah.

Quickly side stepping out of the way, Akisarah barely dodged the blow as he threw a counter punch straight into Sakuris's abdomen. The single blow made Sakuris recoil in pain as he felt the wind leaving his body. He looked as Akisarah merely stood there not having been fazed by the impact of the blow.

Sakuris merely coughed and clutched his stomach as air slowly went to his lungs. "*I have certainly underestimated this one.*" He thought to himself. He quickly saw Akisarah coming toward him just in time to dodge the aero kick he threw. Sakuris felt Akisarah's foot go by his face as the blow narrowly missed him, as he threw his hand up into Akisarah's back.

Akisarah flew past him with so much momentum he was unable to land properly and fell to the ground. He merely stood up and looked at Sakuris watching him carefully, "*His keeps his guard up, even when injured.*" He thought to himself. Barely having enough time to dodge the wind blades being thrown by Sakuris, he back flipped over each one as they narrowly missed him, wondering how he would get close enough to attack Sakuris. He then realized he had his own ace in the hole. His telekinetic powers he had been born with as a child.

He quickly flung his hand up causing Sakuris to rise into the air, "Sakuris, I did forget to mention something earlier. I'm telekinetic, that is how I protected Kayah earlier and that is how I plan to protect her in the future." He said closing his hand. Sakuris could feel his body being constricted as he found it hard to breathe. He felt his lungs slowly collapsing. "I can stop, you know. You brought me here thinking I was weak. Well, do you still think I'm weak?" Akisarah taunted

Sakuris merely shook his head and with a forced voice said only this, "No, I think you're a coward resorting to this method of fighting to win.

Why don't you face me without your powers and weapons and I'll do the same."

Akisarah dropped his hands letting Sakuris hit the floor. Once again, Sakuris could only cough heavily as precious air rushed back into his lungs. Akisarah merely stood watching him. He drew his Kali Sticks and threw them aside, watching Sakuris regain his composure and remove his weapons as he threw them aside as well. Both fighters once again went into their fighting stance and proceeded to engage in hand-to-hand combat. Both fighters' skills met each other with equality and uniqueness.

In the end Akisarah had Sakuris to the floor with a hand raised ready for a downward knife-hand strike to Sakuris's neck. He quickly brought his hand down for the finishing blow, but then suddenly stopped, "No, it's not worth it." He said refusing to kill Sakuris.

Suddenly the dream world of Seltah disappeared and both fighters found themselves awake in Sakuris's room. It had been very late in the afternoon almost dusk as the sun had already started to set.

Kayah came in to see them both awake and quickly called out, "Saiera come quickly they're awake."

Saiera quickly entered the room and saw what Kayah had seen. She dropped the tray she had been carrying letting it crash onto the floor and ran over to Sakuris embracing him, "Thank, Elayis, we thought you'd never awake." She said holding Sakuris tighter.

"How long were we there?" He asked rather patiently.

Kayah went over to him. "We've been trying to wake you for the past three days." She said to him.

"Three days?" Akisarah exclaimed rather surprised.

Sakuris looked at him, "The Seltitian planes shares time with the waking world. It allows the fighter to sustain his bodily functions in the real world. The hunger you had was not just on the planes but in this world as well." Sakuris responded. Kayah helped Akisarah up as they left the room. Sakuris merely watched as they left. Saiera could only smile. She knew even though Akisarah and Kayah were still young, they really did love each other.

"What happened to you two?" Saiera soon asked turning to Sakuris.

"My people are able to access a dream world that exists alongside the real world known as the Seltitian Plains. It's difficult and takes a great deal of concentration. For young Akisarah I was forced to use an alternative method. Saiera, I learned more about him there than I could've ever hoped. He is a fine young man and great candidate for the clan." Sakuris responded with a smile and a hint of pride in his voice.

"And he makes Kayah happy." Saiera remarked smiling.

"Yes, that is true." Sakuris agreed, "It is good for her to have a friend closer to her age." He then sat up on the bed and leaned back against the headboard as Saiera smiled and sat beside him.

"I'm just glad to have them back. I can't help but wonder how worried his parents must've been." Saiera commented. Sakuris chuckled and agreed.

In Kayah's room, Akisarah looked into Kayah's eyes as her arms encircled him, "About earlier, Akisarah. . ." She started but was silent as he placed his fingers to her lips.

"Shh, there is no earlier, there is only us." His words were almost as still and silent as the night. Kayah knew at that moment just how much she cared for him. She couldn't resist just one little kiss.

This time, Akisarah welcomed it. He could feel her small tongue rubbing against teeth. What was it about Kayah that made him feel so close to her? At that moment of strength, he felt as if he could do anything, be anyone. Their arms merely stayed wrapped around one another as Kayah finally pulled her head back and gave a small smile. Despite her young age she wanted Akisarah at that moment and had started to work at getting his tunic off. He merely gripped her hands into his own, "All things to those who wait, Kayah."

With frustration, she nodded and pulled her hands away from his tunic, "You're right." She then walked over to her bed and laid down. "You staying tonight?" She asked already knowing the answer to her question.

Akisarah shook his head. "Not tonight, Kayah. I need to get home. My parents are probably worried to death about me." He replied as he walked over and gave her a light kiss on the forehead, "I'll come back to see you, tomorrow." He then walked out of the room and out of the home. Not knowing what to expect in the forest so late in the day he drew his kali sticks and realized the spearheads Sakuris had given on the Seltitian planes were still there. He had no idea how he was going to explain where he had been or what he had been doing in his absence.

He wondered if his parents would ever believe him. Not wanting to stay in the forest for the night he placed his weapons back in their scabbard and hurried home. He arrived to a most puzzling sight, the home was empty, aside from what furniture and wall decorations remained, and his parents nowhere to be found. "Mama? Papa?" He called.

A presence soon appeared behind him. Sensing it, Akisarah turned and brandished his Kali Sticks ready to strike in self-defense but merely found Master Ryuomi waiting for him. "Taylah-sama? My apologies." He gasped lowering his weapons and taking a few steps back.

"You came looking for your parents, young Kamikawi. Come I can show you where they are." Ryuomi responded as he motioned for young Akisarah to follow him. What he led him to, young Akisarah was not prepared for: gravestones marked with his parents name seals.

"No!" Akisarah exclaimed as he stepped towards the graves and knelt before the one marked with his mother's name as he threw his arms around it with tears coming from his eyes, "Mama!" He cried.

"I am sorry young master." Ryuomi responded as he stepped up and knelt behind him putting a hand to his shoulder.

"I've only been away a few days. What happened?" Akisarah managed to ask through his tears.

"Witnesses say they saw a man coming from their home in a hurry. He had been looking for you." Ryuomi responded doing his best to explain the situation.

"This man, what did they say he looked like?" Akisarah asked almost demandingly. Taking pity on the boy, Ryuomi gave the description that he had been given. It was a match for Kenzji Ketsuro, but was it truly Kenzji who did it?

"Leave me, Taylah-sama." Akisarah asked, continuing to stare at his mother's grave.

"Of course, young master, take all the time you need." Ryuomi responded as he stepped away from Akisarah to let him grieve for his parents.

Having taking a few moments to grieve for his parents, the young spirit clansman stood up and stepped in front of his father's grave, but so many questions ran through his mind. Why had he left, if he had stayed he may of been able to protect them, or would have he been consumed in the tragedy as well? Either way, he did not want to think about it. He merely bowed before his father's grave and returned to his home in Kaylah. Looking over to the wall he could see his father's sword resting upon a shelf. It was one his father had forged himself, called the Sword of Hope.

Abandoning every principle Akisarah had about taking a life, he reached for it and took it out of the scabbard. The blade had still retained its sharpness. The double edge made it ideal for combat. With a strength like no other as fire rose in Akisarah's soul, he placed the blade back in the scabbard and strapped it about his other shoulder letting it rest upon his Kali Sticks.

Still stricken with grief, and rage burning in his heart, Akisarah knew there was nothing left for him in Kaylah so he gathered his things and went back to Sinileass's home and walked around the back, to Kayah's room. He took a small pebble and threw it against the wall. Opening the window, Kayah looked to see him there as puzzled expression came across her face, "Akisarah I thought you went home."

He held up his father's sword with tears still in his eye. He tried to hide it; pretending the night was doing it, "I want to come up." He said with a broken voice.

He hadn't been able to hide what happened. Kayah knew by the way he spoke. She quickly went down stairs and outside to where Akisarah had been, "What happened?" She asked concerned for her friend.

"My parents, they're. . ." Akisarah began, trying to respond, but his voice broke, and he buried his face into Kayah's shoulder.

Kayah merely encircled her arms around him, "You don't have to say anymore. Come on I'll take you upstairs. Tonight, I lay in your room." She said to him as they entered the house and went upstairs. They both entered Akisarah's room, but he didn't want to sleep.

He could only think of the gravestones he had seen at Kaylah, "I should have been there." He said blaming himself for what happened as he sat on the bed.

"Don't blame yourself Akisarah. Even if you had been there, there was no telling what could have happened." Kayah said trying to make him feel better. Akisarah pretended as if he didn't hear, but knew she might have been right.

Slowly he laid down and placed his head on his pillow letting tears flow onto it and slowly closed his eyes to fall asleep. Kayah went over to the other side and slipped in, there was no way she would sleep on the floor. She needed to be at his side. She agreed to do the same thing Akisarah had done. She would leave early in the morning before her brother awoke. Outside, the moon hung suspended in the sky as the sounds of the nocturnal animals could be heard throughout the forest. This peaceful setting made it easier for everyone to sleep through the night. Slowly, the clouds drifted past the moon and through the sky making the night seem as still as stone. Rain slowly poured down upon the area making small dripping noises on the trees as it fell.

It rained throughout the night and when dawn had arisen Kayah slipped out of Akisarah's bed and went to her room and laid down in her bed as she pulled the covers over herself and proceeded to fall back asleep. It had not been long before she could hear the sounds of voices downstairs as she awoke. Akisarah had been talking with Sakuris. About what, Kayah couldn't tell. Slipping out of her bed she exited the room and merely looked down at them. Akisarah had been yelling, "Train me Sakuris, I want to be part of the Dragon Clan. My parents' murderer must pay."

Sakuris shook his head. "We are not about in that Dragon Clan. If you act so foolishly, you will lose yourself in anger." He remarked trying to convince Akisarah of the folly of his wish.

Akisarah stared hard at him, "I don't care. I WANT VENGANCE!" He yelled.

Sakuris looked at him, replying "You get a grip on yourself, one who fights for revenge fights for nothing." and getting stern with Akisarah.

"*I want justice.*" Akisarah said in barely a whisper.

"Sakuris, training him won't hurt. If he does meet with the murderer of his parents it would certainly be useful that he know what we do. Especially if it was a Dragon Clansman or an ex-Dragon Clansman." Kayah said as she came down the stairs.

"You speak of Kenzji. Puzzling, why would he be looking for our young friend here?" Sakuris responded taking time to think about it.

"Master Taylah, did say eyewitnesses mentioned someone who matched Kenzji's description leaving the home." Akisarah informed Sakuris.

Sakuris looked at him, "Very well, Akisarah, I'll train you, but now's not the time. You are not ready yet. I'll train you when the time comes." He said to him.

Time moved on slowly since that day, and Saiera soon gave birth to a beautiful girl, whom she and Sakuris affectionately named Iyata. It was not long before the second of the Wyvern Clan elite showed himself. It was the younger of Fei Ling's sons, Doreto. Sakuris stood by Saiera as Ryuomi fought to defeat his opponent. In the end he failed and was beaten back.

Ryuomi retreated to Sakuris's side, "Damn, he's tough. Your turn Sakuris." He said sitting down and taking deep, slow breaths.

Sakuris smiled as he drew his blades and stepped forward. Doreto merely made the come here gesture with his fingers. "Come, son of Kaemouri. Show me what you got." He said encouraging Sakuris to make the first move.

Swords at the ready, Sakuris rushes Doreto aiming the tip of his blades directly at his heart. A quick side step allows Doreto to dodge to the left of Kaemouri as he drives the pommel of his sword handle into his opponent's back.

Thrown forward by a combination of the strike and his forward momentum, Sakuris quickly regains his footing and turns around, making the same come here gesture to Doreto. With a sinister grin, Doreto rushes Kaemouri, sword at the ready. As still as stone, Sakuris takes a stance familiar to Saiera as she realizes what he planned to do. It was the same wind slicer technique he used on her so many months ago. The wind blew warm as summer took over for spring. The sun had been high that day. Vanishing from sight as Doreto slashes down at him with his blade, Kaemouri reappeared as he fell from the sky, charging his blade with the power of wind, and unleashing a mighty battle cry.

Doreto merely dodged as Sakuris brought the blade in his right hand forward for the attack and landed on one knee with his back toward his opponent.

"Some technique, but you left yourself open." Doreto laughes, raising his blade ready to punch it through Sakuris back and down through his heart, but Sakuris was unphased and merely stared back not at Doreto, but past him watching the huge whirlwind that approached him.

Curious to know what Sakuris was viewing, Doreto dropped his attack to look behind him. By the time he see the whirlwind approaching, it was too late. Unable to dodge it, he was lifted high into the air.

Standing to his feet, Sakuris turns around and, stepping back, takes precise aim as he fired three fire balls into the twister. The giant funnel of fire slowly burned Doreto to death as his agonizing screams could be heard from inside the storm. By the time it disappeared Doreto's body was but a charred pile of skeletal remains that dropped to the ground, dissolving into dust that was blown away by the wind. Out of breath, Sakuris stood motionless as he let fresh air rush in and out of his lungs.

Turning to the other two fighters, he returns his blades to their scabbard. Their battle won, the three warriors traveled back to the newly rebuilt Kaylah. Many more months passed and the rebirth of the Dragon Clan slowly took place, growing from a few hundred to thousands as Sakuris, Saiera, and Kayah took their places in the hierarchy of the clan with Akisarah heir to position of Arch-Dragon. Even Reia, whom had finally come to terms with Sakuris's return, took her rightful place within the clan.

Reconstruction of Shikanaca took place as more Dragon Clan members were tested and accepted and soon came the test of someone Sakuris had not expected. Stepping into the forest arena of Shikanaca was someone Sakuris and Kayah had known from their past. Watching as the female fighter step into the arena, Sakuris couldn't help but smile. From the stands, Kayah could see the familiar face of their old friend. "Yu-Ka-Mi." Sakuris remarked.

"Hello, Sakuris." Yu-Ka-Mi responds with a cheerful smile. She was clad in samurai armor and carried with her an extremely long sword, known as a Nodachi.

"You've caught up to me, at last. Are you ready?" Sakuris asked drawing his weapons.

"The question is: Are you?" Yu-Ka-Mi responded as she removed the extremely long weapon from her back and with the help of a nearby Dragon Clansman drew it from its scabbard.

The clansman barely had time to move away as Sakuris made the first move as he lunged toward Yu-Ka-Mi, but due to the extremely long reach of her sword, his attack was cut short. Sakuris knew he would have to get inside her defenses in order to take away her reach advantage, but how?

From the stands, the two fighters could hear the cheers of the other Dragon Clansman as they continued their bout. "She's amazing." Sakuris exclaimed to himself having a hard time finding a way into her defenses, "I must find a way to overcome her reach advantage."

"Come, son of Kaemouri, show me the strength of the child I once took in." Yu-Ka-Mi called, beckoning Sakuris.

Behind his back, Sakuris concealed one of his hands, charging a ball of chi and running towards Yu-Ka-Mi as she prepared to defend herself. Launching his hidden attack, Kaemouri prepares to strike true in order to end the bout, but Yu-Ka-Mi parried with her sword, and quickly drew forth the Tachi that rested at her side and used it to stop Sakuris in his tracks. The tip of the blade rested just at Sakuris's throat as he stopped just in time.

"Impressive, old friend, but look down." He commented bringing Yu-Ka-Mi's attention to his sword hovering just inches from her heart, "We would've joined each other in death."

"Shall we call this match a draw then?" Yu-Ka-Mi ask curious.

"A draw it shall be, welcome to the Dragon Clan." Sakuris responded as he re-sheathed his weapons and the two fighters bowed before each other. "An impressive display of sword skill, my friend." Sakuris continued, "Such skill deserves a position worthy of honor, be my protector, and lead my forces."

"An honorable invitation, Lord Kaemouri, I accept." Yu-Ka-Mi responds as the two fighters bow once more, leaving the arena.

After the test ended, Sakuris went down to a nearby hot spring ready for a hot bath. Kayah, meanwhile, had returned to her room to change clothes for the evening. Her young body had blossomed into that of a young woman as she was now seventeen and Sakuris the age of twenty four. Akisarah, who had just joined, turned seventeen a few weeks earlier and had grown into a strong young man. Iyata, daughter of the elder Kaemouri, was now five years old.

Sitting at the foot of her bed, Kayah stares, blankly, at the wall lost in her own thoughts of Akisarah, *"I am now able to bare children and must soon find a husband. I love Akisarah, but I am afraid he does not feel the same way."*

A knock at her door, and the calling of a familiar voice, brings her back to reality. "Kayah, Kayah, you in there?"

Recognizing the voice to be Akisarah's, Kayah rushes over to open the door, "Akisarah, I was just thinking about you."

With a sly smile, Akisarah enters the room and wraps his arm around her waist, pulling her in close and nudging the door shut with his foot, "And I have not stopped thinking about you ever since the day we met."

The moon had just risen and darkness shadowed the land of Shikanaca. Kayah blushed as Akisarah drew her closer to him, letting his lips meet hers. As he lifted her up, Kayah wrapped her legs around his waist as she opened his tunic and let her hands feel around his strong chest. Their tongues entwined, Akisarah gently laid her back on the bed, opening her kimono and cupping his hands around her breasts, he gently squeezes them.

Her head went back as she stared him in the eye. "I love you Akisarah." She said letting her lips press to his once more as she used her feet to slide his pants and under pants off.

Akisarah pulled back. "I love a woman who takes the initiative, especially the one who is with me now." He responded pressing his lips to hers as he slid his kimono top off and threw it aside, gently laying Kayah back as he slid her kimono off and worked his tongue down her female anatomy.

Lower and lower, he went down to her waist and lower still, letting his tongue work over the narrow opening between her thighs causing Kayah's pelvic region to arch up involuntarily and slam back down on the bed as her legs began to spasm from the pleasure. Lost in ecstacy, Kayah allowed Akisarah to do as he wanted with her. She wanted this so bad, to be his.

"Oh, Akisarah." She moaned with ecstasy in her voice, as Akisarah continued working his tongue over the same spot. Kayah felt the pleasure racing throughout the lower half of her body as it tensed up. "Akisarah! Yes! More!" She begged, clasping his head in her hands ready to scream. Akisarah continued until finally Kayah screamed his name, "Akisarah!"

He looked up at her and smiled. "Hmm-hmm, was it good for you, my dear?" He asked letting his tongue flow back up her body.

"It was great for me, my love." Kayah responded as Akisarah gazed lovingly at her, letting his body slide into hers.

The feel of his body inside her set Kayah's soul ablaze. She had waited so long for this, and now it was finally happening. She rolled him over and straddled him sliding her hips back and forth, "Oh, yes, yes, yes!" She chanted.

Akisarah rose up once again and cupped her breast in his hand, gently encircling his lips around her nipple he began to suck on it. The rocking of her hips along Akisarah's shaft along with her breast being sucked on cause Kayah to bite her lip as she held back another scream.

The young couple continued to make love as Kayah's screams of ecstasy echoed in Akisarah's ears, and when their young adult bodies had all they could take, the two were thrown into orgasm as they finished and laid next to each other in bed. Kayah looked at him, "So that's what sex feels like. Feels good." She said to him, gasping for air.

Akisarah nodded in agreement. "I have been wanting to do that for a while." He remarked as the two of them lie next to each other.

Kayah continued to look at him as her eyes met with his. "Akisarah, this won't change things between us will it. I mean if I get pregnant, you won't run off and leave me, will you?" She said in a troubled voice.

Akisarah merely brushed her hair from her face and looked at her reassuringly, "Never, you're too important to me. I promise no matter what happens I'll stay by your side, I love you." He responded.

Pleased with his response, Kayah smiled lovingly at him and gently kissed his forehead. "Thank you, it makes me happy to hear that." She said kissing him lightly and rolling over to fall asleep.

Akisarah wondered if he should stay with her or not, he did not want to get her in trouble with Sakuris. Slowly rising out of bed, he slid his pants and under pants on. Feeling the weight shift in the bed Kayah rose and looked at him. "Please don't go, I don't want to be alone tonight." She said pleading for him to stay.

He turned to face her. "I would not want to get you in trouble with your brother." He said as he continued to dress.

She merely looked at him. "Too bad, because if you go, you may never see these again." She said letting the covers drop from her breasts.

Akisarah merely looked at her. "Kayah you are positively evil." His voice contained a sarcastic tone within it, "If Sakuris kills me, I'm coming back to haunt you." He said climbing back in the bed and pulling the covers over him as he wrapped his arm around Kayah. Under his arm, Kayah's breasts laid flat and she felt the same security she had their first night together. The warmth from his body had a soothing effect on her allowing her to fall asleep with ease. Akisarah slowly felt his eyes close as he, too, fell asleep.

Back at his room, Sakuris had just returned from the hot spring as it grew late in the night.

He walked in and saw Saiera feeding Iyata. Iyata looked at him. "Daddy!" She cheered as she ran up to him.

Sakuris picked her up in his arms. "Didn't your mother already feed you?" He asked teasing her.

She nodded. "Yeah, but I was hungry again." She responded sweetly as she smiled trying to look cute and innocent.

"Well do me a favor little one, I need to speak to your mother alone for a bit. Why don't you go visit with Grandma and Grandpa" He said to her as he set her down.

Doing as instructed, the kaemouri child leaves her parents in order to venture to Sinileass's room. "Grandpa Sinileass, Grandma Kyusa, I'm came to visit." She called through their door.

Kyusa answered. "Well, Iyata, come in little one." She said allowing her granddaughter to enter the room.

"Daddy said he needed to be alone to speak to mommy." Iyata asked curiously.

"He did? Well, then you just come in and visit for a while then." Kyusa responds allowing her adoptive granddaughter to enter the room and led her to see Sinileass.

In Sakuris's and Saiera's room, Sakuris looked at his beloved with a troubled expression on his face.

"Something troubles you, my love?" She responded as the two of them sat on the bed together. Sakuris merely stripped his gi-top off revealing his masculine chest to Saiera. Unable to resist, she steps behind her husband to rub his shoulders.

Taking a deep breath, he sighed through his nose and smiled as Saiera gently massaged him. "No, just been a long night." He responded.

"The woman who tested this evening. It seemed as if you two knew each other." Saiera remarked curiously.

"Someone from my childhood. She was the first to take in me and Kayah after the death of our parents. Kayah wanted so much for her to be our new mother." Sakuris responded with mixed emotions.

"Seeing her does not please you, my love?" Saiera asked as she continued to rub Sakuris's shoulders. Sakuris merely chuckled as he touched one of his hands to Saiera's.

"It pleases me greatly." He responded as he laid his head on Saiera's lap. Saiera merely smiled down at him as she gently stroked his cheek.

"Reconstruction of the clan seems to be going well." She remarks pleasantly. Sakuris merely looked up at her with a smile.

"I agree with you, and the rebuilding of Shikanaca is ahead of schedule," He responded with pride. Walking over to a nearby window, Sakuris gazes out over the city, "and soon will be strong enough to once again help in the war efforts."

"I hear more villages have fallen to Isura." Saiera responded from the bed.

Sakuris turns his head to look back at her. "Yes, and with Kenzji helping them, many more will fall to its demonic influence. It's a shame really, he is Shikanancan, after all."

Iyata soon came back into the room and went over to Sakuris and hugged him. He picked her up and held in his arms. "Did Grandma and Grandpa send you home?" He asked her. Held in her father's arms, the young Kaemouri nodded in reply

"Well, in that case, let's get you to bed, little one." He responds taking Iyata over to a child-sized basket bed that had been suspended from the ceiling, and laying her down for the night.

Iyata looked up at her father. "Daddy, I want a story. Tell me the one about the dragon who slayed a demon." She said to him.

Having followed her beloved over, Saiera was not pleased by the story her daughter had requested, *"You told her about your fight with Zecuroas."* She whispered in his ear in stern voice.

"I may have mentioned it to her." He whispered back and yawned, "Sorry, squirt, I am too tired tonight. Maybe tomorrow night." He said to his daughter as he kissed her good night. Iyata merely giggled as he did. Once she was tucked in, she rolled over and allowed herself to fall asleep.

Smiling cheerfully at their sleeping daughter, the young couple walked over to the bed together and laid down upon it. "Beloved, we've been together a long time now. We have a beautiful daughter, why are we still not united?" Saiera asked sadly trying to strike up some pillow talk with Sakuris.

"War makes romance hard, I suppose. I guess we've been so caught up in trying to rebuild the clan and Shikanaca that it just never happened."

Sakuris responds turning towards her as the two gaze at each other, "A union could be nice, though. Is that what you want, my love."

Saiera nodded approvingly. "Very well wait here a moment." Sakuris instructed Saiera as he got up out of the bed and went over to his bag that sat on the other side of the room. Rummaging through it, he soon found what he was looking for: A double edged dagger, housed within a gold scabbard, commenting "This dagger is used by my people to perform unions." As he holds it up for her to see.

Saiera walked over and gazed upon it. "It's beautiful." She remarked watching Sakuris draw the dagger and letting it gleam in the moonlight that shone into the room. He placed it about his wrist and looking at her lovingly as he made an incision just deep enough to draw blood and spoke the words he heard so many times, "Do you accept this offering as it my bond to you and yours to me?"

Handing the dagger to Saiera, he told her the words to speak. Nodding approvingly, Saiera gently made the same incision on her wrist. "I accept your offering, and let it mingle with an offering of my own." She responded placing her wrist to Sakuris's letting her blood mingle with his. Gently leaning forward, she kissed her new husband and smiled, "Thank you, beloved."

The young couple took their wrists from each other and bandaged the incisions they had made. Sakuris had always wondered if maybe the union ceremony was a bit useless, but he loved Saiera just the same. Of course, now that her blood was coursing through his veins he may never be parted with her. Even in death she would be with him.

After they had performed the sacred ceremony, Sakuris walked over to the window once more and gazed onto the city. "Think about it Saiera, one day this entire land will belong to Iyata, but I want a son, someone to carry on for me. Every time we tried something went wrong." He said to her refusing to understand her inability to conceive for him a second child.

Saiera merely went over and put her arm around his shoulder. "I know Sakuris, but maybe, Elayis does not yet want me to bare a son for you. Still I can't seem to comprehend my inability to conceive again." She said looking into the night as well.

"Hmm, someday Saiera, I know it will happen. Victory comes through patience, not strength." Sakuris said to his wife as he stared through the night. His gaze seemed to pierce it like an arrow flying through the wind, "Come my love, we should return to bed." Agreeing with her husband, Saiera followed Sakuris over to the bed as the two climbed back in, and fell asleep for the night.

Chapter 9

To the west, in Isura, Norakatsu was showing much displeasure in Kenzji's inept ability to kill Sakuris and retrieve the sacred blade. "Two of my elites have fallen, and you have yet to bring me the sacred blade." He remarked harshly to Kenzji.

Kenzji looks at him, apologetically, from a kneeling position, replying, "My apologies, Lord Norakatsu, I've no excuse."

"Perhaps, I've not given you the proper motivation." Norakatsu remarked harshly as Tesarah was brought in against her will by another Wyvern Clansman. Like Kayah, she, too, had blossomed into a beautiful young woman.

"Tesarah!" Kenzji exclaimed as two more of Norakatsu's guards held him down. "Get the hell off me." He demanded watching Norakatsu walk over to Tesarah and brush a hand to her cheek.

"She's grown quite beautifully." Norakatsu commented as Tesarah pulled away from him.

"Leave her alone, you bastard!" Kenzji demanded.

"Nii-sama?" Tesarah said with fear in her voice as she felt Norakatsu's hand move down her body.

"I'm warning you!" Kenzji shouted.

Norakatsu stopped and took his hand from Tesarah as he looked over to Kenzji. "Bring me my blades." He ordered as Tesarah was removed from the room and Kenzji was allowed to stand to leave.

As he did, he merely shot Norakatsu a cold stare as the two men locked eyes at each other. Releasing his eye contact, Kenzji exited the room to carry out his master's orders.

The next morning, in Shikanaca, Sakuris awoke to the sun in his eyes as he slowly opened them and looked around. Iyata had already woken before him and was playing next to the window. "Good morning, Daddy." She said sweetly.

Smiling as he watched his daughter play, Sakuris went over and gently kissed her on the top of her head. "Good morning, little one." He responded, "Now play quietly so you don't wake your mother."

Wanting to check on his bandaged incision from the previous night's union, Sakuris left his daughter to play and went into a part of the room that was a little more private. He undid the bandage and noticed the wound had stopped bleeding. Using water from a nearby basin, he cleaned the wound thoroughly and used an herb based powder to act as an antiseptic before applying a clean bandage to it.

Returning to the main portion of the room, Sakuris could still see his daughter playing near the window from before. Smiling as he watched her, he merely went over and gazed out the window being careful not to disturb his daughter, but soon felt her tugging at his pant leg nonetheless. He looked down to see her staring up at him with puppy-dog eyes as if to say: Pick me up.

With a chuckle, he reached down and took Iyata into his arms as he stood continuing to look out the window. "All this will be mine someday, won't it?" Iyata asked curiously as she stared out the window at the city.

"Yes, that's right." Sakuris responded with pride.

"Daddy, when will the war be over?" Iyata asked with childish curiosity.

"Well, it's tough to say little one." Sakuris responded quite honestly.

"Will you and mommy fight in it?" Iyata once again asked.

"She and I already have, many times before you were born, and if we have to in the future we will." Sakuris responded as his daughter began to give him a saddened look. He chuckled, "Don't you worry little one. Mommy and Daddy can take care of themselves, and they have Auntie Kayah to help them as well. You just focus on growing up."

While they conversed, Saiera awoke to see the two of them as they looked out the window. *"Oh he is such a wonderful father. Now that we are united I know that we will never part."* She thought to herself. She had been unaware of the vision Sakuris's father gave to him so many years ago. It was this vision Sakuris pondered about night, after night, after night.

Looking over to see Saiera had awoken, Sakuris carried Iyata over to her. "Saiera, will you take her to play for a little while. I need to meditate." He asked politely as he handed Iyata to her and kissed her lightly.

"Eww, kissing." Iyata said giggling.

Sakuris looked at his daughter and ran his fingers through her hair. "Hey, I can kiss her if I want." He said to her as she playfully pulled her head away. Saiera looked at the two of them and laughed as she left, carrying Iyata with her.

"Mommy, why did daddy stay behind, does he not want to come to play too?" Iyata asked curiously as Saiera carried her outside.

"Daddy needs to meditate for a while." She responded.

"What's medidate, you know that M-word that you said." Iyata asked, not quite able to pronounce the word.

"Me-di-tate means think." Saiera said to her daughter breaking the word into syllables for her, "Daddy needs to think for a while."

In his room, Sakuris positioned himself into a ginta stance and closed his eyes opening his Seltitian mind to connect with his father. *"Father, every night I ponder the fate you've shown me. Am I able to change it?"* He said opening a telepathic link to his father.

His father's voice echoed in his mind, *"I'm afraid not my son. I am sorry, but this is the fate that has been foretold for you."*

"No, I won't accept it, I finally have the family I have yearned for, so many times. A beautiful wife, a loving daughter. I will not abandon them." Sakuris said rather crossly.

"Watch your words young man, I am still your father." Lord Kaemouri replied.

"Apologies, father, but if I can't change my fate what can I do to accept it." Sakuris said, speaking to his father through his mind.

"Son, maybe you should meet me on the Seltitian planes." His father responded.

The chance to his see his father again perked Sakuris up a little as he brought himself to an even deeper state of meditation and soon found himself on the Seltitian planes with his father standing before him.

The Lord Kaemouri was a strong man with fair colored skin, dark hair, and the same amber colored eyes that Sakuris possessed. He was shrouded in white robes that dangled to his feet. His ghostly figure merely seemed to lightly float where he stood. He looked upon Sakuris with pride. "Sakuris, my boy, look how you've grown. You maintained your strong build. Your mother's hair flows down to your shoulders. You have retained my eyes I see." He said to him.

Sakuris merely went over to his father and hugged him. "Father, how I've missed you." He said burying his face into his father's robes. Lord Kaemouri merely put his arms around his son, "I wish your mother could see you. But these planes frighten the women. I wonder how strong you've become, choose an arena." He said as Sakuris stepped back from him.

"Very well, the top of the black tower that lies in the center of the forest." He responded. The blackness suddenly changed to the destination Sakuris spoke of, "Hmm, I remember the first time I came here. You had been waiting for me just as I had been waiting for Akisarah." Sakuris said to his father.

"You've brought Akisarah here." His father said to him in much surprise.

"Well, yes, I have no son. Someone has to carry on in my place. So I picked Akisarah. Kayah loves him and he loves her." He replied.

"Kayah, if only I can see my sweet daughter once more." Kalas said sadly.

"Kayah lost her sweetness when you and mom died. In its place remained only nightmares of that fateful day. I grew up training her to defend herself. I did not want her to become a victim. But there is a way for you to see her." Sakuris said to his father thinking of Kayah.

The scenery suddenly changed to Kayah's room where she was happily going about her morning. Lord Kaemouri smiled with pride as he watched his daughter. "She's as beautiful as her mother." He commented cheerfully.

"Yes, I'm quite proud of her." Sakuris responded with a laugh.

"My son, you have done quite well for yourself." The elder Kaemouri remarks placing his hand on Sakuris's shoulder, "I'm proud of you. You're coming into your own as a man."

"Father, I'm concerned. It seems my old friend is still alive, and he's in league with the enemy." Sakuris remarked commenting about Kenzji, "He's already come after Kayah and my beloved, Saiera. Father, I'm not sure I have the strength to face him."

"And there are so few Shikanacans left in the world, now. That is quite a dilemma, my son, but . . ." said Lord Kaemouri placing his other hand on Sakuris's other shoulder, "I have faith in you my son. I trust you will know what to do when the time comes."

"I sense my family is returning to the room, I should go, but before I leave you father, have a look at your granddaughter." Sakuris remarked as he thought about Saiera and Iyata changing the scenery to where they were playing.

Gazing upon Sakuris's new family, the elder lord smiled proudly. "A beautiful wife you have chosen, my son." He remarks noticing Saiera's long knife, "And a sacred blade holder, no doubt."

"Yes and the third is in the hands of a Kaylahn named Ryuomi Taylah." Sakuris responded.

"And yours?" His father remarked. Sakuris merely backed away holding his head down in shame, "Sakuris? Where is your sacred blade?"

"Father, it still rests within my possession, but I don't deserve it anymore. I was willing to trade it for Saiera's life. I'm sorry." Sakuris responded regretfully.

The Lord Kaemouri merely stepped toward his son and held his head up to look him in the eye. "Growing up isn't always easy my son; especially when it comes to the matters of the heart. The sacred blades are safe for the moment, that's all that matters. Now, I've kept you long enough. We'll discuss matters further at a later time." He then then hugs his son and steps back, "Now go, be with your family, prosperous life."

"Restful death, father." Sakuris responded as he awoke from his meditation. Leaving his room and stepping out to the living area, Sakuris could see Saiera and Iyata patiently waiting for him.

"Daddy!" Iyata cheered as she saw Sakuris coming out and ran over to meet him, throwing her arms around his leg.

A knock soon came from the door as Kayah announced her presence. Hearing her aunt, Iyata's eye widened with excitement as she released Sakuris's leg from her grasp so that he might proceed over to answer it. "Kayah, good morning." Sakuris remarked rather plainly.

"Good morning, Nii-sama." Kayah responded as Sakuris invited her in. Gracefully, she entered the room as Saiera bid her a good morning.

"Auntie Kayah!" Iyata cheered as she rushed over and hugged her aunt.

Looking at his sister, Sakuris could tell she was absolutely glowing. "You seem rather radiant this morning, Kayah." He remarked plainly.

"Thank you, brother. I feel especially cheerful this morning as well." Kayah responded as she hugged her niece and sent her off to play in another room.

"Oh . . . and why might that be?" Saiera asked curiously.

Kayah stammered for a moment, but regained her composure as she readied herself to tell Sakuris the news of her and Akisarah. "Nii-sama, about Akisarah and I . . . the two of us . . . well . . . we, oh hell you'd have found eventually, Akisarah and I made love last night." She said to him.

This answer did not please Sakuris at all. "You did what?" He asked her rather sternly. Kayah could see the anger in his eyes, but repeated her previous statement.

"Please don't be angry." She pleaded, "I was the one who started it." She was unsure how her brother was going to react, but remained open with him nonetheless.

Sakuris merely shook his head, "I am beyond angry. You are only seventeen." Suddenly remembering the second law, he calmed down, "But the law states that when a woman can first begin to conceive, she needs to find a husband. I'm sorry for yelling like that." He said to her.

Akisarah soon came into the room and saw the three of them. Sakuris looked at him from a distance, "Hello Akisarah, come here." He said with an evil smile.

Akisarah stopped in his tracks, "Uh, no, I think I'll stay here where it's safe." He said not moving.

Sakuris got up and approached him with arms stretched out and repeated himself. Akisarah slowly backed away and ran out the room. Sakuris followed after him as he called, "Come back Akisarah, I just want to hug my future brother-in-law." He then stepped back into the room and sat down on a nearby chair, "I love that gag." He said as he laughed.

Akisarah hesitantly came back into the room. "Is it safe to come in?" He asked standing at the door.

Kayah nodded. "Yes, it's safe. He doesn't want to kill you." She said to him.

Sakuris looked to him. "Well, not yet, anyways." He remarked sternly.

Akisarah looked at him. "I'm glad to hear that. Sakuris, will you come with me for a bit?" He said still standing up.

Rising from his seat, Sakuris followed Akisarah outside the room. They walked in Silence for a few minutes before Akisarah finally spoke. "I humbly ask for your blessing. I wish to ask Kayah for a union."

Sakuris looked at him. "I see, you know what you did and you wish to take responsibility." He replied plainly.

"Sakuris, I love your sister more than anything, and yes I do wish to take responsibility for my actions last night. But more importantly, I just want to be with Kayah. Please, grant me your blessing to do so." Akisarah said humbly bowing before Sakuris.

Sakuris laughed. "You wish for my sister and you to be united then ask her. Take her riding later and ask her then." He said to him.

Akisarah stood up, "Does that mean I have your blessing?" He asked him.

Sakuris touched a hand to his shoulder, "Do you remember the lesson I taught you on the Seltitian Planes. I wanted you to be stronger, because I felt in my heart you were the one for Kayah. I knew it the first time I saw you." He responded.

Akisarah looked at him. "Thank you for understanding." He said to him.

Sakuris only smiled. "Now go." He said urging Akisarah to take Kayah out for a ride.

Hurrying back as Sakuris followed, he first looked at Sakuris and then at Kayah. "Kayah, I'm taking my horse out for a ride, and wish for you to accompany me." He said to her. Kayah merely looked at him and nodded as she went over to him. Sakuris and Saiera watched as they left the room.

Sakuris then turned to his wife. "When was the last time we went for a ride?" He asked kissing her lightly. She merely looked at him.

"Too long ago, before Iyata was born." She replied and then called her daughter into the room.

Iyata came in a few minutes later. "Yes, mommy." She said unsure if she was in trouble or not.

"Iyata, sweetie, your father and I are going riding for awhile, would you come with me to your grandma and grandpa's." Saiera said to her.

The idea of visiting her grandparents caused Iyata's eyes to light up with excitement, and she happily agreed. With a soft smile and a sweet chuckle, Saiera took her daughter to her room to help her pack a few things. Sakuris, meanwhile, used the opportunity to prepare a couple of horses from the Shikanacan stables for him and Saiera.

Once everyone was ready for their respective afternoon activities, the small family first ventured through Shikanaca until they reached the home of Sinileass and his wife, Kyusa. Still brimming with excitement, Iyata could barely contain herself as she hopped up and down at Saiera's side. "Now, now, little one, you must calm your excitement." Saiera remarked sweetly to her daughter as she knocked on Sinileass's door.

"Yes, mommy." Iyata replied as she settled herself and stood patiently.

Sinileass soon answered the door with a yawn as he stretched. "Saiera, good morning." He remarked, dressed in plain clothing.

Saiera smiled as she put her daughter behind her. "I hope I didn't wake you. Sakuris and I wanted to go riding for a bit, and I was wondering if you could you watch this one for me." She said to him as Iyata peeked from behind Saiera's legs.

Sinileass nodded, "Sure just give me a few minutes to straighten up a bit." He replied and closed the door. A few minutes later he came back and opened it. Iyata approached him as he picked her up. "Besides, it's always nice to have my favorite granddaughter around." He said to her as he used his index finger to tap the end of Iyata's nose.

Iyata laughed as he did. "I'm your only granddaughter." She responded. Saiera then kissed her daughter good bye and left. Watching her step away, Sinileass takes Iyata inside his home and closes the door behind him.

Meanwhile, Kayah was enjoying her ride with Akisarah as they rode through the forest. A cooling breeze blew through the land, rustling Kayah's long, brown hair as they rode. Akisarah put his arm around her waist and rested his head on her shoulder. Her sweet smelling perfume traveled up to him as he smelled the sweet essence of berries rising from her body. "Kayah, how would you feel about a union?" He said to her as they rode.

Kayah's heart skipped a beat at his question as she looked at him with excitement and surprise in her eyes. "What!" She exclaimed, "You mean right now?" She was trying to maintain her composure as best she could.

With a calm and soft gaze, Akisarah looked at her and shook his head, "No, but maybe sometime in the future. You said you loved me right." He responded, giving her an honest answer. He only hoped the answer she would give was the one he wanted to hear.

"Akisarah, I do love you, but it seems sudden for a union, doesn't it?" Kayah responded as she reached down to take hold of the hand Akisarah had on the horses reins. In her heart, she loved Akisarah more than anything, but was she ready for a union?

"What's so sudden about it? We've known each other six years now. Surely there isn't that much more for us to know about each other." He said to her bringing the horse to a stop.

Kayah could only blush as Akisarah tightened his grip about her waist and held her closer. "Well, what can I say? Yes, I'll unite with you." She responded very happily and smiling. With loving stares, the two pressed their lips to each other's and shared a passionate kiss on horseback as their hearts seemed to practically burst with joy.

Sakuris, meanwhile, was riding through the forest with Saiera. The warmth of the sun and the coolness of the air made the forest an ideal setting as they rode through. Around them, the ground was covered with sweet smelling wild flowers and the scent of pine filled the air as their horse came up to a river and stopped to drink. Sakuris dismounted and took a look around as he helped Saiera climb off their horse.

She stood next to him as he looked around. "Saiera, does this spot seem familiar to you?" He asked, looking around the forest.

Saiera took a look around at the forest as well and smiled as it appeared vaguely familiar to her. "Sakuris, this is where we met all those years ago. Look there's the stone the monk sat on." She said pointing to a large, flat rock.

With a loving gaze in his eyes, Sakuris looked at his beloved. "It was smart of you to stop my blade rather than dodge it that day. You may not have been standing with me today." He said as he put his arm around her waist and holding her close as she stood next to him. He felt her shift in his arms so she may face him.

She looked up at him letting her eyes meet with his. "Hmm, so many years ago. I never would have imagined our paths bringing us here again. Don't we still have a match to finish?" She said lightly pressing her lips to his and letting out a soft moan. A few seconds went by as they shared the moment.

Breaking the kiss, Saiera suddenly took a few steps back and drew her long knife. "Come, son of Kameouri, show me how strong you've become." She beckoned with a grin.

"*She's serious.*" Sakuris thought to himself and then smirked, "*Still, we did agree to this. Is this what they mean by 'coming full circle?'*" Reaching for his blades, resting about his waist, Sakuris draws them both. He decides to leave them separate instead of joining them. The two had come full circle, indeed, and now it was time to decide the bout they had started so many years ago. Who would be the victor?

Saiera struck first as she raced toward Sakuris and lashed out with her blade, but just like before Sakuris vanished from sight as he reappeared on the same tree branch from before. Studying his wife's stance as she looked at him from the ground, Sakuris could find no openings as he suddenly found himself crashing toward the ground.

Saiera had called up her knife's power and used it to send a vertical blade of wind into the tree branch as it sliced cleanly through it.

Taking advantage, Saiera seized upon the opportunity and rushed over to Sakuris as she once again lashed out at him with her blade, but stopped just short as the edge of her weapon met with his throat. Wanting to toy with him, Saiera merely kissed him and then leapt away. It was clear this match was merely foreplay for her. Boastfully laughing, she motions for him to come at her.

"*She toys with me.*" Sakuris thinks to himself as he studies Saiera once again attempting to find an opening. He barely had time to perform his next move when he sees the power of Saiera's blade coming at him. Using his own sword, he projects a protective barrier in front of himself to absorb the impact. "*She's stronger than I expected. Is this the power of the Wind Clan?*" He thinks to himself dropping the barrier and rushing at her, charging one of his swords with the power of fire as he readies to make his first attack. Just as he brings his blade down upon Saiera, she's leaps out of the way and into the nearby trees. "*Not just strong, but fast,*" He thinks to himself with a grin, "*But she underestimates the power of Seltah.*"

Opening his mind to his mental prowess of Seltah, Sakuris is able to see the entire area in his mind's eye including where Saiera was hiding. Charging his other sword with power of earth, he plunges his blade into the ground as it begins to tremble around him. Unable to maintain her balance, Saiera is sent falling to the ground from the tree she had been hiding in. Capitalizing on the moment, Sakuris leaps upon her as he mounts his beloved. He then raises his blade and plunges it down stopping just short of her heart, and toying with her as she did, kisses her instead.

Their bout soon turned into a game with each kiss representing a kill shot, and they continued this way until their energy had been spent and the game came to a close with Sakuris scoring the final kiss, and his prize: His beloved Saiera as she allowed him to take her into his arms.

"*You have become strong indeed, husband.*" Saiera whispered in his ear as he held her.

"You Sikonian women certainly know how to show a man a good time." Sakuris teased as the two simply lie upon the ground. The two then released from their embrace and turned to gaze up at the sky. There was no telling how much time had passed as they remained there, watching the clouds drift overhead.

"You know we should probably get back to Iyata." Saiera reminded her beloved as she turned to gaze upon him.

"Who?" He asked jokingly not wanting to leave. Saiera merely laughed as she gave her husband a playful slap on the arm. He laughed as well as he sat up in a more comfortable position. "Yeah, you're probably right, but how are we going explain all the bruises." He joked. It's true that while Sakuris may have made his comment in mere jest, the two looked like a walking domestic dispute.

"Body-hardening drills?" Saiera teased back as she and Sakuris laughed hardily. Not wanting to lose the remaining light of the day, Sakuris stood up and helped his wife to her feet.

"Come on, my love, fun's over, parenthood calls." He remarked as Saiera stood to her feet. Aside from being covered in bruises, the two were in need of a bath for they were now covered with sweat and grime.

Realizing how filthy they had become, the young couple decided to take a few minutes to wash as much of the grime off as they could before leaving. A proper bath would have to wait till they got home. Mounting their horse, the two of them seated themselves and prepared for the trip back, once both were properly seated and ready, Sakuris nudges their horse as they begin the journey back to Shikanaca.

Chapter 10

Having returned from their ride in the forest, Kayah and Akisarah found themselves at the room of Kayah's foster parents to tell them the news of their bethrothal. Knocking on the door, the two waited patiently until Kyusa answered it. She looked at Kayah as she held Iyata in her arms.

"Aunt Kayah." Iyata squealed with delight. Stepping aside, Kyusa allowed the two of them enter so Kayah may tell her and Sinileass the good news. "Aunt Kayah's getting united, oh wow!" Iyata once again cheered in delight.

Kyusa could only hug her foster daughter, "That's wonderful Kayah. Your brother will be thrilled when he finds out." She said holding her tightly.

Kayah looked around the room. "Where is Sakuris, anyway? Akisarah and I haven't seen him since this morning." She asked Kyusa as she released her from her embrace.

"He went riding with Saiera a few hours ago. We're taking care of Iyata until they return." Sinileass responded.

"Oh," Kayah remarked with disappointment, "I was hoping to share the good news with them."

"Why don't you two come on in to wait for them, and you can tell them, then." Sinileass remarked, inviting the newly betrothed couple to have a seat. Thanking Sinileass, Kayah and Akisarah proceeded to seat themselves to await the return of Sakuris and Saiera.

Far to the west, in Isura, Kenzji knelt before Norakatsu once more. "Kenzji, you have yet to bring me the sacred blade." Norakatsu remarked with a harsh tone.

"The third of your elites has already been dispatched, Lord Norakatsu." Kenzji responded in order to reassure his master.

"Perhaps this one has no desire to bring you the sacred blade." A female voice remarked from the shadows. It was Norakatsu's mystery woman from before. It was clear she was questioning Kenzji's loyalty.

"And what of the sacred blade you promised us, from Taldriss. You failed to uphold your end. A failure that cost me the lives of many of my fire clansman, and we're no closer to finding the blade than we were before." Kenzji retorted.

The mystery woman merely hissed at him like a cat hissing at a mouse. The next thing Kenzji felt was a bolt of demonic energy whizzing past his ear as it struck a nearby urn, shattering it to pieces. He had clearly struck a nerve with this woman as he gave a sly smile and chuckled menacingly, not bothering to move an inch from his current position.

"Enough!" Norakatsu shouted, "We'll just have to find another way of obtaining the fourth weapon. For now, son of Ketsuro, I want you focused on obtaining the blade held by your old friend. How you proceed in the matter is entirely up to you, but do not fail me again."

"As you wish, Lord Norakatsu." Kenzji remarked as he stood up, bowed, and exited the room.

Once he had left, Norakatsu's mystery woman looked at him. "My love, why do you continue to waste time with that one?" She asked curiously.

Norakatsu merely looked back at her. "That's none of your concern." He responded in a mildly harsh manner.

Walking through the halls of Isura, Kenzji merely thought for a moment as to what his next move against Sakuris should be. He had already dispatched the third of Norakatsu's elites, Doaratoes, to deal with him, but figured he should have a contingency plan as a precaution. He toyed with the idea of dealing with his old friend himself; after all, he still had a dispute to settle.

"Nii-sama." Tesarah stated as she met her brother in the hall way.

"Kobanwa, sister." Kenzji responded wishing his sister a good evening.

Seeing the puzzled look on her brother's face, Tesarah merely thought to ask him about it. "Brother, something troubles you?" She asked plainly.

She received no more than a chuckle in reply from Kenzji as he ran his fingers through his sister's long hair. "Nothing you need concern yourself with, dear sister." He finally replied as the two of them proceeded to walk the halls together.

"Lord Norakatsu still demands the blade. Brother, with your power why do you continue to serve him?" Tesarah finally remarks braving the question.

"That talk has no place amongst these halls, sister; especially as long you bear Lord Norakatsu's symbol." Kenzji responded rather crossly at his sister.

Looking at the Wyvern Clan crest she bore on her clothing, Tesarah realized her brother was correct. Norakatsu had made her one of his chosen elite. With that honor came a strict sense of loyalty and obedience to the clan. "Apologies, brother, I did not mean to insinuate." She responded as the two of them continued to walk down the hallway.

"You let me worry about Lord Norakatsu. Besides, it his mystery woman that concerns me." Kenzji remarked plainly, "The woman makes my skin crawl."

"You don't trust her." Tesarah asked curiously.

"No, and I don't believe our master should either; especially after her failure to obtain the fourth weapon for us." Kenzji responded. The two of them soon arrived at their room together as they opened the door and walked in.

Taking his seat in his usual chair, Kenzji allowed his thoughts to wander. Smiling at him as she went over to a nearby shelf of liquor, Tesarah pours drinks for each of them in wooden cups; her fingers were long and slender as they grasped the fire hardened clay bottles and brought them down to waist level so she might pour from them. "Here, brother, this will ease your worries." She remarked handing Kenzji one of the wooden cups.

Smiling as he accepts the drink being offered him, he took it within his grasp, replying "You're too good to me, sister." And taking a sip of the bitter alcohol. Despite its taste the liquor went down smooth as Kenzji took a swallow of it.

As he drank, Tesarah watched her brother with a smile. "I remember when you used to tell me stories from that chair." She remarked as she sat on the bed next to where Kenzji was seated. "Brother, do you ever miss home?" She asked out of nowhere.

Tesarah's question had caught Kenzji off guard indeed as his eyes widened and he gasped with surprise. "I guess I never thought of it." He responded, "Times were simpler back then." He then stood up and placed his hands on Tesarah's shoulders. "Isura is our home, now, though."

Outside the sun had already set upon the land as day gave way to night. Sakuris and Saiera had arrived back in Shikanaca as the sun had set and Kayah was preparing to give them the good news.

Akisarah stood close by as he held Kayah's hand in his. Taking a deep breath Kayah delivered the news of her betrothal, to Akisarah, to her brother and Saiera. Joy filled Saiera's heart as she congratulated the young couple. Sakuris was quite pleased, as well, though there was never a doubt in his mind that the two were meant for each other.

With warmth in his heart and a smile on his face, he took his sister into his arms and held her close. With Kayah in his embrace, Sakuris looked to Akisarah and gave him an approving nod as he welcomed his new future brother-in-law into his embrace, as well. The four of them had been standing in the room of Sinileass and Kyusa as Kayah delivered the news. Though not their biological parents, the couple still felt a sense of pride for the siblings.

The next night a feast was held in Shikanaca to honor the young couple on their new lives together. It was a feast of merriment as all were welcomed to the table. "Brother, this feast was certainly a splendid idea." Kayah remarked as she partook of the banquet before her. Sakuris merely agreed with her as he also partook of the feast. Kayah wasn't wrong in her statement. In a war such as the one they were fighting, it was a nice boost to morale for Sakuris and his people.

In attempt to make the feast a safe and enjoyable one, Yu-Ka-Mi focused her efforts on patrolling the grounds with the Dragon Clansmen who had been placed under her command. "Look lively everyone, enjoy the celebration, but stay alert." She called as she rode through the area checking on those who had been stationed, at various posts, throughout the fortress-town.

When she was satisfied all was well, she made sure to give her report to Sakuris. "Lord Kaemouri, initial patrol complete, all guards in place." She remarked dismounting from her horse and coming into the feasting area, bowing before Sakuris.

"Very good, Yu-Ka-Mi, thank you." Sakuris responded with an approving nod. Nodding in return, Yu-Ka-Mi rose to her feet and exited the feasting area. Remounting her horse, she continued her patrol. Despite the celebration going on around her, she couldn't help but feel a looming dread as she patrolled the fortress grounds.

She was right to be concerned, for outside the fortress lurked an approaching threat in the woods. Doaratoes, along with a small contingent of Wyvern Clansmen, came ever closer to the fortress. Using the cover of darkness, they stealthily made their way through the area slaying any of the guards they came across without mercy and then hiding the bodies away as they made their way inside.

With everyone at the feasting grounds and only a small contingent of guards patrolling inside, the intruders made their way through with little resistance, moving from roof top to roof top until coming to the feasting area. Doaratoes was the first to arrive as he surveyed the area. The Wyvern Clansmen with him merely spread themselves out as each one began to arrive.

From horseback, Yu-Ka-Mi thought she spotted movement just as she made her way outside the feasting area and continued to watch just to be sure. Unaware of her presence, Doaratoes drew a short bow from his shoulder and an arrow from a quiver on his hip as he notched it and took to one knee to prepare his shot.

Spotting him as he did and realizing she was still within shouting distance, Yu-Ka-Mi looked back and with all her might shouted, "Lord Kaemouri!"

Hearing her at the last minute Sakuris was able to look just in time to see Doaratoes as he released the arrow from his bow string. The distraction from Yu-Ka-Mi's shout had thrown off his aim; however, and the shot imbedded itself into a post just back and to the left of Sakuris. The guards who were nearby quickly swarmed around him. As they did, he could hear the cries of: Protect our lord, and protect the master rising up around him as his protectors attempted to escort him and his family to safety.

Seeing this, Doaratoes signaled to his men to cut off their escape as a few of them leapt from the shadows and descended upon Sakuris and his defenders. More shouts of protect the master flooded Sakuris's ears as his defenders fought off the attackers. Yu-Ka-Mi knew her soldiers would be able to keep safe the man she had once cared for as a boy. Her target was Doaratoes himself as she watched him descend upon the area. In an attempt to stop him from reaching her friend and master she nudged her horse to a gallop. In her hand she brandished her Nodachi ready to rend Doaratoes's head from his body.

Hearing the pounding of the horse's hooves, Doaratoes had just enough time to duck out of the way of Yu-Ka-Mi's blade as it whizzed past him, just grazing his head as it sliced through a few strands of his hair. Refusing to give up Yu-Ka-Mi turned her horse around for another pass and raced towards him once again.

Brandishing his bow, Doaratoes took aim at Yu-Ka-Mi's horse and released the string sending his arrow deep into the breast of the mighty steed as it fell to the ground taking Yu-Ka-Mi with it as she tumbled about causing her to lose grip of her weapon as it fell from her hand.

She could hear Sakuris shouting for her as he and his family were escorted from the area. "I've no intention of dying today." She remarked to herself as she regained her footing and stood facing Doaratoes. She hadn't quite reached her opponent's dead zone, the area where an archer could no longer use his bow effectively, as Doaratoes notched another arrow to his bow string and took aim.

Not wanting to allow him another shot, Yu-Ka-Mi rushed forward with all the speed she could muster as Doaratoes loosed his bow string sending the arrow towards her. Using Iaijutsu, the art of the samurai quick draw, Yu-Ka-Mi drew her Tachi with blinding speed as it sliced cleanly through the incoming arrow, knocking it away. It only took her mere seconds to close the gap between her and Doaratoes as she brought her blade down upon him.

Brandishing the dagger he carried, Doaratoes parried her blade and the two engaged in close quarters combat. All the while, her men, who were defending Sakuris, continued to fight off those trying to cause their master and his family harm.

"Come, woman!" Doaratoes taunted as he and Yu-Ka-Mi continued their bout. Yu-Ka-Mi would not back down as she engaged Doaratoes in a mix of out fighting and in fighting making sure to take full advantage of her sword's reach over Doaratoes's dagger. Their bout continued for several more minutes until Yu-Ka-Mi managed to land the killing blow as her blade pierced the heart of her opponent.

Out of breath, and with her adrenaline pumping, Yu-Ka-Mi forcibly removed her weapon from Doaratoes body as it fell limp before her, and, with a flick of her wrist, slung his blood from the blade of her sword as she placed it back within the scabbard at her side. "An honorable bout," She remarked as she peered down at Doaratoes's lifeless body, "but a dishonorable opponent."

With their master dead, the few surviving Wyvern Clansmen fled into the shadows, quickly exiting the fortress grounds. The threat having passed, those present managed to assess the damage. In the confusion, most of the feasting tables had been turned over, their contents littering the ground around them.

"Casualties!" Yu-Ka-Mi called wanting a report.

"A few of the outer guards are missing from their posts." One of her soldiers replied from a distance.

"The Kaemouries!" Yu-Ka-Mi called once again. The same soldier acknowledged they were safe sending a wave relief over Yu-Ka-Mi.

It had been a terrible night for the people of Shikanaca, indeed. What was meant to be an evening of celebration had instead turned to one of bloodshed. Still, had it not been for the bravery of Yu-Ka-Mi and her men, all might've been lost.

The rest of the evening had been spent searching for the guards who had went missing. Having found as many as they could, Sakuris allowed them the honor of a proper funeral as large pyres were erected in their honor. Torch in hand, Yu-Ka-Mi watched as oil was poured on each of the pyres. With tears in her eyes, she took a brief moment to mourn the loss of her men before proceeding to light each pyre one by one.

Once she had finished, she took her place next to Sakuris as she watched the pyres burn before her, their flames reflecting in her eyes. Placing a hand to her shoulder, Sakuris merely gave her an approving nod as she looked back at him. *"Lord Kaemouri."* She whispered as Sakuris turned his gaze back to the fires.

The fires burned throughout the night as loved ones grieved for those they lost, but Yu-Ka-Mi, she felt their loss more than anyone as she sat crying in her room, and found herself repeating: I'm sorry, I'm sorry, as though the spirits of the fallen could hear her in the next life.

A knock soon came from her door as Sakuris announced himself and hesitantly entered. "Lord Kaemouri." Yu-Ka-Mi sobbed as she went over and threw herself in his arms.

Holding the woman who once cared for him as a child, Sakuris allowed his arms to close around her as she looked up at him. With a warm gaze he smiled and wiped her tears away. "Hush now, hush now," He said with a gentle tone of voice, "dry those tears. They're not benefitting a warrior of your caliber. You and your men fought bravely tonight, do not dishonor the sacrifice of the fallen with tears. Come now," He continued as he led her over to her bed and helped her lie down, "you've had a hard night, and deserve a good night's rest."

Stripped of her armor, Yu-Ka-Mi wore plain clothing as Sakuris brought the covers over her and tucked her in. "This is a switch." She joked lightly as she composed herself.

With a small laugh and a smile, Sakuris nodded. "I remember those nights. You cared for me and Kayah as though we were your own. We owe you a great debt." He responded as he lightly kissed her forehead, "Now get some sleep. You'll feel better in the morning."

Nearby a candle burned brightly as it lit a small portion of the room. Waiting for Sakuris to leave her, Yu-Ka-Mi blew it out as darkness filled the room. With a soft pillow to rest her head upon, she closed her eyes and slowly fell asleep.

Gently closing the door behind him as he exited her room, Sakuris paused for a moment to reflect before proceeding through the fortress grounds. Around him, his people were busy helping to clean up the mess that had been left by Doaratoes and his men. Seeing his people working together as they were brought gladness to his heart. Ahead of him, Sakuris could see the face of his beloved awaiting him.

"How is Yu-Ka-Mi?" She asked once he was close enough.

"Sleeping, how's Iyata?" Sakuris asked concerned for the well-being of his daughter.

"Shaken up, but unharmed. I've got Sinileass watching over her." Saiera responds as the two of them began walking together, "How are you, husband?"

Sakuris hadn't been paying much attention as he watched the goings-on taking place around him. "Husband?" Saiera said a little louder trying to catch his attention.

Stammering a moment, Sakuris looks to his beloved, responding, "Sorry, wife, my attention appears to be divided tonight." apologetically as they walked side by side.

Saiera merely laced her arm through Sakuris's as she rested her head on his shoulder. "I guess I can't really blame you. It was a bold move trying to attack you in your own territory." She remarked plainly.

"Had it not been for Yu-Ka-Mi, they might've succeeded." Sakuris responded, "Come let's get out of this chilly night air." The two of them had arrived at their room and stood outside the door. They had decided to let Iyata stay with Sinileass and Kyusa for the night as a precaution. Entering their room, the couple changed out of their feasting attire and into some plain sleepwear, and prepared to fall asleep for the night

Back at Isura, Kenzji had just received the news of Doaratoes's failure to slay Sakuris and retrieve the sacred blades. His patience had reached its limit as he unleashed all his rage and fury on the room around him as he began smashing everything in his sight.

Terrified by her brother's actions, Tesarah rushed over to him. "Nii-sama, stop, please stop!" She pleaded as Kenzji turned his anger on her striking her to the ground. "Nii-sama?" She remarked quietly as the realization of what he had done dawned on Kenzji. Kneeling beside her he went to gently touch her cheek where he struck her, but, with tears in her eyes, she turned away as her body froze with fear. Feeling the soft touch of his hand against her; however, relaxed her as Kenzji took her into his arms.

"Forgive me, dear sister." He pleaded as he held her close. That was the first time he had ever struck her, not even their father had struck them growing up. On his shoulder, Kenzji could feel the rubbing motion of Tesarah's head as she nodded, "Perhaps it is not you I should be focusing my anger on." He then helped his sister to her feet. "Come, a good night's sleep will make us both feel better." He remarked helping Tesarah to bed. Smiling gently as he tucked her in, Kenzji merely looked upon his sister as she closed her eyes and gently fell asleep.

Feeling remorseful for having struck her, he merely slipped in the bed beside her and held her throughout the night.

Chapter 11

In the morning, as the sun dawned over Shikanaca, a slumbering Akisarah awoke to the sound of Kayah vomiting in a wooden bucket, asking "Kayah, are you ok?" concerned for his beloved.

Continuing to lean over the bucket, Kayah shakes her head as she wipes her face clean, replying. "Ugh, no, I have been puking all morning."

Akisarah went over and felt her head, "You have a fever. I'll get a healer. Go ahead and lay back down. I'll take care of things." He said removing his hand from her head. Nodded as she started walking back to her bed, Kayah screamed, almost falling as she cradled her stomach.

Not wanting to see his beloved hurt, Akisarah quickly catches her in his arms and carries her to the bed, remarking "Wait here, I go try to find you some help." reassuringly as Kayah nodded and did her best to relax in bed.

Taking a few final moments to make sure his betrothed would be alright, Akisarah hurried out of their room and rushed to find a healer for her.

A few moments passed before he returned with the same healer who had examined Saiera. Turning to Akisarah, the healer instructed Akisarah to wait outside and but reassured him Kayah would be safe in his care. Reassured for his beloved's safety, Akisarah nodded and stepped outside. Going over to Kayah's bed, the healer did a visual examination first. "Let's see, the young man your with tells me you're having stomach cramps, nausea, and you have a fever." He said assessing her symptoms.

She nodded acknowledging he was right. "What's wrong with me?" She asked rather concerned.

The healer looked at her. "That's what I'm here to find out." He responded with a hardy chuckle, "Ok up with the tunic I need to examine your stomach."

She opened the lower half of her tunic baring her stomach to the healer. He smiled and laughed, "You know, you're much better than my last patient. I almost thought she was going to kill me. She had been experiencing the same symptoms as you." He said rubbing his hands along her stomach. "Does it hurt when I do this?"

"Yes, YES! It does." She screamed as the healer quickly took his hands away.

"Any other symptoms or odd cravings?" He asked lighting a candle and putting it close to her eye watching the pupil shrink in size as he held it closer and return to normal as he took it away.

Kayah looked at him. "Now that you mention it I wouldn't mind some sushi, and wine to go with it, and some of my berry-nut pie for desert." She replied watching the healer blow his candle out and placing it aside.

He looked at her and nodded, "You'll be fine, considering. . ." He began but hesitated.

"Considering what? Doc, whatever's wrong with me, I can take it." She said to him.

"Considering, you're pregnant." He replied.

Kayah eyes grew wider than her stomach and she grabbed the healer by his tunic collar. "What the hell do you mean I'm pregnant?" She demanded to know.

"Exactly what I said, just please let me live. I'll tell the young man you're with that the examination's free. Just let go of me." He responded fearing for his life.

As Kay released from her grasp the healer ran out the room and turned to Akisarah. "The examination's free. Just, please, make sure your wife doesn't kill me." He said as he passed him.

Watching the healer as he ran down the hallway, Akisarah felt sure he heard him remark, "I need a new job."

Shaking his head, he entered the room and quickly walked over to Kayah, "What did he say?" He asked rather concerned about her.

Kayah took in a heavy sigh as she looked at Akisarah. "You're going to be a father, I'm pregnant." She responded.

Akisarah looked at her stunned. "I'm going to be a what, and you're what?" He asked surprised by Kayah's news.

Kayah repeated herself as Akisarah sat on the bed next her. She merely looked at him as she closed the lower half of her tunic. She sat up and put her arm around him as she rested her head on his shoulder. "That's right, a sweet little girl." She said holding him close.

Akisarah shook his head. "Please, my boy's going to be a fighter." He responded.

Kayah raised her head so her eyes would meet his. "Another you, Elayis would never be so cruel." she teased as she lay back down on the bed.

Akisarah merely laughed as he kissed her lightly on the head. "Go ahead and get some rest, I'll take care of things until you're well." He said to her getting up from the bed. Walking to the door and pausing for a moment, Akisarah looks back at Kayah and smiles as he watches her close her eyes and drift back into the land of slumber. Nodding to himself, he opens the door and exits the room.

It was still early morning as the sun rose over Kaseo Forest. Two fighters were meeting at an undisclosed location outside of Kaylah. "I've already lost three elites to the Kaemouries." One says speaking to the other.

The other looks at him. "I understand, Master Ketsuro." He says bowing before Kenzji.

"Do not fail me, Master Taylah, or the next time I send the red demon to Kaylah I'll make sure none of it remains standing." Kenzji says to him.

With a treacherous grin, Ryuomi nods as he bows before Kenzji. "I've already set in motion a plan to deal with them. Young Master Kamikawi has been looking these past six long years for the one who murdered his parents. I'll give him what he wants and then kill him. Once he's out of the way, Kaemouri's sister will go running to her brother to avenge his death. Facing him with the sacred blade, I'll claim his sword for Isura."

"Do not bore me with the details, just get it done." Kenzji retorts harshly as he disappears into the forest.

"As you wish, Master Ketsuro." Ryuomi remarks as he watches Kenzji disappear into the dawn.

Later that afternoon, Akisarah was spending time with Kayah in their room when a letter was slipped under his doorway. Seeing this as he sat on the bed with Kayah, Akisarah went over and picked it up. Opening the letter, he read it carefully, astonished beyond words as he turned to his betrothed. "What is it?" Kayah asks curiously as she looks at him from the bed.

"It's from Master Ryuomi, apparently he's finally found out who killed my parents. He wants me to come Kaylah right away." Akisarah responds, walking over to a nearby wall-mounted shelf. Atop the shelf is the sword his father had forged all those years ago. Staring intently at it, Akisarah allows himself to become lost in thought as his mind wanders back to that day.

"What will you do?" Kayah asks curiously, as she watches her beloved stare blankly at the sword before him.

Unsure of what actions to take, Akisarah turns his attention from the sword to Kayah as he turns his head to face her. "Six years I spent wondering why my parents were killed," He chuckles briefly, "yet here I stand wondering: Why now? Why after all these years? Part of me wants to believe, Kayah," He turns his attention back to the sword, "but part of me . . ." He trails off shaking his head.

"If you don't go, how will you ever know?" Kayah gently reminds him as he continues to stare at his father's sword.

Part of Akisarah knew his beloved was right. He could also, somewhere inside him, feel that old fire of vengeance sparking again as he clasped his father's sword in his hand and merely held it without so much as bothering to pick it up. "*Father.*" He whispers as he closes his eyes.

At that moment, it felt as if something snapped inside him as he quickly opened his eyes allowing them to burn with a determined fire. "Kayah, I'm going." He tells his beloved as he lifts his father's sword from the shelf and straps it to his back.

"Beloved?" Kayah remarked curiously. She had never seen such a fire in him before as she watched him with ever loving eyes.

Looking at Kayah as she lie in bed, Akisarah went over and merely hugged her and kissed her on the forehead. "I'll try not to be gone too long. I love you." He says to her as he turns to step away.

As he did, Kayah merely grabbed him by the hand causing him to turn back around. The pleading look he saw next sent sorrow through his heart as the two of them look at each other in silence, but knew what was in the other's heart.

The grip of fear Kayah felt upon her heart as she felt Akisarah slip from her grasp was enough to bring tears to her eyes as she watched him grab some supplies for the trip and walk out the door. "Come back to me." She pleaded knowing he could no longer hear her.

Outside, sun gave way to cloud as Akisarah headed to a nearby stable and saddled up the swiftest and mightiest steed he could find for himself, in order to reach Kaylah in the shortest time he could. He had no intent on leaving his beloved Kayah alone for long, now knowing of the new addition to their family.

Leading the horse outside the stable, Akisarah mounted up and took a deep breath to prepare himself for the journey ahead as he closed his eyes and prayed a small prayer in his heart for a safe return.

Now ready for his journey, he nudged his horse and rode off toward Shikanaca's main gate where he found Yu-Ka-Mi standing guard with a few more of her soldiers. Informing her on the situation, he asked that she open the gate and allow him to proceed. Hesitantly, but empathetically, she nodded and ordered the gate to be opened.

Watching the heavy gate of pine as it was hoisted open, Akisarah saw the vast forest of Kaseo expand out before him. Uncertain, but hopeful, of what awaited him, he thanked Yu-Ka-Mi for her understanding and then nudged his horse as he rode away with his steed at full gallop.

With trees overhead, Akisarah pushed his steed as hard as he could down through the shrub lined trails of the forest, causing a trip that would've taken a day or two to take only mere hours to complete.

When he arrived in Kaylah, the last visible light of the sun shrank below the horizon as day turned to night, and having not been in Kaylah since the day he left, Akisarah was awe-struck by the changes that had occurred, including the transfer of power caused by the passing of its aging former master, Veroas, in turn, making Ryuomi the new, official head of state.

Exhausted from travel, and in need of rest, Akisarah sought the shelter of his former childhood home only to find it was newly inhabited. Unsurprised, but disappointed by this fact, Akisarah made his case with the new tenants and was welcomed in. Graciously thanking his new host, he entered the room and allowed himself to be shown to where he might rest during his short stay in the rebuilt city.

Curious to learn more about their new guest, the young couple who now inhabited the home invited Akisarah to join them for evening meal. Not wanting to be rude, or ungrateful, he graciously accepted.

Having lived among Shikanacans for the past few years, Akisarah found it refreshing to be back around his own people as they conversed over a hot meal, and, wanting to be a good houseguest, decided to help with the clean up afterwards. With a hot meal resting snuggly in his belly, and clean up complete, he became increasingly ready for the comfort of a warm bed and a good night's sleep, which is precisely what he would receive thanks to his gracious hosts.

Morning, however, would come rather quickly for Akisarah as he was awoken by the broken rays of the sun coming into the room through the heavy blanket of clouds in the sky. Finding himself unable to fall back to slumber, and not wanting to wake his still sleeping hosts, Akisarah slipped out of the former home of his parents and into the dusty streets of Kaylah for a morning walk. Feeling the cool air through his clothing, he roamed the roadways of his former home as the wooden planks creaked underfoot.

With the vast Kaylahn market spanning out around him and the noise of the city's hustle and bustle in his ears, he was filled with a mix of both longing and excitement. On the one hand, he was glad to be back in his former home, but on the other knew, he would not be able to stay and decided to take the short window of opportunity to visit his parents' gravesites that were nearby.

"Mother, Father, I apologize for my long absence. Much has changed for me. I recently learned I am to be a father." He said with sorrow in voice as he spoke, "I've returned now because I have recently learned from Lord Taylah that he may have learned the identity of the one who sent you both to an early grave. As a boy, I did my best to learn from you, both, the lessons needed to shape me into a man, and now, as a man, I will do my best to pass those lessons onto my child." He then bows and turns away to leave.

As he did, he came face to face with Ryuomi. "I see you've returned, young Akisarah." He then smiles and chuckles as he places a hand to his shoulder, "Not so young anymore, I see."

"I received your letter, Taylah-sama." Akisarah responded.

"That can wait. Walk with me for a bit." Ryuomi beckoned as he motioned for Akisarah to follow. "By now, I'm sure you've heard of my father's passing." Ryuomi commented as Akisarah walked beside him through town.

"Yes, my condolences." Akisarah responded.

"Yes, it was a tragic loss, but it did present some unique opportunities. Opportunities that could lead to some distinct advantages in this war we now find ourselves in." Ryuomi added as the two of them continued to walk together. Around them the hustle and bustle of Kaylah soon gave way to a calm serene, field of grass.

"I thought Kaylah was on the side of neutrality." Akisarah remarked as the grass crunched under his foot.

"We were for a time, but Isura continues to grow its influence," Ryuomi remarks pausing to look at Akisarah seeing the emblem of Shikanaca on his clothing, "as does Shikanaca, I see."

"You said you had information on my parents' murderer." Akisarah remarked quickly changing the subject.

"In due time, young Master Kamikawi, but first I need to know where your loyalties lie. Are you Kaylahn or Shikanacan?" Ryuomi responded.

"My loyalties are where they should be." Akisarah responded rather harshly as he turns and walks past Ryuomi back to the village. He then pauses and looks back. "Now tell me where my parents' murderer is."

He then suddenly felt the tip of Ryuomi's spear at his back. "Right here." Ryuomi remarked harshly, "My orders were to kill you along with your parents, but you went running off to see that Shikanacan whore of yours. Still I'm kind of glad I didn't get to kill you then, now I have the chance to gauge just how strong you really are."

Akisarah merely looked ahead, his heart filling with hatred at the thought of his parents' death, "Your problem was you were so confident in your dexterity with the spear you never carried a back-up weapon." He said side stepping out of the way of the blade and grabbing the spear by the handle as he threw a back kick into Ryuomi's stomach. The blow caused Ryuomi to recoil in pain as he grabbed his stomach relinquishing his hold on the spear.

Now Akisarah was in possession of the sacred blade as he stared Ryuomi down. "I've waited six long years for this moment." He remarked as Ryuomi looked at him, "Now I have the chance to kill the murderer of my parents. Such a shame, Master Taylah, you were an honorable man at one point. What was the price for your honor?"

"Leadership of the Spirit Clan." Ryuomi responded as he charged at Akisarah stopping just short of the spear tip being aimed at him.

"Pitiful." Akisarah remarked simply as the two fighters stared each other down.

Ryuomi chuckled. "You hold the sacred blade now, Akisarah. Its power is overwhelming is it not? You could kill me and claim clan leadership for yourself."

Akisarah wanted so much to end Ryuomi's life at this point, but shook the thought from his mind. He then threw the spear back to Ryuomi. "We'll settle this through Kaylahn law." He responds as he draws his father's sword from his back letting its double edge gleam in the dim sunlight that broke through the clouds.

"Very well, honor combat it is then." Ryuomi responded as the two fighters each dropped into a fighting stance.

The clouds had begun to get thicker as the fighters stared at each other. Lightning flashed off in the distance and the wind rose as the sky began to grow dark and rain poured down on them and saturated the ground. In the background, low rumbles of thunder could be heard after each flash of lightning as the fighters continued to stare each other down. The first move was made by Ryuomi as he thrusted his spear at Akisarah's abdomen region. Akisarah merely parried the spear and side stepped out the way as he countered with an overhead slash.

Parrying the sword with the shaft of his spear, Ryuomi stared hard at Akisarah's weapon of choice. "Your father's sword I see. My dear boy what happened to your principles on valuing human life?" He remarked harshly as he pushed against the blade and using all the might he could took a hard lunge forward, shoving Akisarah back.

Readying his father's sword once more, Akisarah prepared himself for another attack from Ryuomi as he responded, "Those principles died with my parents."

"Good, this fight would've been boring otherwise." Ryuomi remarked harshly as he threw another thrust of his spear to Akisarah's midsection.

Using his father's sword to knock the spear out of the way, Akisarah stepped in for a lunging thrust, hitting Ryuomi in his weapon arm as the blade pierced through his shoulder causing him to cry out in pain.

His shoulder burning, he relinquished the grip on his spear as it fell to the ground. Staring at him was Akisarah with fire in his eyes as he kicked him back violently forcing the blade from Ryuomi's shoulder as he fell to the ground.

Walking past the sacred blade that had dropped on the ground, Akisarah stood over Ryuomi as he lay on the ground cradling his wound. Holding the tip of his father's sword at Ryuomi's heart, Akisarah prepared himself to deliver the death blow to Ryuomi when he heard Sakuris call out, "Akisarah!" from behind him. Kayah had informed him of where Akisarah had gone and he journeyed as fast as he could to Kaylah to stop him.

"Stay out this, Sakuris! This is Kaylahn law!" Akisarah called back not bothering to turn his eye from his target.

"Don't do it Akisarah. You're a Shikanacan now!" Sakuris called back.

"Beloved!" Another voice quickly cried out. It was Kayah, she had ventured with Sakuris to Kaylah, "Please don't, beloved." She pleaded hoping Akisarah wouldn't give in to his need for revenge.

"Torn between two allegiances, what will you do son of Kamikawi?" Ryuomi remarked arrogantly.

His past in front of him and his future behind him, Akisarah remembered about the seed that grew within Kayah that would one day be his child. He shook his head as he took a few steps back and picked up Ryuomi's spear. "You are no longer worthy of this, so I'll be taking it now." He remarked staring at Ryuomi as he continued to back away to Sakuris's side.

"My parents' death has been avenged. It's time to go home." He remarked as he turned away and walked past Sakuris to Kayah, "Thank you, my love." He said to her gently as the two looked at each other with loving eyes.

"Fool, you would abandon your people. Where's your pride as a Kaylahn?" Ryuomi shouted in anger.

Akisarah merely looked back at him. "They are my people now." He responded as he gave a head nod to Kayah and Sakuris, "As for my pride, I will always hold Kaylah dear to me, but life moves on, so to must I."

"The sentiment of a coward!" Ryuomi retorted as he watched the three friends turn and head back toward the village, "Coward! Come back and finish it!"

Akisarah merely ignored him as he left him on the ground to suffer in disgrace, behind him he could hear Ryuomi laughing as though he had been driven mad.

Having completed his task in Kaylah, Akisarah began the journey back to Shikanaca with Sakuris and Kayah. Staring at the sacred blade he had claimed from Ryuomi, Akisarah thought long and hard about what to do.

"You hold a weapon of power, Akisarah. A great responsibility falls upon you, now." Sakuris remarked to him as they sat by a camp fire. Day had given in to night.

"In my haste to avenge my parents, I have left Kaylah without a leader. Veroas is dead and Ryuomi is disgraced in defeat." Akisarah remarked.

Sakuris merely looked at him as he stoked the fire before him as Kayah slept. The conversation between the two men reminded him of a similar time had spent with Sinileass on his way back from Isura. "Life's funny, years ago, Sinileass and I had a conversation much like the one we are having now around a similar campfire." He responded, "You're growing up, Akisarah. These last few years, I watched you grow from a cocky young boy to a mighty warrior. I think Kaylah has a great leader," Sakuris remarked pausing for a minute to glance at Akisarah, "in you my friend."

"My people will see me as a usurper. They will never accept me, and I can never return." Akisarah responded with sorrow in his voice.

"What will you do then? Keep the spear, or return it." Sakuris asked, presenting Akisarah with a troubling question.

"The spear belongs in Kaylahn hands, but the blade must choose its new master for itself." Akisarah remarked.

"Perhaps it already has, draw the weapon from the scabbard and find out for yourself." Sakuris beckoned as he encouraged Akisarah to find out his destiny.

Nervous to find out his worth in the eyes of the blade, Akisarah closed his eyes and, just as Sakuris had instructed, drew forth the weapon from its scabbard to reveal an aura of blue energy glowing from the blade. Upon opening his eyes and seeing the aura, it was as if a great weight had been lifted from him. "The blade has chosen me." He responded as he watched Sakuris draw forth both of his swords to reveal the same blue energy.

"My father once told me that the sacred blades react to the goodness within a person's heart. When you refused to give in to your rage toward Lord Taylah, the blade sensed it and that is why it chose you." Sakuris responded as he held his weapons up for Akisarah to see.

"Kaylahn law is clear at this point. I am the new master of my people." Akisarah remarked as he returned the blade to its scabbard.

"Yes and more importantly, we now have all three weapons in Shikanacan possession. This means they are safe from Norakatsu and any who would seek to use their power for ruin; which begs another question, what is it about Norakatsu that would make him believe he would be capable of wielding mine?" Sakuris responded as the two men sat across from one another.

Ryuomi, meanwhile, in his disgrace, had traveled to Isura and delivered the news to Kenzji. "You let him escape!" Kenzji yelled striking Ryuomi to the floor as the blow struck the side of his face.

Watching the spectacle taking place before her, Tesarah snickered arrogantly. With a cold stare, Ryuomi shot his glance towards her. "I'd keep your laughter to yourself, bitch." He remarked harshly.

Kenzji readied himself for another blow for the insult Ryuomi had just delivered to his sister, but Tesarah stopped him at the last minute. "Brother, look at him. He's disgraced in defeat. What good will striking him do now. He's a man with nothing left to lose. You should kill him and be done with it."

Fearing that he might do as Tesarah suggested, Ryuomi quickly looks back at Kenzji. "They make for Shikanaca, Akisarah carries the blade with him. Give me a squad of your best and I'll ride out to meet them before they arrive." He begged, pleading for his life.

"Brother?" Tesarah asked as Kenzji motioned for her to keep silent. He then looked to Ryuomi in silence as he drew his sword.

"Please, Ketsuro-sama, don't, there's still time." Ryuomi pleaded as Kenzji brought his sword above his head.

Watching her brother, Tesarah smiled wickedly, ready to see him do the deed, as he brought the sword down only to stop just short of slicing into Ryuomi. This puzzled Ryuomi as he felt the blade of Kenzji's sword touching the skin of his face.

"Fail me again, and next time I won't be so forgiving. Now gather those you need and make haste." Kenzji responded as he sheathed his weapon and watched Ryuomi hurry out the room in a panic.

"Why did you not kill him brother?" Tesarah remarked looking to her older brother.

"Because I can use him." He remarked as he looked back at her over his shoulder, "Bring my armor. I make for Shikanaca, at once. There is still one card I haven't played."

Unsure of what her brother had planned, Tesarah did as she was instructed and hurried to find her brother's armor. Within moments she returned and helped Kenzji to put it on as its layers of mail and leather fit snuggly to Kenzji's body. Under the mail of chain was a padded jacket commonly referred to in the west as gambeson.

"My helmet." He remarked commandingly as Tesarah handed him a helm of darkened steel and mail with the same padding. Slipping it on over his head, he turned to face his sister. "Stay here, should I fail in my task, Lord Norakatsu will need someone to act as his hand."

"I understand, brother." Tesarah remarked as she bowed to Kenzji who returned the bow to her and then left.

Under the cover of darkness, he rode out swiftly on his mightiest steed. *"I should've done this long ago."* He thought to himself. Riding with him were a few of his trusted Fire Clansmen. He knew it would take time for Sakuris to reach Shikanaca while traveling at a leisurely pace. Meanwhile, riding at full speed, Kenzji and his men could reach the city within hours.

"That fool, Ryuomi, stands no chance against the combined power of two blades, but his proposal did present a unique opportunity, and it buys me time to reach Shikanaca where Kaemouri's family awaits." Kenzji thought to himself with a cruel laughter.

Still by the light of their campfire, Sakuris and Akisarah continued their discussion. "Once we return to Shikanaca, we'll discuss further how to deal with the current situation we find ourselves in." Sakuris remarked to Akisarah as the two sat across from each other. They had been unaware of the danger coming toward them. Due to the speed at which Ryuomi had been traveling with his men from Isura, they had managed to cover the distance in a shorter time than normal.

Seeing their fire as they approached, Ryuomi slowed his men to a stop as they dismounted and prepared to ambush the three friends. "Quietly now." He remarked in a low tone of voice as he and his men silently approached the campsite.

Hearing the forest grow quiet around them, Sakuris and Akisarah stood up and looked around. Out of nowhere, an arrow flew directly at

Akisarah. Seeing it at the last minute, he narrowly dodged it as it flew into a tree behind him. "Ambush!" He shouted waking the sleeping Kayah from her slumber as he and Sakuris drew forth their weapons in order to defend themselves.

"Kayah, take the spear, and keep it safe." Sakuris remarked as Kayah gave an approving nod and did what her brother instructed as she quickly grabbed the spear and kept it close to her.

Hearing the sounds of Ryuomi's men all around them, the three friends stood back to back with each other. "We're surrounded." Akisarah remarked.

"Steel yourself, my friend." Sakuris responded as the first of the attackers came at them. His target was Kayah who was holding the spear. Pushing her out of the way, Sakuris readied his swords for combat as the attacker's weapon clashed with his, causing the sound of clashing steel to echo throughout forest.

Another attacker soon made an attempt for Kayah as Akisarah came in between the two of them and used his father's sword to fight off their assailant. *"They'll keep coming for Kayah so long as she holds the spear. Bastard, Ryuomi, I know you're out there."* He thought to himself as he scanned the area for Ryuomi. The attackers wouldn't back down as they kept targeting Kayah for the spear.

"We can't hold them back forever." Akisarah remarked as he fought off another attacker.

"Akisarah!" Kayah soon cried out. In the midst of the fighting, Ryuomi had managed to grab Kayah and was now holding her hostage.

"Kayah!" Akisarah called back as he attempted to rush to her aid, but Sakuris quickly stopped him.

Staring hard at Ryuomi, Akisarah could only feel rage burning inside him as observed the dagger being held at Kayah's throat.

"The spear, woman." He demanded.

"No, Kayah!" Akisarah called.

Kayah had no intention of dying today as she secretly drew her diamond dagger from beneath the knee length kimono she was wearing and plunged it into Ryuomi's left thigh. This cause Ryuomi to cry out in pain as he shoved Kayah to the ground. What he saw next was a dagger, thrown by Akisarah, embedding itself into his heart as he gasped the last few breaths he would ever breathe in this life as he fell to the ground dead.

Their master slain, the remaining attackers fled. Rushing over to Kayah, Akisarah quickly took her into his arms. "Kayah, Kayah, are you alright?" He asked concerned for her and placing his hand to her stomach.

"I'm okay, beloved, we both are." She responded quietly.

"Both?" Sakuris asked almost demandingly as he watched Akisarah help Kayah to her feet.

"I had hoped to tell you more properly, brother. Akisarah and I are to be parents." Kayah responded with plain honesty.

"You're pregnant!" Sakuris exclaimed at a loss for words.

"Please don't be angry. We only just found out ourselves." Kayah pleaded finding herself close to tears.

"Master Kaemouri, we need to keep moving." Akisarah beckoned trying to change subject.

"Very well, we can discuss this once we've returned." Sakuris responded as they packed up what remained of the camp and prepared to continue their journey.

When they arrived, it was not the return they had expected. Shikanaca was in cinders and burnt to ash. There were survivors here and there including Kyusa and Sinileass, with them was Saiera with tears of sorrow in her eyes.

Seeing his beloved in such a state, Sakuris couldn't help but rush over to his adoptive parents as they held her in support. "Beloved!" He called as he jumped off his still moving horse and rushed to embrace her.

"Sakuris?" She said through her tears.

"What happened?" He asked almost demandingly.

Saiera looked up at him. "Kenzji came, with men, and his demon, Sakuris I couldn't stop him." She responded weakly as some tears trickled down her cheeks.

"Iyata, where is she?" Sakuris asked as he wiped the tears away from her face.

"He took her," She responded, "Sakuris, he took our little girl!" She couldn't contain her emotions as more tears flowed from her eyes and she buried her face into his shoulder.

Sakuris held his wife close as he gently stroked her hair. "Where did her take her?" He asked calmly trying not to lose his temper despite the rage building up inside of him. Someone had taken his little girl and that someone was going to pay dearly.

"He said to tell you to meet him at Neiheroghi Temple." Saiera responded.

Sakuris looked to Sinileass and Kyusa as he held Saiera in his arms. "I'm going." He then tilted Saiera's head up so her gaze could meet his. "I'll bring our little girl back, Saiera, alive. I promise." He assured her confidently.

"I'm going with you." Saiera responded as she dried her tears and recomposed herself.

"Saiera, no, I need you here to help with the clean-up. Akisarah can assist me." Sakuris responded trying to talk his wife out of going, but she shook her head and protested as hard as she could.

"Sakuris, I'll stay. I need to be with Kayah anyways." Akisarah remarked.

"Very well," Sakuris responded as he looked to his wife, "Saiera, are you sure you want to come?" Looking to her husband, Saiera nodded in acknowledgment.

"You know he's just trying to bait you into handing him the sacred blade." Sinileass remarked reminding Sakuris of Kenzji's true intent.

"I know, but I can't leave my daughter in his hands." as he climbed back onto his horse. Kayah who had been listening the entire time switched places with Saiera.

"Nii-sama?" She said looking at Sakuris from the ground as he looked back at her, "be careful."

"I will." He responded as he nudged his horse and rode off toward Neiheroghi with Saiera following behind him. The sun had started to come up over Shikanaca and the rest of Kaseo Forest as night turned to day and the young couple rode out to bring their daughter home.

At Isura, Kenzji forcibly brought a bound Iyata before Norakatsu. "A bold move, Ketsuro." Norakatsu remarked as he stepped toward Iyata, who was crying in fear at this point. "Now, now, my dear, those tears are unbefitting of the daughter of Kaemouri."

"Who are you? Where are my mommy and daddy?" She demanded to know through her tears.

Kneeling down before her, Kenzji turned her to face him. "If he's smart, on his way to Neiheroghi Temple, where I'm to meet him." He replied with a wicked grin that sent chills down Iyata's spine, "Now be a good girl and wait patiently with Lord Norakatsu."

Iyata merely kicked Kenzji in his shin as hard as she could, but due to the many years of training, Kenzji's body had become hardened and he barely felt the blow as he chuckled. "You have your father's spirit, but don't press your luck." He remarked harshly as he turns to Norakatsu, "I suggest we move her to another location."

"Leave that to me." Norakatsu responded as he took Iyata forcibly by the arm, "Our informant from Taldriss awaits me at the northern fortress with a small contingent of clansmen. Your sister is with her. Bring Kaemouri there."

"As you wish, Lord Norakatsu." Kenzji remarked as he disappeared into the shadows.

In Kaseo Forest, Sakuris and Saiera rode in silence, each one knowing what was in the other's heart as both were concerned for the safety of their daughter. "I want her back, my love. I want her in my arms." Saiera remarked sadly as she stared on ahead of her.

"We'll get her back, Saiera." Sakuris responded reassuringly taking a look around the forest and suddenly saw two arrows fly towards them, "Sidetsute!" He called raising his hands, causing the arrows to stop dead in their tracks and fall to the ground.

The sound of applause could be heard in the distance. It got louder as a masked fighter approached their horses, "Very impressive, warrior." He said looking at Sakuris.

Saiera studied the fighter as her horse stepped back, "Dayis?" She asked recognizing the voice.

The fighter drew his sword and pointed it at her, "How do you know me?" He demanded.

"Lower your weapon to me Dayis Kanz," She said commanding him to lower his blade, "and I'll tell you."

Housing his blade back in its scabbard, the mysterious fighter looks at her as she looked back at him and responded, "Eleven years ago, you told a young woman to run into the forest and not to look back."

Removing his mask, the fighter looked at Saiera through his own eyes, "Saiera, so you did survive. Who is this with you?" He said motioning toward Sakuris.

Sakuris looked at him from his horse. "I am Arch-Dragon Sakuris 'The Wind Sleeper' Kaemouri of Shikanaca and Saiera's husband." He responded with an almost jealous tone.

With a hearty chuckle, Dayis looks at his sister. "Finally Saiera, your femininity has caught up with you. I thought you would never trust men again."

"Stranger, we've no time for games. Either state your business with my wife or stand aside." Sakuris demanded.

"You mean she never told you." Dayis remarked as he looked to Saiera.

Saiera merely looked to her husband and then motioned to Dayis. "Husband, meet my brother." She remarked to him.

"Brother? I thought you said he was dead." Sakuris exclaimed.

"Dead!" Dayis exclaimed in surprise.

"I thought he was." Saiera responded as she hopped down off her horse and walked over to her brother, "Yet here you stand, Dayis, and on a day like this, I'm glad to have found you again. We could use your help."

"We're traveling to Neiheroghi Temple." Sakuris informed him.

"Neiheroghi, why would you want to go to a place like that?" Dayis asked curiously.

"Dayis, a lot has happened since we last saw each other." Saiera remarked as she and her brother stood facing each other, "Perhaps we should discuss things before we continue on."

The two of them then looked to Sakuris who nodded in agreement. Taking a brief moment of respite, Sakuris and Saiera did their best to explain the situation to Dayis.

"A daughter?" Dayis remarked as the three of them sat under the shade of the forest, "So not only did I find my sister on this day, but I find out I'm an uncle as well."

"Dayis, I know this is a lot for you to take in, but it has been eleven years." Saiera reminded her brother.

"At any rate, family is family." Dayis remarked as he turned to Sakuris, "Tell me more about this Kenzji Ketsuro."

"He's a Shikanacan like me, but he was exiled a long time ago with his sister." Sakuris responded as he did his best to explain about his history with Kenzji.

"I think I understand." Dayis remarked looking back and forth between Sakuris and Saiera, "No point wasting time here, then. I'll get my stuff together and we can be on our way."

Dayis soon went into the forest to gather his belongings. Waiting for him to return, Sakuris and Saiera merely sat in silence. "How reliable is your brother?" Sakuris asked finally speaking up.

"He cares for me the way you do Kayah. It was because of him I was able to get away from the destruction of my home. He stayed and fought while I fled." Saiera responded as though Sakuris had touched a nerve.

"Forgive me, wife, I meant nothing negative." Sakuris apologized as he gazed upon his wife.

Dayis soon returned from the forest with his horse and belongings, and informed them he was ready to leave. Climbing onto their horses the three of them began to journey to Neiheroghi.

Meanwhile, deep in the region of Isura, day turned to night and Norakatsu had just arrived at the northern fortress with Iyata who was being transported by wagon. She was bound and gagged. Looking at her from his jet black steed, he sat tall and proud, his long hair flowed down to his waist. He wore all black, including his armor. On his side was a weapon housed in a black leather scabbard. Looking up at him as she sobbed through the gag in her mouth, Iyata could see just how intimidating Norakatsu was as a man.

Watching her as she struggled to get loose, Norakatsu chuckled sinisterly. "Struggle all you like daughter of Kaemouri, but you'll never free yourself. Still, it amuses me to watch you try." He remarked wickedly. Next to him was the driver of the wagon. Norakatsu turns to him. "Take her inside. Put her with the other women." He instructed as the driver nodded and rode on ahead into the fortress.

Watching the driver as he left, Norakatsu grinned evilly as the moonlight gleamed off his armor. "She'll prove to be a most useful slave." He remarked to himself, before riding through the fortress's front gate.

Inside, Iyata was taken to be placed with the rest of Norakatsu's harem. Sitting on a cushion, on the floor, and filled with fear, she found herself alone, surrounded by strangers, as tears filled her eyes. "Poor, little dear." One of the women said approaching her, "Come, now, child, a hot bath to make you feel better." She said extending a hand for Iyata.

Not recognizing the woman, Iyata cowered away, bringing her knees to her chest as she trembled from fright. "Now, now, little one, don't be frightened, look." The woman said motioning to a grand bath in the middle of the room where several other women were bathing, "Come, now, we won't harm you."

Around her, Iyata could hear the murmurs and chatter of the other woman. They were all gazing at her and whispering things like: Poor child and she looks Shikanacan to each other. Food was soon passed around for the women to eat as another woman came around carrying a tray of a delicious assortment of meat, fruits, and vegetables.

The woman who spoken to Iyata motioned for the tray carrier to come over with the food. "Here, little one," The tray carrier remarked, "you must be hungry. Help yourself." She then lowered the tray to Iyata's height.

Her stomach rumbling with hunger, Iyata's eyes widened at the assortment offered her and not being able to resist the smell of the delicious food reached for a few pieces of meat and fruit and happily began eating. "There now, perhaps with food, you'll feel better." The tray carrier remarked before moving on.

In truth, a few morsels of food turned out to be just the thing to ease Iyata's fright as she looked around the room at the other women. A diverse crowd befell her eye sight as the women ranged in age, ethnicity, height, and various other attributes.

As Iyata ate, one of the women had even draped a blanket over her as she tightly clutched it to her. In the back, she could see a mysterious woman veiled by curtains, thin enough to make out the mysterious woman's silhouette but not see her face.

The woman who originally spoken to Iyata quickly stepped in between her and the mysterious woman. "Never look upon her, child." She said in a low tone of voice so only Iyata could hear as she nodded. The woman smiled warmly upon her as she knelt down and wiped Iyata's tears away. "Tell me your name, little one."

"I-Iyata, ma'am." Iyata responded nervously.

"Such a pretty name." The woman remarked sweetly. At this point, Iyata had stopped trembling but was still nervous as she kept her arms and legs close to her body underneath the blanket. Taking pity on the young Kaemouri, the woman who had originally spoken to her stayed with her throughout the night.

Chapter 12

As morning broke over Kaseo Forest, Sakuris and his two companions found themselves in the village of Tysomi, the home of Sakuris's friend, Yu-Ka-Mi. Having traveled through the night, the small band decided a proper rest would be best for the three of them would present a good opportunity to gather information and formulate a plan for rescuing Iyata.

Having gotten around quite a bit in the last eleven years, Dayis knew the tavern scene so he decided to ask around the local tavern while Sakuris and Saiera would ask around the village market.

Inside, the tavern air was humid and mustey; not like the inn upstairs. Here it smelled of sex, orgasms, and cheap alcohol. As Dayis sat sipping a cheaply made Sikonian whiskey, he could hear the screams of the orgasming tavern whores as the men made love to them. Ignoring the environment around him, he sat dazed staring into the liquid drink as he brought it to his lips to sip from it.

Approaching the bar a young woman orders a drink and looks to see Dayis sitting alone on the other side. The look of sorrow on his face intrigued her curiosity as she watched him drink the cheap liquor. With a slight smile, she walks over taking a seat next to him, but remains silent for some time. Wondering if he had taken notice of her, she decides attempts to engage him in conversation, stating, "I've been watching you stranger. You don't seem to be from around here. Did you come alone?" Startled by her voice, Dayis looked at her. She carried a fair countenance of unprecedented beauty.

He scanned her, taking notice of her supple breasts and long legs that seemed to have a perfect shave. Her liquid, brown eyes gazed into his as her soft, braided, brown hair flowed to her waist. He was stunned that such a beautiful woman could ever be in a dump like this. For a time he could say nothing, but spoke softly, "I'm here with some friends of mine, they're wandering the village."

The young woman looked at him. "I see, and you're here drowning your troubles in, let's see . . ." She started looking into his cup, "Sikonian Whiskey. You certainly have good taste in drinks, stranger."

Dayis laughed. "This drink reminds me of Sikan. As a matter of fact, this drink is probably the only thing that remains of my once prosperous home." He replied with a grin.

The young woman wrapped her long, slender fingers around her cup and brought it to her full lips as she crossed her legs and slowly sipped her drink before placing it back down and staring into Dayis's eyes. "A man of Sikan. So that would mean you're a Wind Clansman?" She asked.

Dayis wanted to slap himself for giving himself away as a Wind Clansman. He would have answered but he felt someone grab him by the back of his collar and throw him to the ground. "What were you doing with my wife?" A male voice demanded.

Dayis looked up at the man. He was firmly built and had short brown hair, his dark Japanese skin seemed to match his brown eyes. Upon his arm he bore a mark that Dayis recognized as the mark of Ninjatta. "He's *Ninjatta*." He thought staring at the jealous husband.

The man's wife stepped in front of him. "We were just talking, please leave him alone." She said hastily.

The Ninjatta pushed her out of the way and she fell to the dusty floor of the tavern. "Stay out of this Sei Lyn." He responded watching his wife fall to the ground.

Dayis quickly stood up. "Look, I don't want trouble." He said trying his hardest to avoid conflict.

Sei Lyn looked at her husband as she stood upon her feet. "Daeloshe, leave him alone. I approached him." She pleaded trying to get her husband to calm down.

"I said 'Stay out of this.' Now get back upstairs." He demanded.

Standing to her feet, Sei Lyn dusted herself off and walked toward the stairs, passing by Dayis as he places a hand to her arm. *"Why are you listening to him? Tell him to shut up and leave you alone."* He whispered.

"I can't, he owns me." She whispered back.

"What do you mean he owns you?" Dayis whispered puzzled.

"I'm his slave, the husband-wife thing is just a cover. Now please let me go." She whispered back.

"Woman, I said 'Get your ass upstairs!'" Daeloshe yelled.

The tavern almost went quiet aside from the screams of the tavern whores. Dayis looked at him coldly. "Shut up, you!" He demanded.

"What, the hell, are you doing?" Sei Lyn asked him.

"Saying what you can't." He responded.

Daeloshe repeated his statement one final time before Sei Lyn slowly made her way toward the stairs.

Making his way past Dayis, Daeloshe merely shoves him aside. As he did, Dayis whispered, "*I know what you are, Ninjatta.*"

With a slight chuckle and an arrogant grin, Daeloshe merely punches him in the stomach and then makes his way up the stairs leaving the winded Dayis clutching his stomach and gasping for air.

Riding out from Isura to Neiheroghi, Kenzji looks about the forest around him as his horse gallops at full speed. "*The thought of my kid sister at the Northern Fortress, alone with Norakatsu sickens me, but I have my duty to fulfill. Sakuris, my old friend, this is the way it must be.*" He thinks to himself as he watches the trees pass by him.

Trees begin to give way to rock as he approaches the base of Mt Iyea. "*Iyea, Neiheroghi Village lies within the pass. Fei Ling should be waiting there.*" Kenzji thinks once more as he continues his hard ride, entering the mountain pass.

Meanwhile, at the northern fortress, Iyata was having problems of her own as Norakatsu forced her to watch as he made love to one of his slave women. "Watch closely, little one, for when you have reached maturity, you will be part of my harem." He remarks sinisterly.

Turning away from the spectacle before her, Iyata closes her eyes, picturing herself being held safely within her mother's arms with her father standing next to her. Not wanting to see the site before her, Iyata clutched her knees close to her chest and sat in the fetal position with tears flowing down her cheeks. Where were her mother and father? Why hadn't they come for her yet? She opened her eyes and once again saw the act of sex being placed on display before her. She could hear the slave woman's screams in her ears and, on reflex, finally shouted, "Stop it! Just leave her alone!"

Norakatsu looked at her, smiling as he rose off of the slave woman. Walked over to the child, he places a hand to her shoulder, stating "Did that little display frighten you? Don't worry, you will be in that same position one day."

Slapping his hand away, Iyata looks at him, retorting, "I want my mommy." under her lamentations. Turning his gaze from the young Kaemouri, Norakatsu looked at the woman in the bed and motioned for her to leave. Dressing herself in dark clothing, the woman rises out of and walks over to the door.

Leading Iyata forcibly by the arm, Norakatsu hands her over to his slave girl, commanding "Take this brat with you." as the woman took the crying Iyata into her arms and left.

Re-entering the room where the rest of Norakatsu's harem awaited, Iyata was passed off to another of the women as the woman who carried her there disappeared into the shadows of the back of the room.

"That woman, such evil I sense within her." The child thinks to herself, *"Mother, Father, where are you?"* Feeling herself being carried by another one of the women, Iyata merely rests her head on the woman's shoulder.

"Such cruelty . . . How could he force a child to watch him with that woman, or any woman?" The woman carrying Iyata remarks to herself before looking upon Iyata as she rests on her shoulder with tears in her eyes. "Hush, little one, it's over now." She remarks as she gently strokes Iyata's hair.

"I want my mother and father." Iyata responds without so much as turning her head, "That woman, who is she?"

"No one knows, little one, she says little, and keeps to the shadows in the back." The woman responds to her as she carries her through the room to an awaiting bath, "Come, a hot bath will help you feel better."

"I don't want a bath. I just want to go home." Iyata protested.

"Little one, you've not had a bath since you've gotten here." The woman remarked.

"Good, maybe if I get dirty enough that mean man won't want me here anymore." Iyata responds struggling to get free of the woman.

Chuckling, the woman places Iyata on the ground just short of the bath "Interesting plan, little one, very well." She says, allowing Iyata to run off to be alone.

"The poor dear," Another of the women remarks as the first strips down and enters the bath, "still there must be something about her that Norakatsu is after, but what."

"She appears to be of Shikanacan descent. You don't think . . ." The first woman responds as a third quickly interjects into the conversation.

"Hush, look . . ." She says bringing notice to mysterious woman in the back watching them, "She's listening." The three women soon go back to bathing and say no more on the subject.

A few minutes pass and the female tray carrier from before, once again, brings food around for everyone. Seeing Iyata alone in a corner she takes the tray over to her. "Here, little one, if you do not wish to bathe then have something to eat." She says offering the tray to Iyata.

Feeling hunger in her belly, Iyata takes a few morsels of the food presented before her and begins to eat away at it. As she does, the tray carrier smiles cheerfully upon her. "There, now, that's better." She says as she watches her eat.

Back at Tysomi Village, Sakuris and Saiera had rejoined Dayis at a local inn as the sun was going down. Sitting in an isolated corner of the inn, the three discussed how to proceed with Iyata's rescue. "It's really not necessary for you two to accompany me." Sakuris remarked, "I'd rather the both of you return to Shikanaca and wait for me there."

"You'd be a fool to go alone, Lord Kaemouri." Dayis remarked as he sipped on a drink he had ordered.

"My brother is right, beloved. Besides, Iyata is my daughter as well. I can't leave her in the hands of that bastard." Saiera said speaking up.

"I appreciate the concern, but neither of you know Kenzji the way I do. He's a dangerously powerful man. I'm sorry, but I cannot ask you to come with me." Sakuris responds, sipping on his own beverage.

"Lord Kaemouri, it might not be my place to say this, but have you ever considered why he would choose Neiheroghi Temple?" Dayis remarked.

"A fair question, brother." Saiera remarks.

"And a wise one," Sakuris responds as he strokes the stubble on his chin, "still, I'm left with no choice if I'm to save Iyata." He then stretches and yawns, "At any rate, it's getting late. We should get some rest."

Taking one final sip of his beverage, Sakuris stands from his chair and pushes it in as Saiera and Dayis stand with him and also push their seats in. In the back of the inn, a set of stairs leads up to the next floor as the three them proceed to their rooms to retire for the night.

Outside the moon hangs high as the night drags on. Stirring awake from his slumber, Sakuris looks over to his still slumbering wife. Taking great care not to disturb her, he rises from the bed and readies to continue the journey to Neiheroghi. "Take care, beloved, I'm sorry, but this is the way it must be." He remarks to himself in a low tone of voice as he straps his weapons about his waist and grabs his rucksack. Exiting the room, he walks downstairs to the now empty inn and exits into the streets. Walking to the nearby stables, Sakuris retrieves his horse as he makes it ready for travel.

Riding hard through the night, he leaves Tysomi and makes the rest of the journey to Neiheroghi alone. *"Hold on, daughter, I'm coming to take you home."* He thinks to himself as his horse gallops on. He could see the temple off in the distance as he approaches. Staring out through the dark horizon before him, he could make out the outlines of shadows that appeared to be a couple of guards.

He then sees a third entering the temple. *"Kenzji, you bastard,"* He thinks to himself, *"to kidnap a child, that's low, even for you."* Slowing his horse to a stop, Sakuris dismounts not far from the temple and turns his gaze once more to the guards. "There are two of them? I could easily break in, but I might alert the other guards. Maybe I could find a harmless way of neutralizing them." He says to himself. Watching the guards from a distance, he knew everyone had one weakness, money.

Fumbling through his saddlebags, he soon found a small money pouch and pulled it out. He opened it up and poured the coins out onto his hand and knelt down to count it, "278. . .279," He said counting the money, "280 gold coins. That won't be enough; I make 300 alone for even the most meager of assassinations." He said as he placed the money back in the pouch and placed it back into the saddlebag.

Fumbling through his saddlebag once more he came across, what could only be described as, a bottle. He pulled it out and looked at it, "Finely aged Shikanacan Mead; this plus the money might be enough." He says to himself as he mounts the horse once more.

Nudging his horse, Sakuris rides down to the temple. Upon seeing him approach, the guards brandish their spears as he approaches them, and looks down upon them from his horse. Upon closer inspection one of the guards turns to the other. "Stand down, this is the one Lord Ketsuro spoke of," he then turns to Sakuris, "proceed inside, but leave your horse behind."

Not wanting to engage in unnecessary combat, Sakuris does as instructed and dismounts his horse as he proceeds inside the temple. The inside of the temple was larger than he expected as he walked through, stating to himself "I'm coming Iyata." Around him, he could see various pagan symbols and tributes to the death god, Zecroas, rather than Elayis. "The fire clan certainly switched gods in a hurry." He remarks as he walked through. In the worshiping chamber of the temple, he could hear the chanting of the worshipers as they sang their various chants and praises.

Shuddering at the pagans, Sakuris continued through the temple until he came upon a remote room. Inside, he saw Kenzi waiting for him. "Welcome, old friend." Kenzji remarked as he entered the room.

"Kenzji, where is my daughter?" Sakuris demanded as he stood in the door way.

"She's safe," Kenzji responded as Sakuris felt a powerful blow strike him from behind as he fell to the floor unconscious with Kenzji watching as he did, "but you on the other hand."

When Sakuris awoke again he found himself bond in a cage stripped from head-to-toe of his clothing, and without his swords. Norakatsu soon entered the room and peered into the cage at Sakuris's naked form, behind him were Kenzji and Fei Ling, whom had struck Sakuris. "So, this is the mighty Sakuris Kaemouri; such a pathetic weakling to be taken down so easily." He remarked aloud.

Sakuris looked up at him as he clumsily lifted his head. His blurred vision made it hard to distinguish Norakatsu's facial features; what he could distinguish were the colors of Norakatsu's Japanese skin and clothing. "I demand to know where my daughter is, overlord of the west." He said weakly.

Norakatsu merely laughed as he held up Sakuris's blade. "From where I am standing, Arch-Dragon, you are in no position to demand anything. This blade of yours, it's quite a show of craftsmanship. Your ancestor, Myuranth, knew what he was doing when he created it." He said to him.

Sakuris looked up at him surprised. "What? What are you talking about?" He said rather weakly.

Norakatsu leaned in toward Sakuris. "You really don't know, do you? Myuranth was the first of the Arch-Dragon line. It's his power that is housed within each of the sacred blades. There were four originally, one was meant to come to Isura, but it was lost throughout the ages. It was almost mine, but it proved to be more difficult than I originally anticipated." He responded very plainly, "Still, as long as I have your blades, that's all I need." Turning his attention toward Kenzji, Norakatsu gives him an approving nod and then exits with Fei Ling following behind.

Sakuris looked at the sad expression in Kenzji's face. "What's wrong Kenzji? You should be happy to see me like this; stripped of the Arch-Dragon Dobok and weapons. But most of all, my honor and pride as a Dragon." He said to him. By *Dobok*, he meant the training uniform of a fighter, also known as a *Gi*. Kenzji reached in and placed his hand on the top of Sakuris's head.

"This is a fate I would not even wish for my worst enemy, which, at the moment, happens to be you." He responded, quite honestly.

Sakuris shook Kenzji's hand from his head and looked at him. "And yet you gloat as you look upon me." He said to him.

Kenzji shrugged his shoulders a bit as he looked at Sakuris sitting helplessly in the cage. He gave a smug laugh and turned away to leave, but stopped when he reached the door. Turning back around he said only this to Sakuris, "Remember, Sakuris, you convinced your father to show mercy on me for my demonic power. The punishment for such practice is usually death, but you convinced Kalas to merely exile me."

Sakuris looked at him. "If it had been up to me I would have lifted the sentence. I was young and naive and did not fully understand the duties my father had toward the clan." He responded.

Kenzji smiled the warm smile Sakuris had not seen since their time as childhood friends. "It is for that reason, Sakuris; that you live now." He said and then stepped out the room. Sakuris merely held his knees to his strong chest muscles in an attempt to regain any warmth he may have lost in his cold, bamboo dungeon.

Back in Tysomi Village, the sun was beginning to rise over the horizon as Saiera awoke and ran her hand across the bed hoping to feel her beloved next to her, only to find he was gone.

Assuming he had awoken and already gone downstairs to get something for morning meal, she rose out of bed and changed into some clean clothing. Feeling hunger in her stomach, she exits her room and goes downstairs where she met up with her brother.

"Dayis, have you seen Sakuris this morning?" She asked curiously hoping maybe Dayis had met up with her husband.

"No, not since last night, why?" Her brother responded as the two of them sat down at a nearby table.

"He wasn't in the room when I awoke this morning." Saiera remarked and then it dawned on her, "Oh no, you don't think he continued the journey alone, do you?" Panic entered in her voice as the realization came upon her.

"Now, now, sister, let's not jump to any hasty conclusions. Let's look for him after we've had a bite to eat. It's possible he's just in town gathering supplies." Dayis responded trying to ease his sister's worries, but knew better than to dismiss the possibility of Sakuris doing something as reckless as continuing alone.

"What if he's not, though, and he did continue alone? He could be hurt or worse." Saiera remarked as panic turned to tears.

Dayis quickly reached over the table and took his sister by the hands. "Now, now, Saiera, I know you're worried, and understandably so, but tears won't help." He remarked as Saiera dried her tears and recomposed herself.

The two are soon disturbed by the sound of clattering dishes and someone calling out, "You worthless harlot! Get up!"

Their attention drawn by the noise, Dayis and Saiera look to see Sei Lyn quickly working to clean up some dishes she had dropped along with a mixture of food and alcohol at her master's feet. "Oh, him again." Dayis remarks as he shakes his head.

"Friend of yours?" Saiera asks curiously.

"Someone I met yesterday. Apparently, the woman is a slave named Sei Lyn. The fellow with her, that's her master: a Ninjatta Clansman, named Daeloshe." Dayis responds as he points out the two to Saiera.

"His treatment of her reminds me of Sikan of old." Saiera responds as she watches Daeloshe's harsh treatment of Sei Lyn.

"Yeah, wait here a moment." Dayis remarks as he stands from his seat and wanders over to help Sei Lyn clean up the mess that had been made by the dropped dishes.

"You again!" Daeloshe exclaims upon seeing Dayis approach, "Apparently you didn't learn your lesson yesterday, did you."

"Actually, I was just wishing I had did what I should've done in the first place." Dayis responds calmly as Sei Lyn looks up at him from the ground.

"What you should've done, and tell me, stranger, what might that be?" Daeloshe retorts as he squares off against Dayis as if preparing for a fight.

"Introduce myself," Dayis responds as he uses the hilt of his curved long sword to strike a blow to Daeloshe's abdomen, "I'm Dayis, of the Wind Clan, of Sikan." Winded by the blow Daeloshe recoils as he takes a step back.

"You sonuvabitch." Daeloshe remarks insultingly as he gasps for air, "You'll pay for that." From his waistband, he draws a hidden dagger as he readies it for combat only to have it become sliced in two as the blade drops to the floor.

Surprised by what happened Daeloshe looks to see Saiera with her weapon drawn waving her index finger back and forth as if to say: tsk, tsk, tsk. She had used the weapon's power to send a weakened blade of air toward Daeloshe's weapon.

"Daeloshe, was it?" Dayis remarks, "Meet my sister, Saiera, Lady-Master of the Wind clan. Now this can go easy for you or it can go not so easy for you."

Recovering from the blow struck upon him, Daeloshe glances to Saiera and then back to Dayis simply to ask, "What do you want?"

"The girl. Her life is now mine. Once my sister and I have finished conducting what business we have in this region, we'll return for her. See to it she is properly prepared for her journey to her new home." Dayis responds as he takes a step toward Daeloshe, "And see to it she's unharmed. I prefer my goods to remain undamaged."

"Too late for that." Daeloshe jokes condescendingly.

Knowing what Daeloshe meant by his statement, Dayis gives him a second blow to his abdomen. "Watch your tongue, you Ninjatta scum." He demands as he looks over to Sei Lyn who, at this point, had a look of shock and fear on her face. Giving her a slight nod, Dayis turns away and walks back over to his sister and sits across from her.

"Well that was interesting." Saiera remarks as she re-sheathes her weapon and sits back down.

"I wish you hadn't interphered." Dayis responds as he looks Saiera in the eye.

"Mind your words, brother, these are no longer the old days." She reminds him as their meal is finally brought before them.

"Apologies, sister, I meant no disrespect, still it may have worked in my favor." Dayis remarked as the two of them ate.

"You think he'll release her." Saiera remarks curiously as they ate.

"He will if he knows what's good for him. We should focus on finding your husband, right now, though. We'll start in town first and then the temple at Neiheroghi."

"I just hope he's safe." Saiera responds solemnly as she eats a few bites of food.

"What would possess him to leave in the middle of the night?" Dayis curiously remarks. Saiera shakes her head and informs her brother that's just how Sakuris was.

Back at the northern fortress, Iyata was unaware that her father was there as well as she remained alone in her little corner away from the rest of Norakatsu's harem. Every so often one of the women would attempt to coax Iyata into a bath or with food, but with little luck.

Entering the room, Kenzji looked around as all the women began screaming while attempting to run from him. Ignoring them, he soon spots Iyata in her little corner of the room and walks over to her. Seeing him approach, two of the women come in between him and Iyata. "Stand aside, I'll not harm the child." He states commandingly as the women move aside.

Seeing his face before her, Iyata retreats further back into her corner with fear in her eyes as tears streamed from them. "Now, now, why the tears little one?" He asks curiously, "Are you afraid of me?"

Slowly, Iyata nods as she brings her knees to her chest. "What do you want with her?" One of the women demands.

"Hold your tongue or lose it, woman." Kenzji retorts as he looks back to Iyata. "Little one, I'm here to do you a courtesy as a fellow Shikanacan. Your father is here looking for you."

"Daddy?" Iyata asks in order to confirm what she had heard.

"Yes, little one, I'm not the monster I appear to be." Kenzji remarks as he leans in and rests his hands on his knees to be eye level with Iyata.

"No you're worse, lying to an innocent child like that." The woman from before retorts. Hearing her words, Kenzji merely stands to his feet and gives her a sharp slap to her left cheek, causing her head to turn smartly to the right as she gasps in a mix of pain and surprise from the sting of the blow.

In the back, Kenzji could hear the laughter of Norakatu's mystery woman as she sits veiled in shadows. Ignoring her, he turns back to Iyata and whispers in her ear, "Continue to act as though you're afraid." He then gently but firmly snatches her up, calling out "Come little one! The master requests your presence!"

His words were merely a ruse for Norakatu's mystery woman as he carries Iyata out of the room. As he did, she was kicking and screaming in his arms. Once he was out of the room he sets Iyata down on her feet and laughs. "A clever act indeed, little one." He compliments as he stands towering over her.

"Who was acting? Now where is my daddy?" Iyata demands ignoring Kenzji's height.

"Come," Kenzji beckons as he leads her through the fortress to the room where Sakuris was being held and leads her in, showing her Sakuris sitting in his cage.

"Daddy!" Iyata cries as she rushes toward the cage.

"Iyata?" Sakuris remarks as he sees her running toward the cage. He then looks behind her to see Kenzji standing tall at the door way, "Ketsuro?"

"Call it a courtesy for the mercy you showed me when we were younger." Kenzji informs him as he steps toward his cage.

"Daddy, I wannah go home." Iyata pleads as she hugs her father through the bars.

"I know, little one, I know. We'll figure a way out of this." Sakuris whispers in response.

Watching the two carefully, Kenzji steps behind Iyata and kneels down to whisper in her ear, "Come, little one, we can't stay for long." He then looks to Sakuris who gives him an approving nod.

"It'll be okay, daughter. Go with him, for now." Sakuris remarks as he releases Iyata from his embrace. He was having trouble containing his emotions but did his best to remain strong.

Ending her brief visit with her father, Kenzji takes Iyata back down to the room from before. "Just like before, little one." He says opening the door and shouting, "Get in there, you little brat!" as he shoves her into the arms of a couple of the women as they gather around her. Exiting the room, Kenzji slams the door behind him leaving Iyata alone with the women.

"Are you okay, little one? Were you harmed?" The women all asked as they helped Iyata to her corner of the room.

"No, he . . . he was telling the truth." Iyata responds in a low tone.

"Ssh, look" A second woman remarks once again bringing attention to the mysterious woman in the back, who was watching them once again, "She's listening again."

"Come, child, while you were away food was brought around. We saved some for you, but you must bathe, first. You're filthy." The first woman said to her.

Having seen her father, Iyata was filled with comfort knowing she was not far from him and allowed the women to bathe her. The water in the tub was warm to the touch and soothed Iyata's fears as two of the women washed the dirt and grime from her skin.

"There, that's much better." A third woman remarks as the two women finish bathing Iyata and help her out of the bath, "Now, come eat." The only clothing Iyata had available to dress in were the clothes she had been wearing the day Kenzji abducted her from Shikanaca.

Feeling hungry, Iyata follows the woman as she leads her back over to her little corner of the room where a small plate of food was indeed waiting for her. Eating happily at the meal before her, Iyata could feel her hunger leaving her as the women gather 'round her to talk about what happened. They keep their conversation to a low tone due to the prying ears of Norakatsu's mystery woman.

Back in his bamboo cage, Sakuris sits doing the best he can to keep up his meditations. Using his seltah, he tries to peer through the fortress walls using his mind's eye. He first tried to find Iyata using her spiritual energy as a guide. By doing so he would be able to retrace her steps to the room where she was being held, but whenever he tried to peer out the door of his room, he would become blocked by an unknown force.

"A barrier?" He thinks to himself, *"Kenzji must've placed it with his dark power. That might explain why he had no problem bringing Iyata here to see me. Still at least I know she is, truly, safe."* It hadn't taken long before he sensed the presence of another as he closed off his seltah and opened

his eyes to see Tesarah standing before him decked out in Isuran clothing embroidered with the emblem of the Wyvern Clan.

Unable to hide his nakedness from her, Sakuris merely rose to his knees and leaned forward in the cage. "What do you want?" He asked in an almost demanding tone.

In Tesarah's hand was a small flask of water. "A small courtesy from my brother." She responds presenting the flask to Sakuris who looked at it rather suspiciously. "Go on." Tesarah beckoned as she reoffered the flask.

"I'm not thirsty." He responds as he refuses the flask before him.

Tesarah removes the flask from sight and stands in front of the cage as she squats down to get eye level with it. "You and my brother are quite the pair of dragons aren't you? So much alike, yet so opposite of each other. Take this rivalry between you two for example. It never lets him go." She remarks curiously.

"What about you?" Sakuris responds plainly as he grips the bamboo bars of his cage.

"Me, I'm just like Kayah, simply along for the journey." Tesarah responds when a voice calls out for her to step away from the cage.

Once again, Kenzji had entered the room. "Leave us, sister." He says to her commandingly. She merely backs away from the cage and quickly exits the room.

"Why is my daughter still here? Your master has what he wants. He has no need of her anymore." Sakuris states, being very direct.

"My master's plans are not your concern." Kenzji retorts harshly as he turns to leave.

"DAMMIT, KETSURO!" Sakuris shouts as he pounds on the bamboo bars of his cage, "What happened to you? I know we haven't seen eye to eye since your banishment from Shikanaca, but you're one of the only remaining pure blooded Shikanacans left. Does that not mean anything to you?"

Stopping just short of the door, Kenzji turns his head to face Sakuris. "Yes, that's why you're still alive." He responds both plainly and honestly. Turning back to the front, he then leaves, hearing Kaemouri shouting behind him.

It was growing early into the morning as night gave way to dawn and the moon began to descend below the horizon.

Chapter 13

A new day dawning, Dayis and Saiera prepared to leave Tysomi village. Having asked around the village the previous night, they were unable to find any clues as to where Sakuris had disappeared to. Their only option was to continue on to Neiheroghi Temple in hopes they might find him waiting for them.

When they arrived, the sun had just begun to peak over the horizon. "It's too dangerous to go in, right now." Dayis commented as they surveyed the guards from a safe distance, "Best we wait till tonight."

As much as it saddened Saiera to have to wait, she knew her brother was correct. "Let's make camp then." She responded as she rode away from their viewing point of the temple.

Agreeing with his sister, Dayis merely followed her into the forest. Weary from travel the two of them set up their small camp as they had agreed. Dirty from the journey, Saiera could smell her own stench as it rose from her skin. "By, Elayis, I need a hot spring." She remarked as her brother finished setting up their camp, "Brother, will you be fine on your own while I have a bath."

"Yes, but don't be gone too long." Dayis responded as his sister nodded in agreement.

Reaching down into her bag, Saiera pulled out a change of clothes for herself and an animal skin to dry off with, and hurried off to find a spring to bathe in.

As luck would have it, they had passed by one during the night and Saiera had managed to come across it. Ready for a hot bath, she wasted no time stripping down and slipping into the warm water.

The warmth of the water wasn't even enough to comfort her as she soaked in the spring. She could only think of her daughter as she cried. Iyata was only five years old, she was just an innocent child, "Kenzji, you bastard-sonuvabitch!" She screamed into the morning.

Reaching for her long knife, she draws it from the scabbard and lets the edge of the blade rest against her palm. "I'll kill you!" She screamed running the blade along her palm as blood flowed from the wound and dripped into the hot spring as it ran off the edges of her hand, "I swear by my own blood, I will!" She then washed the blade of her knife in the water of the spring and, drying the blade on the grass, placed it back in the scabbard. Saiera's hand still bled from the wound as she watched the blood run from it. Tearing off a piece of her tunic that had been resting on the edge, she ties the wound closed.

She had the taste of Kenzji's blood on her lips, that's how bad she wanted him dead. No one treats the Kaemouri family so dishonorably. She had become so enraged that she could feel the heat of vengeance burning within her soul as it seared through her skin. She closed her eyes tightly letting a few tears run from it. She then looked into the sky and called, "Elayis, I know you can hear me. If you see fit to help Sakuris get our girl back then make it so, but if not, then you can go to hell, bitch!"

At that point, the earth began to shake as Saiera was tossed around in the hot spring and a powerful voice rang out from the heavens. "You ungrateful little heathen! After all I have done for you and this how you repay me, with blasphemy!"

Saiera steadied herself in the hot spring, "Don't give me that Elayis, my husband is putting his life on the line to fufill your will and you let his only daughter get kidnapped. You're supposed to be the protector of the Kaemouri family and the Dragon Clan." Saiera snapped.

"I know exactly what I'm supposed to do!" Elayis shouted causing Saiera to cower in the spring.

"Then do it, and leave me and my family out of it!" She cried as she began climbing out of the hot spring and drying off. She then dressed herself and began to walk back to the camp site she had set up with her brother.

"Saiera, I am not responsible for what each person does." Elayis said calming down. Ignoring Elayis, Saiera looks back and screams into the sky as she continued the trek back to camp.

It was mid-morning when Saiera arrived back at camp. Dayis had been making occasional trips to their vantage point of the temple to see if he could spot any sort of gaps in the security, and had arrived back at camp roughly the same time as Saiera. "Still no change in security." He informed his sister when he saw her approaching camp, "Did you enjoy your bath?" He then noticed the bandage on her hand. "Saiera!" He exclaimed, "Your hand, what happened?"

"It's nothing, brother, I'm fine." Saiera responded as she took a seat on a nearby fallen log and laid back upon it, staring up at the sky. Though her rage had subsided, she was still quite upset at the situation. Her daughter had been taken from her, and her husband was now missing. In quiet solemnness, all she could do was stare blankly at the sky.

"Saiera?" Dayis said trying to catch her attention.

A passing glance, in his direction, was all he received from his sister as she turned away and remained silent. Concerned for her well-being, Dayis walked over and knelt down beside her. "Saiera, are you sure you're up for this?"

"A little late to be asking me that, isn't it?" She replied with a mildly harsh tone, "Just leave me be, Dayis."

Sighing through his nose, Dayis got up from his sister's side and began to walk away, pausing just long enough to look back at her. "It'll be dark in a few hours. You should try to get some rest." He responded over his shoulder as Saiera waved him on.

The two siblings spent the rest of the day in silence as the sun made way for the moon signaling the start of the evening. Preparing for what lie ahead of them the siblings made their way to the temple on foot. Stealthily they made their way past the guards in an attempt to avoid having to kill any of them. As they did, they made sure to search for Iyata and Sakuris, only to find no sign of either of them.

"I don't understand." Saiera remarked as she and Dayis met up in a dark corner of the temple.

"I know, it's like they're not here." Her brother responded just as confused, "Keep searching, look for anything that can give us a clue."

Splitting up once more, the two continue their search in an attempt to find out anything they could that might lead them to Sakuris and Iyata's whereabouts. Combing the temple, once again, the two siblings did their best to remain out of sight as they continued to search for clues. During her search, Saiera was beginning to feel the sting of despair upon her heart, for fear of never seeing her loved ones again.

Meeting once again with her brother, Dayis, Saiera couldn't shake the feeling of despair she was feeling as the two met in the same dark corner from before. "Still nothing." Dayis remarked as the two conversed in a whisper so not to be heard.

Beginning to feel overwhelmed by her feeling of despair, Saiera threw herself in her brother's arms. "Dayis," She sobbed as her brother wrapped his arms around her. As Saiera cried into her brother's shoulder, not a word was spoken between the two of them.

Unfortunately, her sobs attracted a nearby guard who was approaching them to investigate. "What goes on here?" He demanded spotting the two, his weapon drawn.

Despair turned to rage as Saiera raised her head from her brother's shoulder to look upon the guard who spoke to them. On the verge of bloodlust shea rushed the guard beating him with everything she had shouting, "Where are they? Where are they?" Rage was overtaking her as she continuously punched the guard in his face demanding to know where her loved ones were.

Worried her actions might attract more guards to their location, Dayis did his best to pull her away, but she shoved him back from her demanding he not touch her as she continued her relentess assault on the guard demanding for the location of those she cared for until he finally gave in, blurting out, "The northern fortress." and giving her the exact location.

Satisfied with his answer, Saiera finally relented and ended her assault as the guard went limp, falling to the ground. He'd been nearly beaten to death before surrendering the information demanded of him.

As for Saiera, she'd become so enraged, she could feel her veins pulsating in her head as her adrenaline was pumped through them. Her heartrate had become so elevated that she fell to one knee trying to catch her breath. "Dayis, something's wrong." She gasped breathing hard and fast, almost as though she was hyperventilating.

"Come on sister, now's not the time. We need to leave, there's no telling who may have heard that." Dayis responded as he helped his sister to her feet and supported her weight on his shoulder, "You need to calm yourself down. Just breathe; deep slow breaths."

"My chest, it really hurts." Saiera gasped weakly as she tried to steady her breathing.

"It's the adrenaline. You need to steady your breathing." Dayis responded as they did their best to get out of the temple without being seen. That was going to be easier said than done as Saiera's fit of rage had attracted other nearby guards who were now coming toward them. Cursing under his breath, Dayis leaned his sister against a nearby wall. "Wait here, I'll be back, just keep breathing."

Using the wall for support, Saiera could still feel the veins in her head pulsating with adrenaline as she watched her brother dispatch the guards before them using his scimitar-like long sword. "Saiera?" He said turning back to her as hurried over and once again used his body to support her weight, "Come on, we're almost out." He informed her as he could see the entrance just ahead of them, "Look, the entrance is just ahead."

Saiera chuckled as she continued her attempt to slow her breathing. Only the guards at the entrance remained between them and their escape as the two siblings hurried toward the door that would lead them outside. Using the art of stealth, Dayis, after leaning his sister against a second wall, was able to dispatch the final two guards from behind as their bodies fell limp to the ground.

Hurrying back, once more, he collected his sister and the two made their way outside, back into the forest as they raced towards their campsite. "Saiera?" Dayis said as he leaned her against a tree to support her weight, "Stay with me. You're gonna be okay. Just keep taking slow deep breaths and let the adrenaline pass."

Merely nodding, Saiera continued her breathing. "I haven't felt like this in a long time." She remarked through her breathing.

"You've never been that angry before either." Dayis responded as he stayed with his sister.

"I'm sorry for my actions towards you." Saiera apologized.

Dayis merely shook his head. "I know you are, and I understand why you did it." He responded as he continued to help Saiera calm her breathing.

"I couldn't control myself. I felt like I could've killed that guard and not thought twice about it." Saiera responded through her breathing.

"Any longer and you would have." Dayis responded as he looked Saiera in the eyes and helped her to focus on him as her breathing finally began to slowly return to normal.

Able to control her breathing, once more, Saiera gave Dayis a nod signaling she was okay. "You okay, now?" He asked trying to confirm she was indeed okay.

"Yeah, but I need to sit now, set me down." She responded as Dayis nodded and helped her sit on the ground to lean against the tree.

"Okay, get some rest, tomorrow we'll send word back to Shikanaca informing them of our progress and letting them know we're safe." Dayis responded as he knelt down in front of his sister.

It was still dark outside as the night drug on. Exhausted from her fit of rage at the temple, Saiera managed to fall asleep quite easily while Dayis simply stared up at the stars as he gazed upon the night sky. He had been lying on the ground which was hard and stiff underneath him. It was quite cool that night as Saiera shivered in her sleep.

Looking over to her, Dayis merely got up and draped his cloak over her in attempt to keep her warm. He would've made a fire for the two of them to stay warm, but it would've risked giving away the position of their small camp. Going over to the vantage point he had used earlier, Dayis merely stared out upon the land expanding before him.

"The northern fortress . . . not much is known about it, and it's secluded deep in Isuran territory so it would make sense to use it as a hideout." He remarked to himself as he pondered over the next action he should take. Chuckling at the situation, it dawned on him he was doing this for relatives he just found out he had, but as he said: Family is family.

"Dayis?" Saiera remarked as she walked up behind him and stood next to him.

"I thought you were asleep." Dayis chuckled as Saiera walked up next to him.

"I was, but I couldn't stop shivering in the night air." She responded handing him his cloak, "Thanks for trying, though."

Chuckling, Dayis accepts his cloak back from her and stares back out over the horizon. "It's so quiet tonight." He remarks noting the silence that had fallen over the forest. Above, only a few stars shone through the clouds drifting over the forest. Even the moon remained veiled in shadow as a chilling, quiet wind blew through the area.

Staring out from their vantage point, the siblings remained quiet as they pondered what to do next. The snapping of a twig soon caught their attention as they both turned around to see Akisarah approaching the camp. "Akisarah?" Saiera exclaimed, "What are you doing here?"

"Kayah was getting worried." He responded as he approached their vantage point and stared out onto the temple, "Where's Sakuris?"

"He came here on his own, but he's gone now; taken somewhere else." Dayis responded, "Iyata, as well."

"That's unfortunate, any clue where they may have been taken?" Akisarah remarked as he stared out toward the temple.

"The northern fortress," Dayis responded, "it's good you're here actually. We could use the help. There's still a couple hours before first light, we should try to get some sleep until then."

The rest of the night moved by quickly as dawn peaked over the horizon. Having gathered up their belongings, the three travelers began the journey to where their loved ones were being held. It was long and arduous as the fortress was secluded deep in Isuran territory. Surrounded by dense forests, it heavily guarded making it the ideal hideaway for those who didn't want to be found, and unless one knew the precise location, they would become lost during the trip.

Luckily, Saiera had been able to obtain that information from the guard she had nearly beaten to death; though the journey wasn't made any less difficult as the small party traversed the dense forest surrounding the fortress, and while the fortress itself was only a short distance away from Neiheroghi Temple, the journey took almost a full day's ride to complete.

This worked in favor of the would-be rescuers as they would be able to use the cover of darkness to attempt to enter the fortress unnoticed. There was another issue; however, none of them knew the layout of the fortress grounds or the number of guards present. They also had no way knowing for sure if Sakuris and Iyata were still being held there or if the guard had spoken the truth. It was too late for second thoughts now, though, as the small group was already past the point of no return. They would just have to do the best they could and leave the rest up to fate.

Inside the fortress, Norakatsu was preparing to return to Isura with the sacred blade he had obtained from Sakuris. Kenzji, along with Norakatsu's mystery woman, would accompany him while Tesarah and Fei Ling would remain behind to keep an eye on the captive Kaemouries. "Stay safe, dear sister." Kenzji cautioned his sibling as he prepared for his journey.

The two of them had been sharing a room just like back in Isura. "I will, brother." Tesarah responded as she hugged her brother and the two parted ways. Outside the fortress, Norakatsu awaited Kenzji as he sat proud upon his horse. Accompanying him were a few guards for escort along with a wagon full of supplies. Not with him, however, was his mysterious guest.

Noting this as he rode out to meet him, Kenzji braved to ask where she was. "She refuses to travel by ground. Though I don't know any other way to travel." Norakatsu informs him as their horses stand side by side, "Now come, I am eager to return home."

Eager to return to Isura, Norakatsu gives his horse a good nudge in its sides causing it to dart off at full gallop toward Isura. With a sinister smile and a slight chuckle, Kenzji nudges his horse and begins the trip back to Isura.

Back inside the fortress, Iyata's new friends were helping her bathe and get ready for bed that night. Having seen her father a couple night's previous, she was in a lighter mood despite her situation as she tried to make the best of it. As they washed the dirt and grime from her skin, Iyata could feel the heat of the water penetrating her skin relaxing her body and calming her fears.

"You know you're very pretty for such a young age, little one." One of the slave girls noted as she helped to bathe Iyata.

"Thank you." The young Kaemouri replied with a smile. In truth Iyata had inherited her mother's beauty. Her hair hung low as it reached down to her lower back and had the same chestnut color as her father's. Her skin was fare and her eyes were same the color as Saiera's.

The girls began to scatter as Tesarah soon entered the room and looked around it. "Where is she?" She demanded to know. A few of the girls merely pointed to the bath where the girls had finished bathing Iyata and were now getting her dressed.

Looking toward the direction the girls had pointed, Tesarah began walking over to her. Seeing her approach, the girls with Iyata merely shielded her from view. "Have no fear, I'll not harm the child." Tesarah remarked as the girls stepped aside for her, "After all, she's a fellow Shikanacan."

She then knelt down as Iyata stood in front of her. "So you're the one my master and brother have been making such a fuss over. I had to come and see for myself." She remarked as she placed her hand to Iyata's face and studied her countenance, "Interesting, you bear the looks of a Sikonian, but I sense a strong Shikanacan spirit in you."

Unsure of what to make of the situation, Iyata merely remained motionless as Tesarah studied her. Taking her hand from Iyata, Tesarah merely stood tall, once more, and allowed the girls to dress her as she looked down upon her. A few minutes passed before Tesarah turned from the child and walked out of the room. Watching her leave, Iyata looked to the girls who were now dressing her. "Who was that?" She asked curiously.

"Her name is Tesarah, she's one of master Norakatsu's elites and sister to Lord Ketsuro." One of them responded as she looked Iyata in the face and studied her much the same way Tesarah had done, "She said, 'you had a Shikanacan spirit', just who are you child?'"

"Iyata, Daughter of Kaemouri." Iyata responded.

"By the gods," The woman gasped in awe, "I knew it. Then the man Lord Ketsuro took you to see . . ."

"My father, Sakuris." Iyata replied as the women finished dressing her.

A second woman turned to the one who had inquired Iyata about her identity. "Do you know her father?"

"Perhaps, but it was a long time ago when I lived in Kaylah. I had become trapped in a house that had caught fire during an attack on the city. A man, whose name remains unknown to me, risked his life to save me from the flames. He was a Shikanacan who had come to the city. I never saw him after that. Seeing this child now though I wonder if her father was the same man." The first one responded as she looked at Iyata and finished helping her get dressed.

Outside the fortress, Saiera and her two male allies prepared to make their way inside. Tension hung heavy on the air as they silently crept through the fortress grounds killing any of the guards they found and then hiding the bodies until they had finally made their way inside. Now came the hard part: Navigating the fortress hallways. Divided into three wings, the fortress was vast leaving plenty of hiding spaces for captives to be held. The three opted to split up as each took a separate route in order to widen the search.

Dayis would take the central part of the fortress, Saiera the west wing, and Akisarah the east wing. Sakuris meanwhile was still attempting to figure out a way to escape on his own. Once again he attempted to use his

Seltah to trace Iyata's spirit energy back to where she was being held only to once again be stopped by the barrier from before.

"The same barrier from before, there has to be a way through it." He thinks to himself and again tries to trace Iyata's energy back to her only to be stopped once more. About to give up he suddenly senses a new energy coming toward him, "Someone's coming, but who?"

"Master Kaemouri?" Someone says entering the room. Looking to see who had spoken to him, Sakuris sees the face of his friend, Akisarah.

"Akisarah!" He exclaims, "Man, am I glad to see you. Get me out of here."

Rushing over to his friend, Akisarah begins to work at opening the bamboo cage that held Sakuris prisoner. Within a few minutes he had his friend free and helped him to climb out of the cage.

"Saiera?" Sakuris quickly asks as he stands to his feet.

"She's searching another part of the fortress. Let's get you out of here." Akisarah responds as they head to the door.

"Wait." Sakuris remarks calling attention to his lack of clothing.

Tossing his pack to the ground, Akisarah quickly began rifling through it and pulled out a spare set of clothing, tossing it to Sakuris. They were a little big on him as he dressed himself, but they would have to do for the time being. "They have the sacred blade." He informed Akisarah as the two of them began to leave the room.

"We'll have to find it later. Where is Iyata?" Akisarah quickly responded as they hurried toward the exit.

"I don't know. I've tried locating her, but was stopped by a barrier of some kind. All I know is that she is here." Sakuris responded as the two friends emerged into the hallway, "Let me try to find her again." Closing his eyes and opening his Seltah, Sakuris once again attempted to locate his daughter using her spirit energy. With no barrier in place to stop him, it took little time to follow her qi trail back to the room where she was being held with the other girls. "Found her, follow me." Having found his daughter, the elder Kaemouri raced down the hall with Akisarah close behind..

Following his daughter's qi trail, it took only mere moments to find the room she was being held as the two of them quickly entered. "Iyata!" Sakuris called as the women cleared the way for him.

"Daddy?" Iyata asked as she heard her name and looked around. Over the chatter of the women, Iyata heard her name being called again.

"Daddy!" She called in reply as she quickly looked to see him coming through the crowd of women as they cleared a path for him.

Excited to see her father coming to get her, the child quickly raced into his awaiting arms as he took her into his embrace. Joy filling her heart, Iyata couldn't hold back her tears as she cried and cried into his arms. "There, there, daughter, you're safe now, daddy has you."

"What a touching reunion." A voice said from behind as the women scattered in fear. Looking to see who had spoken, Sakuris saw the face of his fellow Shikanacan, Tesarah.

Turning to Akisarah, who had followed him through the crowd, Sakuris handed his daughter off to her uncle, instructing him to take her and find Saiera. Not wanting to leave her father's arms, Iyata fought against Akisarah's grip, but was soon taken up in his arms. "Come, little one, your father will be fine. Let's go find your mother."

Looking around at her new friends, Iyata wasn't ready to leave. "Wait, what about the others, we can't leave them." She pleaded.

"Yes you can, little one." The woman who had befriended her from before stated clearly, "This is no place for you."

"Iyata, go!" Sakuris ordered his daughter with fatherly authority. With tears in her eyes, she nodded and allowed her uncle to take her.

"Sakuris, take my father's sword." Akisarah offered presenting the sword strapped to his waist to Sakuris.

"Once I engage her, make for the door." Sakuris remarked as he drew the sword.

With a sinister chuckle, Tesarah drew her weapons as the two combatants prepared to engage in close quarters. Fearing injury, the women cleared enough space for them to engage in their bout. Eager to leave the wretched fortress, Sakuris made the first move, throwing a vertical overhead slash at Tesarah starting the bout.

Using her sword, she parried the blow and countered with a horizontal cross cut to Sakuris's offside. Waisting no time, Akisarah took Iyata and raced to the door way.

"No!" Tesarah exclaimed as she took a concealed dagger from her waist band and threw at Akisarah, but her aim was off as she missed sending the dagger into the post next to the door.

"Tesarah, your bout is with me." Sakuris called as he struck out at her again.

"Very well, let's end it then." Tesarah retorted as she once again parried his attack and countered with an attack of her own sending Sakuris into a nearby wall. Pressing the advantage Tesarah wasted no time closing the distance to strike a death blow only to gasp sharply as she reached him.

Looking down to see the reason for her sharp breath, she noticed Sakuris's blade had penetrated her breast and pierced her heart from below. Wanting to have the last laugh, she smiled wickedly, letting loose a sinister laugh as blood drained from her mouth. "My . . . brother . . . will a-a . . ." she remarked struggling to finish her statement, but was unable as her last ounce of breath left her body and she fell limp as her blade dropped to the floor.

"A Shikanacan's death." Sakuris remarked as he pulled his weapon from her body letting it fall to the floor. Taking one last moment to look around the room, Sakuris turned and exited into the hall way as he began to race down it, once again opening his mind to Seltah and using it to locate his loved ones. Occasionally he would run into a few guards that were easily dispatched as he made his escape. Continuing to follow the qi trail left by his loved ones, Sakuris eventually caught up to Akisarah and Iyata as they met up with Dayis and Saiera in the middle of the fortress.

"Mommy!" Iyata cried as she raced into in her mother's arms.

Wrapping her arms around her daughter, Saiera allowed tears of joy to escape from her eyes. "Oh my baby, my darling girl, thank Elayis you're safe." She cried as she knelt down and held Iyata tightly to her breasts. Seeing Sakuris approach, she had become infuriated by him leaving her in Tysomi. Releasing Iyata from her embrace she stood up and rushed to her beloved not to embrace him, but to give him the sting of her hand across his face. "Bakayarou!" She screamed calling Sakuris an idiot as he stood with a hand to his cheek, "I was so worried about you."

"I'm sorry, beloved." He said regrettably as he turned his head away in shame.

"Perhaps, you can set your squabble aside and focus on more important things like getting out of here." Dayis called pointing out the fact more guards were coming to find them.

"He's right. We need to go, now!" Akisarah remarked agreeing with Dayis. Agreeing with her brother and Akisarah, Saiera scooped Iyata into her arms as the group made their escape.

Outside the fortress, their horses were waiting for them as they quickly mounted with two of the horses carrying two riders: Iyata with her mother and Sakuris with Akisarah.

The morning sun was beginning to peek over the horizon as the group raced away from the fortress towards the forest as arrows from the guards on the roof rained down on them with one managing to penetrate into Sakuris's shoulder causing him to cry out in pain.

"Sakuris!" Saiera shouted.

"Don't worry about me, keep going!" He shouted back.

Harder and faster they pushed the horses as they made their way to the tree line of the forest disappearing from sight of the guards.

Having safely made it to cover, the group slowed down it's pace in order to provide aid to their injured comrade. Helping Sakuris down from his horse, they were careful not to cause the wound from the arrow to tear.

"Careful, careful, watch the arrow." Akisarah remarked as he and Dayis merely set Sakuris down against a nearby tree.

"It's lodged in pretty good." Dayis remarked examining the arrow protruding from the wound, "We'll have to force it through."

"Daddy?" Iyata asked concerned as she stepped forward.

Taking her daughter into her arms, Saiera took Iyata away from the area so she wouldn't have to watch. Once they were out of sight, Dayis gripped the arrow tightly. "My friend, brace yourself, this is gonna hurt, a lot." He informed Sakuris as he forced the arrow the rest of the way through his shoulder causing him to shout out in pain. Quickly breaking the arrow, Dayis removed the part that remained in his Sakuris's shoulder and passed it off to Akisarah.

It was at then Akisarah noticed a weird aroma coming from the arrowhead. "Odd, this smells like . . ." He began as he sniffed the arrowhead again, "poison."

"Poison? What kind of poison?" Dayis quickly asked as he took the arrow from Akisarah and smelled it.

"Unknown, but we'll need to get him to a healer soon. Let's get him patched up and ready for travel." Akisarah responded as he looked to his brother in law.

"Tysomi Village isn't far from here. We can take him there. I still have business to attend to there, anyways." Dayis responded.

"Good thinking, Reia is there waiting for us." Akisarah informed him.

Having agreed on a next course of action, the two of them worked quickly to bandage the wound as they made Sakuris ready for travel to Tysomi.

"Saiera, bring Iyata, we're going." Dayis called to his sister. Hearing her brother call to her, Saiera took Iyata back to where the others were waiting for her, and prepared for the journey back to Tysomi Village.

Once everyone was ready, they made haste to the village as they pushed their horses to full gallop in order to get there in the time.

Chapter 14

The sun had just started to set when they arrived back in Tysomi Village. Quickly entering the village, the small group finds Reia awaiting them. Seeing her friend injured, she immediately asks what happened. Doing their best to explain, the small group informs her of the events that had taken place and that there was no time to lose.

Taking Sakuris to a nearby clinic they were met by a medic, named Tallinyia. A woman roughly the same age as Sakuris. Seeing the group enter with her potential patient, she drops what she's doing and quickly rushes to assist as they place Sakuris on a nearby observation bed. "How long ago was he injured?" She asks beginning her examination.

"A few hours, at most." Akisarah responds as he explains the situation to her. A few minutes pass as he explains the events leading up to what happened. After hearing everything she needed to know, Tallinyia sends the group into a separate room to await word of their friend's condition.

Minutes passed like hours while the group awaited news of their friend. Finally Tallinyia came back out and gathered the group around her. "Your friend's stable, and I've managed to slow the spread of the poison. I can make an antidote to neutralize it, but I need the petals of a fire blossom . . ." She said informing the group of Sakuris's condition.

As Tallinyia spoke, Akisarah had looked around to notice Reia was missing. "Where's Reia?" He asked interrupting Tallinyia's statement. In truth, Reia had exited the room in the middle of Tallinyia's statement and was already exiting the village on horseback as she rode hard through the forest. *"Fire blossoms, they only grow in one place, by Elayis, why there?"* She thought to herself as she rode toward Mt Iyea pushing her horse at full gallop.

Back in the village, a sleeping Sakuris awoke to a familiar face. "I've not seen you for many years." He remarked seeing the face of the monk he encountered the day he met Saiera.

"Yes, the Demon-Dragon has appeared and the prophecy has come true." The monk said to him.

Sakuris shrugged and looked at the monk. "What prophecy?" He asked confused.

The monk only looked at him. "You don't know, I'll tell you. According to ancient text, two dragons will immerge from the skies and fight to unite the four kingdoms of Japan . . . or divide them. If the kingdoms are Kaylah, Shikanaca, Sikan, and Isura; and you, Sakuris, are one of the dragons. That would mean Norakatsu is the second. You must defeat him before he revives as the Demon-Dragon." He replied.

A knock soon comes from the door as Sakuris looks toward the direction the sound came from and then back to the monk to see he had once again disappeared. "Come in." He announces as the door creaked open and Iyata popped her head in.

"Hey, little one." Sakuris says lovingly to his daughter, motioning for her to enter. With a smile on her face, Iyata rushes over to her father as Saiera enters behind her.

"She was starting to get scared. So I decided to let her see you were safe." Saiera remarked as she walked over to Sakuris's bed and sat at the foot of it, "How are you doing?"

Playing with Iyata's hair, Sakuris smiled as he looked to his wife. "The doc says she managed to slow the poison." He responds as Saiera runs her hand, lightly, along Sakuris's leg.

"I was really worried about you. Please don't ever leave me like that again." Saiera pleaded as she looked at her husband with gentle eyes.

"It wasn't my intention to hurt you." Sakuris responded as he ran his fingers through Iyata's hair and smiled at her.

"I know. Anyways get some rest." Saiera remarked as she looked at Iyata, "Iyata, come dear."

Iyata had been resting her head on the bed next to Sakuris the whole time. Hearing her mother's call, she lifted her head and looked at her father once more. "Go ahead, Iyata. Go with your mother." Sakuris said to her as he patted her on the shoulder and sent her over to Saiera.

Leaving with her mother, Iyata turned around and waved good bye to her father as she walked backwards out of the room. With a chuckle, Sakuris smiled and waved back. Lying back on the bed, he merely stared up at the ceiling as he allowed his body to relax.

Wandering the village, Akisarah, meanwhile, had found himself a nice little inn to stay in for the night. Laying on the bed, he heard a knock at his door and a female announce, "Masseuse!"

Getting up from bed and walking to the door, Akisarah opens it to see an older woman standing before him. "I didn't ask for a masseuse." He said to her.

The woman looked at him as she stepped in. "I know, compliments of the inn. The innkeeper figured you might be tense. I'm here to help you relax." She responded. In her hand she carried a leather bag full of various oils and other instruments of her trade.

"A massage would be nice, I suppose. Sakuris always said they are good to have." Akisarah thought as he followed her over.

"Lie down on the bed, face down, please." The masseuse says to him as she motions to the bed.

Doing as instructed, Akisarah lays face down on the bed. Setting her bag aside, the masseuse reaches in and pulls out one of the small bottles. Opening the bottle, she tips it so a few drops of oil drip onto her hand. She then looked at Akisarah, who was still wearing his Kimono. "I'll need you to remove your Kimono, sir." She said to him.

"Oh," Akisarah responded as he stripped off the top half of his Kimono and laid it on the floor, "Sorry, first time."

The masseuse laughed. "It shows. You have a nice build for someone your age." She said to him as she placed her hands on his back and proceeded to massage him.

"By the way, what is your name?" Akisarah asked her.

"It's Kiyanah." She responds, running her hands gracefully along Akisarah's back and shoulder muscles.

"Kiyanah, charming, may I ask what it means?" Akisarah said to her.

"It means graceful angel." She responds as she works her way up to Akisarah's neck.

Akisarah looked forward as she massaged him. "Are you called that because you're good with your hands?" He asked her.

"I'm good with more than my hands. You should see my performance in bed." Kiyanah flirted.

Laughing from her remark, Akisarah lets out a relaxed moan. "That feels good. Just out of curiosity, you ever work on a Sakuris Kaemouri." He asked her quickly changing the subject.

"Ah, Kaemouri-san, how is he? I've not seen him since he was a child. He and his father would come to my mother's parlor every other week for a massage." She responded.

"He's hurt badly." Akisarah responded, "He's being treated at the clinic, right now."

"Will he be okay?" Kiyanah asked concerned for her friend.

"It's a bad wound, but I believe he'll live. That man has never let anything stop him." Akisarah responded.

Kiyanah laughed as she massaged Akisarah's shoulders. "Yes, that sounds like a Kaemouri." She said to him.

"We'll be leaving to go back to Shikanaca once we've finished our business here. Why don't you come with us? I'm sure Sakuris would be pleased to have you."

"Mother always was his favorite." Kiyanah responded, "I'll consider it, and Kayah, how is she?"

"Pregnant." Akisarah responded as he felt Kiyanah's hands running over his back and shoulders again.

"Pregnant? Who's the father?" Kiyanah asked curiously. She wanted to know of the man who Kayah had chosen to sire a child with.

With a chuckle, Akisarah responded, "That would be me."

"You, how did you manage that one? Kayah never let any man near her." Kiyanah asked him.

"We met as children. I saw her walking through Kaylah one day. A few of the other boys decided they would try to have some fun with her. I saw them and let one of them have the sting of my fist, right in his back. Things simply developed naturally from there." He responded.

"So how long have you've known Kayah?" Kiyanah asked, her interest was piqued at this point.

"About six years now. We're to be united soon, actually." Akisarah responded.

"Oh how wonderful for you." Kiyanah said as she finished massaging Akisarah and helped him sit up. She then handed him a cup of water. "Here drink this, the massage released the toxic lactic acids from your muscles and you'll need to get them out of your system." She said as Akisarah sat up in bed and drank the water. "So what of Sakuris, has he taken a wife, yet?"

"Yes, about five years ago, actually." Aksiarah responded as he leaned against the bed's headboard.

Excited by the news of her friends, Kiyanah braved another question. "Does he have any children, yet?" She asked feeling her heart race with anticipation.

"Yes, one daughter. Her name's Iyata." Akisarah responded as he finished the water Kiyanah had given him.

"How old is she?" Kiyanah asked him as took Akisarah's empty cup from him.

"About five, she was kidnapped and Sakuris went to find her. That's how he got wounded." Akisarah responded, relaxing his body on the bed.

"And Ketsuro-san, is he well." Kiyanah asked curious to know of Kenzji as well.

Akisarah shook his head. "He was the one who kidnapped Iyata." He responded.

A perplexed look came across Kiyanah's face. "But he and Kaemouri-san were friends. I don't understand. What happened?" She asked.

Shaking his head, Akisarah merely shrugs. "Sakuris doesn't like to talk about it, so I make it my place not ask him." He responded.

Kiyanah said nothing more on the subject of Kenzji and his past friendship with Sakuris. She merely turned from the bed and walked to the door. "I should be going. I have other guests to attend to. Say 'Hi.' to Kayah for me." She said opening the door and exiting the room.

Looking around the room from his bed, Akisarah spots a nearby window and walks over to it. Standing next to it, he stares out into the night as its shadow envelops the land. "Sakuris was right. That massage felt good." He said to himself as he stared out into the night.

Feeling slumber attempting to overtake him, he stretches and yawns as he walks back over to the bed and lays down upon it to fall asleep for the night.

Meanwhile at the village tavern, Dayis was enjoying a bit of food and drink. Next to him sat the Ninjatta from before, Daeloshe; with him was Sei Lyn. "Alright Sikonian, here she is, unharmed, as promised." He said in a cross tone of voice.

"Good, now be gone from my sight." Dayis retorted as he went back to enjoying his meal.

Nervously Sei Lyn stood in silence as she listened to the two men speak. She wanted to be free from Daeloshe's cruelty, but at the same time she knew nothing about her potential new master.

Before leaving, Daeloshe put one final thing on the counter before Dayis. "You will need this." He said to him placing a vial of colored liquid on the counter.

"Keep it, I know how to handle my slaves." Dayis retorted.

With a chuckle, Daeloshe removed the liquid from the counter saying, "Good luck, then." before leaving Sei Lyn with Dayis.

"Ninjatta scum." Dayis remarked under his breath once Daeloshe was far enough from the area and then looking to Sei Lyn who stood nervously awaiting her new master's orders, "You need not fear me, woman. The old ways of Sikan are simply that: Old. Sit and have a drink with me, Sei Lyn was it?" Dayis said as he ordered a second drink for himself.

Doing as Dayis instructed, Sei Lyn took a seat next to him. "I've heard of the reputation of Sikonian men." Sei Lyn remarked as Dayis ordered her a drink.

"At one point, it was true, but not anymore. That Sikan is no more, destroyed in the great destruction. One day; however, perhaps my sister and I will rebuild it." Dayis replied sipping on his second beverage and taking another bite of food, "Are you hungry?"

"I can't remember the last time I had a decent meal." Sei Lyn responded.

"Order something then, whatever you wish. You're free now." Dayis replied.

"Free?" Sei Lyn exclaimed as her eyes widened in surprise, "You mean you do not wish me for a slave?"

Dayis merely chuckled at her remark. "As I said, those ways are done, my sister saw to that."

Unable to contain her emotion, Sei Lyn quickly stood up and threw her arms around Dayis saying, "Thank you." as tears streamed down from her eyes.

With a smile, Dayis merely held Sei Lyn as he allowed her to cry into his shoulder. "Come now, dry those tears. Have to something to eat instead." He remarked as he felt Sei Lyn's head rubbing on his shoulder as she nodded.

Overjoyed, Sei Lyn took her seat once again and wiped her tears away as she ordered herself a fine meal. Overtaken by hunger as the meal was placed before her, Sei Lyn began to feast hungrily at it, almost choking herself as she did.

"Easy, woman, you'll choke if you continue to eat that way. Slow down, savor it." Dayis remarked with a chuckle.

Swallowing the food in her mouth, Sei Lyn nodded and smiled. "I'm so used to the table scraps Daeloshe would leave me, and even then I barely had time to eat. This is going to be an adjustment for me." She remarked as she sipped from her beverage.

"You'll be fine." Dayis remarked as Saiera soon entered the tavern with Iyata.

"That's your sister over there, isn't it?" Sei Lyn asked seeing the two of them enter.

Looking over to the tavern entrance to see Saiera and his niece, Dayis chuckled. "Yes, and the girl with her must be the niece she told me about." He remarked as Saiera and Iyata came walking over to the two of them and sat down.

"How's your night been?" Saiera asked as she ordered a drink for herself and Iyata.

"Well, given the circumstances, can't say it's been all bad." Dayis responded as he sipped from his beverage cup.

Peering past her brother as a cup of Sikonian Whiskey was placed before her, Saiera spotted Sei Lyn next to him. "Ah, I see, now. Will the two of you be returning to Shikanaca with us?" Saiera asked curiously.

"Shikanaca is your place, sister. The forest is mine. My old hideout is still there though if you ever need to find me." Dayis remarked looking past Saiera to Iyata as a cup of milk was placed before her. "Now, let's meet this niece you told me about. Come here little one." He said motioning for Iyata to come stand before him.

Doing as instructed, Iyata grabbed her cup and walked over to her uncle. "Hello there, little one. You're mother here tells me your my niece and that your name is Iyata." Dayis remarks politely

Nervous at the newcomer, Iyata nods her head as she stands silent before her uncle. "Well, Iyata, my name is Dayis, and I hope we get to become good friends someday." He told her not trying to sound to intimidating, though his daunting appearance made that hard.

Turning his attention back to Saiera, Dayis inquires her of Sakuris's condition. "He was resting when I spoke to him. I just hope we get that antidote soon." Saiera remarked with concern.

"Yes and by the way his friend disappeared out of the room like that, I can only guess she knows where it is and that's why she left in such a hurry. Hopefully she makes it back in time." Dayis responds taking one final sip of his drink as he stands from seat, "Come Sei Lyn, we must make ready for our journey." He then takes one final look at his sister. "I am glad to have found you again." He says to her.

With tears forming in her eyes, Saiera stands and the two siblings embrace. "Come back to me, again." She says as Dayis reassures her. Releasing from their embrace, they trade their final goodbyes before Dayis and his new friend exit the tavern.

It was a hard ride from Tysomi to the cliffs of Mount Iyea, and Reia had finally arrived at the base of the mountain, just as the first winter's snow began to fall. As she ascended the mountain, the cold winter night's air blew harshly on her body as it pierced through her animal skin cloak. They were so strong, at times, she almost lost footing causing her to stumble. Not yet ready to give in to the cold, Reia pulled herself back into position and continued to climb with all her might. She had to get that blossom.

Spotting a small cave on an outcropping just above her, she used every ounce of strength she had remaining to pull herself up into it in order to rest for a bit. Once inside, she gathered various sticks and other tender so that she may build a fire. From her pack, she grabs some kindling along with some flint and steel. Striking the steel to the flint, Reia watched as the first few sparks ignited the small amount of kindling and the fire flared up.

The warmth of the fire was so inviting that she debated about falling asleep for the night, but knew not how much time she had; and that she would have to hurry if she wanted to save her friend. Resting maybe an hour, she had just enough time to grab a small morsel food and recover her strength.

"Don't die on me, Sakuris. I'll get that blossom in time." She said to herself as she stood up and put out the fire.

Stepping out of the cave and continuing her ascent to the top of the mountain, she would not let herself be defeated by the darkness, not here, not now; not ever. A few birds flew high above her as they gave off their various caws and shrieks. Above her, an eagle swooped down and grabbed a small mountain rodent within its talons; and while this fascinated her, Reia knew she had no time to watch in amazement as the eagle finished off the rodent as a meal. She had to get to the top soon or she would lose her best friend.

It was late into the night when she reached the Dark Forest and entered. Wandering through it, Reia soon arrived at a pond with a small island at the center and growing upon it was a single fire blossom. "That's it! I made it! I can't stop now; I need to hurry if I'm to save Sakuris." She said to herself as she ran toward the isle. She was ready to dive in to the water when a huge fiery dragon descended out of nowhere and swooped down in front of her.

"Who dares trespass in the sacred forest of the Demon-Eyes Flame Dragon?" It snarled as it gazed upon Reia; it's immense fiery body whipping about in the night air. Even at a safe distance, Reia could feel the sweltering heat coming from it.

Frozen by fear, she felt her heart skip a few beats. Taking a large deep breath and swallowing hard, she mustered enough courage to respond, "My name is Reia Teaiss, and I've come for the fire blossom. May I please have it?" She asked.

The dragon looked at her as it lowered his head and met Reia at eye level. So near to her, she could feel the intense heat from dragon's body. "That flower can increase the strength of whoever eats it. What is your purpose for it?" It snarled.

Reia dropped to her knees and looked up into the dragon's eyes. "Please, I beg you; my friend's life hangs in the balance. I need that plant to make an antidote for the Red Poison." She pleaded.

Shifting its gaze from Reai to the plant then back to Reia, The dragon responds. "Your intentions seem noble, but how do I know you're telling me the truth?"

"Please, I give you my word as a Dragon Clansman I am telling you the truth, dragon." Reia responded still feeling the intense heat emanating from the dragon's body as it stared into her eyes.

"You're a Dragon Clansman? No, you're lying, a Dragon Clansman would not be out this far." It responded drawing its head back, "The blossom stays where it is."

Reia wouldn't accept this answer. "I've told you the truth; now relinquish the plant, dammit. Sakuris will die without the antidote." She demanded.

"Sakuris!" The dragon exclaimed as it turned back to Reia, "Perhaps I was wrong about you. Maybe you are telling the truth, but why would Sakuris have the red poison running through his veins?" It asked.

Taking a breath, Reia steadied her composure. "He was wounded by an arrow poisoned with it. If I don't get that plant back he will die. Please, will you let me have it now?" She pleaded.

Staring at Reia, the dragon turned his head toward the plant and gripped it in his teeth. He then turned back toward Reia and dropped it before her. "I've guarded that plant for many years. Take it; use whatever petals you need of it and then bring the rest back here." He said to her.

Reia reached over and gripped the orange colored plant. She bowed her head before the dragon. "Thank you and I promise to return what I don't use." She said thankfully as she stood up and turned from the dragon.

"Be warned," It said to her from behind, "If the flower is not returned soon; disaster will fall upon my forest. Hurry and use what you need."

Reia turned her head back toward the dragon and nodded as she bowed once more. "Yes, I will." She responded as she ran toward the edge of the forest. Her descent down the mountain was harder than the ascent. The wind blew her this way and that as she fell a few times and bruised her body up.

When she finally reached the bottom, day had just peaked over the horizon. Mounting her horse, she rode off toward Tysomi Village. Waisting no time as she entered the village, Reia raced to the clinic caring for her friend. "I have it!" She called hurrying inside.

Tallinyia, who had just finished working on another patient, saw Reia rushing inside with the flower and rushed over to her. Taking the blossom from Reia, she immediately went to work preparing the antidote for Sakuris. Once administered, the antidote quickly went to work as Sakuris began to slowly show signs of recovery from the poison.

"The antidote will take time to work completely." Tallinyia said as Reia stood next to the bed.

"Whatever it takes; just don't let him die." Reia responded relieved to hear Sakuris would live, only to collapse in Tallinyia's arms.

"You're exhausted, lay and rest for a bit." Tallinyia remarked as she help Reia lie down on a nearby bed.

"Thank you." Reia remarked as she allowed her tired body to recuperate, "I'll need to leave again soon. The blossom must be returned to where it came from."

"Rest for a bit, first. I'll come and get you so you can return the blossom." Tallinyia remarked as she left the room.

"Reia?" Sakuris said weakly as looked over to his friend in the bed next to his, "What a pair we make."

"I know what you mean. Both of us as reckless as the other." Reia responded as she turned on her side to face her friend.

"You risked your life to find that blossom didn't you, thank you." Sakuris responded with a slight cough.

"Yeah, I guess, too bad I have to make the climb again to return it." Reia responded as she looked at him.

As the two of them conversed, the sun began to rise over the village. An hour or two had passed since Reia returned with the plant and she had to prepare to leave again. Upon horse back, she raced out of the village and into the forest to return the item she had borrowed.

As Reia headed for Mt Iyea, Dayis and Sei Lyn were riding back to Dayis's forest hideaway, as the snow fell, lightly, down around them. Having never ridden a horse before, Sei Lyn tightened her grip around Dayis's waist as she rode seated on the saddle behind him.

Feeling her tension Dayis placed a hand to hers, "This the first time you ever rode a horse?" He asked her. Sei Lyn laid her head on his shoulder to make herself more comfortable. "Yes, I'm used to walking." She replied feeling herself become fidgety in her legs, "Dayis, I have to, uhm, you know."

Dayis looked at her, "What, pee?" He asked receiving a nod in reply. With a chuckle, Dayis slowed his horse to a stop and helped her climb off keeping alert for anything, as he dismounted and stood next to Sei Lyn. Wanting to give her some privacy he started to walk off to let the horse graze before hearing Sei Lyn calling for him to wait.

"Don't leave me." She said to him hastily.

Dayis turned to her. "I thought you might want your privacy." He responded respectfully.

Shaking her head, she replies, "Thank you, but privacy is something I've never had, Daeloshe would always watch when I did this. I'm used to it." Not bothering to look upon his new companion as she slipped her torn skirt off to squat and relive herself, Dayis went over and stood at her side. Upon finishing, Sei Lyn wipes herself clean and stands as she redresses her lower half. Dayis watched as she walked back over to the horse as it grazed upon some forest grass.

Just as he was about to climb onto the back of the horse to help Sei Lyn up, they heard a rustling in the trees around them as a hungry forest wolf peered out from the under brush. "Sei Lyn, wait here." Dayis instructed her.

Looking at the wolf as Dayis approached it sent something unusual flooding through Sei Lyn's mind: Memories of a forgotten past of large wolves and a mysterious island. "What, what was that?" She asked herself as though she had seen the memory before her very eyes as she looked at Dayis.

In his hand rested a curved long sword. The slender blade gleamed in the moonlight as he stared down the beast. Watching Dayis closely, Sei Lyn held onto the reigns of the horse to keep it from getting away.

Before Dayis could react the wolf lunged upon him, causing him to drop his sword, as it pinned him to the ground. He brought his arm up to protect his throat the hungry beast had been longing to chomp down upon. Sei Lyn cried out in fear as Dayis's name escaped from her lips. Wrestled the wolf down to the ground, Dayis plunged a small dagger into the throat of the animal as it gave off a small gurgling sound while blood ran freely from the open wound.

Feeling a vomit taste rising in her mouth, Sei Lyn cringed in disgust as she witnessed the act. Looking at her with a bloodstained face, Dayis wipes the dagger clean with a piece of linen concealed within the pocket of his kimono sleeve before proceeding over to mount his horse. Looking to Sei Lyn he apologizes for her having to witness such an act of defense.

As Dayis looked upon her, the combination of the snow and the moonlight hitting her made her look like a winter queen to him. Looking upon her, he could see an expression of sorrow on her face, as though he had done something wrong by killing the creature. He looked back at the dead animal as its body lay sprawled out across the forest floor, causing him to think back to the first animal he had killed. It had been a tiger found deep within Kaseo forest. He had skinned the animal and used its fur to keep warm and made the head of the animal into the mask that rested upon his face the day he met Sakuris. Looking back at Sei Lyn, Dayis could see her shivering within the coldness of the night.

A thought came to his head as he looked at the beast and then to Sei Lyn as she stood, shivering in the cold. Taking pity on her as she stood silent, Dayis walked back over to the beast and used the dagger from before to skin the animal's hide. Rolling the fur up into a ball, he placed it in a brown leather sack as it became stained red from the blood. Using the grass to clean his dagger, he placed it away before proceeding back over to the horse.

Passing Sei Lyn as he walked back to the horse, Dayis tied the leather sack to the saddle and climbed back upon the horse. Extending his hand to Sei Lyn, he helped her climb up as she grasped his hand in hers. "Come, we should get out of the snow." He said to her as he allowed her to seat herself behind him as she wrapped her arms around his waist to prevent her from falling. Nudging the horse in its sides, Dayis continued on his way to his forest hideout.

Chapter 15

Having made her ascent back up the mountain, Reia stared at the Demon-Eyes Flame Dragon as she stood before it with the remainder of the fire plant she borrowed. Looking at her as its fiery body hover in the air, it growled, "You've returned with the item you borrowed; was it of use to you."

Reia bowed at the waist. "Yes, oh great god of fire." She responded as the dragon drew its head so close to Reia that she again felt the intense heat of its body and began sweating.

"That's good." It responded as it drew its head back from her.

Petrified, Reia could feel the sweat drip from her head. Seeing this creature was one thing, but having it so close to her body frightened her as she hesitated to pull out the remainder of the plant that was in her pouch as she presented it to the dragon.

The dragon brought its head close to the small plant. "There isn't much left, but it will regrow soon enough." It said taking the plant into its enormous mouth and placing back in the center of its island.

The dragon looked back at Reia. "I'm glad it could assist you. If you ever need it again, don't hesitate to return." It said loudly as its voice echoed throughout the mountain's summit.

It was so loud Reia had to cover her ears. She then looked at the dragon. "I'll take my leave of you now, fire god." She said as she turned around.

"Wait!" The dragon called.

Reia turned back. "Yes?" she responded hesitantly.

Flying over and the dragon landed next to her. "The descent will be a dangerous one, and you've done enough climbing for one day. Please, allow me to carry you down." It said to her as it solidified the flames of its body into shimmering gold scales and extended its wing for Reia to climb up on.

Cringing at thought of flying, Reia hesitated, she hated heights, but the mountain climb was arduous and her body was exhausted from the journey. Not wanting to insult the great dragon, she takes a hard swallow of air and braces herself as she accepts the fire god's invitation. "You should feel honored, young human. Not many have gotten to ride atop a dragon." The great deity of flame remarks as Reia seats herself astride the mighty dragon, "Now hold on."

It hadn't taken long for the dragon to ascend into the air and make the quick descent down the mountain. It was more than Reia could bare, however, as she quickly climbs off and stumbles over to a tree, wretching as she leans against it. She felt sick to her stomach as she looked at the vomit on the ground in front of her. Pausing to stare at her for a moment or two the dragon flew back up the mountain. Shaken from the flight down; Reia merely stood where she was for a minute or two in order to regain her footing. She hated heights; riding a horse was bad enough, but she vowed to never fly on a dragon again. Having regained her composure, Reia climbs back on to her horse and begins the journey back to Tysomi Village.

Back in Isura, Kenzji had just received news of his sister's death from the slave girl who had befriended Iyata as Fei Ling forced her to her knees so that they were both kneeling before Kenzji.

Not bothering to take his eye off the slave girl, Kenzji directed his next statement to Fei Ling. "Tell me, Fei Ling, were you not also left there to help my sister guard the captives, and choose your next statement <u>very</u> carefully." He said emphasizing the word: Very.

Stammering over his words, Fei Ling knew by Kenzji's tone of voice that bringing the slave girl before him might've been a mistake.

"I was in another part of the fortress, and was unaware of what was happening. I found her body later." He replied.

The slave girl dared a chuckle. "Good help can be so hard to find." She remarked harshly.

"Hold your tongue, slave." Fei Ling retorted as he shifted his gaze to her with a glare and then turning it back to Kenzji who already had his hand on the hilt of his sword.

Ignoring, Fei Ling's warning the slave girl's chuckle soon turned into uproarious laughter at Fei Ling's expense. She knew as well as he did bringing her there would be his undoing. Her laughter was cut short when she felt the edge of Kenzji's sword blade on the skin of her neck as blood trickled from it, but whose blood was it? Fearfully, she dared to look over only to see the decapitated corpse of Fei Ling on the floor as his head rolled out in front of her, making her shudder in disgust.

Removing his sword from the woman's neck, Kenzji used a flick of his wrist to sling the blood from the blade. "His failure was not your own, slave. As I told the Kaemouri child, 'I am not the monster I appear to be.' Now grant me the honor of telling me how my sister died." He said to her placing the sword back in its scabbard.

"In honor combat doing her duty to you, Lord Ketsuro." The slave woman responded as she shifted her gaze upon him. This news pleased Kenzji greatly as he turned to walk away. "One more thing, Lord Ketsuro," The slave woman called as Kenzji stopped to look back at her, "The one who did it; he said something after ending her life. He said, 'A Shikanacan's death.'"

"My people consider it an honor to be killed by one of their own in honor combat. It was, as he put it, a Shikanacan's death." Kenzji responded as he turned to a couple of guards who were waiting at the nearby entrance of the room, "This woman has brought me word of my sister, and while it was disheartening for me, she deserves to be rewarded for her bravery. She has family in Kaylah, send them a decent amount of gold along with my thanks. As for her, see to it she is cleaned and fed before her journey back to the Northern Fortress."

Finishing his statement to the guards, Kenzji exits the room. Walking down the hallways of Isura, he could feel a seething rage welling up inside of him, along with a mix of turmoil and sorrow over the loss of his sister.

So great were the feelings of these emotions that they triggered the dark power within Kenzji as it began growing uncontrollably making it difficult for him to walk and causing him great pain as he tightly clutched his hand over his heart. Using the wall for support and struggling through the pain he managed to make his way to a nearby dojo he used for training. Inside he made his way to the center of the room giving him enough clearance from each of the walls as he unleashed his dark power in a single red aura, shouting in a mix of rage and pain, "TESARAH!" until all his power was expended and his feelings of turmoil subsided. Weakened by the sudden expenditure of power, he collapses to the ground, falling into deep state of dormancy.

Back at Tysomi Village, Saiera and Iyata were spending time with the recovering Sakuris when a knock came from their door and a voice announced "Masseuse."

Looking at the door, Saiera became puzzled. "Ma-what?" She remarked as she went over and opened it.

There was something about the voice that seemed familiar to Sakuris as he peered from his bed, past Saiera to see an oddly familiar face. "You, I know you, don't I?" He asked curiously.

"It's time for your regular semi-weekly massage, Lord Kaemouri." The masseuse remarked as she stepped inside with Saiera looking at her puzzled. "Beloved?" She asked curiously.

"It's alright, my love." Sakuris remarked getting a good look at the masseuse. "Kiyanah," He said chuckling at the realization of who it was, "I've not seen you since childhood. Come sit." He then looked at Saiera, "Saiera, come, I wish for you to meet an old friend of mine."

"You must be Lady Kaemouri." Kiyanah remarked as she turned toward the approaching Saiera, "I am honored to meet you; Kiyanah, daughter of Kaideshie, at your service ma'am. Your friend at the inn told me you were here. I hope my coming to visit is okay."

"Don't be silly Kiyanah, you and your mother were always welcome in my parents' home no point changing that on my account." Sakuris responded cheerfully as he turned to Saiera, "Beloved, this is the daughter of the woman my father would go to for his massages I once told you about."

"Yes, I remember." Saiera responded as she stepped toward her husband, "A pleasure to meet you Kaideshie-san."

"Mommy?" Iyata asked as she stepped forward and stood next to her mother.

"Oh, and who is this?" Kiyanah remarked taking note of Iyata's presence as she knelt in front of her, "Hello there, little one."

Iyata quickly backed away as she cowered behind Saiera's leg. "Don't take it personally, Kiyanah. Like me, my daughter has been through an ordeal." Sakuris remarked as Kiyanah stood back up, "Iyata, it's okay, little one. She's an old friend. Say hello to her." Nervously, Iyata came from behind Saiera's leg and looked at her father who beckoned her to say hello to Kiyanah.

"H-hello." Iyata said nervously.

"Hello, Iyata, was it?" Kiyanah said cheerfully as Iyata nodded, "Iyata, my name is Kiyanah. I've son who is about your age. His name is Mitsuo.

Perhaps later, if your parents allow, you can come meet him." Shifting her gaze from Iyata to Sakuris and Saiera, Kiyanah smiles warmly, "Kaemouri-san, you have a beautiful family; my congratulations to you. Now, I feel as though I've intruded long enough. Lady Kaemouri, it was a pleasure meeting you. I bid you all good night."

"It was nice seeing you again, Kiyanah. Have a pleasant evening." Sakuris responded as he laid back in bed. Watching Kiyanah as she walked the door, Sakuris couldn't help but chuckle and smile, "Small world, never would've imagined seeing her again after so many years."

"I can relate." Saiera remarked referring to her chance meeting with her brother. Having a guess to what his beloved was referring to Sakuris took Saiera's hand into his own.

"You refer to your brother. Yes I can imagine how meeting up with him again must've been for you. Still it must've done your heart some good knowing he was still alive." He remarked as Saiera touched her other hand to his. Feeling her do this, Sakuris brought her hand up and gently kissed it.

"Sometimes I wondered if he ever made it out." Saiera responded as she sat down on the edge of the bed. Iyata, sensing Saiera's worry, merely went over and hugged her mother's leg as she rested her head on Saiera's knee. Looking at her daughter, Saiera smiled warmly at her as she ran her fingers through Iyata's hair, "Hello, little one."

"I wonder if Dayis would be interested in returning to Shikanaca with us." Sakuris remarked. Saiera merely looked back at him and shook her head.

"He and I already spoke about that. He decided to return to the forest with a slave girl he met." She responded.

"Slave girl?" Sakuris asked curiously. Saiera nodded her head as she explained the events that had taken place in Sakuris's absence, "Shame he won't be returning, but at the same time, I suppose I can understand where he is coming from. Still, at least you know where you can find him now. As for this slave girl, I hope your brother knows what he's doing. Ninjattas have always been known for their cruelty toward slaves along with those who would aid them."

"What's done is done, husband." Saiera responded as she laid her head upon her husband's shoulder.

"Still, if your brother has even half the strength I suspect he does. I'm sure he'll be just fine. Now, perhaps it's time I rested. Why don't you go ahead and return to the inn with Iyata." Sakuris remarked as he hugged Saiera and kissed her on the top of her head. Not wanting to part from her husband, Saiera looked up at him with sadness in her eyes as if to say: I don't want to go. "Go on, Saiera, I'll be fine. Besides, our little one needs some down time of her own."

With tears forming in her eyes, Saiera slowly nods. Smiling gently, Sakuris uses the tip of his thumb to wipe her tears away. "Come now, my love, there's no need for tears. Return to the inn with Iyata." Kissing her gently on the forehead, Sakuris allows his wife to stand from the bed as she wipes the remainder of her tears away.

"Iyata, come dear." Saiera remarks, extending a hand for her daughter. Leaving Sakuris to recover in the clinic, Saiera takes her daughter by the hand and returns to the inn. Excited to be in a comfortable room again, Iyata rushes in and hops onto a bed in the back of the room.

"Mommy, when will we be returning to Shikanaca?" Iyata asks curiously.

"I don't know, dear. Your father will need time to recover from his injury. Soon I hope." Saiera responds as she takes her long knife from about her waist and sets aside on a nearby table, "For now, little one, let's get you cleaned up and ready for bed."

"Okay, mommy." Iyata responds agreeably as she allows Saiera to scoop her up into her arms. Carrying her to a nearby bath, Saiera lights the wood underneath it so that it may heat up. Undressing her daughter, she places her in the bath.

"Mommy it's still cold." Iyata protests, shivering as she hugs herself to stay warm.

"Don't worry little one. It'll warm up soon enough." Saiera responds as she reaches to a nearby shelf of oils and chooses one. Opening the bottle, the sweet smell of flowers fills the air as Saiera inhales the scent, "Here, Iyata, tell me what you think."

As Saiera places the bottle before her daughter's nose, Iyata inhales the scent. "Smells like home." She responds.

"I'd say, 'it's just right then.'" Saiera remarks as she grabs a nearby linen rag and lets a few drops of the oil fall upon it and begins washing the grime from her daughter. As she did, Iyata began to relax as the water became heated to a more desirable temperature. Using a nearby pale of water, Saiera puts out the fire underneath to prevent the water from overheating.

"Iyata, once we've finished mommy has a surprise for you in her bag; something to help you feel more at ease." Saiera remarks as she uses the oil from before to wash Iyata's hair with, "Rinse, little one."

Dunking herself into the warm water, Iyata allows her hair and body to be rinsed of the grime ridden oil as she rises back to the surface. Using one of the linen towels supplied by the inn, Saiera wraps her daughter up as she lifts her from the tub, and removes the wooden stopper in the drain to let the water drain to the outside of the building.

Drying her daughter off, Saiera takes her back up to the front of the room and sets her down. "Wait here little one, mommy will be right back." She remarks as she turns to walk away from Iyata. Going over to her bag, she a rifles through for some clothing for her little one to wear, "Here, little one, get dressed, and then mommy will give you your surprise."

Eager to know what her mother had gotten for her, Iyata hurries to dress herself in an undergarment and a child sized sleeping gown made of silk. Fully dressed and ready for bed, Iyata smiles happily at her mother. "Now then, Iyata, I have one other item for you." Saiera remarks as she once again goes over to her bag and pulls out one final item: A doll, Iyata's favorite. Turning back to Iyata and walking over to her she presents it to her daughter whose eyes widen in surprise.

"MY DOLLY!" The Kaemouri child cheers excitedly as she accepts the doll from her mother and hugs it close to her, "Thank you, Mommy!" Excited by having her doll back, the young Kaemouri hugs her mother in gratitude. Smiling upon her daughter, Saiera wraps her arms around her, happy to have her back with her.

A knock soon comes from the door. "Oh, I wonder who that could be." Saiera remarks as she releases Iyata from her embrace, "Iyata, wait here, little one. I'll go see who it is." Turning from Iyata, Saiera walks over to the door and opens it to see Kiyanah standing there with a young boy just a little older than Iyata, "Oh, Kaideshie-san, was it?" She remarks curiously.

"Kobanwa, Lady Kaemouri, is this a good time?" Kiyanah responds wishing Saiera a good evening.

"Well, I suppose, please come in." Saiera responds watching Kiyanah and the young boy step inside.

"Lady Kaemouri, this is my son, Mitsuo." Kiyanah remarks motioning to her son, "Mitsuo, say hello."

"Kobanwa, Lady Kaemouri, hajimimashite." Mitsuo says sweetly, with a humble bow as he wishes Lady Kaemouri a good evening and acknowledging it is nice to meet her.

With a cheerful chuckle, Saiera acknowledges the young Kaideshie responding "Hello, little one." As she returns his bow, "Awfully polite for someone your age."

"Mother has been teaching me." Mitsuo responds humbly.

Leaning forward, Kiyanah whispers into her son's ear, "*Sweetie, why don't introduce yourself to Iyata.*" She said motioning to Iyata who was now sitting down on the floor playing with her doll.

Mitsuo walked over and sat next to Iyata. "Are you a girl?" He asked her.

Startled by his presence, Iyata looked at him and stood up to back away. "Are you a boy?" She responded answering his question with another.

Mituso nodded. "Yes, I am. My name is Mitsuo Kaideshie." He said to her, introducing himself with confidence.

Iyata stepped back toward the bed. "Mother, I'm afraid. He talks funny." She remarks causing Mitsuo look down to the ground sadly.

"Iyata, that wasn't nice." Saiera said to her scornfully, "Maybe you should say you're sorry."

Agreeing with her mother the Kaemouri child walks over to Mitsuo and apologizes remarking, "I've never seen a boy before".

A gentle smile comes across Mitsuo's face as he responds, "It's alright, because I've never seen a girl before."

Having broken the ice with the young boy, Iyata sits back down to continue playing as she invites him to join her.

"You have any toy swords. I like swords." Mitsuo responded.

Laughing with childish innocence Iyata tells him, "No, silly, I'm mean with my dolly."

"Dolls are for girls." Mitsuo remarked.

"And swords are for boys. What's your point?" Iyata says to him as he shrugs.

"I don't know. It's just that where I'm from, the sons are taught the art of swordsmanship when they're young." He responded.

Saiera and Kiyanah looked their children as they continued to conversation. "Children can be adorable can't they?" Kiyanah remarked.

Saiera laughed a bit. "Yes they can, until they're teenagers." She responded.

Kiyanah couldn't help but laugh, remarking, "Tell me about it. I annoyed my parents to death when I was a teenager; especially when I brought my boyfriend home for them to meet. I've never seen my father so protective."

Saiera laughed a bit. "I know what you mean, my first boyfriend kept me out after curfew, and when I got home my mother was so angry; she had to keep herself from laughing. I was sent to bed without any supper. I didn't mind, I had eaten earlier that night anyways."

Kiyanah laughed and responded, "I remember those days. I thought my husband and I would last forever, but sadly it wasn't meant to be. He died while I was still pregnant with Mitsuo." As the two of them conversed, Saiera offered Kiyanah a seat and asked if she'd like some wine.

Graciously accepting Saiera's offer, Kiyanah sat down at a nearby table as Saiera poured some wine for the both of them. Turning to Mitsuo, Kiyanah calls to him, ""Mitsuo, sweetie, will you be okay while Miss Saiera and I get better acquainted."

Hearing his mother's question, Mitsuo momentarily stops playing with Iyata in order to respond, "Yes, mother, I think I'll get better acquainted with Iyata."

With a chuckle, Saiera takes a sip of wine and remarks, "He is very smart for his age."

Kiyanah looks to her son as she sips from her wine. "He's studied under the best tutors. I keep him well educated. He can read on a high level. What about Iyata, has she had formal education?" She asked.

"Nothing I would call formal. Though, I have been teaching her about her heritage as a Shikanacan-Sikonian." Saiera responds taking another sip of wine.

Kiyanah looked at her. "You're not Shikanacan?" She asks puzzled.

"No, why do you ask?" Saiera responds.

"Oh, no reason, curiosity I guess. I meant no offense." Kiyanah responds as she finishes the last of the wine in her cup and stands from the table, "Well, this has been a lovely conversation, but it's late, and I would not want to overstay my welcome. By the way, your friend Akisarah invited me to come stay in Shikanaca."

"I'm sure it can be arranged." Saiera responds as she stands from the table.

"Thank you, Lady Kaemouri. Well, I should be going." Kiyanah remarks turning to Mitsuo, "Mitsuo, come, dear, let's let the Kaemouries get some sleep. It's past your bed time as it is."

"Yes, mother." Mitsuo responds as he stands and bows before Iyata, "Good night, Iyata."

Watching him as he runs over to his mother, Iyata couldn't help but chuckle as she watches Mitsuo bow before her mother, wishing her a good night.

Night drug on as Tallinyia made her rounds in the clinic. Hearing her announce her presence as she knocks on his door, a sleeping Sakuris slowly wakes up and calls for her to enter.

"Sorry to disturb you, Lord Kaemouri. I just need to change your bandages." Tallinyia remarks as she enters the room with a bag of medical supplies.

Slowly sitting up, Sakuris watches her as she walks over to him. "How are you feeling?" Tallinyia asks sweetly as she opens her med bag and pulls out some fresh bandages.

"I've been better. Still, the antidote seems to be helping. I feel stronger than when I was brought in." Sakuris replies as Tallinyia cuts away his old bandages and checks his wound.

"Well, there's no sign of infection. A few more days rest and you'll be strong enough to travel." Tallinyia responds as she takes the fresh bandages and applies them to the wound.

"We could use a healer where I'm from. Would you be interested?" Sakuris remarks inviting Tallinyia to return with them.

Surprised by the invitation, Tallinyia hesitates to answer, but responds, "You honor me with your invitation, Lord Kaemouri. Business has been rather slow here. Though in my profession, maybe that's a good thing."

"Take the rest of tonight to think it over." Sakuris remarks as Tallinyia finishes bandaging his wound.

"Thank you, I will." Tallinyia responds as she collects her supplies and heads back to the door. Before exiting, she turns to Sakuris and wishes him a good night. He wishes her the same and then watches her exit the room.

Over the next few days, Sakuris recovered more and more from his ordeal, and was soon strong enough to travel. Gathering all their supplies into a single wagon they had purchased in the village, Sakuris and his friends were ready to return home to Shikanaca; accompanying them were Tallinyia and Kiyanah with her son, Mitsuo.

Once everyone was ready, the small group leaves Tysomi Village and makes their way back to Shikanaca.

Back at his forest hideaway, Dayis had used the wolf skin he had obtained the night he left Tysomi to make a cloak for Sei Lyn. As they sat near an open fire in his hideaway, he stood and presented the cloak to her. Gasping in surprise as her eyes widened with excitement, Sei Lyn graciously accepted it into her possession. When she did, a most unusual thing happened. Just like before, memories of a long forgotten past of hunting and a mysterious island again flooded her memory.

"What was that?" She asked aloud as though she had relived the memories.

"Sei Lyn, are you okay?" Dayis asked concerned for her well-being.

"I-I'm not sure. The last few days, I've had these strange flashes of what appeared to be memories. The first one occurred the night you brought me here when we encountered that wolf. I saw a memory of large wolves and an island, somewhere in a great fog, and just now, when you handed me the cloak; I . . . I saw myself hunting on the same strange island." She responded as she wrapped the cloak around herself only to have her head filled with more memories, "It's happening again."

"What do you see?" Dayis remarks.

"Women, an island of women," Sei Lyn responds as she feels a sharp pain starting to rise in her head. Bringing her hand to her forehead, she groans from the pain as the memory continues. "They wear the skins of animals." Sei Lyn continues as the pain in her head gets worse causing her to scream.

"Sei Lyn?" Dayis exclaims taking her into his arms.

"It's . . . it's gone. The memory is gone." Sei Lyn responds, "I don't understand."

Dayis thought for a moment and remembered the liquid Daeloshe had presented to him, saying he would need it. "Now that I think about it, Daeloshe did present a bottle of liquid to me saying I would need it.

Could've been some kind of memory inhibitor. Perhaps, it's best we take you to Shikanaca to see Master Kaemouri. He might know how to help."

Sei Lyn nods in agreement as the two of them gather their belongings and prepare for the journey to Shikanaca. Stepping outside the hideaway, the two of them mount their horse and ride off into the forest as they venture to the Shikanacan stronghold.

Chapter 16

In the months that followed, life slowly returned to normal in Shikanaca. Sakuris, recovered from his wound. Kayah and Akisarah were finally wed and it was time for the birth of Kayah's baby. She was carried to the clinic screaming as she went into labor with her child. Tallinyia escorted her over to a bed and laid her down. She continued screaming as each contraction came; letting out every obscenity known to man. Tallinyia remained calm as she motioned for everyone else to leave. They did so and waited outside the room.

Anxiously awaiting news, Akisarah began pacing the floor back and forth as Saiera watched him, stating "Akisarah you pace anymore and you'll wear a hole in the ground."

"Just nervous, I guess. I've never been a father before. What if I mess it up?" He responded.   "Akisarah you can't think that way. If I had, there's no telling what might've happened with Iyata. You'll be fine. You're a fine young man and an even better fighter." Saiera responded doing her best to reassure him.

Remaining silent throughout their conversation, Sakuris sat on a nearby bench. His expression showed he was as nervous as Akisarah. Kayah may have been Akisarah's wife, but she was still Sakuris's sister and that frightened him. If something should go wrong and Kayah didn't make it, he would be devastated. Having made a silent promise to his mother and father the day they died that he would always look after her, he would be devastated if she died giving birth. Trying not to think about it he kept reassuring himself she would be fine. She was a Kaemouri after all, and not only that, but she was also the sister of the Arch-Dragon. So, silently, he sat and waited.

Time drug on as seconds turned into minutes and minutes turned into hours. What was taking so long? Finally, Tallinyia came out of the room. Sakuris quickly stood up as Akisarah stopped pacing. Both men looking at her blankly, she stood by as Sakuris asked of his sister's condition

Informing him that his sister safe, Tallinyia informs those present that the young KAemouri and her newborn were both safe and ready to receive visitors.

Sakuris held Saiera back as she stepped toward the door. *"Akisarah deserves to go first."* He whispered to her as he watched Akisarah enter Kayah's room.

Saiera looked at him and then Sakuris and nodded in agreement. Also present in the room were Saiera's brother, Dayis, and their newest ally, Sei Lyn. Feeling her brother's arm around her should shoulder, Saiera looked at him with a smile as she allowed him to hug her close.

Holding her new born baby, Kayah awaited her beloved as he entered. "Kayah, how are you?" He asked her.

She looked at him as he sat on the bed next to her. "I'm fine, beloved, exhausted, but fine." She responded as she presented her child to him, "Your son, my love; I haven't named him yet. I wanted you to do it."

Akisarah took his son and held him in his arms. He was small, but healthy. Smiling at the newborn sleeping in his arms, Akisarah thinks of the perfect name for him, "I know just the name. We'll call him Ishiemae; in Kaylahn it means gift of heaven."

"A good name, beloved." Kayah responded with a smile. In awe of the moment the new parents merely gazed upon their new born son who awoke crying.

Chuckling, Akisarah handed the new born Ishiemae back to his mother. "He's hungry, I think."

Smiling, Kayah took her son back into her arms and offered him a breast to drink from. Latching onto her, Ishiemae drink greedily at the nutrient rich milk that flowed into his mouth. Entering the room with Saiera, Sakuris walks over to his sister and hugs her. "How are you feeling?" He asks.

Smiling at her brother, Kayah informs him she is well. Seeing little Ishiemae in his mother's arms, Sakuris smiles with pride at the newborn Shikanacan.

"He looks like his father." He comments looking to Aksiarah, "Perhaps one day he'll grow to be as strong as him."

"Would you care to hold him, Nii-sama?" Kayah asked presenting Ishiemae to her brother.

Smiling at his newborn nephew, Sakuris takes him into his arms and holds him. "Hello there little one; welcome to the Dragon Clan." He says to him softly. Ishiemae merely coos in his uncle's arms. Looking over Sakuris's shoulder, Saiera merely smiles upon her new nephew and waves to him, as Sakuris lays him back in Kayah's arms.

"Sakuris, can you guys give me and a Kayah a minute?" Akisarah asks calmly looking at his brother in law. Gently nodding, Sakuris agrees and leads everyone else outside the room.

When everyone else had gone, Akisarah leaned forward and kissed Kayah gently. She merely smiled at him. "Tallinyia said I'd be able to leave in a week." She said to him.

"I'm happy to hear that." He responds as he touches a hand to his son's head, "I wish my parents were alive to see this day."

"I'm sure they'd be proud of the man you've become." Kayah responds. Exhausted from labor, she lays back in the bed.

Knowing Kayah needs to rest, Akisarah kisses her forehead. "I guess I should go and let you sleep." He says to her.

Once again offering a breast to Ishiemae to suckle from, Kayah nods in agreement with her husband. "Very well, my love, come back and see us later." She responds as she lets Ishiemae latch onto her to drink.

Embracing his beloved one last time, Akisarah exits the room, leaving Kayah to feed her newborn.

Tallinyia soon came back into the room and felt Kayah's head. "How are you feeling?" She asked checking Kayah's temperature.

"Ok, I guess." Kayah responds as Ishiemae releases her breast from his mouth and falls asleep in her arms.

Drawing her hand back from Kayah's head, Tallinyia takes a measure of Kayah's pulse. "Well, your temperature and pulse rate are normal. That's very good." She remarks cheerfully pouring some water into a wooden cup for Kayah to sip on, "You lost a lot of water during the delivery. You should drink some, now."

Handing the cup to Kayah, Tallinyia watches her as she accepts it and begins to sip on the cool water from it. When she had finished she handed the cup back to Tallinyia who then took it and set it aside. In need of rest, Kayah merely laid back on the bed and allowed herself to drift off into slumber.

In quiet contentment, Kayah slept easy as she dreamed of her union with Akisarah. She had worn a beautiful ceremonial kimono, while Akisarah was had worn a formal Gi. The two of them were standing in front of Sakuris who was reciting the traditional words as he handed Akisarah a gold dagger. Kayah enjoyed her dream until she soon woke up to see Tallinyia standing over her. "So, you're finally awake." She said to her.

Kayah looked at her and nodded. "How long have I been asleep?" She asked curiously as she stretched and yawned.

"Not long, about two hours, maybe. How are you feeling?" Tallinyia responds as she changes Ishiemae.

"I can't remember the last time I slept so well. Where's my son?" Kayah asks eager to see her son again.

Smiled as she presented Ishiemae to his mother, she informs Kayah her son fine and allows her to take the new born back into her arms

"There's my baby boy." She saiys cheerfully opening her kimono to offer her son a breast. Taking it willingly into his mouth, the newborn Kamikawi hungrily feeds off Kayah's breast milk. His suckling was so loud Kayah could hear him swallowing. "Oh my, an aggressive little eater, aren't you?" She said teasingly as she looked down at him smiling.

Though things had been going well in Shikanca, all was not well in the rest of the nation. Using the power of Sakuris's sacred blade, Norakatsu had conquered much of the known land as he seized the wealth of the smaller villages and added it to his own. Kenzji had awoken from the slumber his sudden surge of power had caused him to fall into, and during his long sleep his only thoughts were of revenge for his sister's death. He intended to kill Sakuris and would let nothing stop him.

Having amassed a sizable army, he stood ready to attack Shikanaca fortress. At the forefront of his assault force was the red demon that had been unleashed upon Shikanaca the first time it had been destroyed. From horseback, clad in in his family's armor and armed with the Ketsuro family sword, he signaled the attack as he sent his demon charging through Shikacana's southern wall allowing his forces to pour in behind it as they began slaughtering all they found, women and children alike.

Hearing the crashing of the wall as it shook the ground. Kayah gasped in horror. "That was the southern wall!" she exclaimed as Sakuris came rushing into the room, "Nii-sama?"

He was bleeding from his mouth and arms. "The fortress is under attack. We have to leave now." He said hurriedly as he struggled to maintain his stance.

Tallinyia looked at him. "But Kayah's too weak to go anywhere right now." She protested as an Isuran soldier attempted to rush into the room causing the women to scream in fear. Disarming the soldier, Sakuris ran him through with his own blade as he kicked his lifeless body down to the floor.

"I'll carry her, but we have to leave now." Sakuris responds going over to his sister. Setting the sword aside, he takes Kayah into his arms. "Grab Ishiemae." He says quickly to Tallinyia.

Handing Ishiemae over to Tallinyia, Kayah allows her brother to carry her out of the room with Tallinyia following close behind.

As they rushed through the fortress, the scent of blood filled the air. Looking around them, they could hear the panicked screams of the citizenry who were attempting to evacuate. In the center of the fortress, Sakuris could see the red demon as it rampaged through, destroying anything in its path. The guards did their best to fight it off, but each one fell prey to the immense monster.

At the gate, with horses ready to go, Yu-Ka-Mi awaited Sakuris and the others. "Help my sister." He called to her as flaming arrows flew over their heads. The fighters ducked out of the way and watched as the arrows struck several of the homes. Yu-Ka-Mi hurriedly helped Kayah onto her horse.

More of Isura's army poured into the fortress as they began ransacking homes and plundering anything they could find. Observing this, Sakuris climbed onto his horse and made ready to leave with the others. Protesting she be the one to carry Ishiemae out of the fortress, Kayah took him from Tallinyia as she held him close to her.

In horror she watched as the demon once again destroyed her homeland. "My gods, Sakuris, it's happening again." She said with mild panic in her voice.

"No, it's not. Not if I can help it." Sakuris responded reassuringly.

"You don't have the sacred blade, you can't face it." Kayah said beginning to panic.

Riding over to his sister and places both hands to her cheeks and he turns her to face him. "Kayah, I'm right here. I know you're scared, but right now, we can't think about the past. I need to get you and your baby away from here. Now I need you to be brave for me, can you do that?" He says to her as she slowly nods in response, "Good, now come on."

He then nudges his horse and rides off into the forest with Kayah following close behind him. Quickly climbing onto her horse, Yu-Ka-Mi reaches down and helps Tallinyia climb on in front of her. She nudges the horse and the two of them quickly followed behind the siblings. As they make their escape, an arrow flies at them from behind as it pierces into Yu-Ka-Mi's shoulder causing her to cry out in pain.

Hearing his friend cry out, Sakuris turns to see the arrow sticking out from her shoulder blade. "Yu-Ka-Mi!" He cries out, but Yu-Ka-Mi shakes her head and motions for them to continue. There was no time for them to stop now as the travelers continued to flee into the forest until they came across a small Shikanacan camp site, where the others were waiting for them.

Sakuris stopped his horse as he rode into camp. "Yu-Ka-Mi's wounded, help her!" He ordered a few of the remaining guards. They nodded as they rushed over and helped her from her horse, and observed where the arrow had struck her. Tallinyia quickly climbed down and rushed over to the guards as they leaned Yu-Ka-Mi against a tree with her back to them so not to disturb the arrow. "I can treat this. It's not bad." She said; breaking the arrow as Yu-Ka-Mi whinced in pain.

Observing what was left, it had become apparent to Tallinyia the arrow hadn't gone all the way through. "Yu-Ka-Mi the arrow didn't go all the way through. I'm gonna have to push it the rest of the way. Brace yourself, it's gonna hurt, a lot." She says informing Yu-Ka-Mi of she was about to do.

Gritting her teeth, Yu-Ka-Mi prepared herself as Tallinyia took a small dagger from her guard belt and, using the hilt of it, rammed the arrow the rest of the way through her shoulder causing her to cry out in pain as tears flowed from her eyes. Pulling the remainder of the arrow from Yu-Ka-Mi's shoulder, Tallinyia did the best she could to clean and bandage the wound.

Turning Yu-Ka-Mi around, Tallinyia helped her sit to rest. Going over and kneeling beside her, Sakuris took Yu-Ka-Mi's hand in his own. "Yu-Ka-Mi, don't die on me. That's an order." He remarked half humorously, and half seriously.

Looking at Sakuris, Yu-Ka-Mi chuckles weakly, "Funny, Sakuris." With a sly grin, Sakuris gives her an approving nod as Saiera approaches him from behind and places her hands on his shoulders.

"Come on, beloved, there's nothing more you can do." She said to him as she helped him stand.

Turning to Tallinyia, a cold stare rested in his eyes. "Tallinyia if she dies, it's your head." He said with a serious tone. He had known Yu-Ka-Mi since childhood. They had met on the road to Tysomi village after the destruction of the first Shikanaca. She was the first to take him and his sister in and look after them. Now he would protect her like a child would his favorite toy.

Tallinyia nodded as she helped Yu-Ka-Mi to her feet. "She'll be okay. I'll take good care of her." She said to him as she led Yu-Ka-Mi to a nearby empty tent. A few animal skins had been rolled out for anyone to sleep on. She laid Yu-Ka-Mi down on one of them and looked outside the tent. "Bring Kayah and the baby. I can look after the injured here in this tent. Is anyone else hurt?" She called out.

Everyone looked around and shook their heads as a few guards helped Kayah and Ishiemae from their horse and lead them over to Tallinyia's tent to let the two of them rest on the animal skins. Due to the commotion from before, Ishiemae had been crying the entire time they had ridden. To calm him down, Kayah waited for the men to leave and opened her top to offer a breast for him to nurse from as she gently rocked him while singing.

While Kayah nursed her child, Sakuris looked around the camp site. "Is everyone here?" He called out.

Saiera looked at him. "A few of the guards didn't make it, and Dayis and Sei Lyn are missing, but I know my brother. He would've taken her to his cave in the forest." She responded.

Sakuris looked around at the few graves that had been dug, disgusted at the losses. The Dragon Clan was one of the most powerful clans in Japan and it was overtaken. Kenzji was behind the attack and he knew it as he looked into the distance at the burning ruins of the once prosperous Shikanaca.

The Red Demon had left and the Isuran forces had retreated once they had nothing left to plunder or people to kill. Continuing to observe the fortress, Sakuris leaned against the trunk of a tree, banging it with the side of his fist as Saiera stood next to him. *"Kenzji and the demon; there has to be a connection between them but what is it?"* He thought to himself before looking to Saiera, stating "Get everyone together." Saiera could see the fire in her beloved's eyes as she nodded and quickly worked to assemble everyone together.

That night, everyone sat around a small camp fire as Sakuris stood up. His wounds had stopped bleeding. "Citizens of Shikanaca and members of the Dragon Clan, this is a sad day in our history. Isura has gone too far and attacked our peaceful fortress, and while we may have suffered some losses, we are not yet defeated." He announced, "As Arch-Dragon and high master of the clan, I swear by family name; and the name of my ancestor, that the Isurans will pay!" He called holding his fist high. The remaining citizens of Shikanaca cheered as he said this.

Plans were quickly thought out for a counter attack that would decide the fate of the Dragon Clan forever. Though there were some protests, Sakuris knew his plan was the best one they could come up with, but with so few Dragon Clansman left, the probability for success was low. Unwaivered by his present reality, Sakuris knew the Wyvern Clan had to be stopped or it would continue to bring suffering to the people of Japan.

Haunted by the thought as he lay awake in his tent in that night, he sat up and looked around as Saiera rested beside him. Placing a hand to her cheek, he smiles gently upon her and kissis her gently. Awoken by his touch, she kissed him back. Sorrow filling his eyes, Sakuris gently gazes upon his beloved. "What's wrong love?" She asks him.

"Can't sleep, I guess. How's Iyata?" He responded as he laid back and stared at the top of the tent.

"She was fine when I checked on her earlier. Sakuris, what are we to do, now?" Saiera responds as she turns on her side and snuggles up to Sakuris.

Gently kissing her forehead, Sakuris places his arm around her. "I wish I knew. Shikanaca's in shambles, Norakatsu has the sacred blade and our numbers dwindle." He responded despairingly. Things seemed grim for Sakuris and his people as he laid in his tent with Saiera. "Saiera, wait here, I'm going to go get some air." Sakuris remarked as he rose from the animal skin and dressed into some more appropriate attire.

"Will you alright by yourself?" Saiera asked concerned as she watched her husband change clothing.

"Yeah, just wait here for a bit." He remarks as he exits the tent and heads to the edge of the camp to head off into the forest.

"Where will you go?" A voice from behind asked him. Turning to around to see who had spoken to him, Sakuris was met with the faces of Siniless and his daughter.

"Daddy?" Iyata asked as Sakuris knelt down to take her into his embrace. Rushing over to her father's arms, Iyata allows him to pick her up and hold her close to him.

"Hey, little one, it's late you should be asleep." He gently reminded her.

"She had a bad dream and couldn't get back to sleep. So I thought I'd bring her out here for a bit." Sinileass responded.

"I guess we're all having trouble sleeping tonight." Sakuris responded as he looked at Iyata and tapped her nose with his index finger, "What's wrong, little one, bad dream."

Iyata merely nodded in reply. "Grandpa Sinileass brought me out hoping it would help me go back to sleep."

"He did, well I'm also having trouble sleeping." Sakuris said to her, "I was just about to go for a walk to clear my head a bit. Why don't you go back with Grandpa Sinileass and try to get some sleep, okay?"

"Okay, Daddy." Iyata responded as Sakuris smiled and held her close as he gently kissed her forehead before setting her down.

Walking over to them, Sinileass took Iyata by the hand as he looked at Sakuris. "Will you be alright on your own?" He asked concerned for Sakuris's well-being.

"Yeah, I just need to clear my head for a bit. Go ahead and take Iyata and see if you can put her bed." Sakuris responds as he watches Sinileass take Iyata by the hand and lead her away.

He turns back to Sakuris just long enough to say, "Be careful" before leading Iyata back to his tent.

Leaving the camp, Sakuris finds himself walking through the forest for a little while, making sure to keep the camp within site. Standing in the stillness of the night, a deathly quiet fills Sakuris's ears. *"It's so quiet. Is this what's it's like to stand on the eve of battle? Father, I need you here with me. I can't do this alone."* Sakuris think's to himself as he feels the cool night wind blow against him.

Tension hung heavy on the air. Sakuris knew not what he was about to face. Without the Sacred Blade, would he even have a chance of facing

Kenzji and the Red Demon? Closing his eyes, and inhaling deeply, Sakuris stilled his mind and in a single moment of clarity realized some hope remained. His forces still possessed two of the sacred weapons: Akisarah's spear and Saiera's long knife.

There was a chance, a small chance, but a chance that with the combined might of his force of fighters and the two remaining sacred blades that they could possibly succeed after all. With this renewed confidence, Sakuris felt a glimmer of hope spark within him as he returned back to the small camp and entered into his tent to see Saiera sleeping peacefully.

Gazing at her lovingly, Sakuris crawled over beside her and kissed her gently whispering, "*Sleep well, beloved.*" Before falling back asleep.

When morning came, Sakuris awoke to the sound of Akisarah calling his name from outside the tent. He cleaned himself up and dressed as he stepped outside to meet his brother-in-law. "Yes Akisarah, what is it?" He responded when saw him.

Akisarah looked at him as the sun rose slowly over the forest. Looking back at his brother-in-law, Sakuris could see a fire in his eye he had never seen before. "When do we attack?" He asked eagerly, his hands aching with blood lust.

"Get everyone up." Sakuris responded, "I want the women and those who shouldn't be fighting escorted somewhere safe. Everyone else is to assemble in the center of camp in one hour."

Akisarah bows in acknowledgement of his orders and walks away to carry them out. Returning to his tent, Sakuris opens a small chest of a few of the belongings he had been able to save from Shikanaca. Among them was a suit of mail overlaid with dragonscales known to Sakuris's people as dragonmail.

"Beloved?" Saiera asked as she awoke to see Sakuris holding the exquisite armor.

"It belonged to my father. It's the perfect thing to wear into the upcoming battle. It should be just the right size for me." Sakuris responded as he stared at the armor.

"I thought you and Kayah had lost everything after the great destruction?" Saiera said puzzled.

"In our haste to leave, we thought we had, too. When I was old enough, I returned there with Kayah to see what I could find. This, by some miracle, survived. Help me put it on, would you?" Sakuris responds as he strips down out of his tattered old clothing and changes into something more appropriate for combat. Once properly dressed, Sakuris receives Saiera's assistance in putting on his father's armor. As he suspected, it fit him near perfectly. Turning to his beloved, he gazes upon her and places a hand to her cheek as he gently kisses her lips. "The women and most of the children are being escorted to safety. There would be no shame if you were to go with them, my love."

"What, what are you saying?" Saiera asked in surprise, "I can't walk away from this. That monster destroyed my home as well." She then reached down and clutched her Sacred Blade, bringing it to her bosom. "As a blade holder, I cannot let you go alone."

"What of Iyata?" Sakuris reminded her gently, "Saiera, I cannot have her go through what Kayah and I had to." He then clutched Saiera's hand in his as he brushed back a few loose strands of Saiera's hair, "Allow me to carry your sacred blade into battle with me."

"Master Kaemouri," Akisarah said leaning into the tent, "It's time."

Looking at Akisarah and then back to Saiera, Sakuris could see a pleading look on his wife's face. "Where's Iyata?" Sakuris asked without bothering to look back at Akisarah.

"She's safe with her grandparents." Akisarah responded.

"Saiera will be joining us in battle. She is after all, a blade holder." Sakuris stated as continued to gaze into his wife's eyes, "Get ready, beloved, and join the rest of us outside."

Leaving his wife to prepare for battle, Sakuris exits the tent and walks through the campsite with Akisarah where those who were to go to battle awaited, little Mitsuo among them, standing next to him was Kiyanah.

Seeing this, Sakuris turned momentarily to Akisarah. "Go wait with the others. I'll return shortly." He says to him before going over to speak with Kiyanah and her son. Looking at Mitsuo and then back to Kiyanah and then back to Mitsuo, he kneels down before the man-child. "Is this your son, Kiyanah?" He asks curiously as he looks the boy over.

"Yes, Lord Kaemouri. He wishes to participate in the battle." Kiyanah replies as Mitsuo bows before Sakuris.

Curious as to Mitsuo's reasoning, Sakuris turns to him and speaks. "What's your name young man?" He asks curiously.

The overwhelming confidence in his voice made Mitsuo hesitant, but he found the courage to answer nonetheless. "Mitsuo, Son of Kaideshie." He responds with equal confidence.

"I hadn't intended for children to fight in this battle. Why then do you now come before me wishing to do so?" Sakuris asks curiously.

"You are mother's friend, Lord Kaemouri, and I am the only male in my family; therefore, I am duty-bound to fight." Mitsuo responds, "I may be a child, but I am trained." He then motions to the dagger, commonly referred to as a tanto, strapped about his side.

"Good choice of weapon, for a boy your age. However, tantos are not without their drawbacks. The men we'll be fighting will have weapons capable of further reach. They will be bigger, stronger, and possibly more agile than you currently are, you understand?" Mitsuo nods his head as Sakuris continues, "Still, I think I may have a use for you. If you wish to help, go over to where Tallinyia is treating the wounded and sick. She may have tasks suited to someone of your courage."

"As you wish, Lord Kaemouri." Mitsuo responds as Sakuris hurries him along to speak with Tallinyia.

With a chuckle, Sakuris smiles as he turns to Kiyanah. "I do not doubt your son would be brave in battle, but I cannot risk his life either. I'm sure Tallinyia will find a task suited for him. Besides, my sister is in that tent with her newborn. I will feel better knowing he is there to protect her if needed." He says to her quite honestly.

"And I will feel better knowing he is away from any real danger. Your decision is most acceptable; thank you, Lord Kaemouri." Kiyanah responded with a humble bow.

"Rise, my friend." Sakuris remarks with a chuckle, "You need not bow before me. Your son's bravery is more than enough."

Rising to meet Sakuris's gaze, Kiyanah peers over his shoulder to watch as Mitsuo does as he was instructed, "I should be going with the rest of the evacuees now. Take care of my boy, Lord Kaemouri."

"I will, my friend, stay safe." Sakuris responds, watching Kiyanah as steps back and turns away to leave.

Once Kiyanah had safely joined the others who were being taking somewhere to wait out the battle, Sakuris joined those who were to fight and had gathered them around a fallen tree.

Climbing onto the tree, Sakuris looks around at everyone who was to participate. "My friends, now is the time to strike. Norakatsu thinks he has us beaten and will let his guard down thinking our small force won't be a match for his army, but I know each and every fighter here, like I know my own scent; therefore I know there is nothing to fear. You are all great fighters, and now is the time for us to rise up and make sure the Dragon Clan lives on; now and forever." He called out to everyone.

Plunging their sword into the air and cheering loudly, every armed fighter present watched as Sakuris raised a closed fist to quiet everyone down. "I need everyone to hurry and get ready. Make sure you say good bye to your loved ones and tell them you love them. I know I'm speaking as though some of you won't return, but this is war after all. We attack at night fall, good luck and dismissed." He said as he hopped down from the tree log and walked over to Saiera who had been standing amongst the crowd.

He took her into his embrace and kissed her gently. "It's time my love." He said to her.

Saiera nodded. "Yes and I know we'll be victorious." She responded.

Walking through the camp, Akisarah watched everyone as he made his way to the medical tent and steps in, looking for Kayah. Seeing her lying in bed with their newborn son, he walks over to her and gently kisses her forehead, "Beloved, it's time for me to go."

Kayah nodded as she let Ishiemae suckle the milk from her breast. "Would you like to hold your son before you leave?" She asked him as she presented Ishiemae to him. Not wanting to release from Kayah, Ishiemae merely whined a little as Kayah tried to calm him down.

Akisarah nodded as he took Ishiemae from Kayah and held him as he fell asleep in his father's arms. Kayah sat up and looked at him. "Promise me one thing, Akisarah; that you'll return to me safely no matter what." She said to him. A hesitant look came to Akisarah's eyes. He knew that was a promise he would not be able to make. Wanting an answer, Kayah reaches out to put both her hands to each side of Akisarah's face, "Promise me."

"I promise to do all I can to return, but beloved . . ." He began but trailed off when he saw the pleading look in his wife's eye as he leaned forward and kissed her gently, "I promise, my love; take care of Ishiemae until I return." He responded handing Ishiemae back to his mother. Taking her son into her embrace, Kayah allows him to continue nursing.

Exiting the tent, Akisarah sees Sakuris standing before him. "Are you ready?" He asks as Akisarah nods in return, "Then go join the others. They prepare to march as we speak. I'll be there shortly." Patting Akisarah on his shoulder as he passed by him, Sakuris gave an approving nod and a self-assured chuckle as he entered the tent.

"Nii-sama!" Kayah exclaimed as she saw her brother walking over to her.

"Kayah, since childhood, I have done my best to fulfill the promise I made to father. As such, I've protected you the best I can. Now, I see you before me with child in hand. You've become a true woman. I can protect you no longer. You must find the strength within yourself now." He said to her as he knelt beside her.

"I understand, brother." Kayah responded as the two embraced for what could possibly be the last time, "You be careful out there." As the two siblings released from their embrace, Sakuris looked over to see little Mitsuo hard at work for Tallinyia.

"Mitsuo." He said commandingly, calling Mitsuo over to him.

Stopping what he was doing, the young Kaideshie went over to see what it is Sakuris needed of him. "Yes, Lord Kaemouri." He responded confidently.

Motioning to Kayah, Sakuris looked at Mitsuo, not as a boy, but as man of equal stature. "Mitsuo, this is my sister, Kayah. In addition with helping Tallinyia with what she may ask of you, I am charging you with the protection of all those in this tent. I know you wanted to participate in the battle, but this task is of the utmost importance and all men of fighting age will be on the battlefield. That is why I must leave it to you. Do you understand?" Sakuris said to him.

"Nii-sama?" Kayah exclaimed, but Sakuris motioned for her to be still. Following her brother's instructions Kayah said no more as she watched him speak with young Mitsuo.

"I'll not fail you, Lord Kaemouri." Mitsuo responded with a humble bow.

"I know you won't. I never got to meet your father, but if you are any indication of the kind of man he may have been, then I'm sure I would've been honored to. You have a strong heart, Kaideshie Mitsuo. I wish you luck." Sakuris said to him before looking to Kayah and then back to Mitsuo.

Nodding approvingly, he steps out of the tent and joins the others who were preparing to march on Isura. Looking around at everyone, he mounted the horse Saiera had waiting for him, as he looked at his beloved and then to Akisarah who had also been sitting on his horse, with his spear lashed to the side of it.

Preparing to march, the three fighters looked at the small band of warriors which numbered within only the hundreds. "We're taking a small militia force to lay siege to an entire fortress, and battle an army many times larger. We're short one sacred blade, and supplies are limited." Akisarah remarked as he looked around.

"I know my friend, things do seem grim, but with Elayis on our side I know we'll prevail. Besides we still have two sacred blades. Even Norakatsu's army won't be able to withstand that." Sakuris responds as he looks at the faces of those who are to fight. Amongst them he sees Sinileass and even the recovering Yu-Ka-Mi.

With an approving nod, he turned to face Saiera and Akisarah. "Let's go." He said to them as he nudged his horse and slowly trotted off. Following behind him, the two of them rode up next to him and the march had begun. As the small militia made its way to Isura, Yu-Ka-Mi made her way through the ranks to take her proper place at Sakuris's side.

"I knew you wouldn't be able to resist." Sakuris commented as the two of them rode side by side.

"My place is at your side, Lord Kaemouri. Not rotting away in some medical tent. Besides, Tallinyia cleared me for combat." She responded.

"All the same, watch yourself out there. You were the closest thing Kayah and I had to a mother after we lost our parents." Sakuris gently reminded her.

"Yes, I know, and I am glad to have been such. You have grown into a fine young man." Yu-Ka-Mi responds with a smile.

"All thanks to you, my friend." Sakuris remarks as they rode alongside each other.

It was early evening when they arrived at the base of Mount Iyeia. Stopping his horse and raising a fist, Sakuris signals for his forces to halt their march momentarily. Seeing his signal, the rest of the militia halt their march and await further instructions. Riding up to her husband, Saiera awaits at his side. "It'll take a day to cross over to Isura, plus the fire clan resides along the mountain rodes." He says to her, "We should wait till nightfall; have everyone break out water and rations. We'll let them rest before we cross. It'll be easier under the cover of darkness, anyway." He says dismounting his horse.

"As you wish, beloved." Saiera responds acknowledging her husband's orders as she passes them on to Yu-Ka-Mi who then passes them on to the rest of the militia. Taking what time they could for respite, the small army takes food and drink along with what rest they could.

When night had fallen, the small band of fighters gathered up the remainder of supplies and prepared to cross Mount Iyea and over into Isura. Nudging his horse forward, Sakuris prepares to lead his militia force through the mountain pass. The journey through was a quiet one as the small force of Shikanacans remained on alert. "It's quiet." Akisarah remarked as he rode alongside Sakuris.

"Yes, too quiet, remain alert." Sakuris responds, turning to Yu-Ka-Mi who rode behind him, "Open the gap between us and stay with the others." Following Sakuris's instructions, Yu-Ka-Mi slowed the pace of her horse allowing room between her and the three fighters in front.

Looking around, as he rode next to his friends, Sakuris extended his hand to Akisarah. "Akisarah, your father's sword, please." He remarked asking permission to use Akisarah's sword of hope.

"Yeah." Akisarah responded as he removed his sword from his side and handed it to Sakuris, who then strapped it about his waist. Above them a loud shrieking sound rang out as the ground became enveloped in shadow.

"What was that?" Saiera exclaimed as the three of them slowed their horses and turned them this way and that to look for the source of the sound.

"Sounded, almost, like a bird." Akisarah remarked.

"I know of no bird that sounds like that." Saiera responded as she looked about the sky.

"Yes, and by the shadow it cast, whatever it was, it was large." Sakuris remarked as the shrieking sound rang out again.

This was causing the three friends and the militia force, behind them, to become nervous. "Let's not tarry here, my friends." Sakuris remarked as the shrieking stopped, "Whatever it was; it appears to be gone, now. We should keep moving." Continuing to lead the way to Isura, Sakuris pushed his militia force forward through the mountain pass.

It was almost early morning when they had arrived at the border of Isura. "The border; that means the fortress town won't be much further." Sakuris remarked as he and his friends emerged from the mountain pass, "We'll let the militia rest here for a bit while the three of us scout out ahead to see what we're up against. The journey through the pass was too easy."

Riding back to the rest of the army, Sakuris heads over to Yu-Ka-Mi to pass his instructions on to her. Bowing in her saddle, Yu-Ka-Mi rides away to carry out her orders as she passes them on to the rest of the Shikanacan forces. Watching her as she does, Sakuris nods approvingly and then rejoins his wife and brother-in-law. "Come, but be cautious; the sun will be up soon." He remarks as the three of them continue deeper into Isuran territory.

As they neared the fortress, the three of them slowed their horses as they led them to a concealed position. "The horses should be fine here. We're far enough away that it will be hard for the guards to see us. We'll continue on foot." Sakuris remarked as the three dismounted and made their way toward the fortress, using the shadows for cover. Along the fortress walls, archers patrolled the battlements, prepared to rain arrows on those who would intrude.

On the ground, a single gate remained guarded, around the clock, as it separated the inner layout from the outside world. Motioning for his friends to stay low, Sakuris gave the signal to split up to cover more ground. As he moved through the trees surrounding the fortress, Sakuris was careful not to alert any of the guards that came across his path until he met up with Saiera and Akisarah on the other side.

"Archers, on the walls." Akisarah remarked as the three of them met up with each other.

"One entrance guarded by two soldiers." Saiera added as Sakuris looked at the two of them.

"Let's get back to the others." Sakuris said to both of them as they quickly left the area and headed back to their horses. Leaving the area, the three of them returned to the small encampment where the others were waiting. As luck would have it, there was a hot spring nearby, and weary from travel, Saiera had decided a good soak would do her body some good before battle.

Feeling the warmth of the water penetrating into her skin, Saiera relaxed as she leaned upon the edge of the spring. Staring at her hand, she still bore the scar from the day she made the blood oath to end Kenzji's life. Even now, she still longed for the chance to kill him herself.

Over the horizon, the sun rose, spilling its light out onto the land below as a misty haze rested upon Kaseo forest. Finishing her bath, Saiera climbed out of the spring as the water receded from her naked form leaving only tiny droplets that glistened in the sunlight. Though no longer as young as she once was, she was still beautiful and fit. Her muscular body, relaxed by the water, felt renewed and ready for battle. Though she carried no armor, her clothing was made from a thick silk along with the clothing she wore underneath, acting as a make-shift padded armor. Being a woman, she was also naturally more flexible than a man, making her both nimble and agile.

Using a cloth made of linen, she dries herself off and dresses her body. Standing confident in the sunlight as it shone down upon her, she straps her sacred blade to her waist and heads back to camp. The day drug on slowly as a heavy tension hung on the air. Rations were passed for everyone to have food in their bellies before battle.

Eager to go to battle, Akisarah worked on the kata of his martial arts in order to calm his nerves and focus his mind. Gracefully he went through the motions of assorted blocks, punches, and kicks as he practiced his breathing and targeting.

As the day moved on, the tension thickened as everyone stood on the precipice of battle till finally the moment came, and the army began the final march to the fortress.

Chapter 17

It was nightfall by the time they arrived, and the gate was sealed up tight while the guards remained at their post. On the walls, the archers still patrolled the rampart. Seeing Sakuris and his two companions within the dim light of the torches that lined the fortress walls, one of the archers fired a warning shot as it landed just short of Sakuris's horse causing it to rare up on its hind legs.

"That's far enough, stranger. What business have you here?" The archer called down to him.

"Tell your master we've something he wants, and that we're prepared to give it to him." Sakuris responded as Akisarah and Saiera held up their sacred blades for the archer to see.

Laughing with villainous glee, the archer sends a messenger into the fortress. "I hope you know what you're doing, my friend." Akisarah remarked quietly as he stood by Sakuris.

"There's no other way in. Our only hope is to draw them out, and the blades are the best way to do it." Sakuris responds, sharing Akisarah's reservations.

A few minutes went by and Kenzji appeared on the fortress ramparts. "Ah, Kaemouri, so you did survive." He gloated victoriously as he motioned for some of his men to ride out and retrieve the blades. Unknown to those within the fortress, the rest of the Shikanacan army was waiting under the cover of darkness for Sakuris to signal the attack.

Peering from the forest was Yu-Ka-Mi as she watched and waited for Sakuris's signal. Behind her the Shikanacan forces awaited for their attack orders. Watching as the Isuran riders drew closer and closer to Sakuris, she finally saw what she was looking for. The blue glow of Sakuris's sword as it became charged with the power of frost.

Seeing this, she immediately signaled for the rest of the militia to begin the attack. Charging at full speed, the militia had weapons drawn as they rushed toward the fortress.

Seeing the oncoming forces, Kenzji's gloating soon turned to panic as he ordered his troops back into the fortress. Following behind them as they turned around, Sakuris and his two companions immediately rushed inside after them to avoid being shut out. Using the frost power he had charged his weapon with, Sakuris froze the chains of the fortress gate in place making them so brittle that they broke as the guards on the ramparts attempted to shut the gate, causing it to fall back open, allowing the rest of the Shikanacan militia to enter into the fortress and begin engaging targets in combat.

"NO!" Kenzji shouted in anger as he saw what was happening. "Archers!" He shouted signaling the archers to open fire upon the fortress grounds. However due to the confusion caused by the combat below, in addition to the dimness of the torchlight, it was hard for the archers to decipher friend from foe causing them to hesitate.

"What are you idiots doing? Open fire!" Kenzji shouted as he looked at his archers.

"Sir, those are our people down there!" One of them retorted. Out of frustration, Kenzji went over and shoved him off the ramparts to his death as he took his bow and arrows in hand and began shooting at any target that moved.

Witnessing this from below, Sakuris ordered his people to seek cover as he cut a bloody trail of bodies to clear a path into the inner workings of the fortress itself. Due to the construction nature of the Isura castle town, Sakuris and his companions would have to fight their way through a maze of districts and dead-ends before reaching the keep, where they suspected Norakatsu would be waiting for them. Using this fact to his advantage, Kenzji left his archers on the ramparts and headed down to ground level to join the battle.

Slaying one of Sakuris's horseman and stealing his steed, he quickly rode to overtake Sakuris and his companions in attempt to hinder their progress. This wouldn't stop Yu-Ka-Mi as she gave chase to him. Armed with her Nodachi, she rent the heads off of every Isuran she passed as she hurried to catch Kenzji.

"Lord Ketsuro!" One of the other Isuran soldiers shouted as he saw Yu-Ka-Mi giving chase. Turning to see what the shouting was about, Kenzji saw Yu-Ka-Mi just in time to parry her blade as she struck out at him.

"You'll not touch my master." She remarked harshly as she rode past the young Ketsuro and turned to face him with an icy glare in her eyes.

"Be gone from my sight. I've no desire to kill a woman, but if you continue to stand in my way . . ." He retorts, pointing his blade at her.

Ignoring the blade, Yu-Ka-Mi stood her ground as she readied her weapon. "I am Yu-Ka-Mi of Tysomi Village, retainer to the Lord Kaemouri, and I am prepared for death, are you?" She retorts ready to engage Kenzji in combat.

"So be it, then." Kenzji remarked as he nudged his horse forward and engaged Yu-Ka-Mi in mounted combat. The echo of clashing metal rung out through the fortress as their blades bore down on one another.

Hearing the sound of the echoing metal, Sakuris stopped just long enough to turn and see the two opponents locked in combat. "By Elayis, Yu-Ka-Mi!" He shouted as he hurried to ride to her aid, but was stopped by both Akisarah and Saiera as they held him from each side.

"No, my friend! She's buying us the time we need." Akisarah reminded him, "I suggest we use it."

Watching in horror as Yu-Ka-Mi dueled with Kenzji, Sakuris was frozen in decision. "Sakuris! I know you care greatly for her, but we must press on." Akisarah remarked trying to get his friend to see reason. Looking to Akisarah and then back to Kenzji, Sakuris knew what he had to do, but to leave his friend to possibly die was not something he was prepared to live with.

"Beloved, come." Saiera said calmly as she gently shook Sakuris to snap him back to reality.

Seeing her friend frozen as he was, Yu-Ka-Mi parried another sword blow from Kenzji shouting for Sakuris to continue on.

For the first time in his adult life, Sakuris felt tears coming to his eyes as he shut them tightly, turning his head away. Turning his horse back around, he stilled his heart and continued forward with his two companions following behind him.

"I've no time for this." Kenzji remarked harshly as he kicked Yu-Ka-Mi off her horse, knocking her to the ground. Landing on her still recovering shoulder, Yu-Ka-Mi cried out in pain as some of the Shikanacan forces came rushing to her aid.

Smiling sinisterly, Kenzji chuckled victoriously and nudged his horse forward as he hurried to catch up to Sakuris and his companions.

Knowing the fortress layout better than Sakuris and the others, Kenzji would have a far easier time navigating its grounds as he quickly caught up to them just as they entered the stone walls of the keep.

Entering the stone walls behind them, Kenzji leapt from his horse as he landed on one knee shouting, "KAEMOURI!"

Stopping in his tracks, Sakuris turned to face him. He could feel Saiera tugging at his arm urging him to continue on with her and Akisarah. "Sakuris, come on, we have to hurry." She pleaded trying to get him to continue on with her.

Sakuris merely shook his head responding, "No, I have to do this." He then turns to Akisarah, "Akisarah, take Saiera and continue on without me. Defeat Norakatsu and reclaim my weapons, then get everyone else out of here."

Taking Saiera by the hand, Akisarah pulls her from Sakuris. "No! No!" She protested as Akisarah pulled her down the hall. "Sakuris!" She called letting her cry echo down the hall.

Once they were far enough down the hall, she pulled away from Akisarah and gave him the sting of her hand across his cheek, shouting, "That's my husband back there!"

"Yes and he can take care of himself." Akisarah responded as though he hadn't felt the slap he had just been delivered, "I know you're scared for him, but we need to continue on. We are the only ones who can stop Norakatsu. Sakuris knows this and is fighting to buy us the time we need to do so."

In tears, Saiera nodded her head as she threw herself into Akisarah's arms, sobbing into his shoulder, "I don't want him to die."

Softly stroking Saiera's hair, Akisarah did his best to reassure her. "Saiera, look at me." He said tilting her head up so he could make eye contact, "After everything he's survived through, do you really think he would come all this way just to die?"

"No." Saiera sobbed in response as she shook her head.

Using his sleeve, Akisarah dried her tears. "Then dry those tears, and let's finish this." He said softly as he released Saiera from his embrace allowing her to compose herself as she dried her tears and nodded signaling she was ready as they continued on to the inner sanctum of the keep.

They arrived just in time to see Norakatsu and his masked mystery woman standing near an open balcony only to leap from it.

Running over to the balcony to catch them, the two fighters saw something they were not prepared for: a giant, bird-like creature carrying the two Isurans away.

"What the hell?" Akisarah remarked to himself witnessing the giant creature rising into the sky.

"What is that thing?" Saiera exclaimed as she and Akisarah watched it fly away into the night as the laughter of the woman echoed through the darkness.

Back in the hallway, Sakuris looked at his opponent as he watched him unstrap his weapon from his waist and throw it aside as it hit the ground with a thud. Removing Akisarah's sword from his waist, Sakuris leaned it up against the wall.

"Now we'll see who the true Arch-Dragon is." Kenzji remarked dropping into a fighting stance, "I've dreamt of this moment for a long time."

Sakuris stares at him hard and coldly as he drops into a fighting stance. "Now you'll pay for ever trying to harm my family." He responded harshly.

"Come on." Kenzji said motioning for Sakuris to make the first move, before quickly spinning around and back fisting a nearby torch, sending it straight at Sakuris. Dodged it nimbly, he looked to see Kenzji coming toward him and throwing a double front kick. The blows landed perfectly as Sakuris was knocked to the ground. He responded with a front sweep bringing Kenzji down with him. As he fell, Kenzji brought his elbow down upon Sakuris and landed a blow to his stomach, winding Sakuris as he attempted to rise up on all fours.

Seizing the opportunity, he quickly threw his arm around Sakuris's neck as he brought him to his feet squeezing hard upon his throat. "You killed my sister." He remarked harshly.

Feeling the precious life giving air leaving him, Sakuris knew he was in danger as he opened his mind to Seltah. Clearing his airway, he gave a powerful shout; releasing an aura so powerful it threw Kenzji back and caused a few of the walls to crumble from the impact. The power Sakuris unleashed was so tremendous; it actually frightened Kenzji as he crawled backwards away from him. Still he wouldn't back down as he stood to his feet and brought forth his Kyuroksho, unleashing his own powerful aura as more of the building collapsed. That part of the building had lost so much of its support that it began collapsing under its weight, burying both fighters within the rubble.

Feeling the effects of Sakuris's bout with Kenzji, and knowing the building wouldn't hold up much longer as it shook around them, Akisarah quickly looked around for a means of escape. Quickly spotting another nearby door, he took Saiera by the hand and the two of them began to run for their lives as the building begun to collapse behind them threatening to bury them as well.

Feeling a sharp pain go through her heart as she and Akisarah made their escape, Saiera quickly stopped and looked back, quietly stating "Something's happened to Sakuris."

Akisarah could feel it too as he looked back down the hall and then to Saiera. "Come on, Sakuris can take care of himself." He said to her as the building continued to collapse under its own weight from the battle between Sakuris and Kenzji, but Saiera didn't want to leave her husband even though she knew she had no choice but to follow Akisarah out. Narrowly making it to the entrance, the two of them hurried outside where they found Yu-Ka-Mi awaiting them after a hard fought battle. Behind them, the fortress keep collapsed under its own weight shaking the ground below

Running up as soon as she saw them, Yu-Ka-Mi inquired to Sakuris's location, nervous of the answer she might receive.

Akisarah looked at her and then at the ruins of Isura, shaking his head. "He didn't make it." He responded sadly, "I'm sorry."

Yu-Ka-Mi felt her heart sink in her chest as she fell to her knees, overwhelmed by grief as tears flowed freely from her eyes.

Kneeling before Yu-Ka-Mi, Saiera quickly took her into her embrace letting her cry over her loss for a bit before helping her to her feet as the three of them headed back to camp. The Shikanacan camp site was set up just outside the border of Isura, and night had just fallen when the three of them had arrived. In need of a hot bath, Saiera proceeded to the hot spring she had found before and stripped down.

Slipping into the warm waters of the spring, she relaxed her battle-ridden body as she thoroughly bathed the scent of death off her skin. When she finished, she merely soaked in the spring as she stared at the ruins of Isura. "I know you're still alive Sakuris. Please return to me." She said to herself staring up at the full moon of the night sky; wondering if she would ever see her beloved Sakuris again.

Was he alive, and what had become of Kenzji? Did he survive the fall of Isura? And who was the woman that helped Norakatsu escape? Most importantly, what would become of the sacred blade?

Pondering these questions as she soaked in the spring, Saiera merely stared up at the sky wondering: What tomorrow might bring.